D0360324

"Jade Lee has the heart-stopping tension,
wonderful characters, and compelling voice to
sweep you away to another time and era."
—Sabrina Jeffries, *New York Times* bestselling author

Wedded in Sin

"Jade Lee's *Wedded in Sin* is the charmingly seductive tale
of a white, but rumpled, knight who will steal your heart as
he puts his lady's problems to rest."
—Courtney Milan, *New York Times* bestselling author

PRAISE FOR

Wedded in Scandal

"Lee's diverting historical suggests that while scandal may
strip one of one's title, breeding will out . . . Lady Helaine
Talbott has enough spunk and pure sex appeal to turn the head
of Robert Percy, Viscount Redhill . . . [Robert] recognizes
class when he sees it; harder for him to accept is that a lady
could have the wits or sense for business . . . Charming verbal
fencing ensues [as] Helaine matches Robert clever retort for
clever retort . . . [An] entertaining read."
—*Publishers Weekly*

"Filled with both heated sensuality and emotional depth. . . .
A beautiful, haunting tale of love overcoming the seemingly
greatest of odds." —*Night Owl Reviews*

HILLSBORO PUBLIC LIBRARIES
Hillsboro, OR
Member of Washington County
COOPERATIVE LIBRARY SERVICES

Wedded in
Sin

JADE LEE

BERKLEY SENSATION, NEW YORK

THE BERKLEY PUBLISHING GROUP
Published by the Penguin Group
Penguin Group (USA) Inc.
375 Hudson Street, New York, New York 10014, USA
Penguin Group (Canada), 90 Eglinton Avenue East, Suite 700, Toronto, Ontario M4P 2Y3, Canada
(a division of Pearson Penguin Canada Inc.) • Penguin Books Ltd., 80 Strand, London WC2R 0RL,
England • Penguin Group Ireland, 25 St. Stephen's Green, Dublin 2, Ireland (a division of Penguin
Books Ltd.) • Penguin Group (Australia), 250 Camberwell Road, Camberwell, Victoria 3124, Australia
(a division of Pearson Australia Group Pty. Ltd.) • Penguin Books India Pvt. Ltd., 11 Community
Centre, Panchsheel Park, New Delhi—110 017, India • Penguin Group (NZ), 67 Apollo Drive,
Rosedale, Auckland 0632, New Zealand (a division of Pearson New Zealand Ltd.) • Penguin Books
(South Africa) (Pty.) Ltd., 24 Sturdee Avenue, Rosebank, Johannesburg 2196, South Africa

Penguin Books Ltd., Registered Offices: 80 Strand, London WC2R 0RL, England

This is a work of fiction. Names, characters, places, and incidents either are the product of the author's
imagination or are used fictitiously, and any resemblance to actual persons, living or dead, business
establishments, events, or locales is entirely coincidental. The publisher does not have any control over
and does not assume any responsibility for author or third-party websites or their content.

WEDDED IN SIN

A Berkley Sensation Book / published by arrangement with the author

PUBLISHING HISTORY
Berkley Sensation mass-market edition / August 2012

Copyright © 2012 by Katherine Ann Grill.
Cover art by Judy York.
Cover design by George Long.
Interior text design by Kristin del Rosario.

ISBN: 978-0-425-25103-4

BERKLEY SENSATION®
Berkley Sensation Books are published by The Berkley Publishing Group,
a division of Penguin Group (USA) Inc.,
375 Hudson Street, New York, New York 10014.
BERKLEY SENSATION® is a registered trademark of
Penguin Group (USA) Inc.
The "B" design is a trademark of Penguin Group (USA) Inc.

PRINTED IN THE UNITED STATES OF AMERICA

10 9 8 7 6 5 4 3 2 1

ALWAYS LEARNING   PEARSON

Chapter 1

❧

Samuel Morrison's mind was racing, but that was not unusual. His mind was always racing. Even on this most beautiful morning as he strolled down Bond Street at the height of a shopping day. His thoughts wandered to Lady Pierson, who had just slipped a note to the flushed and very young Mr. Cooper. Then it hopped to Lord Simpleton, er, Simpson, who appeared to have left his home without his hat. Or a clean shirt. Ah, that was because he was coming from the brothel, Samuel realized, mainly from the unmistakable scent of smoke and perfume that trailed in the man's wake. And from the man's smile. Obviously, poor Lord Simpson was arrears in his funds, because he was walking down this side stretch of Bond Street rather than hailing a cab from Nightingale Street.

Samuel's mind wandered on, noting everything from the style of one person's clothing to the rubbish on the street. He did his best to ignore his thoughts. It was really the only way to survive without complete lunacy, but his mind kept chattering away, this time about the dark-haired boy with the bad cough who was trying to get up the nerve to pick someone's pocket. About four yards away, a gypsy woman was watching closely, most likely as the boy's instructor. Not mother and son, he realized, because of the different facial features. More likely from the same gypsy family, though, because of a certain twist of the head. An aunt, he guessed.

Following their gazes, Samuel realized their victim was likely to be Lord Histlewight, who had obviously just returned from Northampton because his shoes were new. The fine stitching of his footwear proclaimed them as Northampton made. Unlike Samuel's own; his feet had lately begun to throb from his very cheap and poorly made shoes.

With a sudden veer, Samuel decided to turn left rather than suffer the moral choice of preventing a pickpocketing crime or keeping a silent witness. Normally he would have warned the child off, but the boy was thin and ill and would probably make better use of the coin than Histlewight ever would.

But a moment later, Samuel spun on his heel and turned back. His sense of justice prevented him from allowing any crime, even against an ass like Histlewight, to go unchecked. He made it to the street barely two feet ahead of the boy. Quick as he could, he grabbed the child's arm and hauled him up. It was pitifully easy. The boy was stick thin and too frightened even to scream, so Samuel had ample time to speak harshly into his ear.

"No thieving today, my boy. There's a butcher shop seven blocks that way." He jerked his head in the right direction. "Talk smart and polite to Mr. Braun, and compliment his smoked bacon. He's extraordinarily vain about his pork. The man's looking for a new apprentice, as the last one ran off. No matter what your aunt says, thieving leads to the gallows or worse. Not every man is blind or stupid. Someone always sees."

He held the child a moment longer. The boy was shaking

in terror, but Samuel didn't release him until he had caught the aunt's eye a block away. The boy was too young to know better, but the older one would see that Samuel would not be crossed on this. It was a lie, of course. They could move their business two blocks over and he would not be there to prevent it. But perhaps it was an illusion that would hold. Perhaps the woman would make the right choice, apprentice the boy to the butcher, and turn from their life of thieving.

So he held the woman's dark gaze and whispered a quiet prayer on the child's behalf. And then he let the boy go. The kid dashed away on wobbly legs, catching up to his aunt before tugging the woman away down toward the butcher. Perhaps he had done a good deed, he thought, though he doubted the lesson would stick. Gypsies, as a rule, did not like to be tied to regular jobs or regular homes.

Meanwhile, his mind had tired of the gypsies and wandered off to notice other things. Mrs. Worthington had lost some weight. She had a new charge this season—two girls fresh from the nursery. One was pretty, the other canny. He gleaned that in an instant from their clothing, the way they moved, and the way the canny one kept her head down but her eyes always roving. Her gaze stopped on him and she flashed him a flirtatious smile, but he was already turning away down a side street to avoid having to chatter with the females. Meanwhile, he noticed that the meat pie cart had a weak spoke on its left side wheel. And perhaps he ought to check his own pocket to be sure it hadn't been picked while he was about his good deed.

He shoved his hand into his pocket and was relieved to feel that his few meager coins were safe. He had enough to last him until quarter day, but not much beyond that. Perhaps he ought to avail himself of his own advice, he thought. Find a regular job, focus on a regular task as so many younger sons were forced to do. He didn't truly need the money, except for right now. His investments would return handsomely in the next few years. But for the moment, a job would relieve his cash flow difficulties and, much more important, give him something to do.

Then the most extraordinary thing happened. His mind noticed one thing more before falling absolutely silent. It was a woman with a too thin build and above average looks. She was carrying a child and a satchel while being bodily evicted from a shoemaker's shop. No one else noticed what he saw, though there were a dozen people watching the spectacle. She was arguing, the child was crying, and none of the constabulary appeared to care despite her large gestures and vehement protests. Only he saw that all her noise was for show, covering the fact that she had just tossed a small bag at a pile of rubbish.

It was a poorly tied bag with thin seams. As it landed, to wedge between the brick wall and leather scraps, the stitching burst and something distinctive tumbled out. Something that silenced the noise in his head and left his thoughts utterly speechless.

She'd just discarded Lord Winston's left foot.

Penny Shoemaker was furious. And not the kind of fury that made tears burn in her eyes. This anger was like a living thing under her skin that drove her to madness. If someone had given her a knife right then, she would have easily sunk it hilt deep in the constable's throat. A tiny part of her was horrified by that, but it was only a tiny part lost beneath the weight of anger fueled by humiliation.

She was being thrown out of her home. While she'd been quietly feeding Tommy a real breakfast of bread and eggs— their first in weeks—armed men had banged on her door. She'd picked up her nine-month-old brother and answered the door. She'd been told in round flat tones that she was no longer owner of their home. That everything they owned— from the tools in the shoe store on the first floor to the clothes in their home right above—had been sold to that bastard Cordwain, a small-time hack of a shoemaker.

Well, she'd told them flatly that they were mistaken. She'd never sold anything, hadn't been paid a groat, and they could bloody well leave. Then she slammed the door in the constable's face.

She knew it wouldn't work. She recognized the face of Authority when it came in the guise of armed men and a constable's badge. It didn't matter that her eviction was wrong. That she hadn't sold their home or that for the first time since her parents' deaths, she'd found a way to support herself and her brother. It didn't matter to those bastards outside. To them, she was a woman alone with a babe. Her parents had been murdered less than two months ago, and she was now vulnerable to every kind of horror that the uncaring world could throw at her.

"Bleeding curs," she spat as she dashed for the workroom. There was only one thing of true value in her home and she would be damned if Cordwain got his hands on it. It was in a satchel because her father had been a slob. He had always planned to put everything on display or at least organize it in a closet, but that had never happened. And now Penny had cause to be thankful for his forgetfulness. She was able to grab the bag and her coin purse. Then she was back upstairs, Tommy crying in her arms as she stuffed clothing and the like into another bag.

But she was out of time. Their door burst open and the men tromped upstairs. Before she could do more than scream, rough hands wrapped around her waist. She kicked and screamed, but she had no purchase as she was lifted off the ground. The bastard was strong, his grip bruising, and his smell even worse. She knew without looking that the greasy head of hair belonged to Jobby, Cordwain's nephew and all-around brute. He flipped her over his shoulder and carried her outside. How she kept hold of both Tommy and her bags, she didn't know. Except that it was her life and her brother that she held and she'd be damned if she dropped either one.

Jobby banged her head three times on the way out of the house. She barely cared. She was more interested in protecting Tommy's head than her own. Still, the pain made her head throb and gave birth to that living fury just beneath her skin. Once outside, the constable ordered Jobby to set her down. Normally she wouldn't have heard it, but the man had a whistle that he blew right in Jobby's face to get the idiot's attention.

"There's no cause for that!" the constable bellowed. And so Jobby put her down, copping a feel of her bottom as he did. She kicked him hard as she could right in the privates. Luck was with her. She connected. Not as hard as she would have liked, but enough that Jobby went down with a howl. Every man there winced in sympathy, and that gave her time to toss the satchel of important things to the side, where hopefully no one would notice. Then she started screeching like a madwoman by way of covering. If anyone had noticed what she'd dropped, hopefully they'd get distracted and forget.

She focused on the constable, as he was the authority here. His eyes had darkened as he watched Jobby writhing on the ground, but now he focused on her.

"There were no cause fer—"

"He had no cause to be doing what he was doing to me bum either," she snapped, her language deteriorating as her fury grew stronger. "And you've no cause to throw me out of my home!"

The constable sighed, the sound coming from deep within him. If she were less furious, she might have felt sorry for him. He had the air of a man keeping doggedly on simply because there was nowhere else to go. A soldier, she thought, in a forced march. But then the image was gone as Cordwain blustered forward.

"Got the bill of sale right here, my girl. As of dawn this morning, yer property is mine."

She snatched it from his hands, all but ripping the document. She would not have him waving the thing in her face. Problem was, she still had Tommy wailing in her arms, clinging to her like he was terrified. Which he was. Just as she was, but she controlled it better than the toddler. And while she was struggling to control the boy, Cordwain turned to Jobby, who was just now getting to his knees, his face a pasty white.

"Get inside. Make sure she didn't steal nothing!"

"It's not yours!" Penny snapped in reflex, but the constable just shook his head, his hands shoved deep in his pockets.

"I'm afraid he's right, Miss Shoemaker. I made sure of it before I came. Everything's sold to him."

"By who? How can someone up and sell my home right out from under me?"

Cordwain rolled his eyes. "Aw, listen to the tart. Lying bitch. I paid you all my damn savings for this place. You're rich, you bloodsucking whore. And you won't be denying me what's mine!"

Penny gaped at him, her mind rebelling at all the things that were absolutely wrong with everything he'd just said. But before she could get a word past the dam of fury clogging her throat, another man sauntered up. A gentleman, by the looks of him, and a useless one at that, given the worn state of his clothing. He was tall and somewhat thin, and his dark curly hair went every which way about his head as if his brains were exploding by way of his hair.

"If I might have a word, Constable—"

The official all but groaned. "Sir, this is hardly the time."

"Yes, I know, but in the interest of the writ of law, I thought I'd point out something." He gestured with his hand, and in that one movement alarm bells began to ring in Penny's mind. He was looking at the satchel. He knew and was about to tell. Bloody hell.

"You want justice?" she snapped. "Here, hold Tommy

for a moment." Her words made no sense, but she had to distract him somehow. And how better to distract a toff than to hand him a squirming, screaming toddler?

"What? No!"

Too late. She'd shoved the boy into his arms, much to both males' terror. And with her hands free, she could finally look at Cordwain's false bill of sale while keeping half an eye on whether the toff hurt Tommy or not. He didn't, thank heaven, but neither boy nor man was pleased with the situation.

"Can you read it?" sneered Cordwain.

"'Course I can. Enough to see that you didn't pay me for my property. And as I'm the one who owns this place, I'm the only one who can sell."

"I did, too, pay!" snapped Cordwain as he grabbed the bill out of her hand. "Right here. Payment to one Thomas Shoemaker."

"Tommy! That's Tommy!" She pointed at the squirming babe. "And he can't sell anything but his drool."

"Look, you lying piece of—" Cordwain's next words were drowned out as the constable blew one long shrill note on his whistle again. The noise was so loud that everyone stopped to clap their hands over their ears, Tommy included. Then, while their ears were still ringing, the constable stepped forward, speaking in a low, reasonable tone.

"It wasn't Tommy himself who sold your home, Miss Shoemaker. It was his guardian."

"I'm Tommy's guardian," she snapped.

"No, miss. You're not." As proof, he lifted up the bill of sale and pointed at a signature. Right there in dark ink she saw the signature of Mr. Reginald Addicock, solicitor and trustee of Thomas Shoemaker.

"What's a trustee?" she asked.

"Legal term for guardian," inserted the toff from behind Tommy's head. Apparently during that shrill whistle blow, Tommy and the gentleman had come to some mutual agreement. Tommy was wrapped around the toff's neck like a monkey and he wasn't screaming anymore. Meanwhile, the man supported Tommy's bum with one hand while angling for a better view of the bill of sale.

"But he can't sell my home!" Even as she said the words, a worry niggled at the back of her mind. She knew Mr. Addicock. He had been one of her father's friends. But surely her father would have said something if he'd named Addicock guardian. Or had that been just another thing her father had meant to do but forgot?

"He can and he did!" bellowed Cordwain.

"You've never even heard of him?" asked the gentleman. "How long have your parents been gone?"

"Seven weeks! Don't you think that in nearly two months, the man would have presented himself?"

"Well, yes, that would be typical, wouldn't it?" The man reached over and picked the bill of sale right out of Cordwain's hand. No one disagreed. He had that kind of confidence that people went along with. As if he had the right to step in and solve the problem. Which he didn't. But as he was working on her side, Penny saw no reason to stop him. Meanwhile, he was frowning down at the document. "It does look official, but—"

"'Course it is," said Cordwain. "It's this lying—"

"Call me names again, and I will scratch your eyes out!"

"You will not!" inserted the constable. "But I will blow this whistle until you are both too deaf to hear it. So stubble it, Cordwain. You got no cause to be saying things like that to her. Especially since you got the law on your side."

"His side!" Penny cried. "But none of it is true!"

The constable grimaced. "Everything I got is legal and true, Miss Shoemaker. It says he purchased your shop and everything in it."

"But how? I haven't received any money, I haven't talked to this solicitor, I don't know anything about this at all!"

The constable just sighed again, and the sound seemed to pull his shoulders down. It was the look of a miserable individual, but one who would do his duty no matter if it were wrong or not.

"It's not *right*," she said.

"Don't matter," inserted the toff. "It looks right from his end. He's got no cause to stop it."

"But it's *wrong*," Penny repeated, trying desperately to find a way to stop this. "All of it is just . . ."

"Legal," said Cordwain with a sneer. "All legal. Now get gone from here, girl. And take your brat with you. I can't have the likes of you around my place of business."

That was the final insult. The living fury beneath her skin broke free. She launched herself at Cordwain with the only weapon she had—her nails and her fury. But she never connected. Before she even realized she'd leaped, the toff had her around the waist. It was no small feat, given that he still had Tommy wrapped around his neck. And for a too tall, no-good toff, he was damned strong.

"We'll have none of that," he scolded, not winded in the least despite the way she was flailing in his one-armed grasp. "It's too late; surely you can see that," he continued.

He was right. While she was trapped by the toff, the constable had stepped between her and the bastard Cordwain. Jobby, too, had recovered and was now looking as dark and violent as she felt. Still, she would have fought on if it weren't for Tommy. All her struggles were putting the toddler in danger. Apparently the stranger knew that, too, because he was quickly shoving the boy into her arms even as he set her back onto her feet.

"There, now, hold the boy before he gets hurt," he said.

"That's right, you b—"

"Enough, Cordwain," cut in the constable. "Damned if you don't know how to make a bad situation worse every time I see you."

The bastard puffed himself up, his face flushed and his mouth starting to open, but the toff was there beforehand, his manner somewhat bumbling but his eyes very keen.

"One question, Mr. Cordwain, if I may. Did you know this solicitor before the sale?"

"Wot? Why—"

"How close were the two of you?"

"I didn't know the damned man before he took my money!"

"Well, that's clearly not true," said the gentleman with an eye roll. "You don't just give a man money for a store out of the blue. How'd you know he was Tommy's guardian? 'Specially since the lad's sister didn't even know."

Cordwain's brows narrowed and he looked to the storefront. "Everybody knows I've wanted this property. Been trying to buy it, but her dad wouldn't sell."

"I see," said the gentleman, his brows drawn together in a frown. "But what has that to do with Mr. Addicock?"

"He contacted me. Said as he knew I wanted to buy it, and would I do it now? And for a bloody high price, too!" Cordwain's face snapped around to glare in their direction. "Had to spend all my savings for it. Every last groat!"

"Well, every last groat except for the men you're paying right there." He gestured to the three sour-looking thugs loitering around the shop's front door. "Five men plus the constable to evict one woman and a babe? Seems rather excessive, doesn't it?"

"I knew she would be trouble," the bastard growled. "And I was right."

"Huh." That was it. Just a grunt more than a word, accompanied by a glance at the constable, who simply shrugged.

"No!" Penny cried. "No!"

"I'm afraid so, Miss Shoemaker. It's the law. Do you have someplace to go? A relation perhaps? Or a friend?"

Penny stared at them. Cordwain, the constable, Jobby and his henchmen, then the toff last of all. They all stared at her like mutton. Blank male faces of differing personality, but all dumb, all blind. "Can't you see . . ." she began, praying that one of them would help her. After everything she'd done since her parents' murder, everything she'd survived, this final humiliation was too much. It was—

"I'll see to her, Constable," the gentleman said. "Just let me get my bag." Then, without so much as a by-your-leave, he strolled straight over to her satchel and flipped it over his shoulder.

"But—"

"Best go with him," the constable said, giving her a sad smile. "Nothing to be done here."

"But . . ." Her gaze traveled to her home. She'd been born in the upper story of that building there, as had her father. The shop had been her grandfather's pride and joy, and her father's after that. One month ago, she had found a way to save it. She'd just begun to dream of opening its doors again to show her wares just like a Shoemaker had for over fifty years. It couldn't be taken from her. Not without warning. Not like this.

"Come now," said the gentleman as he gently cupped her elbow. "There's stuff to be done and it isn't here."

"But—"

"Just walk," he ordered. Not harshly, but with enough authority that she obeyed. She spoke not a word, and to her added fury she found she was crying. Big, wet tears leaked down her face. She couldn't stop it, and she damn well couldn't hide it.

They were three blocks away when the toff finally said something that jolted her out of her misery.

"Tell me why I'm carrying a bag of body parts."

Chapter 2

❧❧

"They're not body parts!" she cried. Then she forcibly pulled her emotions under control. By all accounts, this man was trying to help her. She shouldn't be taking out her frustration on him. "They're called 'likes.' They're wood blocks cut into the shape of our customers' feet. A shoemaker then makes the shoe to fit the mold."

He glanced at her, and she was startled to see his eyes twinkling in the sunshine. Was he teasing her? Perhaps, but when he spoke, his words were very serious. "I know what they are, Miss Shoemaker. What I want to know is why—when armed men were bursting through your door—you took the time to grab a bag of wooden feet."

Penny resettled Tommy on her shoulder, using the time to think how to respond. Now that they were away from all the frightening things at home, the child was starting to droop against her. He'd be asleep before long.

"They're the only thing I have left from my father," she said softly. Even added a slight sniff as if she were teetering on the very edge of despair. She was teetering, but not headed toward despair. Seething anger was her particular demon.

Apparently, the toff wasn't fooled. She hadn't even finished her sniff when the man burst out laughing. "My dear, you will have to do a great deal better than that if you want to fool me."

She sniffed again, but not in tears. Damn the man for being smart. "I'm sorry, sir, but I don't even know your name."

"Oh! Bother, of course." He stepped back and executed a rather florid and formal bow. "Mr. Samuel Morrison at your service."

She frowned, searching through her memories of the different gentlemen who had frequented her father's shop. Her job had been to smile sweetly at them as she served them tea or something stronger. She'd learned very young that delicate line between being charming without actually flirting. And if she ever crossed the line, her mother had been there to haul her back by her ear. But she didn't remember a Samuel . . .

"Oh wait! Your father was Baron Hugh Morrison. His feet might be in that bag you're holding! And your brother . . ."

"Gregory."

"Yes! Oh, he was such a serious little boy."

"We call him sullen."

"But I don't remember . . ."

"A younger son?"

She flushed. She knew something about being passed over by a parent. Apparently, Samuel did, too. "Er, perhaps I was away when your family came for shoes," she offered.

"You weren't. I never had the joy of a Shoemaker boot, but my father swore they were the very best."

Now she really was touched by a bit of melancholy. Her father had been the very best shoemaker in England, and times like this, she missed him terribly. But rather than dwell on what was lost, she glanced over at Mr. Morrison, only to find him watching her closely. His eyes were the dark brown of fine leather stained honey. Most would call it a simple brown, but she saw the lighter streaks, especially now with the sun shining on his face.

And she shivered. Not in fear, but in sudden awareness. There was a banked intensity in him. He spoke casually and sometimes with a touch of irritation, as if he couldn't be bothered with whatever it was that you were saying. But the way he looked at her said that he was anything but casual about his environment. Indeed, she believed he saw *everything*, and that worried her. She was too used to hiding things for her to be easy around someone who *noticed*.

"Um," she said, scrambling for some way to distract him. "A pleasure to meet you, Mr. Morrison."

"Hmmm, that remains to be seen. I was about to turn you in to the constable, you know. The bill of sale stated everything in the home and shop. Including, I'm sure, these very body parts that I'm hauling around."

"They're not body parts!" she huffed. "Stop saying that!"

He chuckled. It was a nice sound, though surprisingly gruff. As if he weren't used to laughing and was as surprised as she by his amusement. "But I like saying it. Tickles my admittedly macabre sense of humor."

She opened her mouth to say something to that, but really what could one say? Exactly what did he mean by "macabre"? She knew the word, though only vaguely. It had to do with death, funerals, and gloomy things. But he had said "sense of humor", so that couldn't be right. Meanwhile, he had begun swinging the satchel left and right, talking in an almost singsong way.

"This is not a well-made bag, you know. I noticed it because the seams were old and weak. Any little provocation could have it splitting wide open and spilling wooden body parts all over the street. Just imagine what might happen if I accidentally knocked it against a tree."

He was fitting word to action and she nearly leaped out of her skin to catch it. But with Tommy now asleep on her shoulder, she couldn't move fast enough and he kept it maddeningly out of reach.

"Please, sir!" she gasped as she looked hurriedly about her. "Please don't throw that around!"

"But you threw it right in a pile of rubbish."

"I didn't—" She snapped her mouth shut. Of course she did. And he had seen. And now he was looking for an explanation. He was looking at her, the bag still swinging back and forth. He didn't even look like he was paying attention to her, but she knew that was an illusion. Especially when he arched a brow. "I detest repeating myself, Miss Shoemaker. Why did you risk everything on grabbing a bag of wooden feet?"

"Because they are mine! And that bill of sale is completely false!" Damn the man for turning her into a shrew in the middle of the street. Back there was bad enough when she was fighting against armed bullies, but now they were strolling along near Bond Street on a beautiful day. And now he'd managed to poke at her until she was as furious and *helpless* as she had been back there.

As if he knew he'd pushed her to the very brink, he stopped swinging the bag. It slowed, then eventually came to rest against his leg. She stared at it, unable to meet his gaze. It took her a few moments to get her temper back under control, but when she did, she spoke in low tones.

"They are the feet of all of Father's most prestigious clients. Nobs as a rule don't like coming in to get their feet measured. They'd much prefer to send a messenger. *'I'd like a pair of riding boots like Lord Whomevers. I need a new left shoe as my old one is terribly scuffed.'* They can't be bothered to come in and get a new foot whittled, and besides, that takes time to get the mold right."

He nodded, taking up the flow of her words, his agile mind easily understanding what she was saying. "So that makes the molds rather valuable, I would guess. Whoever has the wooden feet is most likely to get the nob's business."

"Yes."

"But that still doesn't answer the question. Why would *you* care about that? Your father was the shoemaker, not you."

She didn't answer. She couldn't because everyone knew that women couldn't be shoemakers. They were too weak, too soft, too mutton-headed. Everyone knew that, which was why she couldn't get a job as a shoemaker's apprentice even though she'd been making shoes all her life. Her father's hands hadn't always worked so well, and she was right there, eager to help. She'd learned every aspect of the trade by the time she was twelve, but still no one would buy from a girl.

That was why she had started selling shoes made by Tommy's "father," whom no one had ever met. And yes, at the moment, she only made women's shoes, but one day that would change. One day, Tommy's "father" would open the shop again and send notes round to all the nobs with feet in her bag. He would offer them new shoes at a discounted price if only they would send a drawing of what they'd like. But it would be her, of course, making the shoes in secret and sending them on.

Except now a damned toff was looking at her much too clearly. It was bad enough that she'd just lost her shop and home. Now he could expose everything else. People wouldn't buy shoes made by a woman. And if she couldn't sell shoes, then how would she and Tommy survive?

"Is your father still alive then? Or an uncle or . . ." He glanced at the babe asleep in her arms. "Tommy's father?"

"Yes," she said, forcing herself to meet his eyes calmly. "Tommy's father. I measure the customer's feet, manage the leather and cording, and he makes them."

"I'm sure he does. At night, in secret, and no one has ever met him, have they?"

"Tommy's mother did."

"Ah. Yes. Of course. But I hardly think they were discussing shoes."

Penny flushed and looked away. She knew everyone thought Tommy her bastard son. Hadn't Cordwain just bellowed that to the world? She'd given up protesting her innocence. No one ever believed her, but the innuendo still made her angry. And that made her skin flush. Let him believe she was blushing in embarrassment.

"Do you make good shoes, Miss Shoemaker?"

Her chin shot up, but anger pushed her to say the truth. Much too loudly. "I make the finest shoes in England."

His brow arched at that. "England is a very large place, Miss Shoemaker. With lots of shoemakers in it."

"I learned at my father's knee. And my grandfather's, too."

"And you whittle new molds as well. Don't bother to deny it. I can see the marks on your hands."

She looked down at her palms. There were rough patches and nicks, to be sure, but it would take a keen eye to notice that.

"How long does it take to make a new likeness?"

"Days if I have nothing else to do."

"And that's if the customer cooperates and comes in to be measured. I begin to understand why you risked everything to grab a bag of wooden feet." He tilted his head, his eyes narrowed in thought. "Do you really think you can make shoes for the likes of Lord Winston?"

She nodded slowly. She was not used to telling her plans to anyone. Certainly not a man she had just met. But the truth was, she had absolutely intended to become a very successful shoemaker. And then, when everyone was wearing her shoes and she was buried in gold up to her ears, then she would finally reveal herself as the shoemaker. Her. *A girl.* A woman passed over by her own father because he couldn't see past the fact that she was female. She would be the most famous shoemaker in the world because she was that good. And because she was a woman.

"I am amazed," he said slowly. "And I assure you, that doesn't happen very often."

"Because a girl can't make shoes?"

"Because people, as a rule, don't think clearly enough to plan such an elaborate deception. You quite take my breath away."

She gaped at him, her words torn away by his admiration for her . . . mind? No one appreciated her thoughts. No one understood what it took to survive as a woman alone with a babe. No one but perhaps her new friends at the dressmaker shop. And certainly no man had ever seen such a thing in her. But he had, and she was totally overwhelmed by a sense of gratitude. Good Lord, he *saw* her. And she was equal parts joyous and terrified by that.

Then the moment was over. With a jaunty whistle, he started walking again, swinging her satchel back and forth as if he hadn't just warned that a stiff breeze could have it splitting open. Then he looked back at her, his expression pulled into a slightly irritated frown.

"Well? Are you going to tell me the rest? I can't solve the puzzle without all the pieces, you know."

She rushed to catch up to him. "Pieces? Puzzle? Whatever do you mean?"

"Your parents' murder, of course. Tell me everything."

Samuel found it hard not to dance in the street. Here he'd been thinking that the Season would be beyond dull this year. Certainly it was a necessary part of his life, given his current financial straits. But free food aside, nothing at all of note was happening. And then what should appear before his eyes, but a mystery! Complete with murders and villains and a damsel in distress! He couldn't be happier if the Prince Regent himself popped by to ask for popularity advice.

Sadly, the whole problem probably wouldn't take more than a few days. He'd already solved the most intriguing bit. And how gratifying it was that the distressed damsel was not touched in the head when she grabbed the bag of feet, but of a surprisingly logical bent. Imagine, a woman who could think things through and settle on a practical plan! He was still shocked by it.

Meanwhile, the lady in question was peering at him with narrowed eyes. It wasn't an unusual look for him to receive, usually by someone who was not at all pleased to discover Samuel's unusual intelligence, and so he slid straight into a bit of charm. It was silly, really, how easy it was to distract some people.

"Oh, dear," he exclaimed. "I can see that it has been much too much for you today and no wonder. But don't you worry. You have too much to handle as it is, what with a babe and all. Is there someplace we are headed? We can get you settled there in a trice, and then sort this whole thing out. It won't be too hard. I promise."

Far from helping matters, the lady's eyes narrowed almost to the point of fury. "Yes, sir, I do have a place to go," she said in cold, clipped tones. "But you won't be going there with me, and I won't be talking of my parents or lifting my skirts for a toff who's too bored to find his own life." Then she held out her free hand. "I'll be taking my bag now, if you please, and you can be on your way."

Samuel stared at her, his mind once again stunned silent. How had this woman—this little slip of a girl, really— managed to silence him twice in the space of an hour?

"Magnificent!" he murmured. Her eyebrows shot up at that, and he scrambled to explain. "I have no interest in your skirts, lifted or otherwise, Miss Shoemaker, so you can be at ease on that score." It was a lie, of course. Any woman who could so effectively put him in his place had him harder than a rock. She was comely and all, but a woman who could trade verbal barbs with him was rarer than Helen of Troy and infinitely more exciting.

And smart as she was, she called him on his bluff. "You've got a gleam in your eye and a swelling that calls you a liar."

So he did, which he acknowledged with a slight bow. "Excellent! I'll call that point yours. But what I want isn't of the usual sort." She gasped at that and he rushed to explain. "I wish to solve your puzzle. It's a worthy one, you see. An injustice done to an innocent who hasn't the where-withal to solve it on her own. I could do that for you and count it as a good deed on my way to heaven."

She snorted. "You are *not* a Good Samaritan."

"No, I'm certainly not." He waited, looking at her with as open an expression as he could manage. But she had to know she was running out of time. Already his mind was beginning to wander. They had reached Bond Street, where the fashionable wandered. He had already seen two new couples and one decidedly bad choice in waistcoat. Much longer and he would lose interest, his mind dragging him along to something that was likely more trivial than this, but decidedly more immediate.

"You cannot be *that* bored," she snapped.

He sighed. "I assure you, I am. And worthy mysteries are hard to find."

She tilted her head as she looked at him, and for a moment his mind centered on the shift in color as the light hit her hair. She was a dishwater blonde with streaks of hair going from nearly white all the way to a dull brown. But in the sunlight, her hair appeared like textures to him. An infinite variety of multifacets that boggled his mind for the complexity of it. And yet, taken as a whole, it was simply stunning.

"You're a daft toff and I'll bet a lazy one," she said, dismissing him with a sigh. "But if you want to carry my bag to the dress shop, then I won't say no."

"Will you thank me?" he asked, startled to hear himself flirting. With a shoemaker of all people! And yet he found Miss Shoemaker to be intriguing. And that was not something he ever took lightly.

She snorted as if he'd just confirmed her worst opinion of him. "If you give the bag straight back to me with no argument, yes, I'll thank you." Then she pointed to where they were heading. "Lady Caniche's shop is a few blocks that way."

"Caniche? That's a decidedly unfortunate name." She didn't disagree—and how could she with a shop named "Lady Poodle" in French? So together they headed off while his mind began sorting through the pieces. The shop was a nothing place struggling to survive in a location too far off Bond Street to be noticed by anyone at all. Except that someone had noticed it. Lady Gwen, now a baroness, had commissioned her trousseau from them and everything went as it usually did. Lady Gwen's attire was sumptuous, and Mrs. Mortimer (the owner) was well on her way to fame and fortune.

Then the quiet dressmaker did the unheard-of and wildly fantastic feat of snagging Lady Gwen's brother Robert, Lord Redhill, in matrimony. It wasn't quite the bizarre situation it appeared. Unlike everyone else, Samuel had known Mrs. Mortimer's true identity the moment he'd seen her. But that was a secret he had no interest in exposing, and besides, it had nothing to do with his current mystery.

"I thought Lady Redhill renamed the shop to A Lady's Favor," he said.

He watched as the woman's step faltered. "I—I'm sorry. You are correct. It was renamed two years ago when Mrs. Mortimer took ownership." He nodded. "Perfectly understandable. I surmise you have lived all your life in this area. When one's life is in upheaval, it is easy to forget minor changes in the environment."

"Except *you* remembered." She tilted her head, her eyes

once again narrowed. As if it were his fault that he remembered practically everything, trivial or not.

"My life is not in upheaval."

"Neither is this your usual environment."

He nodded happily. "Thank you for noticing. I assure you, it is the rare soul who does so. Now to continue, I believe you are the shoemaker making all those lovely slippers for Lady Gwen's family."

"No, sir," she said stiffly. "I am merely the girl who takes the measurements. Tommy's father fashions the shoes."

"Of course," he said, understanding that was a fiction she needed to maintain for now. Until such time as she became famous enough to reveal her true identity. But that was neither here nor there. "They will let you sleep in the shop?"

She shrugged. "Mrs. Mortimer married—"

"Yes, I heard."

"But her mother still stays in the rooms above the shop. They've made up Helaine's old bedroom for Tommy for when I'm working and can't watch him."

"And now it shall be for you both. At least until we can get your true home back."

She looked at him, her light blue eyes almost colorless in the sun. He could see she was fighting tears of frustration. She was not one to waste them on pitying herself, but fury could make one's eyes water just as well. He had much the same reaction to lawlessness.

"How?" she asked. "How will we do that?"

She was overwrought, and no wonder; otherwise she would likely have figured it out for herself. Still, he was grateful that she couldn't see the answer because that gave him a purpose. "It is the solicitor, of course. Wills, trustees, and sale of property all require a solicitor, and they can be as criminal as a bloody burglar. They just do it on paper. But one has to admire the cheek. He hears your father's dead, draws up the documents declaring himself the trustee, and then sells your property right out from under you. And if you were to complain—"

"Of course I'm going to complain!"

"Well, when you complain, you're a woman alone and a distraught one at that. Probably won't even admit you to his office. Then what would you do?"

She lifted her chin, a blaze of fury flashing in her eyes. "I'd go to Helaine, is what I'd do," she said firmly.

"Ah, but Mrs. Mortimer is now Lady Redhill and on her honeymoon. Not much help to you there, is she?"

He watched the lady glare at him, her agile mind realizing that she would either have to wait out Lady Redhill's honeymoon or be grateful for his help. He wondered how long it would take her to ask him for it.

"I could hire my own solicitor," she said. "One who will open his door to me."

"You could, but that will take time and, I suspect, money that you do not have. And even then the man would not have my skills—"

She snorted at that because, of course, she had no idea how very extensive his skills were.

"Or my connections."

He let that hang in the air between them. She had no true idea who he was. Certainly she guessed that he was a hanger-on in society, a jester invited because he was entertaining. But that also meant that he had friends. A few at least, who would stand him in good stead provided that he did not tax them too much.

Meanwhile, she came to her decision. "Very well," she said. "I will hire you on my behalf. You'll get ten quid when I move back into my home all free and clear. Fifteen if you put that bastard solicitor in jail."

He raised his eyebrows, startled once again. "I had not asked for payment."

"I detest favors, Mr. Morrison. Nobs never stop collecting them, and men always want something I won't give. We'll be writing down our arrangement on paper. I'll be paying you for your time, and if you treat me badly and get nothing done, then you'll be the one paying me. Same amount."

"Ten quid if I can't get you back into your home?"

"And fifteen if you can't put the bastard in jail."

"So this is more of a wager, then. With you betting that I cannot do what I promise."

She shrugged. "Nobs like wagers, treat them more fairly than they do their honest workmen."

"Or workwomen."

She nodded, but refused to be distracted. "As you're a nob and a daft one at that, I should like the wager written down. Doesn't have to be public, unless you don't pay when you fail."

He rocked back on his heels, surprised for the third time that day. She had neatly created a win-win situation for herself. If he succeeded in everything he planned, then she would have her life restored to her. If he failed, then she would have fifteen quid to help pay her bills. And she had found the one thing that would keep him interested beyond the usual attention of his very fickle brain: a wager. Not on a turn of a card, but on logic and action.

"You are a remarkable woman, Miss Shoemaker."

"Do we have a deal?"

"We do. And now, truly, you must tell me everything you know about your parents' murder." She opened her mouth to argue, but he raised his hand to stop her. "You have hired me, Miss Shoemaker, or bet me. Either way, you must allow me to work as I will. And that includes revealing every terrible detail of a painful crime. I am sorry, but I really must insist."

She closed her mouth and eyed him with exasperation. But she didn't say anything.

"Miss Shoemaker?"

"I'll be happy to tell you, Mr. Morrison, but not in front for your jilted lover."

"I beg your pardon?"

Instead of answering, she gestured vaguely to the area behind him. He spun around, nearly splitting open her bag of feet on a nearby tree. But that was nothing compared to the horror he felt when he saw the woman who was right then breaking speed records as she ran pell-mell at them.

"She's not my mistress!" he snapped. "She's much, much worse."

"Oh?" came Miss Shoemaker's amused response.

"Yes. She's my brother."

Miss Shoemaker snorted. "How can a woman be your brother?"

"Same way Tommy's father is your shoemaker." He sighed because she clearly didn't understand. And because there was no way to avoid Georgette. "You'll see," he said darkly. "My brother, his wife—they both have the same brain. And it's not that fond of me."

Chapter 3

Penny knew enough to keep her mouth shut when the stern-looking German woman finally stopped, huffing and puffing, right in front of them. She was fast, despite her bulk, which meant that Mr. Morrison had no time to run, though his gaze darted left and right, obviously searching for an escape. Meanwhile, Penny had time to look at the woman more clearly.

Under normal circumstances, Penny would have called her cheery. The woman looked exactly like the mother in a set of nesting dolls she'd once played with. She was rosy cheeked and dressed in a bright gown of yellow with light blue accents. But the gimlet eye she trained on Mr. Morrison was just short of evil. Fortunately, she hadn't the breath to speak, which allowed Mr. Morrison to try an escape.

"Ah, Georgette!" he cried, in clearly false cheer. "Lovely to see you, having fun shopping? Well, I can see that you've got other things to do, so I shall leave you to them. Good day!"

He made to move away, but the woman grabbed hold of

his arm and clutched tight enough to make Mr. Morrison wince.

"Hold still, Samuel," she snapped. "Your brother needs a word."

"Then I shall contact him in due time—"

"Just a moment! I shall tell you it directly."

"But you never stop at just one word," he drawled as he eyed the midday sky. "And it'll be dusk before you're done."

Penny raised her eyebrows at that, but Georgette looked positively thunderous.

"We wouldn't use so many words if you would but *listen* to us."

Mr. Morrison heaved a mighty sigh. "You make a common mistake, Georgette. Listening is not the same thing as obeying. I do listen. I can hardly help but listen."

"And then you forget and go about your merry way without a thought in your head."

"Never that, Georgette. Never, ever without a thought in my head." He sounded downright morose at that. Meanwhile, Penny realized that she ought not to be standing there listening to what was obviously a family squabble. So with a slight nod, she started to step away.

"I shall leave you to your family," she began, but Mr. Morrison was quick to grab her elbow.

"No, no. We have business, you and I. Urgent business, that cannot wait."

"Urgent!" the woman scoffed. "As if you have anything urgent in your life! Your brother was just commenting the other day about the company you keep! Tarts and artists." She sniffed and curled her lip.

Up until that moment, Penny was inclined to be neutral toward the woman. After all, she understood how men could be exasperating, and so she was prepared to remain silent. But at those words, she stiffened her spine. This woman had no cause to be bringing her into her family spat. But long before she could say anything, Mr. Morrison stepped forward, his face dark and cold as Penny hadn't seen before. Not even when he was facing the thugs who had stolen her home.

"You forget yourself, Georgette," he snapped. "May I present Miss Shoemaker and her brother, Thomas."

"Does she write poetry?" the woman sneered.

"She's my client, Georgette. Miss Shoemaker, my brother's shrew of a wife, Baronness Georgette Morrison."

Penny smiled politely and nodded. She managed to force herself to say, "Baronness," in greeting, but that was all. Meanwhile, the woman's expression slid from disdain, through outrage, to a slow but very clear shock. In fact, her mouth opened and closed twice before she found her voice.

"Client?" she finally asked.

"A small legal matter. Miss Shoemaker hired me to help her sort it out."

"You're working? You have a job, Samuel? Sweet heaven, that's wonderful! Your brother is so pleased!"

"My brother is nothing of the kind as he does not know. Now if you'll excuse us—"

"Wait! Wait!" She huffed out a breath and had the grace to look ashamed. "I am terribly sorry for misjudging you," she said to Penny. But then she turned to her brother-in-law, and her eyes went cold. "Your brother is most vexed with you."

"That is hardly news—"

"It's about Maximilian."

Mr. Morrison froze and even Penny could see the sudden wariness in his expression. "Yes?" he said slowly.

"You forgot!"

"I could hardly forget I have a nephew, Georgette. I—"

"Idiot! You forgot his birthday!"

"I most certainly did not! His party is . . . It's . . ." He frowned and looked at Penny. "Oh, bloody hell, what day is it today?"

"It was yesterday!" his sister-in-law snapped. "Yesterday

was the party and yesterday you were not there! Please, God, tell me you were busy obtaining work or abducted by pirates or something meaningful!"

Both women looked at his face, hoping for a ready excuse, but he had none. The guilt was written plain as day, and all he could do was shake his head. "I was sure it was tomorrow."

"Harumph!" snorted his sister-in-law. "I cannot tell you how disappointed Gregory is in you."

Mr. Morrison rolled his eyes at his sister, and truly Penny was a half breath away from doing the same thing. It was clear the man felt guilty enough. The woman did not have to heap on more blame. And in the way of families, Mr. Morrison only made it worse.

"Really, Georgette? Gregory is disappointed? One would think it would be the boy who expressed dismay. Or do you simply tell the boy what to think as you do everyone else?"

"Max? Max is a boy. He doesn't say anything but kicks furniture and mopes about! If you have a brain in your head—"

"Oh, my God!" snapped Penny, her patience completely exhausted. They were on Bond Street, in full view of everyone, and were picking at each other like a pair of magpies. "Mr. Morrison, pray say that you are sorry and that you will bring round a gift immediately. And, Baroness Morrison, please will you simply accept his apology? Scolding at a man never does anything but stop his ears up tighter than a drum."

Penny expected to be roundly cursed by both parties. After all, she was the interloper here, but really, they had both lost any semblance of reason. Far from cursing her, however, the lady stared at her in shock. And then a moment later, she rocked back on her heels as her gaze swept the street around them. They hadn't attracted much attention. Truly, family squabbles happened every day on Bond Street, and this one had progressed in icy cold tones, not screeching yells. But it was embarrassing nonetheless.

"Of course, you are quite correct, Miss Shoemaker," the baroness finally said. "You are a clever girl and quite above his usual company. Are you sure you want to employ him?"

Penny had nothing to say to that, though naturally Mr. Morrison did. "Oh, leave off, Georgette. And I shall do you one better than a promise of a gift. Here, give the boy this." He passed the woman Penny's satchel of molds.

"Hey!" cried both women, but for entirely different reasons. Penny had just risked everything to save the likes from Mr. Cordwain. She did not want them passed to some relation's son! What the baroness thought of the heavy satchel was written in her very curled lip. But before either woman could say more, Mr. Morrison held up his hand.

"Please, ladies, give me a moment to explain. Georgette, the bag is not the gift, but the puzzle is. Have Max inventory it and make a list of all the people who might want to kill for it."

"Kill!" the woman gasped. "He's just a boy!"

"Exactly! He will love it. Not a boy alive who doesn't love murder and mayhem."

Apparently the baroness couldn't argue that, so that left time for Mr. Morrison to turn to Penny.

"And, Miss Shoemaker, your things will be quite safe there with Max. He's a most clever boy, very careful with his things, especially my presents to him."

His sister-in-law nodded, oddly in accord on this point. "They are like two peas in a pod, those two. I cannot understand it, but rest assured, my Max will treat this like gold."

"But—" began Penny, only to be overrun once again by her daft toff.

"And what will you say if a certain gentleman claims that they are lost? He will come round looking for them, will he not? And this way you can truthfully say that you have no idea where they are."

"But I will know," she said with a sigh.

"Do you know where my brother lives? Of course not—"

His sister-in-law spoke up. "Well, that's easy enough. Our house is in—"

"Georgette! Hush! My God, what are you thinking? She cannot know where you live."

"But—"

"Oh, spare me from a woman who cannot think!"

Baroness Morrison was about to snap back at him, but Penny intervened. "I believe Mr. Morrison is playing a game with the constable. Pray do not argue with him. He believes he is being very clever. But he doesn't understand that I am not one to lie to the authorities. That will only make my problems worse."

Mr. Morrison grimaced at her words, but he didn't have time to speak before his sister-in-law cried out in horror.

"Constable? Authorities? My God, Samuel, you cannot involve Maximilian in such things!"

"Do not be so dramatic!" he returned, his brow furrowing as he glared down at the cobblestone. "Miss Shoemaker, it matters not what you say to the constable, so long as you don't have the thing at hand. We need time, don't you see? Time to prove the fraud. And if Cordwain gets his hands on that bag, you will never see it again. Of that you can be sure."

He had a point. She had just risked everything to take it out of the shop. She did need a good hiding place for it. Why not leave it with a young boy who would take great care of it?

"He will not harm them?"

"I assure you," the man continued, "this will be a great treasure to Max. And you would have my deepest gratitude as well. Pray, do not disappoint the child. That would be very cruel."

He was charming her, his expression so earnest she couldn't help smiling. To the side, Baroness Morrison was similarly exasperated and amused. "I never understand half of what he says, Miss Shoemaker. Your word of honor that no harm will befall my boy for taking . . . whatever it is in this bag?"

"Oh, good God, Georgette. They're not dangerous!"

The two were about to start squabbling, so Penny once again stepped between them. "There's nothing dangerous about them," she said gently. "And I would be grateful if your son could keep track of it for me for a bit. Now if you'll forgive me . . ." Penny rehoisted her sleeping brother on her shoulder. "Tommy is rather heavy and it has already been a long day."

The baroness took the cue and her leave. She carried the satchel awkwardly, but with a firm grip. And a moment later, she was stepping into a hansom cab, presumably on her way home to her son.

Meanwhile, beside Penny, Mr. Morrison was releasing a sigh of relief. "Good God, but the woman's exhausting!"

Penny snorted and began walking again toward the dress shop. "I rather think she says the same about you."

"I don't doubt it!" he said as he fell into step beside her. "Thing is, she's the perfect woman for my brother. And she gave birth to a wonderful boy, that Max. Smart as can be. But she can't get it into her head that I'm not part of her circle of management."

Penny nodded, unsure how to take that comment. After all, the baroness did indeed seem to be a managing sort of woman. But on the other hand, she suspected that, as men went, Mr. Morrison could do with a little direction. He seemed to be a little—or perhaps a lot—out of step with the rest of the world. She could only be grateful that his current step was alongside hers. Assuming, of course, that he was able to help her. To that end, she turned to him.

"Do you really think you can expose the solicitor as a fraud?"

"Hmm? Oh, yes. That shall be easy. Proving that he had your parents murdered, now that will be a challenge!"

Penny stumbled, the bluntness of his words cutting straight to her heart. They had been talking about this, of course, before his sister-in-law appeared. He had asked her about their murder, but her mind had been so preoccupied with losing the shop, with who exactly he was, with everything that had happened this day, that she had not comprehended his thoughts. The solicitor had her parents murdered? But . . . but . . . They had been killed by footpads or so the constable had told her. Could all of this be one piece? The idea was monstrous and it was more than she could handle at that moment.

So she stumbled, jostling Tommy and stubbing her toe at the same time. Samuel caught her quickly. A hand beneath her elbow to steady her. And then when he looked at her face, he released a soft but heartfelt curse.

"I wasn't thinking," he said by way of apology. "My mind, you know, it runs on. But you needn't worry about any of it. We have a wager, you know, and I shall take care of it all. I swear."

"But how," she whispered. How did one go about finding justice in this world? It simply wasn't something she'd had any reason to expect.

He flashed her a smile that was half shrug, half apology. "By being me, of course. I know I'm odd, Miss Shoemaker. But when I set my mind to something, I am rather excellent at it. I shall see things set to rights."

"Will you?" she asked, wondering not about his promise but his mouth, of all things. His lips were nicely formed and his teeth marvelously straight. In his whole face, his mouth was most appealing, though his eyes took a very close second. They were warm and honest as they looked at her. And she had the strangest desire to do more than look at him. He sensed it, too, for she saw his eyes darken and his nostrils flare. She was used to noticing when men found something attractive. It was usually the sign for her to disappear. But for the first time in years, she didn't want to run. She wanted to learn more. And she wanted to touch and be touched in return.

But that was a ridiculous thing to do with this odd gent. He wasn't even all that physically attractive, though he did make her smile. He was too gangly, his clothing too shabby, and his hair really did need a comb. And most important, she needed him to help her, not be distracted into other thoughts.

And yet, his mouth was right there and he was looking at her with a surprised kind of interest. As if he, too, had no intention of being attracted to her, and yet found himself suddenly interested.

Then, thank heaven, they were saved. Tommy woke up and began to cry. The mood was broken and she had to readjust her hold on the child to comfort him. That meant that Mr. Morrison let go of her elbow and took a step back.

All over. No more unwanted attraction. Everything sorted itself back to where it ought to be. Or so she told herself.

Except that when she looked over Tommy's shoulder at Mr. Morrison, she saw that indeed everything had changed. He was looking at her with alarm that he quickly tried to cover by staring blandly at a storefront window. Tommy had settled again, having found his thumb to soothe himself. While Penny was holding her breath, wondering if things were about to become very awkward indeed, Mr. Morrison changed. He squared his shoulders and lifted his chin. Then he slowly, carefully turned back to look at her. And she saw as clear as day that he wanted her as a man wants a woman.

Penny licked her suddenly dry lips, and then roundly cursed herself for doing so. His gaze riveted on her mouth.

"Mr. Morrison," she began, wondering all the while what she intended to say.

"Never fear, Miss Shoemaker," he returned, "I shall sort things out to end up just how they ought to be."

She raised her eyebrows at his arrogance. He truly believed he was that powerful. And yet, everything she'd seen of him so far proved him to be an extraordinary gentleman. "But what if I think your arrangement is completely wrong?"

"Well, then," he said with a wink, "I expect we will have a jolly good row. But eventually you'll come around. Everyone always does."

She snorted. Really it was hard not to laugh at such vanity. "Do you know, Mr. Morrison, I believe you are every bit as managing as your sister-in-law, but in your own way."

He reared back. "Now you are being needlessly insulting."

"No, sir, I don't believe I am. But as our wager has you working toward my ends, I think I'll let you have your head, so to speak. Go on," she said, waving airily at him. "Manage my home back." Then she began to walk away, her back prickling the whole time with an awareness of him watching her.

He didn't stay behind her for long. His longer steps easily caught up to her. But what made things all the more disconcerting was that he never said a word. He just matched pace with her. And when she glanced his way, she found him watching her with a rather intense expression. The kind of expression that made her breath catch as shivers slipped down her spine. It was part awareness, part terror, and wholly disconcerting. And it didn't help in the least that he seemed as unsettled as she was.

Good God, the woman was whip smart! Samuel could barely keep his pace steady as he thought on that remarkable fact. Miss Shoemaker was perhaps one of the top twenty females of his acquaintance for intelligence. It wasn't her education, of course. Like most females, she was sorely lacking in that area. As the daughter of a successful merchant, she probably had the equivalent training of a vicar's daughter or a forward-thinking cit. That was deplorable, given her natural talents, but the way of things for a female.

He did not fault her for it. Far from it, actually, because it made her abilities all the more impressive.

He tallied up her accomplishments in his head. First, as a woman alone with a child, she had still managed to find a way to ply her trade—shoemaking—without anyone realizing their foot ware was being made by a woman. Second, when armed thugs appeared at her door, she had not lost her head to hysterics, but had grabbed the most valuable thing she owned—the foot molds—and staged a drama such that she could escape with her booty intact.

Third—and this was most significant in his mind—she had quite accurately read his character regarding his sister-in-law. He roundly hated Georgette for the exact reason that Miss Shoemaker stated: his sister-in-law was immune to his usual mixture of flimflam and cool logic. Georgette's stubbornness stemmed from a marked arrogance. She simply could not understand that her way was not always the best. Miss Shoemaker, on the other hand, accurately saw right through his charm and his logic, then coolly manipulated things to *her* liking.

He was both horrified and horribly impressed. And that led to a *situation*. Whenever he was horribly impressed, two completely separate things happened. The first was that his mind rapidly went about searching for a way for him to become *less* impressed. Like a boy searching for the magician's trick, he scrambled for some way to explain away the magical and replace it with something terribly mundane.

And the second, at least where females were concern, was that he became completely and totally infatuated. Rockhard infatuation complete with heart palpitations and myriad schemes intent on bedding the woman.

He would succeed. He always did, but it never lasted. Eventually his mind would find a way to dismiss the woman's brilliance. No person—male or female—could withstand critical scrutiny for long. In time, flaws would appear, and his mind would gleefully seize upon them, holding them up like dirty laundry. The infatuation would fade, and he would once again return to his normal world filled with trivialities and soul-eating boredom.

But that was for the future. In the present, he was flush with his infatuation, both for the woman and the rather weak mystery of her evil solicitor. And even more fortunate was her position in life. She was unmarried and of a class that would allow him to dally with her without repercussions. Perfect!

So while he went about solving her problems with the solicitor, he could bed her to their mutual satisfaction until his mind ferreted out her flaws. And then, the interlude would be over. He would return to his normal life, and she to hers with the added benefit of a restored home after he brought the solicitor to justice.

An excellent plan, he decided. Suddenly the next couple weeks were looking rather exciting. Sadly, it likely wouldn't last more than that amount of time. Possibly less than a week. He was, after all, extraordinarily intelligent, and therefore able to spot flaws very quickly. But Miss Shoemaker was also pretty and the day was rather fine. He would do his best to focus more on bedding the woman than finding her flaws. Probably as soon as tonight, after he exposed the solicitor to the proper authorities. She would naturally be grateful to him and therefore easily seduced.

It was all quite logical, and he was eager to get on with it. To that end, he pasted on his most brilliant smile and began his seduction of the pretty shoemaker with the even prettier mind.

Chapter 4

~✦~

The dress shop seemed quiet, but Penny guessed that was because all the activity was in the back workroom. Helaine's notoriety as the new Lady Redhill had brought scores of new customers to their door. But as she was gone on her honeymoon, the rest of them were scrambling to keep up. Helaine's mother was doing her best as the new front woman—the person who greeted the guests, talked to them about what they wanted, and in general tried to sell them things. Fortunately, she was pretty good at the task, enticing people to prepay for a special design once Helaine returned. Others accepted the lower-cost option of an existing design in the sketchbook, but with some tiny alteration in color or embellishment. That could be created immediately once the customer had been measured.

Which meant that almost all the work from the measuring, through the cutting, and on to the sewing was done by Wendy Drew, the seamstress and co-owner of the dress shop. Penny hadn't a clue how the woman kept up. She'd been working nonstop since Helaine's wedding two weeks ago and had even been induced to bring on an apprentice. Sadly, Tabitha wasn't very capable, and Penny very much feared she wouldn't last. But she was an extra pair of hands, at least, and so for now, she was welcome.

Penny hesitated on the shop's steps, knowing that she was bringing extra work to her already overburdened friends. But there was no help for it. She had nowhere else to turn. Still she couldn't push through the door until Mr. Morrison touched her elbow.

"Hesitation is against all logic. If you have decided, why wait?"

"I wasn't hesitating," she lied. "I was . . . I was . . . Oh, bother," she snapped, then she pushed through the door.

She didn't look behind her to see if he was following. Or smirking. She merely went through the front room to the back workroom, where Wendy was snapping orders at the sobbing apprentice and Helaine's mother was looking on with dismay. But they all looked up at Penny as she stepped slowly into the room.

"What 'appened to you?" cried Wendy, her refined accent slipping as she turned her back on her new apprentice to look Penny up and down. "You look all twisted and angry."

"And who is this?" asked Helaine's mother as she turned to frown at Mr. Morrison. "I'm sorry, sir, but we don't as a rule allow gentlemen in the workroom."

"Of course, my lady. I'll withdraw immediately. Miss Shoemaker, we can depart for the solicitor's as soon as you are ready."

Penny nodded while Helaine's mother released a nervous titter. "My lady?" she gasped. "No, no, I'm just simple Mrs. Appleton. It's my daughter who is the lady now."

Penny bit her lip, damning herself for bringing Mr. Morrison here. Of all the toffs in the world, this one was sure to know "Mrs. Appleton's" true identity as Lady Chelmorton. And his one slip had shown that he knew the truth, but apparently he chose to pretend ignorance. He nodded and flashed his too charming smile. "Of course, Mrs. Appleton. I apologize. I tend to be a little mutton-headed sometimes."

If that weren't a bounder, she didn't know what was. Meanwhile, Penny stepped forward and introduced the man. She ran through everyone's names for his benefit, and then gestured to him. "Everyone, this is Mr. Morrison," she said as neutrally as she could manage. "He's going to help me with a legal problem. My home was stolen from me this morning. The shop and everything!" Her attempts to remain calm failed. As she spoke, her voice wobbled and tears flooded her eyes. She tried to stop them, but she was standing with her friends after having lost everything.

"Stolen! But—"

"My God! How could—"

"Ladies, ladies, please." Mr. Morrison held up his hand, effectively silencing the room. Even Tabby stopped crying to listen. "I'm sure Miss Shoemaker will be pleased to explain everything in due time. But I must express that the faster we get to the solicitor's, the faster we can get everything set to proper order. We have come here, I believe, in the hopes that—"

"Oh yes! Tommy!" cried Mrs. Appleton. "Give me the lad. Set your bags upstairs. You can stay there are long as you need."

The woman bustled forward and gently lifted Tommy from Penny's weary arms. The boy went easily, still drowsy as he sucked his thumb. And as he knew Helaine's mother very well, he settled into her arms with barely a whimper.

"Go on now," Wendy said. "Wash your face and change your clothes. Best not to keep them legal types waitin'."

Penny nodded but she didn't move. And to her humiliation, the tears began to leak out, slipping down her cheeks in misery. And once again, it was Mr. Morrison who saved her, though his tone was gruff as he spoke.

"The thing is, she hasn't got any bags except a few nappies. It was all taken by a Mr. Cordwain."

"Cordwain! That blighter—" Wendy snapped, then she obviously stopped herself from spitting a curse.

"Probably isn't the thief," inserted Mr. Morrison. "But we'll have to visit the solicitor to find out." Then he touched Penny's arm, gently drawing her gaze to his. "Go on. You should at least wash your face." Again, his tone was gruff, but not unkind, which was exactly what she needed to stiffen her spine. Then he undid it all by gently stroking his thumb across her cheek. He didn't speak more, but his expression was quietly miserable. That was too much for her, and she started weeping again with fresh intensity.

"Oh dear!" Mrs. Appleton cried. But her arms were filled with Tommy and so she couldn't do anything. That left Wendy to spit a curse for real this time and bustle forward.

"You'll be wearing a new dress to see that solicitor. I've got two that will fit you right and proper."

Penny shook her head. There weren't any extra gowns here at all and she would not steal a customer's dress.

"Shush," said Wendy as she enveloped Penny in a fierce hug. "You'll take the gowns. They're stitched badly and I'll not have our name on them." She took a moment to glare at her apprentice. "But they'll do for you in a pinch. Come on. Tabby, you come, too. You can help pick some of Helaine's dresses. She's a lady now and will have all new things afore long, so she won't mind a bit. Mr. Morrison, we'll be just a few minutes."

Penny tried to object, but she was overruled. And truthfully, she didn't fight very hard. She did need a better gown for a visit to a solicitor, even if he was a lying thief. And even more than that, Wendy's brusk hug felt beyond wonderful. She hadn't realized how rigidly she'd been holding herself until her friend bustled her up the stairs. Penny didn't even have to look to know that Mrs. Appleton and Tommy were following behind. And Tabby, too, apparently.

And then for the next half hour they washed her face, brushed her hair, and sorted through the gowns. They generally mothered her in the way that only a group of dear friends can. And by the end of it, Penny felt stronger. Perhaps even strong enough to face an evil solicitor.

Or at least that was what she thought until she finally made it back downstairs and discovered that Mr. Morrison had disappeared.

Samuel was bored. He knew from experience that women never took "just a few minutes" to do anything. And even if they did, it only took a few seconds for him to become bored. Or for his mind to start wandering, and once it did that, his body often followed. And that was exactly what happened.

He settled in the front sitting room, just as he'd promised. But that only lasted long enough for all the women to make it upstairs. Then he stood and began inspecting the room he was in. Everything he saw confirmed his suspicion that the dress shop had just recently been in very dire circumstances. But the amount of work in the back room and the piles of receipts on the desk there indicated that the hard times were behind them. Or at least they were for the moment.

But there was something that had caught his eye in the workroom. Something out of place even in the chaos of a women's dressmaking shop. If only he could remember it. Normally he had perfect recall, but apparently Miss Shoemaker had the unwelcome attribute of distracting him when she was near. Things that would normally be burned onto his memory were inconsequential shadows instead. And this particular shadow drew him out of the front parlor and into the now empty workroom.

He stood there frowning as he surveyed everything. What had been out of place? He wandered aimlessly through the tables laden with piles of fabrics and patterns. He spent a little time inspecting the desk placed to the side, and he couldn't resist peeking at the books. Yes, the shop was definitely on the financial mend. But the aristocracy were a fickle bunch, and the news had yet to break that the new Lady Redhill was actually Lady Helaine, the daughter of the Thief of the Ton. Who knew what would happen here when everyone started talking about that?

Meanwhile, he wandered on. He stepped through the new apprentice's tiny area. As small as her corner of the shop was, every part of her work space seemed to be set at maximum distance from her chair. A bottle of buttons, a box of pins, even the thread she used was placed neatly but very far from where she sat. He made his conclusions there, then moved on to the seamstress's primary work area. That was when he found what had seemed so out of place before. He hadn't noticed it immediately because it was covered up by a half-made dress. But when he'd first walked into the room, Miss Drew had been stitching and so he had seen the pack of cards half slipped under a pile of fabric. As if someone had been practicing with them when they had been surprised and then quickly tried to hide them.

He picked up the deck and saw that they were relatively new. New enough that one might not suspect that they were marked. He held them up to his nose, not in the least surprised to detect the scent of tobacco and opium. He had already guessed where the seamstress got the pack, but this just confirmed his suspicion that she'd fallen in with the likes of Demon Damon, owner of one of the worst gambling dens in London.

Bad lot that and bad for the future of this little dress shop. He would have to warn Miss Shoemaker to distance herself from these people immediately. Of course, that would be hard given that they were obviously her friends and the only people who would take care of her and Tommy.

Best resolve the situation with her shoe store immediately, then. He was on the verge of grabbing Miss Shoemaker and doing just that when a woman entered the workroom. Sadly, he was so engrossed with thoughts of

Miss Shoemaker, that he didn't hear her entrance until she all but screamed.

"Who are you?" she demanded in a voice that would carry upstairs should anyone up there be listening.

He spun around, dropping the marked deck into his pocket. Cheating offended him as a general rule. Demon Damon went well beyond the usual type of villainy, so Samuel had no qualms about keeping an illicit deck of cards if it in some way tweaked the miscreant.

Meanwhile he pasted on a genial smile for the newcomer. She was a thin woman, dressed in mourning, but of the highest cut and style. He did not recognize her, which meant that she did not frequent the usual rounds of *ton* parties. That told him she was not an aristocrat, but a wealthy cit. And most telling of all, there was the unmistakable odor of the docks about her. She might be well dressed, but expensive wools absorbed scents just as much as the cheap ones did. Given that she had come into the back area as if she ought to be here that told him that she was the buyer for the shop. And therefore a formidable woman if she went toe to toe with ships' captains as she negotiated for wares.

"Good afternoon, ma'am," he said with a slight bow. "I am Mr. Samuel Morrison, and I'm here to assist Miss Shoemaker."

"Miss Shoemaker isn't here. And that is not her station."

"No, it's not. They are all upstairs, I believe. Doing . . ." He lifted his shoulders in the universal male gesture of ignorance.

"Hmph," she said, and he could tell that she tended toward the suspicious sort. But then a moment later, she appeared to change her mind. "Come along then," she said as she jerked her head out the workroom door. "If you're here, you might as well be useful."

It wasn't until they were outside that he realized she was cannier than he'd expected. Her intention was to grill him while she kept him busy with hauling for her. She had a small cart loaded down with bolts of fabric and a few boxes of buttons. He hadn't really thought of the different types of buttons in the world or that a single box could weigh a ton, but there were and it did. And the woman hefted it as if it were no more than a hatbox. Then she dumped it in his arms.

"So how long have you known Penny?" she asked as she plopped another box on top of the first.

"Ugh!" was all he managed to say and she paused as she grabbed no less than three bolts of fabric to peer at him.

"What's that?"

He swallowed. "Just met," he said.

"Really." A statement, not a question, but there was a wealth of meaning hidden in there and most of it was suspicion.

"Really," he answered firmly. They started moving toward the workroom door. There was no way he could open the door for her like a true gentleman, not with his arms filled with two ton of buttons, but she paused nonetheless, her brow arched as if in challenge.

He rose to the occasion, though his muscles were screaming as he braced the boxes between the wall and his shoulder to free up one hand for her.

"Mind, don't drop that," she said as she sailed inside. "They're precious, you know."

"They're heavy," he answered, though she already knew that.

"Set them over there," she said, waving to an open spot on the floor. "And mind you, bend your knees as you squat down. Don't lean over. My uncle threw out his back thinking he was stronger than he was. But then that's the way with all men, isn't it?"

He glanced back at her, wondering if she truly expected an answer. Apparently not, because a moment later, she was shooing him back out the door. And if he didn't step quickly, she was right there on his heels to keep him going back to the cart.

"There's more out there, you know. Don't dawdle. And what did you say you hired Penny for? New shoes? Must say yours could do with a good polishing if nothing else."

He didn't have the luxury of looking at his footwear because she was already at her cart and dropping bolts into his arms. These were lighter than the buttons, thank God, but still heavy enough.

"She hired me, ma'am," he answered, as she no doubt already knew. But he was being tested and he wondered why. "Do you think I am a spy or something? For another mantua maker?" The idea was somewhat ludicrous, but then again, he wasn't exactly sure how cutthroat the dressmaking business was.

"Hmm? Of course not," she said, lying. Then her eyes scanned about the street on both sides. He followed her gaze and immediately spotted what had her worried. A fellow of rather large size strolling casually down the street, whistling as he moved.

"The big one isn't your worry," he said. "Whistling draws attention and brutes as a rule don't like doing that unless they're about to attack." He carefully set the bolts back down into her cart. "The boy over there, on the other hand, seems to be keenly interested in you."

She spun around with a gasp, being absolutely idiotic for a smart woman. The moment she turned in the boy's direction, the child took off. Samuel had no choice but to give chase. It would save him from hauling more fabric, for one. And besides, his curiosity wanted to know why someone was following a buyer for a dress shop.

Sadly, he was so intent on the boy, he completely missed another thug. This one wasn't whistling, though he did have a fist of iron, which landed right on Samuel's temple. And that was the last he knew for quite some time.

Chapter 5

Penny felt her hackles rise as a wave of equal parts
panic and fury burned through her. Where had he gone? She
needed him! She walked as quickly as she could throughout
the shop. She wouldn't run. She wouldn't betray to everyone
here just how terrified she was at the idea of his absence. It
didn't really make sense to her. After all, wasn't she always
on her own? Didn't everyone leave her eventually?

On her third pass through the shop, Irene Knopp came
trembling into the back room. She was pale, her hands were
shaking, and she looked terrified. The sight was so unusual
in the normally self-possessed woman that Penny drew up
short.

"What happened?" she asked though part of her kept
screaming that she had no interest in what was happening
to someone else when she had her own crisis to deal with.
But Irene was the shop purchaser and a good woman. Perhaps even a friend. And she was obviously distressed.

Irene pulled herself together. She spoke haltingly at first
but with growing strength. "There was . . . I have . . . Lately

I have thought I was being watched. I hear about a new attack every day. London has become very dangerous, and I felt it today. Then there was this man who was whistling, but it wasn't him. It was this boy, and your man chased him for me. I waited but they haven't come back. I'm not sure what to do. Do I go look? I thought if we could go together . . ." She bit her lip. "I don't like being so afraid, but it has been happening for a while. It's . . . unnerving."

By this time everyone was back downstairs, adding to the general commotion. Helaine's mother ordered the new apprentice to get tea. Wendy had stopped looking at the new fabric to frown at the door. It took Penny much too long to sort through Irene's words to realize she had said "your man" as in . . . as if . . .

"Did you say 'my man'?" she said.

"Yes, a tall, gangly sort of fellow with wild hair."

"Mr. Morrison?"

"Yes, that was his name. I didn't know if he really was here to help, so I thought I'd best keep an eye on him. I made him carry things. But then there was the boy, and he took off after . . ."

Penny barely heard the rest. She hauled open the workroom door to scan the alleyway. She saw Irene's small cart, still with a few bolts of fabric on it. There were the usual number of people passing by, but no Mr. Morrison.

Making a swift decision, Penny turned back to the women and began issuing orders. They were all dear women, but sometimes they lost sight of the proper order of things.

"Mrs. Appleton," she said to Helaine's mother. "You stay here with Irene and Tommy. Wendy, if you and Tabby could take care of the cart of fabric? We can't just leave it out there alone. I shall go look for this boy and Mr. Morrison."

Irene straightened her shoulders. "Don't be ridiculous. You can't go out there alone. I shall—"

"You are the one being followed. Just point out the direction they ran. Never fear, I will be quite safe." Mr. Morrison, however, would get quite the tongue-lashing from her if she ever saw him again. It was irrational of her, she knew. He was probably just being helpful as he chased the boy. But at the moment, she had all this anger and it needed an outlet. So long as she never voiced her thoughts out loud, there was no harm.

And so a moment later, she was out on the streets, wandering as she searched fruitlessly for an unknown boy and a missing man. She had no belief that she would find them, but she had to go through the motions nonetheless.

She'd gone only a few blocks when she saw a small crowd gathered. They were milling about and some were arguing. Already her mind had linked the crowd to Mr. Morrison. He seemed to be a man who created a stir wherever he went. So she shouldered her way to the center only to curse under her breath when she saw him.

Mr. Morrison lay sprawled on the ground. A lump had already formed on his temple and a bit of blood was already matting his hair. He was blinking, so that meant he was alive, but his expression was vague and rather dull. That, more than anything, alarmed her. She was on her knees beside him before she even realized she'd moved.

"Goodness gracious," she said as she used her skirt to wipe away a small trickle of blood on his forehead. "You got laid out by a boy?" That wasn't at all what she meant to say. She'd meant to ask how he was feeling, if he could stand, if they needed to call for a surgeon or something. Most of all, she wanted to know if his brains were still intact. But instead, what had come out but the most shrewish comment?

He blinked again, his eyes coming into focus on her face. And bit by bit, his expression shifted into a frown. "Wasn't the boy," he said. "Dunno what, but it weren't the boy." She was still wiping uselessly at the bit of dried blood and he winced in pain. "That doesn't help, you know."

She stilled her hand with an act of will, slowly dropping it into her lap. And when had she knelt beside him like a long-lost lover? She forced herself to calm down and study him dispassionately. The color was coming back into his cheeks, along with a myriad of other lovely shades by his temple. And intelligence had returned to his gaze.

"Do you need a surgeon?" she asked.

He shuddered. "Goodness, no. Damn bastards just make things worse." He pushed himself up to a fully seated position against the wall. Then he glanced beyond her to the folks peering at him. "Nothing exciting to see. Just a gent who got knocked sideways. Happens all the time."

A couple people chuckled at that; others just shrugged. But bit by bit, everyone wandered off. He even helped them disburse by waving good-bye. But despite his carefree attitude, Penny couldn't shake the horror that he'd been knocked unconscious.

"Surely this can't be a common occurrence for you," she said.

He shrugged. "Me? Never. Well, perhaps a few times when I was younger. Well, more than a few times, in fact. Happened at school all the time. As a rule, people don't like know-it-alls, and schoolboys hate them more than most."

That she believed, both that he had been an annoying know-it-all and that he had received a few knocks on the head from it.

"But never," he continued, "in the last few years. Been a paragon of nonviolence ever since I left the army."

She frowned. "You were in the army?"

"It didn't take." Then possibly to cover his embarrassment, he pushed up onto his knees then all the way up onto his feet. She stood as well, a hand out to help him if he needed it. He didn't, and in the end, she let her arms drop uselessly back to her sides.

"Though," he continued in the way he had of sometimes

nattering on, "I am touched that you were so worried about it. Nice thing to wake up to a woman terrified that you had expired. Most gratifying."

"I wasn't afraid you were dead," she said. "I could see you breathing." Her words came out harsher than she had intended because, truthfully, she had been worried. Terrified even. And she wasn't entirely sure why.

He glanced at her. "Of course. A most practical woman. I'd forgotten how levelheaded you are in a crisis. Must be because I'd just had my brains knocked sideways." Then before she could respond to that, he narrowed his eyes and got the thoughtful look that on him could be rather frightening. "But you were worried. Pale, shallow breaths, and your eyes. Miss Shoemaker, your eyes were so wide I believe I could see all the way into your brain."

"Don't be silly."

"Not at all silly. It's a sight that I shall remember all my days. A woman as beautiful as you, terrified for me."

She had no answer to that. He thought her beautiful. She shouldn't be flattered by that, but she was. Lord, she was even blushing!

"Except," he continued as he rubbed at his chin, "you saw me breathing, so you knew I hadn't died. But there was definitely terror on your face." Then he released a rather dramatic sigh, one worthy of the stage. "Oh, bother! You weren't afraid for me, were you? You were afraid I had abandoned you." He glanced about the street, and she could all but see the wheels turning in his head. "You rushed out here searching for me, didn't you? Certain that I had left without completing my task."

She looked away, this time the heat in her cheeks coming for an entirely different reason. Blast him for being so logical and for figuring out exactly what she'd been thinking.

"Men don't tend to stick around for you, do they?" he asked, his voice surprisingly gentle even though he was exposing one of her darkest fears. "I shouldn't let that concern you much. Men, as a rule, are rather stupid."

"So you'll be staying?" she asked, trying—and failing—to make her voice sound casual. "You still intend to take me to this bad solicitor."

"Of course! Miss Shoemaker, I might get distracted by urchins spying on intrepid cits, but I never go back on a bet. And you have bet me that I can't fix your particular problem when I most assuredly can."

She exhaled, relief washing through every part of her. "But perhaps we should go another day," she offered, though every part of her screamed not to. "When your head isn't so . . ."

"Black and blue?"

"Red and black right now. And it probably throbs."

He shrugged. "It does. But here is what I think. We should see your evil solicitor first, then afterward when we go to report his terrible crimes to the constable, I can add in the assault on my person. Two birds with one stone, so to speak. Or two crimes with one visit."

"He will think you the most unlucky of gentlemen."

"Well, then he would be wrong. Also, sadly, not an uncommon occurrence with the constable."

She had no answer to that. He was clearly back to his normal odd self. Only an hour in his company, and she was already well versed in the unusual rhythms of his conversation. But she liked him, she admitted to herself. And she was very glad of his company.

"Well, then, Miss Shoemaker. Shall we go straight to the solicitor's? Or stop by the dress shop first?"

"The dress shop. I'm afraid things were somewhat in disarray there. And my guess is that you want to ask Irene more about her mysterious boy."

"I shall ask, I assure you, but I doubt she knows anything. She thought she was being followed by a whistling stable hand. But I do wonder why someone would pay a child to spy on her."

Penny nodded, her mind too cluttered to sort that out. What possible threat could Irene be to anyone? "Penny."

Mr. Morrison frowned at her and no wonder. She hadn't intended to say her name out loud. "What?" he asked.

"Penny," she repeated. "My Christian name is Penny, and . . . and I, um, give you leave to use it."

His smile was slow in coming, but no less charming once it filled his face. "And you may call me Samuel." He managed somehow to grab hold of her hand and perform an elaborate bow over it. Then he kissed her knuckles while stroking her palm with his index finger. It was quite the grandiose gesture—and a surprisingly intimate one—and once again her cheeks heated in a hot blush.

He noticed. He was a man who noticed everything, but he didn't comment on it. When he straightened, he merely held out his arm to her. She took it as she had seen countless highborn ladies do. And together they walked back to the shop as if they were a lord and lady out for a stroll.

It was the most marvelous thing that happened that day. Or that week. Or most likely for her entire life. Sadly, the interlude didn't last. Eventually they made it to the shop, where Tabby was standing in the doorway and pointing at them. Wendy stepped up a moment later, narrowing her eyes as she peered down the street. Eventually her eyes widened, and her face relaxed as she saw them. Then her keen eyes must have picked out the lump on Samuel's forehead. She gasped and immediately ordered water and a cloth while Penny marveled at how easily Mr. Morrison had become Samuel in her mind. She had only known the man for an hour or so, and yet she felt as if he might be a friend. The concept was odd, to say the least. Certainly she had friends. Women, mostly, and there had been some male playmates when she was little, plus a couple men who had come calling later. No one who stayed, of course, but that was the way with things.

What made Samuel different was that he was a toff. He didn't have a title in front of his name, but he was a gent nonetheless. He wore a gentleman's clothes, talked like a gentleman ought, and knew the kind of people gentlemen knew. Those men, as a rule, did not talk to her except to order her to do something. Or ask to get beneath her skirts. Never had they approached anything like friendship with her.

Except for this man, and the thought was unbelievably exciting. She, Miss Penny Shoemaker, friends with a toff. An odd one, to be sure, but friends nonetheless. She patted his arm as she gestured to the shop. "I believe you are about to be coddled and fussed over."

He gave a mock shudder. "Heavens. Lovely women fussing over me. I shall insist everyone stop immediately after a day. Maybe two."

Penny chuckled as he had intended. Obviously he had not been fussed over much in his life. But even the nicest women could be irritating after an hour. "You must tell me if it becomes too much. And if your head truly pains you, we can get you a cab to take you home." She had to force herself to say the last part. She was beyond anxious to get on with their visit to the solicitor, but his health was most important. Especially as he was now a friend.

He smiled and gently covered her hand with his. His fingers were long and his palm was warm, but nothing matched the understanding in his eyes. "I am fine, Penny. You are the only woman I want ministering to my no doubt colorful bruise. And we shall leave for the solicitor's in fifteen minutes. Mark the time."

"But—"

"I begin to think you want to be rid of me."

"No!" she gasped. Then she realized that he was teasing her. "Oh, I am an easy gull, aren't I?"

"You have just lost your home and your livelihood. I count that as an excellent reason to be distracted." Then there was no more time to talk privately. They entered the shop and were immediately surrounded by anxious women.

Tabby brought the water, and Penny—feeling an irrational surge of possessiveness—took the cloth from Wendy's hand and began to dab at his wound. There was little point. The area was swollen, not bleeding anymore, but it was cool water and so she pressed it against the bump and prayed it helped. And all the while, a fluttering in her stomach had her flushed and unsettled.

Meanwhile, Irene stepped around Mrs. Appleton and Tommy to begin her questions. "Did the boy do this to you?"

"Oh, heavens no," Samuel answered. "I make it a man of above-average height but at least fifteen stone weight."

Penny peered at him. "I thought you didn't see him."

"I didn't. The blow to my temple came from a haymaker punch, but at an angle." He gently removed her hand and the wet rag from his forehead. "Do you see how it is more on my cheek than my temple? That indicates a shot from a man less than my height, but not short. A shorter man would have caught my chin instead."

"Oh," she said, impressed anew by his intelligence. Especially after receiving such a blow.

"And," he continued, "given that the force was enough to knock me unconscious for a few minutes tells me he had weight behind his blow."

"But who was it?" Irene asked.

He turned to look at her. "I have no idea. Tell me why you believe someone has been following you."

She shook her head. "I have no idea, but I have been feeling it lately. Like an itch between my shoulder blades."

He pressed his lips together and said nothing, which obviously irritated Irene.

"You are thinking that I am a ridiculous female, new to this stuff as a buyer and a widow. Clearly I am imagining all sorts of nefarious things."

He tilted his head at her. "Do you generally imagine nefarious things?"

"Of course not!"

"Then why would you start doing so now?"

Her mouth went slack for a moment, obviously startled and a bit ashamed by her accusation. "My apologies. I have tried to talk to my father-in-law about this, but he thinks I am a silly fool. Thinks I'm imagining things because of all the robberies lately."

"Men generally underestimate women. Sadly, I was unable to catch the boy, but it doesn't matter. He was a common street child, bought for a coin. Someone hired him to watch you."

"But why?" gasped Mrs. Appleton from where she had picked up Tommy as if to protect him.

Samuel leaned back, his gaze going slowly about the shop until his eyes landed—and lingered—on Wendy.

"I can think of only two reasons, but there may be countless more," he said, his gaze returning to Irene. "The first is that this is a newly successful dress shop. No doubt there are any number of competitors who would happily send you to the devil."

"But no one else has been followed. Just me," said Irene in a small voice.

"You are the buyer. You are the most visible and probably most vulnerable, especially with Lady Redhill on her honeymoon."

"And who knows if we have been followed?" inserted Penny. "Perhaps we just haven't noticed."

"True," agreed Samuel, "but you have recently lost everything. Perhaps your recent difficulties are part of a larger pattern."

Penny was both reassured and horrified by that thought. Reassured because she was not alone in her problems and horrified that she had just brought all her friends into her own nightmare. "I don't know what to think," she murmured.

He gently pulled the wet rag from her fingers and wrapped her hand in his. "You needn't think for now, Miss Shoemaker. That is what I am here for."

Penny smiled back, caught by the reassurance in his eyes and the warmth of his touch. Indeed, she might have stood there soaking up his touch, but Irene interrupted the moment.

"What is the second?" she asked. "You said you could think of two reasons that someone is spying on me. What is the second?"

Samuel shifted his gaze back to the room in general, and Penny felt the loss keenly. But as he continued to hold her hand, she was able to control her reaction.

"Have you ever heard the expression that where there's smoke, there's usually a fire?"

Irene nodded, her eyes wide.

"I find that when one person associates with dangerous thugs, dangerous things happen. Usually to her friends first." At this, his gaze shifted, looking long and steady into each person's eyes. He began with Irene, who blinked in shock, then to Mrs. Appleton, who simply hugged Tommy and looked worried. Tabby had stepped far back from the group, but he held her gaze as well. Then he looked to Wendy, but the seamstress was looking at the floor while her hands worried in her skirts.

"Wendy?" asked Penny. "Is something amiss?"

The seamstress flatted her lips and glared up at Penny. "Everything is amiss, and there is nothing I can do to change it." Her voice was hard and angry, but Penny read an apology in her eyes. "I cannot understand why you have been thrown from your home, I don't like people being followed or their friends getting noshed on the head. Helaine would know what to do. She always does for things like this. But all I can see is that the shop must stay open. And for that, I must sew a dozen more dresses by week's end and with a girl more thumbs than fingers." She shot Tabby an angry glare. "I fear for all of you and I want to 'elp, but all I can do is sew."

Irene nodded and stepped over to the desk. "Of course,

of course. You're right. Whatever else is going on, we must make sure the shop thrives."

"And to that end," Samuel said as he hopped up from his chair, "Miss Shoemaker and I shall be off to inspect some smoke." He winked at Penny. "That's me being clever as I refer to seeing the solicitor."

"Yes," she returned. "I understood that."

"Oh!" he added as he turned to Tabby. "There's a man near Bond Street, has a room right above the Salty Dog. Name's Bert Keigley and he owes me a favor. Tell him that I sent you—Samuel Morrison—and he'll fit you with glasses right away. Should help with your sewing."

"Glasses!" gasped Wendy. "But she can see better than anyone. Spotted you when you were still down the street and I couldn't see a thing."

"Ah, but that's just the problem, isn't it?" he said to the girl. "You can see at a distance, but up close is a blur. You're farsighted, my dear, and that can be corrected with a pair of glasses. Then I expect your stitches will be as neat as a pin."

Tabby didn't say a word, but the way her eyes widened and she pressed a hand to her mouth told them everything they needed to know. She was indeed farsighted.

"But how did you know?" asked Penny.

"Look at her workstation," he said as he gestured over to the corner where the girl usually worked. "Everything as neat as a pin, but set far away from her chair and with as much wide space as possible from each other. That plus her terrible work and the fact that she did indeed point us out when we were over a block away make the conclusion obvious." Then he turned and rapidly wrote out a note on some paper lying on Helaine's desk. When he was done, he sanded it quickly and handed it to Tabby. "Give this to Bert and he'll fix you up right and tight. Give you a good deal, too, and let you pay in pieces as you get the coin." He glanced significantly at the bolts of cloth stacked six high on the nearest table. "Best go now. He needs time to grind the lens and you need to be back here earning your keep as soon as possible."

Tabby took the note in a shaking hand, at last finding her voice. "Thank you," she whispered. "Oh, thank you, sir!" Then she was gone in a flash, disappearing without even grabbing a coat.

Meanwhile, Samuel was turning his winning smile back to Penny. "Ready to sniff at some smoke then, Miss Shoemaker?"

"Of course, Mr. Morrison. Let us go immediately." She didn't say that when he smiled at her, she was more than willing to go to an evil solicitor's office. Indeed, she was willing to go anywhere at all with him. She would put her hand in his and happily walk right up to the devil himself.

And that, she realized, was a very worrisome state of affairs. Fortunately, she was too distracted by his smile to allow herself to dwell on that fear. Besides, she rationalized, he was a nice man and a gentleman. How dangerous could he be?

Chapter 6

꩜

Penny had never been in a solicitor's office before. It was the province of men and so she was predisposed to awe the moment she stepped in the front door. But even with that, she could see that the offices of Mr. Addicock, solicitor at law, had seen better days. It wasn't necessarily the dirt on the floor or the odor of smoke, but the complete absence of a woman. She saw a boy barely into his teens hunched over a desk writing something and that was all.

Perhaps this was how law offices worked, but Penny guessed that the most prestigious ones had a woman to serve tea and another to dust and clean. Butlers, footmen, and the like were all well and good, but there was something about a woman's eye that made a place brighter. Or at least a good deal cleaner.

She glanced at Samuel and saw that he was observing everything with his own keen eye, but she read no judgment on his face. Simple observation without emotion. Then he abruptly rapped his knuckles on the boy's desk and shifted into a charming and rather stupid smile.

"Ho there, boy. Busy copying, what? Tedious work. I quite admire the way you do that, hunched over all day. Been doing it long, what?"

"Ever' day, all day," the child mumbled.

"Ugh! Tedious, I'll bet. And you have been working here forever, I'll wager. Probably feels like an age, when you've only been here, what? A year at most?"

"Three months. Next week."

"Oh, early days then. But at least the pay's good, right?"

The child rolled his eyes, and now that he'd actually lifted his head, Penny could see that he was older than she'd expected. More like eighteen or nineteen.

"Pay's shit, and that's when he remembers t' pay. But he's nice enough." Then he leaned back and stretched out his back with a grunt. "You'll be wanting to see him, then, but he ain't here."

"Nothing to worry about," Samuel answered with a shrug. "This lady here's his client. Managing a trust for her brother. Thomas Shoemaker? She's here to talk—"

"Oy, that's you then," he said as his gaze turned to her. "He said you'd be round, probably screaming and wailing. That I wasn't to let you in and to call the constable directly."

Penny lifted her hands and tried to force a smile. "I'm not screaming or wailing."

The boy frowned. "No, you ain't."

"Nor is she likely to," added Samuel. "I'm here and this is a happy visit. Not often that a woman's brother gets a fat lot of money for the sale of her home, what?"

Penny looked at Samuel in surprise. She didn't want to sell her home. She wanted it back! But of course, he was smiling happily down at the boy, sparing her the smallest glance. Obviously, he had a plan, so she reinforced her genial smile. She ought to be worried at how quickly she had come to trust Samuel, but that, too, was pushed aside as she focused on looking as far from a hysterical woman as possible.

Meanwhile Samuel gestured to the only other door in the room. "That go to his office then?"

The boy stood up, obviously alarmed. "But he ain't in there—"

Samuel dropped a friendly hand on the boy's shoulder. "I know, I know. If I were to guess, I'd say he's holed up somewhere close. Left you high and dry to deal with a wailing woman."

The boy's expression shifted to a disgusted grimace. "'At's me job," he said with a kind of grunt.

"Really? I thought your job was to copy papers and such. Filings and the like. You know, the job of a clerk. Not to play nursemaid to screaming women."

Obviously the boy hadn't thought of that, and obviously this was just the right tack to take. His expression tightened in a sulky kind of disobedience. "'At's what I says," he grumbled. "But 'e don't listen."

"No, his type never does. But tell you what, old boy, turns out that this is a happy day, the lady isn't screaming, and you don't have to call the constable on anybody." Then he tossed the kid a tuppence. "Why don't you run over and tell Mr. Addicock that the lady's excited to see him while we wait here."

The boy shook his head, but with some regret even as he pocketed the tuppence. "I ain't supposed to let anyone in here. Not without Mr. Addicock."

"Of course, of course," said Samuel with a nod. "But we're not just anybody. The lady's a client. And you'll be going to get Mr. Addicock, won't you? His office is locked, ain't it?" Just to prove it, Samuel rattled the doorknob. "'Sides, he'll be happy to know that she's not screaming, won't he? Come on. It ain't your job to be sitting here nursemaiding anyway. Not when your hand is so neat and the copying so perfect."

He pointed to the papers the boy had been writing so carefully.

The boy was giving in. Penny could see it, but he wasn't quite convinced yet. So she decided it was time she played her own hand, though it turned her stomach to do it. She smiled sweetly in just the way that she did for very difficult customers. She was warm and friendly, and she lowered her head slightly in a show of humility.

"I'd be very grateful," she said. "And I promise not to descend into any sort of hysterics at all. I swear!" She said it with a kind of giggle that only the very birdbrained released.

It worked. The boy colored up to his ears and ducked his head. This was, of course, exactly why women acted the fool. Because it made men fools. She glanced sideways to see if Samuel was affected.

He was, but not how she'd hoped. He was watching her with his eyes narrowed, and his color raised. She had no idea what that meant. For all she knew, he could be suffering a moment of dyspepsia. But then the expression was lost beneath his congenial expression.

Meanwhile she touched the boy's arm. "I am afraid you have the advantage of me, sir," she said as breathlessly as possible. And when the boy didn't answer, she smiled. "You know my name, but I don't know yours."

It took him a moment that involved several blinks and a gasp. But then he ducked his head. "Um, Ned, mum. Ned Wilkers."

She gave him her best curtsy. "Pleased to make your acquaintance, Ned Wilkers."

Beside her, Samuel grimaced. Probably at how easily Ned was becoming flustered. Rather than allow the boy to see Mr. Morrison's disgusted expression, Penny stepped forward right up to poor Ned. Any closer and she'd be in his lap.

"Please, Mr. Wilkers, I want so much to thank Mr. Addicock in person. I'm so thrilled with what he's done." It was a miracle she didn't choke on her words. "Would you get him for me, please?"

He hesitated even as she lifted him out of his chair and began guiding him to the door. "Um—" he began, but she giggled again.

"We won't bother a thing. I promise."

"But—"

"Go on," Samuel urged the boy. "Bad form to keep a lady and a client waiting, what."

Ned took a breath, looked a little sweetly at her, and then nodded. "Right away, miss. Right away!" Then he dashed off without even remembering his cap.

The moment the door shut, Penny exhaled in relief and turned to Samuel. "He's gone. Now what?" But her voice trailed off. Obviously, Samuel already knew what he wanted to do. He was at Mr. Addicock's door with a lock pick in his hands.

"Lock the front door. It'll delay them when they return."

She did as he'd bade, using the key that was hanging on a peg right in plain sight. By the time she'd finished, he had opened the door to Addicock's office and was releasing a low whistle.

"Our intrepid solicitor is not a man who likes to file."

Penny looked around and couldn't help agreeing. She had thought her own father was a slob with everything but his tools. He used to leave receipts everywhere, mixed in with leather scraps and the odd pound note. But at least her father had both herself and her mother to keep things in order. Apparently, Mr. Addicock had no such females in his life. Pile after pile of papers rested haphazardly next to cold tea and the remains of a very old meat pie.

She grimaced, scanning the floor for the telltale signs of vermin infestation. Sadly, she found them easily. "Mind where you step," she warned. Who knew what creature might attack if its nest was disturbed.

Samuel apparently didn't hear her as he was already sorting through the pile on the man's desk. She stepped to a different pile—on a rickety bench like a schoolchild might once have used before it was discarded to the rubbish bin—and began looking at the papers there.

"What is all this?" she asked.

He didn't even glance up. "Can you read?"

She stiffened, knowing it was a reasonable question, but insulted nonetheless. "I had an excellent education," she lied.

He did look up at that, a slight frown on his face and a gaming token in his hand. "I didn't ask about your education, I asked if you could read."

She grimaced and spoke in stiff accents. "Yes, I can read."

"Excellent. So read. We are looking for your father's will or anything that has to do with you or your brother. Try not to disturb the piles overmuch. We are working in secret, though I doubt Mr. Addicock would notice if we tossed everything here into the air." Then he returned to the pile on the desk. She stared at him a moment, watching the way he worked. His eyes were narrowed, his entire body focused and intent. Then without even glancing up, he added, "We are working against time, Penny. After that display of yours, young Ned will rush back to your side. I would have preferred it if you had begun some waterworks. That would have pushed him out the door faster and delayed his return."

"Or it would have had him calling for the constable as he was told to do once I descended into hysterics."

He shifted to a different pile, his hands moving methodically. "Which would have left us alone in here as well. It is not as if he could snap his fingers and have the man appear. One has to go *search* for the constable who, I'll wager, would not be anxious to appear. Yes, all in all, waterworks would have been the more logical choice."

"Of all the—"

"Please, Penny. We are short of time. If you do not wish to search the pages, at least step outside and watch for Ned's return."

She clenched her teeth against the words that were burning like acid on her tongue. "High-handed bastard" was the kindest epitaph she had for the man. But that would have served no purpose. So she held her tongue—though only barely—as she set to searching her pile of documents.

She was inordinately pleased when she came across exactly what they were looking for. Her father's Last Will and Testament. She held it up with a gasp, reading the document as best she could. Many of the words were unfamiliar to her, the legal language looking closer to French than anything else.

"Damnation," he cursed, and she jumped because she hadn't even realized he'd made it to her side. "No wonder the man pays young Ned. His own handwriting is deplorable."

True, but Penny's father's hand had been equally cramped. She could make out the letters easily enough. It was just the meaning that was lost. So she pointed, reading the words aloud.

"'This is the Last Will and Testament of Carson Shoemaker. In the name of God. Amen. I, Carson Shoemaker—'"

"Yes, yes. I can see that." He pulled it out of her hand, then promptly stuck it under her nose and pointed. "Is that your father's signature?"

She looked, her heart dropping into her stomach. It certainly looked like her father's signature. "But it can't be true!" she gasped. "He'd never do it!"

"Is it his signature?" Samuel repeated. "Or just a reasonable copy?"

She shook her head. She had no idea. She'd seen her father's signature perhaps a dozen times in her life. She knew his handwriting like the back of her hand, but his signature? "He usually just wrote an S in the shape of a shoe."

"That would not be his legal signature then. What about these other names? The witnesses, do you know them?"

She frowned and shook her head. "Never heard of them."

He nodded as if he had expected as much. Then he took the paper to the desk and began rooting about for something. "Look for the bill of sale for your property. And if it mentions the bank, all the better."

She nodded and began searching, all too aware that they were running out of time. But she still kept an eye on him as he found a sheet of paper. "What are you doing?"

"Copying the signatures," he said as he carefully placed the blank paper over the fake will.

She wasn't finding anything about the sale to Cordwain, so she returned to his side. "Just rip up the thing. It's not true!"

Samuel didn't answer, too intent on his work. She wasn't sure how he managed. The foolscap was thin, but not thin enough to see through clearly. But when he lifted up the page and compared it to the original, the ink was surprisingly accurate.

But it didn't matter. If a piece of paper could declare Addicock as Tommy's guardian, then ripping up the lying paper would return things to normal. So thinking, she grabbed the page. Or she tried to. The damn toff was faster than she was, easily lifting the sheet out of her reach.

"You can't destroy it," he said as he moved back to the pile where she'd first found it.

"I bloody well can!"

He carefully replaced the sheet exactly where she'd first lifted it. How he knew the place was beyond her, but he did. "You're supposed to be a lady, Penny," he said without heat. "Do watch your language."

She stepped up and meant to shove him aside. That damned will was going to be destroyed, but the toff was a great deal stronger than he looked. He easily held her off.

"Be logical, Penny. This is not the only copy. The important one was already filed into the courts. That's the one that must be proved false."

"But it's not true!" She knew she wasn't being reasonable. She knew that it was not the way to argue with Samuel. She knew, but she couldn't stop the tears from threatening or the frustration from burning in her gut.

He sighed, looking at her with an impatient kind of sympathy. He opened his mouth to speak, but there wasn't time. They both heard voices arguing from the front office.

They shared a panicked glance, then quickly dashed out of the office. "Get ready to delay them while I relock the door."

"Delay them?" she hissed. "How?"

"Hysterics, anger, drunkenness. Good heaven, how should I know?" he shot back. "Now be quiet. This requires concentration."

She would bloody well like to tell him what required concentration: trying to think of a way to hide a gent who was in full view, but she bit back her retort. Instead she laughed loudly and leaned against the door.

"Imagine me w' all that money. Why, Tommy and me can finally have new clothes again." She could already hear that Mr. Addicock and Ned had discovered the locked door and were trying to open it. So she slammed her hand against the door to hold it closed. "Ooh! I think they've returned!" she said loudly.

She looked back at Samuel, whose face had flushed red and she was pretty sure she heard him mutter a very impressive curse.

The lock slipped back with a thunk and the doorknob turned. "Oooh, wait!" she cried. "I'll get the door. Here. Let me unlock it." Bracing the door shut with her foot, she shoved the key into the lock and relocked it. Then she made a show of turning the knob. "Here now, Mr. Addicock. Oh, blimey! Did I lock it?"

On the other side of the door, she could hear Mr. Addicock cursing her. She laughed loudly. "Silly me! Just a moment! I dropped the key."

She turned back to Samuel, glaring at him even though he couldn't see. Damn the man. He'd gotten the door open in half the time. Below her hand, she felt Addicock insert his own key and twist it open. She hadn't the time to relock it again. She was just about to fling herself bodily against the door when Samuel crowed softly and straightened up. Success!

"About bloody time," she hissed as she stepped back.

"Language, my dear," he shot back. Then the door flew open as an obviously angry Addicock stormed in. He was a fleshy man with sagging jowls and florid skin. But his eyes were disconcertingly pretty with long lashes over his brown eyes.

"What cause have you to lock me out of my own office?" he bellowed.

Samuel was at Penny's side in an instant, his manners congenial, but his general stance protective. It was such an odd moment for her. Not even her father had ever done such a thing. Only her mother when she thought a customer was getting too friendly. And that had been more to shoo Penny into the back than anything else.

So when Samuel suddenly stepped between herself and Mr. Addicock, it left her startled and flustered. Part of her wanted to shove him away, and truthfully if it were a usual day, she would have. But today had been the worst of all her days, except for the night she'd learned her parents had died. So when a handsome man stepped between her and the thieving man who'd stolen everything from her, she allowed it to happen. She even exhaled in relief.

It gave her time to search for a weapon with which to kill the bastard.

Meanwhile, Samuel was smiling his generally flustered, half-mad smile. "Ah well, Miss Shoemaker has been feeling a bit unsettled ever since her parents died. She was scared, you see, so I locked the door myself. As a way to calm her nerves. Delicate creatures, women, but it's usually best to humor them."

Addicock wasn't fooled, but Ned obviously was. He stepped forward to offer her his hand. "No need to be afraid now. I'll make sure everything's right and tight for you, Miss Shoemaker."

Penny smiled. She wanted to roll her eyes that this boy had obviously gone sweet on her. She was much too old for him, not necessarily in years, but in experience. And yet, that same experience told her that she should never disdain kindness even if it was from an earnest young man. *Especially* an earnest young man who was apprentice to her enemy.

But it made her feel like the lowest worm to play on his sympathies as if she were interested in him. Still, she took young Ned's hand.

"Thank you," she breathed with enough huskiness to make poor Ned color up to his ears. Then she turned to Mr. Addicock. "Could we not go into your office now? I should like to understand."

The man's brows drew even more tightly downward but he didn't so much as twitch. It was obvious he couldn't decide what his next move should be—whether to throw her out or allow her deeper into his clutches. Fortunately, Samuel was there to force the decision.

He smiled and spoke gently. "She just wishes to understand the terms of her father's will. She has that right, Mr. Addicock. And I am here to see that nothing untoward happens."

Addicock's gaze snapped up to Samuel's. "Untoward? There's nothing untoward about any of this!"

A guilty confession if ever there was one, and Penny twitched with the need to scratch the man's eyes out. Fortunately, Ned was already moving her toward the office door.

"Of course you want to know, Miss Shoemaker. I'm sorry I didn't know your father. I wasn't working the day he made up his will. But Mr. Addicock was just telling me that he was a kind and generous man. A good man. They were friends, you know. And he did right by picking Mr. Addicock here as his solicitor. He'll make sure everything is right and tight for you."

Penny stared at the boy. He couldn't possibly believe everything he was saying. For one thing, her father was not a kind or generous man, or at least he wouldn't have been to poor Ned. Her father, as a rule, was as pinchpenny as they came and had little respect for apprentices. But one look at Ned's earnest face told her that he did indeed believe in her father's good nature and Addicock's as well. "But don't you work every day? Saturdays, too?"

The boy frowned. "Yes, miss."

"Then how could you not have been here—"

"It was a Sunday," Addicock snapped as he stepped in front of Ned, probably to block the doorway. But when everyone stopped to stare at him, he had little choice but to open it. He glared at Penny as if all this were her fault. And then once again, Samuel stepped in the way.

"By 'untoward,' I meant that I would keep Miss Shoemaker from any unseemly displays of emotions. She's delicate, as I said. And it's excruciatingly hard to do business with a wailing woman in the room. I assure you, it's my only purpose here."

Delicate? Wailing? Good God, the toff was giving her a hard role to play. And right there, as if to spite her, the seething anger roiled in her throat. She'd have choked if she weren't so used to swallowing it down.

Addicock spent one moment more staring at Samuel, and then he gave a slight nod, which Samuel echoed. Right there, plain as day: the silent communication between men who promised to keep their dirty secrets away from the women. It fueled the anger inside her, burning it to a fever pitch. All of a sudden, everything she had ever doubted about Samuel—the crazy toff—surged to the fore. He was supposed to be *her* ally, and yet here he was trading nods with the bastard who had stolen everything from her.

"Why, you bloody—"

Samuel whirled around, his eyes blazing with alarm. "A moment more, Penny. I promise you, everything will be all right in a trice."

It was a lie and they both knew it. The question was, would she trust him to play out his game? Or was he yet another man intent on cheating her?

She bit her lip. She'd already made her choice a few hours ago. Only a stupid fool would throw away her last hope on a temper tantrum. So she swallowed down her fury— again—and forced herself to act wilting. *Wilting*, for God's sake.

"It's just been a rather difficult day," she said through clenched teeth.

"Of course," Samuel said. Then he threw a warning glance at Addicock. "Please, let's progress with this quickly. No need for dramatics, what?"

The bastard nodded—obviously feeling a masculine kinship with Samuel in the need to avoid female hysterics—and quickly opened his office door. Ned and Samuel together led Penny to a chair as if she hadn't spent most of her life hauling wood and working leather. She sat gingerly in the seat, more because she wanted room to leap up and scratch the bastard's eyes out than because she was feeling "delicate." Either way, Samuel and Ned hovered solicitously over her while Addicock went straight to the pile that held the will.

He pulled it out and waved it at her face without really showing her the document. "Here's the will." He pointed to the bottom. "Here's your father's signature." He pointed again. "Here's my name. Makes me guardian of young Tommy. That means I control his money completely.

Everything he owns goes through me and I'll take care of him right and tight."

She reached for the document, but he set it behind him on his desk. Then at an arch look from Samuel, he huffed, grabbed it again, and handed it over. To Samuel.

Men!

"I don't understand," she said. "Why would my father do this?"

"Well, somebody has to look after Tommy."

She glared at the man. "I have been. Every night. Every day."

The man had the grace to flush, but that didn't stop him from softening his expression in the warmest, kindest way. It was startling really. She knew he was a scoundrel, possibly a murderer, and yet, he was also rather handsome in a fatherly kind of way.

"I know this is hard, Miss Shoemaker. You have been doing an excellent job of raising Tommy, but I was referring to his financial affairs. Even if you could manage to sort through the mess of documents . . ." He gestured behind him to the piles that she knew for a fact had nothing to do with Tommy. "You have enough to do with his daily care. This needs to be handled by a man who understands finances and the law." Then he paused, tilting his head in the way a kindly uncle might. "Miss Shoemaker, don't you remember me? Your father and I were friends. We used to meet at Bert Harvey's pub, but surely you remember me."

She did, now that she was looking at him. He'd come around the shop many times. Bought a pair of boots, but never paid, as she recalled. And yes, he and her father had seemed friendly enough. But then her father had been friends with anyone who might be a customer. Still, with all eyes on her, she was forced to nod. "I remember you," she pushed through a constricted throat. "But I don't remember anything about a will."

"Well, not the thing to speak of to a delicate woman," he

said gently. "Talk of death is always upsetting to the fairer sex."

Beside her, Samuel nodded. "This seems to be in order. Who are these gentlemen here? The witnesses? John Smithee and Thomas Baker."

Penny wanted to know that, too. "I don't know them."

"Hmm? Oh, friends of your father's," Addicock answered. "This will was done at the pub, you know. And on a Sunday. Didn't even want to come to the office. But it's filed, you know. All legal like."

Bollocks, Penny snarled in her thoughts.

"So you never met them before?" Samuel pressed. Then he turned to the boy. "What about you, Ned? Ever seen them or heard of them before?"

Ned shook his head. "But I wouldn't. Not if it were done at a pub."

"Well, then I suppose all that's left is to sort out the details of Miss Shoemaker's monthly allowance and the delivery of cash from the sale of her home."

Addicock jerked in what was obviously a practiced move. "What?" he gasped overly loud. Truly the man had *no* future on the stage. He was a terrible actor. "What sale?"

"A Mr. Cordwain appeared just this morning with armed men and the constable. He took possession of the Shoemaker store and all the property contained within. Had all the right documents with him."

"Couldn't have!" Addicock cried. "I never authorized such a sale."

"He had all the correct documents. Both myself and the constable checked them."

Addicock shifted behind his desk. Now that he was into his performance, he seemed to be moving more securely. His acting skills improved and Penny could almost believe he was outraged on her behalf. "Well, false documents can be hard to spot unless one is well trained. Bloody hell!" he cursed, then immediately looked up with a perfectly done rueful look. "Pardon me, miss. I am certain that everything can be sorted out right and tight and that villain Cordwain tossed in jail."

Samuel nodded. "And what, may I inquire, can you do against a man like Cordwain?"

"Oh, many things, many things! Documents to file. Notices to be served. That sort of thing. All legal things, you understand. Never you fear, Miss Shoemaker. I'll sort things out right away."

She had to force herself to nod. She recognized a man who was lying through his teeth. Especially since he wasn't doing anything with the papers on his desk but rearranging them. And surprise of surprises, one glance at Ned's troubled face told her that he suspected something amiss as well.

"How?" she pressed, knowing that details were the best way to catch a liar. "How exactly, Mr. Addicock? And don't say legal things. I need to know. That was my home!"

"Of course, of course," Mr. Addicock soothed. "Of course you are upset. Ned, get the lady some water."

Ned leaped up to do just that, but Penny kept her eyes trained on the solicitor. She wanted him to know she would not be distracted by a glass of water.

In the end, he sighed. "You see, Miss Shoemaker, the thing is that Mr. Cordwain may be our villain. Or he may have been duped by a canny thief who pretended to be me. It's all very havy cavy, but I assure you, I shall sort it out."

Samuel leaned forward. "And while you are sorting things out, you will need to provide funds for your charge to survive. Without their home, Tommy and Miss Shoemaker are on the streets."

"Wot?" gaped Addicock.

"As Tommy's legal guardian, you must provide for his well-being. I assure you, sleeping on the streets is not being well."

"But there was no money in the estate. Only the shop and the like. And Cordwain stole that." He turned to Penny.

"Haven't you a place to stay? A, um, gentleman's home?" he asked as he glanced significantly at Samuel. "Just until things get sorted out."

Penny stiffened. "What kind of woman do you take me for?"

Addicock gave her a sad look, as if he were a disappointed father. "My dear, I know all the details from your father. Perhaps you could stay with Tommy's father?"

"Bloody hell," she cursed as she pushed to her feet, but Samuel grabbed her hand to hold her still. And when he spoke, it was with freezing accents.

"Mr. Shoemaker was Tommy's father."

"Yes, yes, we all know he *claimed* that. Adopted his wife's sister's son, and no husband to be found. But . . ." His eyes slid to Penny. "The boy's true parentage—"

"Is my aunt and her husband," Penny snapped.

Addicock didn't say anything. He didn't need to, especially as Ned had returned and pressed a glass of water into her hand. Penny glanced up to thank him, only to have the words die in her throat. Even the boy had changed how he looked at her. No more worship or sweet blushes. His gaze had turned almost dirty somehow because he assumed she was a tart.

It was all she could do not to throw the water back in his face. She sure as hell wasn't going to drink it. So she set it back down—forcefully—on the desk. Then she pushed to her feet.

"Here's what's going to happen, Mr. Addicock," she said in freezing accents.

Samuel was on his feet as well, pushing forward to cut off her words. "You're going to give her a hundred pounds to get through the month—"

"A hundred pounds! The devil—"

"And then you go to the constable immediately, showing the proper documents of your guardianship and demand that he look into this heinous fraud!"

Addicock leaned over his desk, his face florid and his handsome eyes narrowed in fury. "I haven't bloody well got a hundred pounds! I haven't even got the quid to pay Ned here and he's a damn sight more useful than your Tommy!"

"Wot?" That came from Ned, the tone both surprised and indignant. And it was enough to recall Addicock to himself.

The man straightened his coat, tugging on the fabric in what was obviously a nervous habit. Then he spoke slowly and clearly, his eyes calm and his expression grim. "Guardianship of one Tommy Shoemaker has not brought me any money at all. There has been no income from the property; therefore, I have nothing to give Miss Shoemaker." He turned to Penny, his expression cold. "I suggest you find a husband. Quickly. Or ply some other trade." His tone left no doubt as to what trade he referred to.

She gasped, but Samuel tightened his hold on her arm, silently willing her to keep quiet. It was a near thing, but she obeyed. For the moment.

"But you will go to the constable to show proof of guardianship? And you will report this crime? This is what a *legal* guardian would do."

Addicock released something between a growl and a grunt. As answers went, it meant nothing. Fortunately, Samuel wasn't going to let the man get away with that.

"You know, I intend to stop by the constable's this afternoon. Should I send him around to you? But of course, once here, he might take it into his head to look into more documents. As long as he's here—"

"I said I'll go to the constable. It's what a guardian does, and I take my responsibilities seriously."

Samuel gave a brusque nod, then turned to Penny with a smile. "Very well, Miss Shoemaker. I believe we are done here now."

"What?" she gasped. "I have no home, no money, no—"

"Yes, yes, I'm aware. But these things take time, as I'm

sure you know. Let Mr. Addicock do his job. He'll get it all sorted out."

"But—"

"Please," he said, his expression congenial, but his eyes intense.

She wanted to argue. She wanted to choke Addicock with her bare hands. But she wasn't going to get what she wanted, and so in the end, she spun on her heel and headed toward the door. Samuel followed at a slower pace, as if thinking of something.

"Oh, one more thing, Ned. I believe I know your aunt. Is it Mrs. Saynsberry? Husband owns a printing shop down by Picadilly Circus?"

The statement was so odd that it caused Penny to turn around. But her confusion was nothing compared to Ned and Addicock's. They both stared at Samuel as if he were the daft toff she knew he was.

"Er, no, sir," Ned answered. "My family's the Wilkers. Live down in Shoreditch."

"Of course they are! Now I remember. I saw one of your father's plays once. Or read one. Or was it a poem?" Penny could tell he was guessing. Shoreditch was known for its writers and artists, and given that Ned was a clerk, it made sense that his father was a writer. But it was just a guess. Fortunately, given Ned's surprised expression, she could tell that Samuel was right.

"Poem, sir. He's had a few published."

"That's it. Excellent man, your father. I'm sure he's right proud of you."

Ned flushed, as all young men did when praised in so casual a fashion. Looking at it from outside the conversation, Penny could see the brilliance of her mad toff. If he'd been more earnest in his compliment, it would have been suspected as flattery. But spoken so offhand, and as he was reaching for his hat, no less, Samuel managed to both flatter the boy and make it sound completely genuine.

Not that she understood how flattering Ned and his father would get them anywhere. But she was working on trust—a very rare and surprising thing for her—so she kept silent. A moment later, she and Samuel were out the door and strolling steadily down the street.

"Well," said Samuel with a hearty sigh, "I count that a good day's work."

"What?" She whipped around to glare at him, at last able to vent her spleen. "And what have we accomplished? I've still got no home, no money, and no bleeding shop!"

Samuel flashed her a grin. "But we do have a clue. A whole slew of them now, and the beginnings of a theory."

"A theory! Oh," she mocked, "the toff has a theory. Well, how is that going to feed me and Tommy? How will that get my shop back or—"

He held up a hand, and when that did not work, he pressed his fingers to her lips. She wanted to slap his hand away. She should have bitten off his fingertips. But what she did do was curse under her breath even as the press of his fingers against her mouth threw her thoughts into turmoil. It was bleeding cheeky of him to do it, and yet she liked the touch of his fingers on her lips. Then her mind flashed on the question of what it would be like to have his mouth on her lips. And if that weren't startling enough, he then removed his hand and dropped a quick and startling kiss right on her mouth!

Then she did raise her hand to slap him. It was a normal reaction, more habit than thought. But he caught her wrist and held the hand away.

"I know that was terribly bad form for me. But we have made such progress and you did so splendidly, what with charming young Ned, that I couldn't resist."

"I am *not* a whore and I will *not* be spreading my—"

"A what? A what! Good God, did I offer to pay for that kiss? I'm sure I would have remembered it if I had."

"I am *not*—"

"Yes, yes, I know you are not!" He glanced significantly around. More than a few people were looking at them curiously. "I was cheeky and rude. Pray let me apologize over luncheon. I don't know about you, but I'm starving. Are you starving? Mind the pickpocket to your left. Let's go to a place that has the most wonderful meat pies in London, shall we? It's almost the perfect time."

She frowned at him. "Luncheon was nearly two hours ago for most decent people."

"Good thing I just proved I'm not decent. Come on, Penny. Do let me apologize."

"What I want is—"

"An explanation. Of my theory. Well, yes, but that shall have to wait until we have full stomachs. Hard to appreciate my brilliance without food, you know."

"But—"

"Pray say yes, Penny. It would be the decent thing to do."

Would it? She wasn't sure. But what she was sure of was that she wasn't leaving this man's side until he'd solved her problem. So that meant going with him to dine.

"Very well," she said with a reluctant nod that was completely false. After all, she was starving.

"Excellent!" he cried as he hailed a cab.

And as she climbed in the dark interior of the carriage, she began to wonder exactly what she would do if he tried to kiss her again in this terribly dark and intimate space. She wasn't exactly sure, and that thought bothered her as much as anything else that had happened this day.

Chapter 7

※

Well, that was expertly done! thought Samuel with a grin. Not only had he made great strides in discovering her thief, but he had also begun Penny's seduction with a clumsy but effective move. Samuel regretted that their first kiss had been fumbled and by necessity brief. But "clumsy" and "awkward" were the perfect descriptions for his social skills. Fortunately he was brilliant enough to make that seem endearing.

So he relaxed back into the perfume- and sweat-stained squabs of the carriage and tried not to grin. He failed, of course, as he always did when things were going well. But that was just as well, too, because it was relatively dark inside the carriage and he liked that she might be able to see his teeth. Of all his physical attributes, he believed his teeth were the best. Hadn't many a lady told him he should smile more often? But then his grin faded as he began tallying accomplishments from this morning and which questions they led to and in what order those questions would need to be answered . . .

"Exactly how am I to get my home back from Mr. Addicock?"

Samuel blinked, forcibly bringing his mind into the present. He did not like doing that. He thought much better when he was not interrupted. "Mr. Addicock doesn't have your property. Cordwain does."

"And how am I going to get it back from him?"

"He doesn't have the property either. He's just living there."

"But—"

"Please, I'm sorry. But I'm trying to think. Did we not just agree to allow all explanations to wait until after a meal?"

"You might have agreed, but—"

He raised up his hand and glared through the gloom at her. She glared right back. "I believe," she said in frosty accents, "that I am the employer here. As my employee, you have an obligation to answer my questions."

"What an amazing thing that accent is. Where did you learn it? Your background is decidedly middle class, and yet you sounded just like a duchess right then. Do it again. I think I recognize the accent. You learned it from the Duchess of—"

"Astonberry," she said with a tight-lipped anger. "Her husband got his boots from my father—"

"No, I was going to say Westbrook. You sound much more like the Duchess of Westbrook. You should work on the vowels a bit if you want Astonberry—"

"Samuel!"

"And as this is a wager, not an employment arrangement, I owe you nothing until the wager is complete."

"But you told your sister that I was a client."

"Sister-in-law. Do try to be precise—"

"Samuel, I believe I am about three heartbeats away from kicking you. As hard as I can manage."

He paused a moment, waiting in silence for exactly four heartbeats. "No. I don't believe you had that right—*ow!*"

She did. She kicked him hard right in the shins. But he believed the trigger was his words, not the count of her heartbeats. And as he grasped his aching shin, he couldn't help grinning at her.

"You are a most lively woman. I believe I like you. Damned if I don't. Most lively!"

She stared at him hard. Glared actually, in exactly the perfect imitation of the Duchess of Astonberry. He was on the verge of saying so when her expression crumpled. It simply wrinkled up as her jaw clenched and she started to blink past tears. Not of weepy sadness. That was not Miss Shoemaker's ilk. He'd already deduced that her tears stemmed from fury. A frustration so deep that it etched itself into her features and slipped out of her eyes.

It made him immediately contrite. After all, this was mostly a game to him. He tended to forget that her very survival was at stake. Or so she believed.

"You know you will get your life back, Miss Shoemaker. Even were I to fail completely—which I assure you I will not—you will continue to live above the dress shop until you earn enough money to find a new shop. Then with the likes you have—or rather my nephew Max has—you will send round a special note from 'Tommy's father' expressing your desire to make a special boot or shoe or whatever at a special price. That will bring in a few gents, to be sure, especially if I drop a word here and there."

"I doubt you're a fashion leader," she snapped.

He waved away her objection. "You'll hire a front man or someone to pose as Tommy's father. In the end, if the workmanship holds up—or should I say workwomanship? Difficult thing, language. For all its marvelous ability to allow one to order lunch and the like, it's terribly imprecise. In any event, before long, you shall have everything just as it would have been whether at your father's shop or elsewhere. In truth, I believe selling shoes for ladies will likely take all your time anyway and that has already been established at the dressmaker's shop. And really, I'm very glad Lady Helaine changed the shop's name from Lady Caniche's. She looks nothing like a poodle, so A Lady's Favor works much better."

He wound up his words and smiled benignly at her, pleased to see that she was no longer making fists or leaking fury. Instead, she was staring at him, her mouth compressed into a long flat line.

Oh, dear. He'd forgotten that she was possessed of a marvelous intellect. Especially for a woman. Her next words confirmed that.

"Do you usually babble when confronted by a woman's tears?"

"Fists and feet," he corrected. His shin still ached like the devil. "Sometimes tears. But usually fists can be most easily deflected with a wall of words."

"Male or female?"

"Both, really. If the mind is occupied with interpreting a rolling wave of words, then it cannot order the fist to strike. And if it does, the blow is usually slow and obvious."

She nodded slowly. "I can see that you do it well. And you are correct. I am not likely to hit you now."

"I am gratified to hear it."

"But I am not reassured either. I have lost everything this day to a thieving solicitor. And I intend to get it back."

He huffed. "But Mr. Addicock did not steal your home. Did you not hear that he had not profited from his work?"

"He's lying!"

Samuel ignored her outburst as an emotional reaction and therefore not relevant. "And neither was it Mr. Cordwain. He spent the money—a great deal of money—and was quite put out about it. Those two are merely pawns in a larger game. Both are villains of a sort, Addicock more so because he created the theft. But we have to find the larger game."

"There is no larger game," she growled. "I need my home and my shop back. Cordwain has it, Addicock sold it."

He sighed. She was a practical woman, focused on the simple necessities of life. "But what of justice?"

"What of food and shelter?"

"Both of which you have at the moment. Or will in a moment." He glanced out the window. They were nearing their destination.

She shook her head and he could see her shoulders bunch with tension. She didn't speak but he could feel the anxiety pressing upon her. In truth, it had been a very hard, long day for her and it was barely half over.

"They say patience is a virtue."

"*I* say that I shouldn't put all my eggs in the one brain basket of a mad toff."

He blinked, startled. "That was very clever."

She sighed, the sound coming from deep inside her. He was well versed with the sound, hearing it often from friends and family alike. But he felt hers more keenly. Something inside him did not like that he frustrated her. So he leaned forward and touched her hand. It was a gesture he did not usually make. A comforting touch had never been something he excelled at. But with her, he did not mind making the effort, and she seemed to need it.

"I will not fail you," he said, stunned by the weight of his own words. Especially as he continued, his mouth working despite the fact that his mind was reeling. "You shall have a home and a shop. This I swear."

She narrowed her eyes. "Double the wager?"

He nodded. "Done."

Then the carriage stopped at his brother's home. Odd how he usually despised the time spent traveling from one home to another, and yet, he wanted to stay here in the dark with her. He leaned forward.

"Penny . . ." he began, his thoughts on how he could manage a kiss before they had to disembark.

"I will kiss you, Samuel, when the wager is done and I have a home again."

His mouth curved into a rueful kind of smile. He might be a master of deduction, but she was a master of motivation. And with that thought in mind, he pushed open the carriage door.

Penny was just stepping out of the carriage, blinking at the afternoon sunlight, when Samuel stepped in front of her, blocking out everything but the worn fabric of his coat.

"Pray remember not to look around. We are at my brother's home, and if you recall, you do not wish to know where it is."

She sighed. They were back to this ridiculous game? "I am perfectly capable of lying when asked where my 'likes' are. I have no idea where they are. After all, I don't know where Max has put them or even if they are in your brother's home. And as I absolutely do have an idea—or could deduce their location—it would be a lie whether or not I looked about this lovely . . ." She looked past his shoulder, narrowing her eyes. As she had spent many a year running shoes to customers throughout London, she quickly figured out their location. "This lovely home on Portugal Street." Though it wasn't quite the neighborhood of the *haut ton*, she recognized it as a respectable location near enough to the city's elite. Clearly, his brother was doing well.

Samuel nodded slowly. "Lying is difficult for most people to accomplish credibly. At least to a trained observer." Then he frowned. "And you told Georgette that you are a terrible liar."

She snorted. "I lied." Then as he gaped at her, she shrugged. "Fortunately, I doubt the question will ever be posed—"

"Of course it will!" he said as he grabbed her hand and began escorting her up the steps. "Mr. Cordwain is likely right now demanding their location from your friends back at the dress shop."

She winced at the idea of dropping such a disaster on her friends' doorstep, and she glanced behind her, wondering if she should return. But he gripped her arm.

"Don't be foolish. That is expressly why you are here. So as to avoid being put in the awkward position of trying to lie."

Meanwhile, they were halfway up the step when the cabbie called after them. "Oi! What about me fare!"

Samuel waved distractedly at him without even turning his head. "Braxton will see to it." Then he stepped up to the door as it opened, where a large and very imposing butler was grimacing at him. "Ah, there you are, Braxton—"

The butler looked over their shoulders at the angry cabbie. Then he nodded and held up a small purse. Penny frowned at Samuel.

"Your brother pays your cab fare?"

"What? Oh, no. It's a loan of sort. Braxton keeps the total. I'll repay it on quarter day." Meanwhile, the butler had not gone out to pay the cabbie, but was grabbing Samuel's hat. "Mind you go straight back and don't make noise. Mum has the headache."

"Worse than usual?" Samuel asked.

Braxton didn't answer except to roll his eyes. Samuel snorted and grabbed Penny's hand, ducking his head as he pulled her along. She had the feeling that they were two children rushing through the hallway on the way to some mischief. But halfway through the house he stopped to whistle like no bird she'd ever heard. It was a rolling cascade of notes that ended with a flourish. Penny turned to stare at him, but his attention was focused upstairs to where a boy's head abruptly appeared over the railing.

"That's a new one," the boy said in a whisper.

"White-browed scrub robin from Africa."

The boy—presumably Max—frowned down. "Really? From Africa?"

"So says Professor Lowth, who has just returned from there, but I sometimes wonder if the man is completely sane."

Max nodded sagely, then pursed his lips and echoed the birdcall back exactly—near as Penny could tell, at least.

Samuel grinned. "Excellent!" Then with another tug, he pulled her quickly through the house and into the kitchen.

The cook was there, already setting out two plates on the long servants' table. But as Penny stumbled in, the woman narrowed her eyes. Fortunately, the toff was already making introductions even as he pulled out a seat at the table for Penny.

"Chef Winnie Cook, may I present Miss Shoemaker? Miss Shoemaker, this is the woman who can make even the most horrible meat divine."

The woman grimaced but blushed prettily. "Don't be Frenchifying me name. I'm just plain Cook as it should be in all decent homes. So you're the fancy piece." She narrowed her eyes at Penny. "Don't look fancy or a fool. Means the mum's got it wrong."

Penny opened her mouth to say something—she had no idea what—but was forestalled as Samuel tugged her into the chair. She flushed, embarrassed that he'd had to remind her to sit. What was he doing holding out a chair for her? No one held out a chair for the likes of her.

Meanwhile, Samuel was gesturing to a maid. "Jenny, sweet girl. Been out back, have you? Come, luv, get us another plate and a pie, what, and give me a gift?"

A young girl with a flushed face and mussed hair giggled and grabbed a plate from the cupboard. "I heard that Lord Harker's younger brother Benny is in the suds again. Actress wants money for the babe."

Samuel shook his head. "Too easy. That boy—"

"Actress wants a hundred quid a month!"

Samuel paused, his eyebrows rising with surprise. "What does that tell you, clever girl?"

The maid pranced. "That the babe really is his, otherwise why would she demand so much?"

Penny snorted. Even she knew Benny's reputation. And

that his brother would rather pay any claim than investigate it. "It means there really is a babe, but I doubt it's poor Benny's."

Samuel turned his dark eyes onto her. "Really? Why do you think that?"

Penny shrugged. "I met Benny once when I was younger." She'd been younger, sweeter, and at an age to try out her feminine charms. Specifically, she'd tugged her blouse down to a nearly scandalous level and tried to flirt with the man. Benny hadn't even noticed. His eyes were trained on one of the workmen who'd been hauling in a shipment of heavy leather. The workman had stripped out of his shirt in the stifling heat and was quite the picture of steamy masculine health. "Benny didn't father any babe on an actress."

Samuel nodded slowly. "Exactly correct." Then he glanced at the maid. "Sorry, Jenny. Miss Shoemaker wins."

Jenny pouted prettily, but it was the footman who had just joined them that chuckled. "Go on then, give 'er the prize."

Penny frowned. "Prize for what?"

"Best deduction for the day," answered the boy Max as he climbed into his seat. Penny hadn't even noticed him as he entered, but he slapped a couple sheets of foolscap on the table then eyed the tarts that Cook was just bringing over.

"Yeah," agreed a second footman. "And the prize is always the same."

Penny took a second to look at Jenny's flushed face, the two footmen's laughing expressions, and Cook's roll of her eyes. She didn't have to ask, but Cook answered anyway, her voice deadpan.

"A kiss. And not on the hand."

Bloody hell. Men everywhere were all the same. "As if your kiss is any prize at all."

"True, true," agreed Samuel with a grin. "But we have to play the game. Those are the rules."

"No, we—"

His lips were swift, sweet, and very perfunctory. Damn it. Some part of her wished he'd taken his time.

"There now, all right and proper," he said as he took his seat and tucked into his own meat pie. Another had appeared on the plate in front of her.

Meanwhile, the footmen jeered. "That ain't how it's done, gov," they protested.

"It is with Miss Shoemaker," Samuel responded as he ate. "Now, Max, my man, what have you figured out?"

The boy looked up. Somewhere during all the hooting, he had picked up a cherry tart. And like his uncle, he spoke as he was eating.

"Got the list of likes," he said, pushing one sheet of foolscap forward with a red-stained finger. "Can't see anybody killing for 'em. Except maybe another cobbler."

"No," Samuel said, shaking his head. "Wasn't the cobbler. He paid dearly for them, but I don't think he's the type to kill. That takes a particularly ruthless mind."

The boy frowned up at him. "Unless in rage. Lots of people might kill by accident." Meanwhile, one of the footmen was inching closer to see the list. He stretched out a hand, only to have it slapped away by the cook. And with a wooden spoon, no less.

"That's Master Max's birthday present. You ain't got the brainbox to play."

The footman stepped back with a sulky glower, but Max flashed a grin. Penny wasn't looking at Samuel, but she guessed he was equally pleased though he didn't allow the boy to gloat. Instead, he continued to ply the child with questions about possible villains. He even slid the list of customers over to Penny so she could look at it.

"Does the list seem accurate, Miss Shoemaker? Nothing missing?"

She had to think a bit, run through the customers in her mind, but in the end she nodded. "That's correct."

"No one missing?"

She leveled him a look. "That is what you asked, isn't it?"

He gave her a pleased grin as he reached for the remaining pastry. "I am very glad to see that you are learning to be specific in your answers."

She all but rolled her eyes, but then he was extending the last sweet to her.

"I believe this is for you."

No, it wasn't. As she was the unexpected guest, it had obviously been meant for him and the boy. She counted herself lucky to get a meat pie, and an excellent one at that. So she shook her head.

"No, sir. That one was meant for you."

"Of course it was," he said cheerily, "but I am extending it to you. It was because of me, after all, that you missed your lunch."

It wasn't. It was because she couldn't afford a lunch now that her home was gone. And before she could protest, he flashed her another grin.

"My mother would have my ears if she heard that I took a tart from a lady." Then he blinked and frowned. "A tart from a lady. My goodness, there's a joke in there somewhere, isn't there?" Then he glanced up at Cook. "Set the pot for tea. Mum's about to wake."

A collective shiver went through the group as the entire room began to empty. The only ones who did not move were herself and the boy. Max looked up at his uncle with a challenge in his eyes.

"Mum will not be down here for another twelve minutes."

The entire room slowed, then paused, everyone turning back to look at the child, including Samuel, who had been in the process of climbing out of his seat.

"That cannot be correct, Max," said Samuel. "Your mum is cross with me today and would have heard our whistling. Five minutes debating what to do, another fifteen in a doze, but then she would have roused. Ten-minute toilette—"

"Seven because she is angry with you," corrected Max.

Samuel nodded. "Very well. Seven. Which means she will arrive all the sooner."

The boy shook his head. "Mum always likes a fresh pair of stockings after a trip into town."

Samuel nodded. "Yes. So why would—"

"I hid all her fresh stockings. It shall take her twelve minutes to find them."

The two footmen released identical low whistles while Jen cursed then glared at the boy. "Coo, why'd you go and do that for? She'll be extremely cross, and who'll be to blame? Me, that's who!"

The boy turned to Jen and slowly shook his head. "I left her a note saying I reorganized her clothing to a more logical pattern. She'll never find anything now." The boy shrugged. "She is always saying I don't put things away or that I never help her."

Samuel turned to Penny. "It's not true, you know. Max is ten times neater than either of his parents, but they feel they must say something to the child to show who is in charge."

Penny eyed the servants as they hung on every word. She recalled that the butler had paid their cab fare, the cook had served them food without even a token protest, and that the maid and footmen would clearly do whatever Samuel asked. "Looks to me as if you are the one in charge," she said. "And the boy in your absence."

Samuel's eyebrows rose. "You deserve another kiss for that, clever girl."

She held up her hand. "There will be no more kisses," she said sternly, though inside she sighed. When was the last time any gent had kissed her? Mad toff or not?

Meanwhile, Max finished off the last of his cherry tart. "Ten minutes now," he said with absolute certainty.

Samuel nodded gravely. "Very well, young Max. Why is it that you hid your mother's stockings just to have twelve extra minutes with me?"

Max looked up. He was seated quietly at the table, his

hands folded and his eyes grave. If it weren't for his lack of height, he might have been a judge sitting at a trial. He was that composed.

"I wish to know the real reason you missed my birthday party."

Samuel looked down, abruptly uncomfortable. He hid it well, but Penny was sitting beside him, listening closely. She heard his breath stop, knew the moment his foot ceased tapping.

"I'm sure your mother told you I'm a brainless idiot who just forgot, then slap dashed together your present." He inclined his chin toward the list of customers.

The boy nodded gravely. "I do not believe it."

Samuel grimaced. "I do have trouble remembering dates. You know that."

"Not mine. Not my party."

Samuel sighed. She heard it distinctly, and suddenly she realized that the boy was correct. There was a special bond between these two, and mad or not, Samuel would not have forgotten this child. So what had happened?

"I was at a brothel, Max," he said softly.

Penny winced. Sure enough, men were all the same the world over. From a quick glance about the room, every one else jumped to the exact same thought. Except the boy didn't seem to take the statement at face value. He just sat there and stared at his uncle. Finally, he said quietly, "Why?"

Why? Penny would think that was obvious even to a boy as young as Max. Especially as Samuel's ears had colored red.

"Your mother would not want you to hear this."

That made no impression on young Max at all. In the end, Samuel sighed and gave in.

"A gent became violent and the girl killed him. As I am a friend to the madame, she called me to assist in making sure that the constable came to the correct conclusion. The law can be rather thick sometimes when it comes to a woman of the lower orders hurting—killing—someone of a more wealthy sort."

"And that took all your time?"

Samuel rolled his eyes. "And more. Made me fill out a form as a witness."

Penny frowned. "*Were* you a witness?"

Samuel shot her a frustrated glare. "I was a witness to the *evidence*."

"And you are certain of your conclusion? The . . . girl was only defending herself?"

"Absolutely."

Penny looked into his eyes. Truthfully, it made no difference to her if a whore killed one of her gents in self-defense or not. Ugly things happened every day. But she could see that it made a difference to Samuel. And apparently to the boy, because Max nodded gravely.

"Thank you, Uncle."

Samuel flashed the boy a grin. "Your present was going to be a description of the crime scene so that you could figure out the clues. But then I chanced upon Miss Shoemaker and thought this was a better present after all."

The boy's eyes sparkled. "Can we do both?"

"Of course. But not today. Your mother is due in two minutes."

The boy nodded and everyone scattered. Everyone, that is, except Penny and Samuel, who glanced down at the uneaten tart. "But you haven't eaten it!" he cried.

"It's yours."

Samuel flashed her a grin, then wrapped up the food in his handkerchief. "We'll just save it for Tommy, then."

And with that, he took her arm and led her out the back door.

Samuel apparently didn't have the money for another cab—or perhaps she should say, he didn't have another butler to pay for his fare. Either way, they had to walk back to the dress shop. Penny chaffed at the time, but in truth, she was grateful for the forced reprieve. Her day had begun with armed men throwing her and Tommy out of her home. She could scare credit that it was less than eight hours ago, but it was. And now, after the bizarre meeting with the solicitor and an equally strange luncheon, Penny was hard pressed to think beyond the placement of one foot before another.

And yet, her mind refused to quiet. She tallied out customers at the dress shop and the slippers they might buy. She thought of the leather she needed to work, and groaned inwardly at the soles that were left behind at the shop that was now owned by Cordwain. She would have to remake them with leather she would have to buy at a premium since it was urgent.

Thoughts, worries, and calculations piled up in her head until she was fairly swimming with exhaustion at them all. Then she felt herself being pulled to a stop. She glanced about. They were yet a mile or more from the dress shop, but Samuel had stopped walking and had pulled her to a standstill.

"Don't be afraid," he said gently.

Normally she would have said something acidic. It was all well and good for him to be so casual when he had his brother's household supporting him. But she—

He pressed a finger to her lips. "Don't be afraid," he repeated. "It's not logical."

She nearly bit off his finger then. "I'm not afraid," she snapped. "I'm angry. And it bloody well is logical—"

She cut off her words. He was lifting her chin, stepping in close, and lowering his head toward hers. He was going to kiss her and it wouldn't be any chaste quick buss either. They were in the middle of an alleyway in the middle of London, and yet he was about to kiss her deeply, sweetly, and thoroughly.

She didn't want that to happen, didn't want to be kissing

any toff right then, crazy or not. But that was her mind speaking, not her body. Even before his lips touched her, she melted. Her resistance faded; her frustration and anxiety, it all just drained away. It was too exhausting holding on to them. And he was right here, tall and strong and offering to help her with her overwhelming problems.

She felt his arms wrap around her and his mouth descend. She opened her lips when his tongue traced the seam between them. And then she felt him invade.

She had been kissed before. Scores of boys had tried to take liberties with her, especially around Christmas. She'd even let a few succeed. There had been one young man, back when she was a bare nineteen, who had caught her fancy. A baker by trade who had brought her a fresh bun every morning. They had kissed like this, too, deep and passionate, with hands that roamed and a pounding of her heart.

For a full month they had stolen away for kisses and a bit more. She had been thinking about marriage when she'd learned he'd gotten a maid pregnant. That was the last time—until today—that she had allowed anyone to kiss her.

Today was no different than then, back when kisses were exciting and new. A sweep of the tongue, a press of bodies against each other, and the invasion of all her senses by him. Her eyes drifted closed, but the last thing she'd seen was his gaze hot with desire as he leaned in. His scent filled her nostrils—sharp, musky, and so very male. She heard his breath catch, as if kissing her filled him with the same excitement that tingled through her. She felt his arms wrap about her, touching her back, her waist, her hips as he drew her tight against his groin. And of course, she tasted him. His tongue, the sharp tang of the meat pie he'd eaten, and the essence that was him: confidence. She had no idea how a man could taste of confidence, but he did. His every breath was filled with assurance when she was plagued by doubts and anxiety.

Such a thing was a potent drug to her outside of the thrust of his tongue and the press of his groin. Confidence that consumed him and seemed to invade her with his every caress. With him in charge, nothing could hurt her and all bad things just disappeared.

Or perhaps he simply made her forget her cares. His mouth left hers to press kisses into her cheek and down toward her neck. She felt his hands tighten on her hips as he pulled her close. His organ—thick and hot—pressed rhythmically against her, an act that should have alarmed her, but instead added to the wash of sensation. Her heart thundered and she couldn't catch her breath.

"We cannot do this in the middle of the street," he whispered against her throat. Then he opened his mouth wider and she felt the slight scrape of his teeth across her neck. How could teeth feel so erotic? She shivered and her breath stuttered in her chest.

He lifted his head and she saw that his eyes were dark with passion. He looked around, his eyes narrowing.

"Samuel?" she whispered. Her mind was returning to her, and with it all the thoughts and frustrations that so consumed her.

"Come," he said, starting to pull her along. "I have rooms nearby."

He turned her slightly and started guiding her. But his legs were longer than hers, his command of the path better than hers. She stumbled. He caught her, of course, but the alarm that shot through her body was like a scream. It jolted her mind into thought.

She slowed her steps. He didn't notice at first, but caught on fast enough. Then he turned, his eyes still dark with desire.

"Don't be afraid," he said gently. "I have everything well in hand."

She nodded, but slowly. Her mind was fighting an uphill battle toward reason. She looked at him but saw the alleyway. She thought of London and which way they had walked. Not a direct path to the dress shop, but slightly out of the way. As if he had intended all along to head toward his home and not hers. She had been so absorbed in not-thinking that she hadn't noticed that little thing.

She remembered his words, the repeated, "Don't be afraid." But she wasn't really afraid. She was angry and frustrated. If he had understood her better, she probably wouldn't have had the presence of mind to figure things out. But that discordant note had been enough.

She looked back at him, seeing his eyes widen in surprise. He knew she was figuring things out. He knew that she was not a stupid cull like any number of other women. Because at that moment, she realized he was not a bumbling mad toff. No, Mr. Samuel Morrison was bloody brilliant. His mind was ten times faster than the average man's. His ability to sort through facts, to see what was around him, and to come to his own conclusions was beyond anything she'd ever imagined.

And what did this man do with all that brilliance? Played games with his nephew and seduced women. That's what this particular moment was about—seducing her. He'd planned it, executed it, all while she was simply walking beside him on her way home. If she hadn't stumbled, she might now be entering his bedroom.

She blinked, stunned by her own stupidity. Fortunately, the humiliation didn't last long. The fury built in her blood, taking the time between one breath and the next to reach boiling.

"You bloody ass!" she bellowed. Then she slugged him as hard as she could right in his lying mouth.

Chapter 8

❧

Samuel stumbled backward, his mind already working furiously. He caught himself on the brick wall, his feet finding their purchase immediately. It took his mind, however, a few seconds more to reorient.

She had hit him. She had figured out that his last half hour had been a scheme to seduce her and reacted as a moral, upstanding woman ought. Or rather as a woman without brothers or protectors ought: she'd slugged him. Right hard, too! His jaw was numb where her fives had hit.

"Blimey, you're brilliant," he murmured.

She didn't hear him. She'd already spun on her heel and was tromping angrily away. He caught up to her easily. His jaw was numb, not his feet. But she barely spared him a glance as she ground out her words.

"Don't bother," she practically growled. "If it's an apology, I won't believe it. If it's a carefully contrived lie, I still won't believe it."

"And if I were to admit that I was a scheming cad?"

"I would hit you again."

He nodded, agreement with both her judgment and her punishment. "You intrigue me more and more every minute," he finally said.

"And you disgust me more and more," she snapped.

Again he agreed. "That is because you are a discerning woman. Quite the most amazing one I've ever met."

She glowered at him. "Do all the women in your life fall at your feet?"

He thought about it then finally nodded. "All except my brother's wife. But she is also possessed of uncommon intelligence. Sadly, her moral pomposity detracts far too much to make her the least bit interesting."

She didn't answer except to increase her speed. Fortunately, his longer legs easily matched her pace.

"This changes nothing, you know," he said congenially. "I still intend to win our wager."

"Then go do it," she groused. "Because I have grown heartily sick of you."

He sighed. "Well, that is with uncommon speed. Usually it takes women a week or more to tire of me. But as I said, you are highly discerning. I find that most amazing."

She slowed then and cocked her head a bit as she studied him. Bit by slow bit, he saw the anger fade from her eyes. Not completely. She had too much fury built up for it to fully disappear. But there was a lessening, and for that he was grateful. Meanwhile, she was speaking, and for the first time ever, he heard the weariness in her. As if the weight she bore had finally taken her to the last dram of her strength.

"I cannot decide if you are daft or brilliant, my savior or simply annoying. Either way, I am done in for today, Mr. Morrison. Pray just leave me alone." And with that, she started walking away again. Her steps were steady, but heavy. Gone was the energy that had livened her aspect all day. And that saddened him as nothing else could.

He had hurt her, he realized with shock. Not the situation, not the bastard who had killed her parents and stolen her home. No, it had been he who had given her the last blow. The only reason she hadn't crumpled here was that she had to keep moving, keep living, or she and her brother would starve.

And rather than ease her pain, he had added to it by playing at her life and toying with her affection. Ladies, as a rule, treated him as a plaything, and so he played right back. He solved their silly mysteries, delighted them in bed, and when they grew tired of him, he went on his merry way looking for another to interest him.

But Miss Shoemaker was not of his usual ilk. She was not a bored society woman, nor was she a silly maid like Jenny to be teased and flirted with, but never touched. She was somewhere in between, and her life was not a game. Her affections certainly weren't. And he was the veriest cad for what he had done.

"I'm sorry," he said, though she could not possibly have heard him. And worse, he knew she would not believe he truly felt remorse.

How odd that it was beyond his prodigious brain to determine what he could do to make amends. All he could do was follow along behind her, making sure she did not come to harm on the walk back to the dress shop. He didn't speak to her. He could tell that it would be more of a burden to her. So he stepped along behind her, resolved not to speak, not to seduce, but simply to give her exactly what she wanted: her home and her livelihood back.

So he set his mind to that difficult task. He already knew the steps he needed to take, but it entertained his mind to guess at what the results would be based on a variety of possibilities. Sadly, that took only a part of his attention. The rest remained fixed upon the shift of Miss Shoemaker's bottom as she walked, the determined tilt to her pert chin, and the tight ripple of her shoulders.

Quite an impressive woman, he decided as he watched her walk. But where was all that anger from? He speculated on a number of possibilities, but mostly he thought of the many ways to release her tension. Pleasurable ways. With him. In bed.

And so passed a rather pleasant half hour as they made it to the dress shop.

When they finally arrived, Miss Shoemaker stopped at the door. She leveled a long, heavy stare at him that made him decidedly uncomfortable. His mother used to look at him that way sometimes, and it never failed to make him feel guilty. Usually because he *was* guilty of something.

"Go and win our wager, Mr. Morrison. I am ho—" Her voice broke and he knew she had been about to say "home." But of course, this shouldn't be her home. Her real home was currently being occupied by that ass Cordwain.

"Yes," he interposed smoothly. "We have arrived, but please allow me to—"

His next words were lost as the door was abruptly pulled open. He should have seen it coming. By God, he should have heard the footsteps if not the twist of the doorknob, but his mind had been on Miss Shoemaker. Never had a woman so absorbed his senses as to obliterate all else. So he was caught unawares as Penny started to fall backward. Fortunately a rather large young lady was rushing out just as Penny was falling in. The two collided in an embrace that was startling for everyone except the virago who had hauled the door open.

"Oh, goodness, Penny. I have just heard. Of all the dastardly things! I swear I have never heard the like. Oh, Penny!"

Penny recovered easily, returning the embrace with a soft sob as she twisted to press her face in the girl's shoulder. Samuel watched, the feeling of being unneeded growing inside. This was a female moment, one he usually shunned as being frivolous. But he couldn't force himself to leave Miss Shoemaker's side. Not until he was assured that she wanted this girl's attention.

It was a silly thought. From the way Penny was gripping the girl, he knew that they were friends. But he allowed himself the lie as sometimes even the best of friends could be an annoyance. He would not allow anyone to bother Penny more this day.

Meanwhile, the girl was still hugging and talking all at once. "Never you fear, Penny. You shall have work and money aplenty. I have seen to it."

Penny drew back, a frown on her face and her eyelashes spiked from tears. "What?"

"Why, my wedding, of course. I have just doubled the size of my bridesmaids and I have insisted that they all come here for their clothing and their shoes. And my mother and Anthony's mother, too. Plus all the aunts and cousins. I swear! And you shall be my maid of honor. Say you will, oh please, say yes."

Penny stared, her mind obviously overcome. "But, Francine—"

"You have become a dear friend over these last few weeks. Please, will you stand with me?"

Penny blinked and Samuel watched with surprise as a myriad of emotions slid across her features. He cataloged at least surprise, delight, confusion, and worry. But at the end, she landed upon a quiet kind of pleasure. "It would be my honor, Francine. Thank you." The words were heartfelt. Even standing to the side, Samuel could hear the gratitude in her voice. And then she took a deep breath, exhaled as if she were drawing her focus in, and spoke. "How many are in the wedding party, Francine? How many ladies need shoes? Your wedding is just a few weeks away."

Samuel groaned inwardly. He could see it as clearly as he saw the rubbish on the side of the street and the soft fold of the excellent-quality wool that made up this Francine's dress. Penny was pleased at the honor, but shuddering under the weight of the work. So many shoes in so short a time. It would help her financially, but the work . . .

Samuel shook his head, speaking clearly and firmly

though he had no right to do so. "Not today, Miss Shoe-maker. Not today."

Both women turned to stare at him, their mouths opened in shock at his audacity. But it was the bride-to-be who recovered first.

"I'm sorry. Do I know you?" The words were delivered as tartly as any duchess might address an encroaching mushroom. In fact, if he had to guess, he would say that she had learned just that tone from Penny.

"Oh," said Penny with a shake of her head. "I'm sorry, Francine. This is—"

Samuel raised his hand to cut her off. Then he said the eight words that had never passed his lips before. "I am not of any significance at all." There it was, his secret fear spoken aloud. Sadly, it had no impact whatsoever. Francine drew breath to speak, but he rushed on, reaching for his wall of words to hold her off. "Miss Shoemaker is exhausted. And whereas I am sure that she is enormously grateful for the position in your wedding as well as the additional shoe work, it cannot be addressed today."

At that point, Penny drew breath, no doubt to attack him for daring to interfere with her business choices. Again, she was quite right in her outrage, but he prevented it while continuing his wall of words.

"Furthermore, this is not something that should be addressed in the doorway. The air is growing chill. Miss Shoemaker should be inside by a fire, her brother playing at her feet and a lavender compress on her eyes. It must be lavender, mind, and if you have not got any, then someone should send round for it. I believe there is a shop not more than two blocks away that should have an adequate supply at an acceptable price."

He began walking forward, using his larger size to push the ladies into the shop. But once inside, they were met by the rest of the shop workers, including a tall man who hovered near Francine. They were all drawing breath—almost like a Greek chorus—but he forestalled them.

"Upstairs, if you please, Miss Shoemaker. You will wish to cool your face and sit down for a moment. I am sure Tommy can be brought to your side. Ah, here he is, and chewing on a very handsomely wrought glove. Lord Redhill's, I wager. Nonetheless, upstairs, if you please. Ladies, Miss Shoemaker needs a moment to compose herself. You can direct your questions to me, if you would."

"Just one bloody moment, you cheeky toff!" bellowed Penny.

That was it. The words he was dreading. He had already learned that his usual techniques didn't work on Penny. That she stood strong against him now when she was so clearly done in just emphasized how formidable a woman she was. Especially as everyone grew silent to stare at Penny.

"Yes?" he asked sweetly, though inside he quailed.

"You have no right to take control of everything like this."

He nodded. "True enough, but I am. Do you wish to have me thrown out?"

"Yes," she snapped. Then she immediately shook her head before Francine's man—probably the groom-to-be—could do the deed. "No." She turned to the room at large. "Everyone, this is my cheeky daft toff, Mr. Morrison. If you could get a straight answer out of him, then you are better at it than me. I am going upstairs."

"To sit by the fire and close your eyes for a moment." He was pushing his luck for sure, but he saw a flash of gratitude in her eyes.

"Yes. But just for a moment."

"And I shall bring you tea." When her eyes narrowed in suspicion, he held up his hands. "Just tea, Miss Shoemaker. I shall be the soul of propriety, I swear."

He didn't like swearing something that wasn't true, but in this, he assuaged his guilt. He would deal with the ladies, brew the tea, and then he would proceed to give Penny exactly what she needed.

A physical pleasure that only he—and a few Tantric masters—could give.

Chapter 9

⋙✦⋘

Penny felt her nose twitch, the scent of strong tea filtering through her mind. Then between one breath and the next, she bolted upright.

She'd fallen asleep!

Even before she could blink and focus her eyes, she heard his voice, low and soothing. It both quieted her slamming heart and cleared the cobwebs from her mind at the same time. Even before she could understand the words, she thought what a nice voice he had. She could wake to his words every morning and not grow tired of it. It wasn't that he spoke sweetly. Far from it. But the simple recitation of facts settled her as nothing else could.

"You have been asleep for nearly two hours. Tommy is downstairs along with the other ladies being pampered as any boy—toddler or not—would enjoy. In fact, I heard laughter not more than three minutes ago, so I am sure all is well below. I have learned nothing else of note except that Cordwain did indeed appear this afternoon while we were at my brother's home."

Her eyes shot open at that, but she didn't speak. Instead, she focused on his face, where it was illuminated by the fire. She saw the harsh angles of his jaw and nose, smiled slightly at the wildness of his hair, and then steadied herself by looking into his calm, steady gaze.

"Nothing untoward happened," he continued. "Cordwain demanded to see you. They said you were not here. He made blustering threats which, as you may guess, got him nothing but the door slammed on his nose." Samuel shrugged. "He wants the likes, as you anticipated, but will not find them here."

Penny exhaled slowly, her body sinking back into the chair as she reviewed everything he'd said. Nothing more than she expected and a good deal less than she'd feared.

"Tommy is well then?" she finally asked. She didn't need to. She could hear the low murmur of happy voices rising up from below.

He answered anyway as he poured a cup of tea for her and passed it into her waiting hands. "He is doing very well. I gave him Cook's tart that you saved. Last I saw, he was covered in it and the ladies were discussing a bath in the workroom tub."

Actually, he had been the one to think of saving the tart, not she, but she didn't say that. She was too busy sipping her tea. Good solid brew, thick, dark, and hot. She frowned at the steam, wondering how he had managed it. He answered even before she could ask.

"I guessed that you would wish to be woken within a couple hours' time. My mother used to enjoy waking gently with the smell of a hot pot of tea."

"It is the best way in the world," she concurred.

His smile flashed for a brief moment. "Perhaps I could suggest some other ways. Maybe at another time."

She blinked, wondering if he was flirting with her by suggesting something scandalous. Of course he was, but he did it so gently—when he was usually so blunt—that she wondered if he knew what he was about. Of course he did, she thought as she sipped her tea. But that didn't mean it was any less effective. She was intrigued.

She smiled over her teacup at him, marveling at the quietness of the moment. A nap followed by strong tea. She shifted in the chair. Someone had put a blanket over her, so she was warm and comfortable. And a handsome gent was being kind.

"Will wonders never cease?" she drawled to herself.

He heard, of course, and he cocked his head. She didn't answer except to shake her head. And to her surprise, he accepted it with a nod.

"You will want to be about soon," he said softly. "I know that is inevitable. I have already tallied the ladies associated with Miss Richards's wedding. Most will need likes made." He indicated a page of foolscap and the names he had written down. A single glance told her it was easily a dozen names. "Is this the design for the bride's shoes?" he asked, holding her sketch pad open to one of her best designs.

"Yes," she answered, surprised she wasn't more annoyed with him for finding her sketches.

"It's beautiful," he said as his hand stroked over it. "I have not spent much time studying women's footwear, but even I can see the art in all your work." He carefully turned through page after page of designs.

She flushed with pride as he touched the embellishments she'd added, the rosettes and ribbons. A stroke of his finger across one sketch of a heel told her he'd noticed the curve to the wood as it echoed the upper stitching. She'd labored well into the night on each one of those designs. She knew every stroke and shaded pearl. And now he was seeing them, too.

"You have a startling talent," he said, still paging through the designs. "And quite a fascination with wedding shoes."

She flushed. Every bride in England cherished her wedding shoes. The bride and groom's names were inscribed in the sole along with the date of their wedding. And then, after the wedding, the shoes were placed on the mantle for their children to admire. Of course she would dream of wedding shoes. What little girl didn't? And of course, as a shoemaker, she had sketched her ideas.

"I started creating designs well before I could read," she said, completely avoiding the topic of weddings. "I knew the process of making shoes by the time I was six. By seven, I was begging to create something of my own."

"He never let you?" Samuel asked. "Your father?"

Penny shook her head. "No. Not ladies shoes and nothing of my own design."

"You will be a great success," he stated as simply as if he were speaking of the evening's meal. In his mind it was a foregone conclusion, and she was stunned speechless by that. He flipped back to the sketch of Francine's bridal shoes. "You won't have the time to do this design for all the brides-maids, not with full likes for a dozen women. But I believe you are clever enough to find a solution."

She nodded slowly, forcing her mind back to the logistics. She'd need an apprentice for the carving. She already had her eye on a likely child. A daughter of a furniture maker who was also being overlooked by her father. The girl was smart and had clever hands. She would do well in the shoe trade.

After the base measurements were done, the slippers could be made quickly enough. Without even a fully ac-curate like. She was not to make walking boots, but fine slippers for a wedding. Those were more delicate to stitch, but with a steady enough hand, they could be made faster and in time for the wedding.

Her mental list skipped on to the money she would make from these shoes. To what it would pay for and how she would survive these next weeks or months. For the moment, she and Tommy would survive. And if things continued like this, they might even thrive.

Her breath exhaled in relief.

"Better then?" he asked. "You have worked it all out?"

She frowned at him. "Worked out what?"

"Everything to your satisfaction. The money, the business, the timing of it all? Whether or not I manage the return of your home, you and Tommy will be fine."

She frowned at him even as she was nodding slowly. "Yes, I have worked it all out. But our wager still stands."

He sniffed as if insulted. "Of course it does."

"And have you worked out how to accomplish the task?"

He nodded, but his words contradicted it. "Not exactly. Shall I explain my thinking?"

Her mad toff offering to explain? Tonight was a night of wonders. "Yes, please."

"And would you mind terribly? In the evenings when I was a boy, I used to rub my mother's feet. She had terrible bunions, you understand, and after a long day, she would sit by the fire and I would rub her feet. And we would talk." He spoke so wistfully, that she was already shifting to accommodate him without even thinking of the scandalousness of it all.

"What did you talk about?"

"Oh, any number of things. What I had learned that day, what the workers had done, who was cheating whom in the village. Everything. Whatever came into my head to share, and she listened so patiently." His eyes grew distant. "I should like to visit her soon. She says the dog isn't nearly as good as I am on her bunions."

"The dog rubs her feet?"

"What? Oh, no. He lays on them. His body heat helps, I think. But she says my hands are miracles."

A man's hands on her feet? She couldn't imagine. But he seemed so eager and she was equally interested in hearing his thoughts, so she nodded.

He grinned like a little boy, which she found really endearing, and scrambled down to the floor beside her chair.

He was tall and lanky, so it took a moment of arranging for him to settle with his back against the wall. Then he reached under the blanket and took hold of her left foot with a firm touch. She gasped and felt her shoulders tighten, but his touch was strong and impersonal. Or so it seemed, though she felt his every movement as if it were the only thing of true import. As if nothing else in the world mattered except his hand on her ankle as he worked off her shoe.

"This is very wrong," she murmured as she tried to draw back.

"We shall leave your stockings on. Your foot is covered by the blanket. I can see nothing untoward. It is perfectly acceptable."

"It is not, and you know it."

He looked at her, his expression honest and a little disappointed. "Penny, forgive me, but you are not a fine lady to be worried about your reputation. If you were, my presence here would already have ruined you."

"Tommy already ruined me," she said under her breath.

"Your cousin, now brother? How could he ruin you?"

She frowned down at him. Surely he knew. "Everyone believes him to be my illegitimate son."

The man grunted, the disgust on his face clear. "That is the problem with most people. They notice only one fact and forget all the others. Tommy does not have your features. There is some family resemblance, to be sure. In the ears and in the shape of your lips. But that is all. If you were truly his mother, there would be many more similarities, not to mention the changes in your own body."

"Changes in me?" she asked, surprised.

"Wider hips, fuller breasts. Often the gait changes. Even the rhythms of speech can change, but perhaps that is more a result of chronic exhaustion or screaming after stubborn toddlers. I don't know. But I can assure you, there are changes that happen to the body when a girl becomes a mother."

She looked down at her chest. Her breasts had never been small, but . . .

His grip caressed along her ankle. "Rest assured, my dear, it is quite plain you have never had a baby, never been pregnant. Tommy is your relation, but not your child. And anyone with eyes to see will know it. I did immediately."

She looked at him, her mind struggling with what he'd just said. He had known immediately that she was an honest woman. He had known and stupidly believed that everyone else saw it, too. The idea was so unsettling, so wonderful, that she could only stare. In her experience, *no one* saw, *no one* believed. Not even her friends here at the dress shop.

"You knew," she whispered, her voice choked and her eyes misting with tears. Stupid woman that she was, crying over such a silly thing. And yet she was touched all the way down to the core of her soul.

"Immediately," he answered firmly. "But if you are going to cry about it, then I shall pretend you are a fallen woman. Would that be better?"

She laughed. He intended her to, of course. How the man could be utterly charming now when he was so hideously annoying earlier, she didn't know. Perhaps it was just the magic of this moment. So she shook her head and leaned back in her chair. He knew she was an honest woman. And so she would allow him to do the very scandalous act of rubbing her feet.

What a contradiction it all was. And yet as he firmly pressed his thumb into the arch of her foot, she found the particulars didn't matter. She was in heaven, his hands were truly magical, and she would not move even if Armageddon began.

"Please," she said as she closed her eyes. "Tell me what you have surmised about my home."

He settled back against the wall while his thumb pressed deeply into her heel. She could feel the texture of her stocking as it imprinted on her skin. But it didn't matter. Nothing had ever felt this good.

"All we need do is prove the will false. That is a simple matter of comparing the signatures to your father's. A marriage certificate would be best. Do you have that?"

He was curling her toes around, stretching her foot into a point and then arching it back the other way. Oh, God, did that feel wonderful.

"Yes," she murmured. "In the Bible." Then she groaned. "But it is at my home."

"Which is currently occupied by Cordwain. No matter. He certainly has no use for your family Bible. We can surely persuade him to give it to you."

"He wouldn't give me the mud off his boots." She spoke the words without heat mostly because Samuel was rolling his thumb along the ball of her foot, sliding between the ridges. She felt as if her toes were separating, stretching open as never before. "Where did you learn to do that?" she asked.

"What, break wills? Truly it is a matter of deduction. As for why other people cannot make such logical deductions as easily is a mystery that I have wondered all my life."

She smiled. She didn't know if he had meant to be funny or not, but she was pleased nonetheless. "No, silly. To rub a woman's feet like that."

"Ah," he said as he set her foot down. She would have objected, but he was already picking up her other foot. She wiggled her toes in anticipation. "There are Chinese texts on the channels of energy that flow through the feet. Through the whole body actually, but there was a great deal of literature devoted to the feet."

She lifted her head to look down at him. "You speak Chinese?"

"Goodness, no! Well, only a little, but these were written texts and I could not make much sense at all of them."

"Then how—"

"I found someone who could and had the man explain it to me."

"Of course you did."

He sniffed. "It was the logical thing to do. I was interested, my mother's feet hurt, and there was a visiting professor at school who knew. I took the time to ask, and he to explain."

She reached out. If she shifted just the tiniest bit—which she did—she could touch his shoulder. She set her fingertips there and smiled when he looked at her. "Thank you," she said and was pleased when his skin flushed in response. She waited a moment, happy to watch his expression shift from embarrassed to content. She did not think he was often content. Sure enough, all too soon, his gaze grew distracted again as his mind began to churn.

"If necessary, we can challenge the witnesses."

She shook her head. "John Smithee and Thomas Baker? There are dozens of men with those names."

"Yes, but they would have to prove that they could sign exactly like what was on the will. That is a great deal harder to do. But it's best if we simply challenge your father's signature."

"Addicock said he would go to the constable. He said that the bill of sale was false."

"Yes, but recall that the constable already told us he checked out the bill of sale. It was legitimate." His hands shifted to stroke down the back of her ankle. She hadn't thought it would feel so lovely, but everything he did was perfect. Meanwhile, he kept talking as if his mind would not stop. "Of course, you know that Addicock is simply playing a stalling game. Next time you see him, he will claim there was a delay with the constable. And then the next time that he has filed a complaint, but with the courts these days everything is slow."

She picked up the thread of the game, having played it with some of her father's clients—both aristocrat and not—all of whom had wished to avoid payment. "Then he will say that Cordwain is a villain, but he is working night and day to see the man brought to justice."

"Years will pass and in the end . . ."

"He will be very sad, but unable to help me at all." She sighed, her shoulders dropping with the movement. Or perhaps it was because he had found a hole in her stocking. The heel was worn through, so it was an easy thing for him to find. But she hadn't expected that he would slip his fingers through the opening and begin to work on her flesh. Amazing how much better it was when he touched her skin to skin.

"So we must prove the signature false now. Still, I cannot believe Addicock the true villain here. He seems much too bad at it."

"He is good enough that I would have no recourse without you," she pointed out, both frustrated and grateful for his presence. Why were women so vulnerable without a man?

"Never fear. I shall get it sorted out."

"But how? I don't have the Bible," she said, half on a sigh.

"Tell me where it is. I shall get it tomorrow."

She was silent a long moment. Part of her was trying to remember exactly where the massive tome was. Her parents' bedroom, she thought, high on a shelf. But she wasn't sure. The other part of her was feeling his fingers press against the arch of her foot. He seemed to be caressing on a part of her deep inside her body. Not quite her spine, more a tight ache that was echoed throughout her every muscle. And the more he stroked it, the more everything in her eased.

It took a long while for her to remember that he was waiting for an answer. And even longer for her to find breath to answer. "I think it's in my parents' bedroom, but I'm not sure. It could be a dozen different places."

He grunted. "Never fear. I shall find it."

"No, I will go with you. It is my home. I know where

things are. Besides, Cordwain can't have moved in already. He has a home. All he wants is the shop."

Samuel's fingers paused as he frowned at her. "He will have guards, Penny. It will not be safe."

Her gaze did not waver. "My home, my Bible. If you mean to sneak in to find it, then I will be with you."

He grimaced. "I mean to talk to Cordwain and get him to see plain logic."

She snorted. "He's not a logical man. And he's angry."

"Nevertheless—"

"And then when that fails, you mean to pick the lock as you did at Addicock's."

She could tell she had him there. He pressed his lips together in frustration. She wasn't sure why. It wasn't as if she were stopping him from breaking in. Only insisting she help him.

"It's only logical," she said calmly. "You cannot find it as quickly as I can. And the less time creeping about a guarded home, the better."

He humphed and twisted such that he wasn't looking at her. She chuckled. She'd wager everything she owned— which wasn't much at this moment—that very few people ever got the better of him in an argument. She was extraordinarily pleased that she was now one of them.

Meanwhile, he had begun tugging on her stocking. The ties—high on her thigh—had loosened while she slept. Her position on the chair kept the stocking on her leg, but a tiny shift would allow it to slip down.

"This is in the way," he groused, referring to her stocking. "It seems silly to have it on while I am doing this. Doesn't it feel better without it in the way?"

He knew it did. She looked at him, feeling at war with her conscience. If her mother were alive, the woman would be screaming and swatting at Samuel with a broom. Or with a shoemaker's awl, which was very sharp and could be deadly. But Mama was gone now, and Penny had spent many weeks learning exactly how vulnerable a woman alone could be. She'd defended herself and Tommy from all manner of cads.

But Samuel wasn't a cad or a villain. He was helping her merely because it amused him to do so. Yes, she knew he wanted to seduce her, but this was not a seduction. At least not in the usual way. Besides, her friends were downstairs. A single cry, and they would run upstairs, brooms and other weapons in hand.

Meanwhile, he was looking at her closely, as if reading her thoughts right off her face. "You are quite safe with me, you know. I would never hurt you."

She dismissed that with a soft snort. "Men never mean to hurt women. They are simply unthinking, and it happens."

He all but rolled his eyes. "I am *never* unthinking. Good God, my thoughts rarely stop. Why—"

"Samuel," she said softly, effectively stopping his words cold. "You are a strange, mad gent, but you are also kind and smart. Still, I don't want to strip down my stockings for you." That was a lie. A part of her did want to. A part of her wanted it very much.

"Of course," he said. "I understa—"

"I want you to kiss me."

His eyes widened and she could tell she'd shocked him. Here he'd been trying to subtly seduce her, and she had leaped straight to what they both wanted. It was a conscious decision on her part. She was her own woman now, the sole support of herself and Tommy. Her parents were gone and she had no one to watch out for her except herself. She would honor her parents and the morals that they had taught her. But she would also please herself. There was precious little pleasure in her life. She would take it now and not feel guilty about it.

She watched as Samuel rose up before her. She didn't move on the chair, didn't even shift the blanket away from her. She let him come to her, his eyes intense, his shoulders impossibly wide as they blocked out the glow from the fireplace. She saw his nostrils flare, even as she saw his mouth shift and pause, then shift again. He wanted to say something. His mind was likely clamoring some nonsense. But she didn't want to hear it just then.

"Penny—"

"Just a kiss," she said as she pulled her arm out from beneath the blanket.

He nodded gravely. "Just a kiss. Or maybe just a few kisses?"

She smiled and lifted her chin to meet him at a better angle. "Maybe a few. If they're very good kisses."

"Ah," he said. "A challenge. I do like challenges."

It was on the tip of her tongue to respond something sarcastic. Something about men and challenges, and always being ready for some things. But the words never left her mouth. Instead, they were stopped by the stroke of his finger against her mouth. It was a simple brush, a touch then gone, but it left a tingling heat in its wake.

Then he was smiling wryly at her. "We both talk too much."

She couldn't agree more. Then he was kissing her. His mouth pressed to hers, his fingers delved into her hair to support her head. And his tongue teased along the seam between her lips.

"Sweet" was the word that filtered through her thoughts. He was kissing her sweetly, like a boy with his first girl. She wasn't his first. She couldn't be. Any more than this was her first kiss. But it felt that sweet, the way he teased her lips, pressing lightly against them, almost hovering, silently waiting for her consent.

She gave it. She opened her mouth, she pressed herself forward, and she gave herself to his kiss. He supported her head, and he angled his mouth. His tongue swept inward with the confidence that was so much a part of him. Oh, the sensations he evoked with just a thrust of his tongue. She released a sigh and let her herself enjoy what he did to her.

He thrust his tongue in and out, he touched the roof of her mouth and dueled with her tongue. He pressed her backward into the chair and thrilled her as no man had ever done. Just his mouth and his tongue, his teeth, and his presence. He filled her, he challenged her, and she found she wanted more.

He pulled back slowly, and her lips clung to his. His breath was short, and her heart was pounding. The firelight was behind him, so his face was in darkness. But still she knew that his eyes would be dark and hungry. Or perhaps that was her own hunger she felt.

"Was that good enough?" he asked.

"No," she answered. "I think you will have to try it again. Better this time."

"Better how?"

She knew what she wanted. She had married friends. She knew the mechanics of what went on between a man and a woman. She couldn't do all of it, but there was a little she could feel. A tiny bit more that she could enjoy.

She pulled her other hand out from under the blanket. Shyly, she touched his near wrist and slowly lifted it up. She couldn't say what she wanted, but she guessed that, with his mind, he would understand.

"Will you touch me a little, Samuel?"

"As much as you want, Penny. Are you sure you want more?"

She nodded. "Just a little." Then she boldly brought his hand to her breast.

Chapter 10

❦

Samuel felt his mouth go dry while all of his blood rushed straight south. He knew he needed to go slow. She was not a bored society woman. For all that Penny was a woman on her own, she was an innocent in the ways of sexuality. No matter how blatantly she asked for his touch, he had to go slow.

That's what he told himself, but his mind had little control over his body. Even as she brought his hand to her breast, he was already adjusting his fingers to hold her, to caress her in the way all women enjoyed. He lifted her breast slightly, he squeezed just a moment, then he rolled his thumb back and forth over her nipple.

The situation wasn't ideal. She had shift and dress on, but her nipple was tight, and in her innocence, she was extraordinarily sensitive. The first touch had her breath catching on a gasp and her eyes turning soft as she let her head drop back against the chair. He couldn't resist such an invitation. So as his hand continued to mold and tease her breast, he pressed kisses to her lips, her jaw, and down along her neck.

She trembled in reaction. He felt it clearly—a slight shudder against his lips—and it so affected him that he physically jerked his groin against her. He hadn't meant to. He'd always thought it a rather crude act, but his body had taken control as he pressed himself rhythmically against her leg.

Her eyes widened at that. Or perhaps it was because he had begun tasting her skin, pressing nibbles with his teeth along her jaw. Good Lord, he was out of control. But even as his mind tried to remind him of the people downstairs, that anyone could walk in on them, and that this was not the way to seduce an innocent, his body continued assaulting her. He tried to be gentle. And by all accounts, she was enjoying his every stroke. But he knew how beyond the bounds his actions were.

His mind railed in a distant kind of harangue as his free hand began working at the buttons of her dress. For a man out of control, he had remarkable dexterity. She wore a workwoman's gown—one that fastened down the front—and so he began teasing the fabric open one button at a time. And as her flesh was revealed, he shifted to press his lips to the pulse at her neck, the expanse of her throat, and then to the top ridge of her shift.

It was a cheap muslin, worn thin and too small for her. He wanted to tear it apart with his teeth, but she had so few things—only the clothing on her body—that he could not do such a thing to her.

So instead, he slipped both hands beneath the fabric of her dress but above the shift. Her body was hot now, her skin flushed, and her lips parted as she panted. He let his mouth wet the fabric of her shift as he kissed lower. He wanted to suck on her nipples, to bite and to tease, but her clothing was in the way. There wasn't room. And bloody hell, his back was beginning to strain as he knelt in front of her.

He pinched her nipples and she gasped. Her back arched to give him better access, and he lost all sense of control.

He pulled her dress open, straining the buttons but not breaking them. He didn't rip her shift, but only because he was too impatient to bother with the effort. Instead, he set his mouth on her left breast. He sucked through the muslin. She cried out in surprise and he felt her hands on his shoulders. Neither pulling him close nor pushing him away, her fingers just seemed to clutch there, holding him steady as his mouth worked and his right hand left her chest to slide down her leg. He would work it under her gown and . . .

She pushed him backward. It wasn't a strong push, but it was a growing pressure. It took him a while, but in the end, he left her breast. In truth, he had little leverage, so even her little bit of push was enough to force him onto his heels.

"Penny?" he said, his voice thick.

"Thank you," she said, her words a soft pant in the semidark.

He frowned. His mind felt dull. "What?"

Her back curved, slumping her back into the chair. And with shaking hands, she released him to begin buttoning up her dress. With the release of pressure against his shoulders, he nearly returned to her. But her arms were blocking him, and he was fighting too hard to regain control of his thoughts. Why could he not think?

"Penny?"

She glanced up at him, and her lips curved into a soft smile. Her skin was still flushed, her mouth an enticing red, but her gaze was steady as she looked at him. "Thank you, Samuel. That was . . ." She released a happy sigh. "That was wonderful."

"It doesn't have to stop," he said. "Your bedroom is close. There is so much more to show you." Bloody hell, what had happened to the sweet words he usually spoke to women? He usually was able to speak them without actual thought. He should be complimenting her beauty, expounding on how lost he was in the glory of her body. Any number of things. Except this time he actually *was* swept away, his mind scrambling for purchase. And there she was calmly buttoning *up* her dress! "Penny—"

"I wanted to feel it," she said as her gaze dipped to the closures on her gown. Her hands were shaking on the buttons, so at least she wasn't as calm as she sounded. But bloody hell, women as a rule did not re-dress until afterward. They'd barely even begun!

"There are ways to preserve your virginity. Please, Penny, there is so much to know," he said. Good God, was he actually begging her? This was ridiculous. And yet, he wanted nothing more than to teach her, to show her the delight he could give her. He wanted her screaming in ecstasy, and he needed to be the one bringing her there. The idea gripped him so hard that he lost all other thoughts completely. And that was the surest sign that he had gone mad. He saw it, noted it with a clear dispassion, and completely ignored it.

Instead, he grabbed her hands before she could completely close her gown. He brought them to his lips, sucking gently on her bent knuckles.

"Please, Penny." Lord, he had to stop. He could hear the voices downstairs clearly now. They didn't appear to be coming upstairs, but the door to the workshop was open. It was probably late enough that Tommy would be ready for bed soon. And yet, the hunger to disregard all of it consumed him and he groaned. As a gentleman, he had to strangle his baser instincts. That had never been hard for him before now. He was a man of intellect after all.

"Samuel," she reproached him gently. "I said a little. That was a wonderful little, but I will not do more."

"I know," he said. "I know. How lowering to realize that I am a base creature after all." He looked into her eyes, and damn it all, his groin pressed against her leg like a dog begging for a treat. "Bloody hell, I am a bastard!"

She laughed at that. A light, happy sound that frustrated him as much as it made him want her even more. Then he felt her hands on his cheeks, gently lifting his chin to look at her. He stretched forward, hoping she meant to kiss him, but she didn't. She held him back even though her gaze held desire. He was sure it did. She wanted him! And yet she held him back, so perhaps it was his own base desires he read.

"Penny," he groaned.

"Go home, Samuel. Get me back my home."

He ground his teeth together. "Of course I will do that. This has nothing to do with that!"

She smiled and then indeed did press a kiss to his lips. But she slid her hands down to his shoulders, so that when he would have deepened the kiss, she held him back. "I am not one to separate the two, Samuel. It is all wrapped up together in my mind. I will not bed you like a tart as payment—"

He actually growled at that. He did not think of her as a whore. He could *never* think of her that way.

"And if this is something else, then you must know I am an honest woman. I will not bed you out of marriage. It would be a sin."

He wanted to argue her statement. He had not studied overmuch into religion as he thought most of it created for the convenience of the priesthood and not for a rational man. But the moral code was deeply entrained in women, and the penalty for an accidental pregnancy was very high. So he wrestled his lust down and forced himself to pull away.

"I have never thought you a sinful or immoral woman. Nor could I ever."

She smiled and would have said something, but at that moment, they both heard steps on the stairs. He scrambled back to his feet, picking up the tea tray as he did. She double-checked her gown and her hair, though everything could be explained away by her having been asleep in the chair. Meanwhile, he called upon his acting ability and stepped to the side of the staircase.

"Excellent timing, Mrs. Appleton," he said. "Miss Shoe-maker has recently awoken and was asking after Tommy."

The lady smiled warmly at him, but didn't speak. The reason was obvious. The boy was fast asleep on her shoulder. Behind him, Penny stood up and moved to open her bedroom door. Samuel noted the crib in the room and that both women were fully occupied with settling the child.

It would take but a moment. They merely had to lay the child in bed. But then there would be women talk—God only knew what about—but there was *always* women talk. Normally he would run as fast as he could from such a discussion, but he found himself lingering, the tea tray growing heavier by the second. He wanted to catch Penny's eye one last time. To connect with her silently if only to say he was leaving.

But she was busy, and very soon, the other woman had appeared. The seamstress had mounted the stairs and was clucking at him.

"Oh, 'ere. I'll take that. No need to have you standing about holding a tray when everyone's heading to bed. I'm sure you have a great lot to do setting things to rights. Constable's useless when it comes to folks being tossed from their homes. He's got too much to do with the cutpurses and thieving rings. Damned shame, but it makes everyone afraid."

She was babbling on, her own wall of words filling the air as she took the tray from his hands and started back downstairs. He had no choice but to follow. There could be no decent reason for him to hang about upstairs. So with an internal sigh, he followed the seamstress downstairs.

The woman continued to chatter, but he could tell her true intent was to push him out the door. He allowed it to happen because he had no reason to stay. And yet a melancholy had crept into his thoughts, every bit as annoying as the ache in his balls. He was not generally a maudlin sort of person, but when the mood gripped him, it held on with sharp claws. And it growled in his ears so loud that he had trouble hearing his own thoughts above its noise.

The meaning was always the same, merely the details

different. The mood told him over and over that he was unimportant except in how he could solve a mystery or answer a trivial question. As proof, the mood replayed how easily Penny had set him aside. Despite the passion that burned in her eyes, she had stopped him and turned her thoughts to Tommy. Clearly, his only value to her was in the solving of her mystery.

So that, he thought with a depressed sigh, was exactly what he would do. But in the morning. For the moment, he shifted his steps to a brothel. He had no interest in the women there. The ache in his balls would not be satisfied by any tart. But the men who drank and whored at this particular brothel were of an elevated sort. They would not mean to, of course, but all sorts of secrets dropped from their lips as they were pursuing their other passions. And as he was a man who collected secrets, the brothel was a wonderful place for him to pass an evening.

Odd how the coming evening held no attraction whatsoever to him.

Penny slept very well that night, except for the dreams. Asleep dreams she could handle very well. Even the nightmares that sometimes came—jumbled images of her parents as they died or any other such demon visions—were a natural part of life. She brushed them aside as soon as she focused on the next day's tasks. No matter what time of night it was, a single mental list of what she needed to accomplish either had her getting out of bed or huddling back to sleep, the nightmare long since forgotten.

No, asleep dreams held no power over her. It was the not-yet-asleep dreams that haunted her. The memories of the way Samuel had touched her, and the silent yearning for more that unsettled her mind.

She knew he was a mad toff, playing at her life as easily as others played with a deck of cards or a roll of the dice.

She knew with a certainty that gentry—even the second son of a nobody baron—would never marry a tradesman's daughter. And yet, as she closed her eyes, she remembered the touch of his hands on her breasts, the desire in his eyes, and more potent still, the way he had looked at her with surprise and admiration. More than once that day he had looked at her, obviously impressed. Entire dream fantasies were built on such moments.

She had them married in her mind, in a church decorated with flowers. She pretended her friends stood by her side and that young Max stood as ring bearer. She wished she were as happy as Francine was, eagerly planning her nursery. She pretended all these things, and no simple list of tasks could banish the desire that sparked in her soul from these fantasies.

Eventually she fell asleep. Eventually Tommy woke her, babbling in the way of toddlers. So she pulled him into her bed and played there with him, all the while wondering what games Samuel's son might play. Could a daughter by him be equally smart? Would that girl find a place in this world with ease?

She was perhaps ten minutes away from banishing her daydreams. Tommy would get hungry soon. There were ladies to fit and slippers to sew. But she lingered in bed and dreamed only to have it all interrupted by loud banging on the door.

Twice in as many days, she heard the hated bellows of Mr. Cordwain. Thankfully, she could not make out his words, but the tone was clear enough. To Tommy as well, who started crying immediately.

Penny's daydreams disintegrated as she leaped to dress in the nearest clothing at hand. It was what she'd worn yesterday, of course, as she had nothing else. Thankfully, Helaine's mother was equally fast. The two women met at the top of the stairs, their jaws identical pictures of angry determination.

"Here," said Penny as she held the frightened boy to Mrs.

Appleton. "You hold Tommy. I will handle that bastard. He's got no right coming here. None at all!"

The woman took Tommy immediately, but the martial light didn't fade from her eyes. Instead, she lifted her chin. "We'll face him together."

There was little an older woman carrying a babe could do against the likes of Cordwain, but Penny was relieved nonetheless. Compared to yesterday morning, this would be almost easy because she had a friend with her. Though inside, she wished Samuel would magically appear, just as he had yesterday. Logically, she knew it wasn't possible, but that didn't stop her from wishing.

The three of them went downstairs, pausing only long enough for Penny to grab a heavy broom. She might not be as large as Cordwain, but she had strength. And a broom handle could crack a man's skull if wielded correctly. Then, after a last shared strengthening look, Mrs. Appleton hauled open the door while Penny prepared to wield her broom.

As expected, Cordwain immediately went on the attack. "There you are, you thieving whore! Where are my likes? You give them to me now or I swear by God—"

A man's loud voice interrupted the bastard's tirade. "And I swear that I'll crack your skull in two if you try." Then a heavy hand grabbed Cordwain's collar and hauled him back off the front step.

Penny had been too busy blocking the ass from entering the shop to say anything. Even now she was too startled to do more than gape. She knew that the voice wasn't Samuel's but she couldn't help scanning the area, hoping to see his face and wild hair.

He wasn't there. But the constable was, his face set and two of his men standing nearby, one of whom already had Jobby, Cordain's nephew and thug, pinned against the outside wall.

"Get off me, you—"

"Oh, shut yer yap. You got no cause to be waking decent

people at the crack of dawn." The constable spoke calmly, but with no less authority. Then he chanced to glance at Penny. "You can put the broom down, Miss Shoemaker. We have him well in hand."

Penny swallowed, none too anxious to set her only weapon aside. She did, however, relax her grip and shift it to a less threatening position. Meanwhile, Cordwain was not to be stopped. He whipped about in the constable's grip, breaking free as he held up his paper in a clenched fist.

"I got a bill o' sale! You need to be arresting her, the whore "

Crack! Penny had the satisfaction of knocking Cordwain backward a good step. She'd only landed a blow on his shoulder, but he'd sport a welt for sure. Meanwhile, she stepped into the doorway. "I warned you about calling me names yesterday," she said.

Cordwain had his fists bunched and was leaping forward, but the constable was faster. He had his billy club out, but didn't need it. Just as Cordwain took a step forward, the constable swept his feet out from under him, then followed the man down to the ground, pinning him there with his knee. The baton was out merely as a threat to keep the bastard down.

"She did warn you," the constable said in calm tones. "Now keep quiet. Let me have a look at your bill of sale."

It took a while and Cordwain was none too gracious about it. But in the end, he released the paper as the constable lifted it from the dirt.

"This is the bill of sale from yesterday," the constable said calmly. "It says you own the property you took yesterday and all its contents."

"Yes!" screamed Cordwain. "And she took my likes. She took—"

"I didn't see her take anything but a sack of nappies for the boy," interrupted the constable.

"She's got my likes!"

"I don't see anything in this bill of sale about any likes. But what I do see is a man intent on harassing a woman to no reason. You got her home and her clothes, though what you'd want with a pile of women's things, I've got no idea."

The words were meant as a slur on his character, and Penny had the satisfaction of hearing a few chuckles in the street. Just like yesterday, they had drawn an audience. But unlike yesterday, it was Cordwain who was taking the brunt of it. Meanwhile, the constable continued talking as calm as could be despite the fact that he held a roaring Cordwain pinned beneath his knee.

"So what I see is a man intent on causing mischief to an honest woman. Is that what you're doing? Causing mischief to a woman who wants no part of you?"

Cordwain opened his mouth, no doubt intent on spitting some obscenity. But the constable had his baton at the ready.

"Now mind before you speak. I've got no interest in hearing ugly names this early in the morning. Not when I've been chasing footpads half the night already."

She could tell the words had an effect. Cordwain's face twisted in fury, but he moderated his tone. "I got a bill of sale. Says I get those likes and she stole them!"

The constable heaved an exaggerated sigh. "I told you, I didn't see her take any likes. But in the interest of fairness, Miss Shoemaker, do you have the likes he's talking about?"

Penny straightened, silently thanking Samuel for his foresight. "No, sir. I don't. I'll let you search the shop, sir, and upstairs if you want. All you'll find is molds for ladies' feet. Nothing like what my father used to work on." Then she stepped back, but kept her broom at the ready. "You can come in, but I won't let him inside," she said, glaring at Cordwain.

"Thank you, miss," the constable said with a friendly smile. "Thank you, but I got no cause to be searching an honest establishment. I didn't see you take any likes yesterday, so I have no reason to believe you've got anything now." Then he straightened up, pulling his knee off Cordwain even as he stepped to block the bastard from entering the shop. "All I see right now is a loud and angry man unnecessarily disturbing the peace. And if it continues," he said loudly, "I'll have to arrest him."

Cordwain scrambled to his feet. Fury twisted his features and the sight startled Penny. Certainly she knew the man was a villain, but at that moment he was more beast than man. The only thing that kept him from sinking his fists— and likely his teeth—into her was the steady presence of the constable between them.

Penny took a frightened step backward. So, too, did Mrs. Appleton as she pulled Tommy closer into her arms and breathed a low prayer. In truth, the constable was the only one who didn't so much as flinch. Instead, he spoke in the low, tired voice of a man used to dealing with angry animals.

"Go on now, Walter. Yer likes aren't here."

They all watched, frozen in place, as Cordwain regained some sanity. He glared at the constable, and shot a venomous look at Penny. Then he spat a dark and angry glob at her feet. It landed splat on the stoop, before he spun on his heel and stomped away. A moment later, Jobby followed, having been released by the constable's man.

Everyone waited. Penny held her breath in true fear while, beside her, Mrs. Appleton was still muttering a soft prayer. It was some five minutes more before the constable turned around to face her.

"You haven't got his likes now, do you, Miss Shoe-maker?"

Penny took a moment to gasp a breath. It was hard but she managed, and as she did, the constable gently pulled the broom from her hands. He leaned it against the wall, then looked back at her.

"He's a dangerous man when riled, Miss Shoemaker. Got a temper meaner than a mad dog. And he won't stop looking until he finds those likes."

Penny opened her mouth to say something but he held up his hand.

"You got a bad deal, no arguing, Miss Shoemaker. And if you were to have taken those likes, then I wouldn't blame you. But the law's the law, and besides, what's the sense in keeping something you can't use? You ain't going to be making boots for any lords and you can't sell them without him knowing you have them."

The constable stepped forward, his eyes kind but no less firm. Penny shied backward, not because she was afraid but because the man had a dependable kind of presence about him. And she was lying to him. She *did* know where those likes were. But her words were stopped in her throat as the man reached out to chuck Tommy under the chin.

"You got a babe to watch out for and friends here who don't need any more problems. So if a bag of likes was to appear at the station house, then I wouldn't look deep into it. I'd just be sure to get the things quiet-like to Cordwain. No questions. No fuss. And I'd count it as a personal favor to me. Can't be a bad thing having the constable as yer friend, now can it?"

Penny nodded because he so clearly wanted her to. And besides, he was a good man. "No, sir," she said softly. "I would like it very much if you were my friend. But, sir, he's got my home and my shop illegally. That will was false. Neither Tommy nor I have gotten any money for it. The solicitor Addicock—"

"Yes, yes, I know. But I can't do nothing without proof. All I can do is what I see before me. And what I see is that Cordwain is going to be dogging your every step trying to take a bite out of you and yours until he finds those likes. You've suffered a very great deal, Miss Shoemaker. I'd hate to see the troubles piled higher."

So would she, she realized. But the anger was still inside her, the simmering fury at the injustice of it all. It made no difference to anyone else—or at least not enough of a difference—that everything that had happened was *wrong*. She was still being asked—and by a very reasonable and kind man—to give up the last connection she had to her father. And the last hope she had of giving Tommy his birthright: a shoe shop a block off Bond Street and a livelihood that would support him and his family for generations.

So she lifted her chin and spoke a bold-faced lie. "I don't have the likes and I don't know where they are."

The constable nodded slowly, his mouth pressed into a weary line. "Then I'll be swinging by here more often just to check on you. Can't promise more than that."

Penny swallowed, her gaze darting nervously to where Cordwain had disappeared. "I understand," she said softly. Then just before the constable moved away, she touched his arm. "Sir!"

He swung to her, his look patient. "Yes?"

"How did you know to come here this morning? How did you know this would happen?"

The man gave a halfhearted shrug that was part embarrassment, part amazement. He was thinking of Samuel, she realized, even before the man spoke. Everyone reacted to her mad toff like that.

"Well, had a visit from a gent," he said. "Told me all about Addicock and his thieving ways. We had quite a talk about needing proof, which he says, by the by, that he's going to get. Then he said Cordwain'd be here this morning. Probably before I wanted to be out of bed. And that he'd be causing mischief to a shop of ladies that haven't done anyone any harm."

"So Mr. Morrison convinced you to come?"

The constable smiled ruefully. "It's my sworn duty to protect the people of my district, and that includes you, Miss Shoemaker. And when a man tells me when and where a disturbance is going to be, then I'd be derelicting my duty to ignore it, now wouldn't I?"

"Yes, sir. Thank you, sir."

The man tipped his hat with a smile. "Wouldn't be me that you need to thank, miss. That would be Mr. Morrison. And if you don't mind my asking, exactly what is your relationship with the gent?"

Penny felt her cheeks heat, but she forced herself to say the truth. "He's helping me, sir. Nothing more than that. Just . . . helping me right now."

"Ah." There was a wealth of meaning in that one word, but for the life of her, she couldn't interpret it. Instead, she shifted uneasily and asked the question that had pressed in on her from the moment her eyes opened this morning.

"Um, you wouldn't know where he is right now, would you?"

The man shook his head, and a frown creased his brows. "Not a single idea. But it worries me what a man might do to help a pretty miss." Then his gaze got very heavy, very strong. "If you see Mr. Morrison, would you tell him what happened here? Would you tell him what I said about the likes?"

"Of course—"

He cut her off. "Tell him Cordwain's dangerous. And it'd be safest for everyone if someone was to find those likes and get them to me. You tell him, Miss Shoemaker. And then you look to young Tommy there and you think on what to do."

Penny felt her gaze drop to the floor in shame. Was she risking everyone by her stubbornness? "Yes, sir," she said softly. "I'll tell him. And . . . and I'll think about it."

"Good girl," he said. Then he turned and walked away.

She might have done it right then. She even lifted her head to call the constable back, a half breath away from telling the man everything. She would have except her gaze fell not on the constable but down the street to where Samuel was running pell-mell right toward her.

Chapter 11

~×~

Samuel rushed to the dress shop, his brain spinning uselessly about his own failure. He'd had it all planned, but he'd never accounted for the disorganization of other people's homes. Bloody insane! How could anyone find anything? It was all well and good for his own rooms to be somewhat cluttered, but at least he had an excellent memory and a general sense of organization. Apparently not the Shoemaker household. Everything had been stored haphazardly, as if placed where it had been last used, not where it *belonged*.

How could he have been expected to find anything? And now because of that, his entire plan for the day had been wrecked. It had been a simple plan. He knew Cordwain would try to catch Penny before she was fully awake. Indeed, Samuel had counted on just that possibility, waiting an interminable amount of time in the alleyway outside the former Shoemaker shop.

Once Cordwain and his thick-necked nephew went to terrorize the ladies, Samuel had picked the lock and entered the establishment looking for Penny's family Bible. A quick search of the house would give him the proof he needed to establish the will false, and then he'd rush back to Penny's side in time to see that Cordwain did not get out of hand.

Except, of course, he had *not* found the Bible. He had found a bloody mess. In fairness to the Shoemakers, it appeared that Cordwain had rampaged through the entire house looking for the likes, but still. A book ought to be on a shelf with other books. Except the shelves which still contained their items were filled with clothing and toys. And the ones that had been spilled about the floor had held crockery. As if Cordwain had expected the missing likes to be in the kitchen!

The illogic of it all gave him a pounding headache. He'd searched as long as he could, but in the end, he'd had to cry defeat. He might have pushed it a bit longer, but he'd had a nagging pressure in his thoughts regarding Penny's safety.

What if the constable had been late? What if the man hadn't been able to contain Cordwain and Jobby? What if Penny took it into her head to attack when she ought to allow the men to handle the potentially violent bastard? Or much more likely, what if her temper got the best of her? She'd strike out when she ought to stand back. And in the ensuing melee, who knew what could happen or who might get hurt?

It was the pressure of those questions that had him leaving the Shoemaker residence without the Bible. And when he would usually walk to the dress shop, pretending to merely be out on a morning's stroll, he had increased his speed until he was running full tilt. He only eased up his pace for a half breath when he saw the constable speaking calmly to Penny and Mrs. Appleton. There was no crowd, nothing untoward at all unless he counted the broom leaning oddly against the outside of the building.

Penny was standing in the doorway, Mrs. Appleton and Tommy a step behind. They were safe. Everyone looked safe. He exhaled in relief until he noticed that the constable was taking a deuced long time talking to the women. A deuced long time.

Bloody hell. The constable was no fool and he had a way about him. He had a discerning eye and a surprisingly logical mind. Who knew what he could be saying to Penny and what she might be induced to say in return?

He'd barely eased up his pace when he leaned forward and ran again. He knew the very moment she saw him. She was looking up to call to the constable, who had just started to turn away. Then her eyes narrowed and her body jolted. At least that was what he thought happened. It was hard to tell given how much his vision was jumping around from his run.

Then she took a step forward, her mouth open on a soft cry. Their eyes locked and everything about her seemed to soften. Her shoulders eased down, her chest shifted as she inhaled, and best of all, her mouth curved into a soft smile. He would remember that look for the rest of his days. It was a smile of relief and of welcome. And he hadn't seen its like since he was a boy and hours late coming home. But a smile from his mother was nothing compared to this from Penny. Without even realizing it, he closed the distance between them. She'd barely stepped a few feet outside of the doorway when he skidded to a stop before her.

Then they just looked at each other. He would usually have reached for his words. Wasn't his mind sputtering a mile a minute? And yet nothing found its way to his lips. He just stood there staring at her as he struggled to calm his racing heart.

"You missed everything," she breathed.

"I couldn't find the Bible. I looked and looked. Whole place was a bloody mess."

"It was awful. I was so afraid."

"I'm so sorry."

And then nothing. Just a long pause as they stared at each other and his heart thundered in his ears. Then she frowned.

"You went looking for the Bible?"

"Did he hurt you?"

"No."

"Good. That's good. I had it planned, but I couldn't find it."

"I was thinking about that this morning. I think I know where it is. And then there was the banging again. And you weren't here this time."

"I'm so sorry. Tell me where. I'll go again."

"The constable was here. Everything's fine. Thank you for sending him."

Again they both lapsed into silence. He was staring at her, cataloging the shadows under her eyes, the places where the sun caressed her skin and where her mouth had tightened in fear. Or anger. With her, it was usually anger.

He was reaching out to touch the crease by her mouth, soft now but ready to pull deep at a moment's notice. His hand was halfway to her face when he heard a snort from beside them. Both of them jolted, and then Samuel cursed himself for being so unobservant. How had he missed that the constable had sauntered up to stand right beside them?

"Yes, miss," the man said with a chuckle in his voice. "I can see that he's just helping you through this rough spot. Not a thing more to it, is there?"

Across from him, Penny blinked and flushed a dark red. Samuel reacted more to that than anything else as he stepped forward.

"What happened here, Constable? Are the ladies all right?"

"What happened is just what you said would happen, and I thank you for the tip." Then he glanced significantly at Penny. "But Cordwain's an angry bear of a man. I doubt the ladies will be safe until he gets what he wants."

Behind him Penny drew breath to object, but both men raised their hands to stop her, each speaking over the other.

"I'll see it gets set right. I swear it," Samuel said.

"You think on what I said, Miss Shoemaker," said the constable. "Most things ain't worth a body's life."

Samuel eyed him sharply. "You think he's that violent?"

The constable grimaced. "Not usually. Not in a thinking kind of way."

Samuel nodded, agreeing completely. Cordwain was not the kind of man who thought through his passions. But catch him at a bad moment, and there would be lethal rage. "I'll watch out for the ladies as well," he said.

The constable grinned. "Thought you might." Then with a tip of his hat, he sauntered on his way. Samuel and Penny watched the man walk on, his step not exactly jaunty, but not that heavy either.

"I believe I like that man," Samuel said, surprised by his own words. There weren't many people who impressed him. Fewer still that he actually liked. The constable met both categories, and that was quite the surprise.

Beside him, Penny murmured her agreement. Her words were almost too soft to catch, but he heard them. "He's a kind man. I didn't like lying to him."

He processed immediately how she felt and exactly what she had lied about. He knew he should say something soothing. Perhaps promise again to fix everything, though he was beginning to fear that he couldn't. But before he could speak, she lifted her chin.

"I will not tell you where the Bible is. First of all, you couldn't find it, even if I were very precise."

"If you were exactly precise, I wouldn't fail to find it."

"And you're not leaving me again. Not with that bastard banging on my door two mornings in a row."

What she said wasn't logical, but the sentiment was plain as day on her face. She'd been frightened this morning, and when Penny got frightened, she usually responded with fury.

"Did you get him with the broom?"

She blinked, then flashed him a quick grin. "Square right

on his sewing arm. He'll remember that whack with every stitch he pulls for the next three weeks."

He nodded slowly, enjoying her satisfaction at the blow but not liking that Cordwain would be thinking of her at all.

"He didn't bother Tommy, did he?"

"You're not distracting me, Samuel. I'll go with you tonight after the shop's closed. I was born in that house. I know where all the hiding spaces are and all the noisy boards."

"Absolutely not!"

"Then I'll be going without you. That's my Bible and my home. I'm getting it tonight." She paused. "Though it would be a damned sight easier with you picking the lock."

Samuel grimaced, his belly tightening with an unwelcome and unaccustomed fear. But in the end, he had to surrender to the inevitable. He knew her words were no idle threat. It would be illogical to argue with her when he knew she would do it no matter what he said.

"Very well," he said. "But you will do exactly as I say, when I say it."

She snorted. "I'll do nothing of the sort and you know it."

He sighed. That, too, was exactly logical.

She was ready the moment Tommy fell asleep, but she knew Samuel wouldn't arrive for another hour yet. He had tried for a good ten minutes to convince her to wait another day. Probably so he could sneak in and try to find the Bible on his own again. She had adamantly refused. So with a huff, he'd said he'd come by at eleven o'clock precisely. Late enough, he hoped, for Cordwain to have given up work for the night. Cobblers as a rule tended to work when they were able, night or day, but daylight helped enormously.

Meanwhile, he went off to try and track down the other "witnesses." He expected it would be a fruitless waste of time, but he felt certain aspects needed to be investigated simply for thoroughness. In the meantime, Penny went about her day as usual, stopping now only to put Tommy to bed and then . . .

Then pace about the shop wondering what to do for the next hour. She tried to work but her mind wouldn't focus on the task. So when there was a discreet tap on the back door, she opened it without thinking. Samuel stood there looking anxious, his hair curling every which way and his eyes darting left and right. Except for when they riveted on her.

"Good God, Penny. Don't just open the door to anyone! At least ask who it is first."

She grimaced, knowing he was right. "Um, who is it?"

He glared at her. "Not now! It's to be sure—" He cut off his words at her nervous giggle. "Ah. You were teasing me."

She smiled, her hands twisting in her skirt. "I'm sorry. I seem to be a bit nervous."

His expression relaxed as he exhaled in obvious relief. "No, no, that is an excellent thing," he said as he shut the door behind him. "Breaking in is a dangerous business, even if you are breaking into your own home. I am glad that you are thinking better of—"

She pressed her hand to his mouth. "I am going."

He grimaced and spoke beneath her fingertips. "Truly, I can accomplish this on my own."

She shivered. Not because of his words, but because the feel of his mouth moving beneath her fingers was unexpectedly erotic. A tingle centered in her palm, but she felt an answering tremble throughout her body. Without her willing it, she let her hand slide across his face to smooth the nearest wild coil of his hair.

"I am sure you could, but I am going nevertheless. I have decided that there are a few more things I wish to get other than my Bible."

He frowned down at her, then released his breath in a huff. "Do you know I used to believe that knowing a smart woman would be a godsend?" He stepped forward, neatly pressing her backward until her bottom hit the worktable.

"Turns out intelligence only makes her more stubborn and prone to taking ridiculous chances."

Penny bit her lip, her heartbeat thumping faster. "So you think I am intelligent?"

"And stubborn and taking a ridiculous risk." He pushed himself closer, his legs trapping hers, his torso close enough to touch. Which she did. She pressed her hands to his chest and held him still. Or rather he stilled. As strong as she was, he could still overpower her if he chose.

Meanwhile, she lifted her chin. "It is my home, my risk to take. If I knew how to pick a lock, I would have gone already without you."

His hands hit the table on either side of her, caging her between his arms while his upper body pushed forward, forcing her to arch backward. Soon he was all but lying on top of her.

"You will *not* go alone," he stated loudly.

"I already did. I walked by this afternoon. I have a key to my own home," she said. "But Cordwain has already changed the lock. Probably did it the very first day." She grimaced as a surge of anger heated her blood. "But I don't think he is living there. Just working at the shop. If you can pick the lock, then we should be very safe."

He pressed his head against her forehead. The gesture was unexpectedly defeated and his next words confirmed it. "I do not understand this, Penny. I am a man who sees the truth in everything. But this"—he closed his eyes—"this I do not understand."

"What?" she whispered.

He pulled back just enough to look into her eyes. He opened his mouth to speak, but no words came out. Then his expression flickered to desperation, almost despair. Still there were no words.

She was about to say something. His name if nothing else. But she got no further than to draw breath because, at that moment, his mouth was on hers. His tongue was pressing inside. And his groin was thick and hot against her pelvis.

Oh! She didn't speak the word aloud. It was more a word felt through her entire body. *Oh, yes. Oh, please. Oh, more.*

His kiss was deep and heady. He thrust inside as if to stake a claim there. She felt his hands leave the table to grip her hips, steadying her as he ground against her. She had no thought to what he meant by that. Only that she enjoyed the pressure, and she raised her right leg to wrap it around him as much as her skirt would allow. He groaned as she did that, and his kiss deepened in frenzy. In and out he thrust into her mouth.

She played back as best she could, but this was not a game to him. That was what that flash of despair had been before his kiss. The knowledge came as a kind of whisper into her body as she stroked his arms and soothed his back. This was not a game—*she* was not a game to him—and that frightened him as much as it startled her.

He was a mad toff who played at life, but this was deadly earnest for him. For perhaps the first time in his life, he took something seriously. He took her situation seriously. And that pleased her as much as it seemed to frighten him.

Or perhaps it was merely what he did that pleased her. One of his hands had left her hip to stroke upward. As he broke the kiss to press his mouth to her cheek then her neck, his hand worked between them to finally find her breast. His thumb rubbed across her tightened nipple, and her toes curled in delight. Her breath was coming in gasps as she arched into his touch.

Never had anything felt like this! So wild, so passionate. It was so thrilling that she would not end it even as he started to lay her backward on the table. She resisted the movement, more because she wanted the hard press of his body. She had no desire to yield. But he was stronger and with better leverage. She was halfway to the table when he froze.

He lifted his head, his eyes wild as he looked about the

room. "Good God," he gasped. "On the table. In the work-room. Good God!"

He eased himself upward, his hands pulling off her body with a kind of a jerk. She mourned the loss of his touch. The heat of his body, the press of his organ—all of it excited her, and she did not want it to end. But he was relentless as he pulled away, though he did cup her elbow to assist her back to a stand. She did as he bade though her heart was still thumping in her ears, and her body ached with hunger.

"I am a cad. I should leave immediately. You are not a woman to toy with."

"Then who will pick the lock on the door?"

He groaned and rubbed a hand over his face. "Can you not tell me where the Bible is?"

She shook her head.

"Very well then. Let us go now. Smart of you to wear something dark. It is warm tonight, but you still might want a cloak."

She was dressed in an old work dress of serviceable wool. It was one of Wendy's and fit fairly well, except that she was taller than the seamstress. The hem barely reached her ankles and the bodice was a little tight, but it was serviceable enough.

"I don't have a cloak to use," she said as lightly as possible. That was, in fact, one of the things she wanted to grab once they were inside. She stepped past him to pick up an empty satchel. He frowned at it, but she merely folded it up and headed for the back door. "I told you," she said firmly. "I wish to take a few more of my things."

He didn't answer except to rush to open the door for her. That gave her a moment's pause. She was used to opening doors on her own. That he hurried to do such a thing for her made her smile. As if she were a highborn lady and he, her knight errant. The idea kept the excitement simmering in her blood, but gave it a softer feel. A more romantic, dream-like air that she cherished. With him, she felt more daring, more special, more alive than ever before.

It was beyond odd. Not more than fifteen minutes ago, she would have scoffed at such silliness. She was a practical woman who dealt with harsh realities. Never would she have valued a tingling excitement in her blood. Of what use would that be in putting food in Tommy's mouth? And yet she did value it, and she liked Samuel all the more because he gave her such moments.

She glanced at him as she walked outside, her mind quietly turning over the feelings she was still experiencing: excitement, passion, happiness. How could all these things be happening now when she and Tommy had just lost everything?

Meanwhile, he took her hand and placed it on his arm as he guided them down the street. She glanced at him, startled anew at his actions. Then she grinned. It almost felt real. As if she really were a society lady out for a stroll with a handsome gent.

"Thank you, Samuel."

He shot her a glance. "For what? Risking your life on a dangerous errand better suited for a thief? A *male* thief, I might add."

"Yes," she said with a low chuckle. "Thank you for that."

He snorted. "And you call *me* mad."

Chapter 12

✳

Penny knew it wasn't safe to wander through the streets of London at night, but against all logic, she felt safe with him. So she didn't mind that they made it to the shop at a leisurely stroll. As the night air was lovely, the meandering path they took was a delight. They didn't speak much. He talked a bit about Max, the affection in Samuel's voice obvious. The boy was beyond clever and was clearly the closest Samuel had to a son. It didn't take much prompting for him to expound on a half-dozen smart things the child had done in his short seven years.

But then they arrived at the door. The shop was dark as were the family rooms above. Penny stepped to the side, giving him room to pick the lock. He set to it immediately, and yet still managed to chatter on about his nephew's first experience with insects. Amazing that his mouth could be doing one thing while his hands and his mind were somewhere else entirely.

Then the lock clicked. With a twist of his wrist, the door was open and she slipped inside the showroom, breathing in the air of her home for the first time in too long. Except even in the dark, she knew that something was wrong with the place. Behind her, Samuel shut the door then she heard the sound of him lighting a lamp before holding it aloft. It was only then that the horror hit as the flickering light fell on the debris of what had once been her father and her grandfather's shop.

Everything was in disarray. Not broken, she realized as she looked about, but slammed to the floor in fury, some of it probably kicked into the corners. Beside her, Samuel released a low whistle.

"It wasn't like this this morning," he said. "You must have deeply upset the man."

"Good," she said. She hoped he broke every single one of her father's tools in his fury. She'd rather the implements were broken than used by that bastard.

Meanwhile, Samuel headed for the back stairs, the ones that led to the family quarters. She stopped him with a touch on his arm.

"Not up there. The Bible's in here."

"What? Why ever would you keep your family Bible in the middle of a shop?"

"That's what I remembered this morning. My father had it on his worktable one day. I saw it and asked him why and he said that someone wanted to see the family history."

"Someone?" Samuel asked, obviously latching on to the one thing that she found most interesting as well.

"I don't know who. I don't think he ever said. But knowing my father, he would never have remembered to take it back upstairs. He would have left it on the bench until it got in the way. Then he would have set it aside, intending to put it away later, but forgetting."

She moved into the back workroom, seeing that Cordwain's fury hadn't destroyed much of anything there. He probably had enough intelligence to see the value in the tools scattered about the room.

She crossed quickly to the workbench, seeing the tools but nothing else of value. To the corner was a pile of rubbish, and right on top of it were the leather soles she'd been working before all this happened. As they were already cut for ladies' slippers, they would be useless to Cordwain. She gathered them quickly and pushed them into her sack.

"The Bible, Penny. Where would he have put it?"

She frowned as she scanned the room, her gaze landing on the shelving next to the closet where the likes *had* been stored. There was nothing on the shelves and likewise nothing left in the closet when she opened it. Everything had been thrown on the floor, no doubt as Cordwain searched fruitlessly for the likes.

Samuel was moving about the room, searching methodically. But she was the one who had lived here all her life. She was the one who knew her father's habits. Where would he have set something valuable to be out of the way and yet not back in its place upstairs?

She snapped her fingers. "Of course!" She crossed to her father's desk. It was a small thing, more suited to a child than a man, mostly because her father never used it. It was where she used to sit, sorting through the receipts and cataloging bills. But her work had always been on top of the desk—bills and receipts which were now thrown willy-nilly about the floor.

What few people realized was that the top lifted completely off. It was meant to be a child's secret compartment for toys. Instead, it was where her father kept a plate and a cup for when he ate a meal in the shop. Her desk—papers and all—would be lifted off and set aside. Then he would sit as if at a table and eat his food. The compartment was deep enough for his cup and wide enough for anything he meant to take care of but forgot about.

"Here!" she cried, picking up the heavy tome.

"Excellent!" Samuel said as he rushed to her side. They

stood breathless as she flipped through the pages. She did it quickly, moving to the beginning where her family's names were written. There it was, her father's bold handwriting clear as day. He wrote his name married to her mother and then her own name came below.

Beside her, Samuel pulled out the piece of foolscap he'd written on before. The one with a copy of her father's signature from the false will. They both looked and then he cursed softly. The signatures were not identical, but they were close enough.

"But that can't be," she cried.

Samuel didn't answer. Instead, he touched her hand gently. "What about the marriage license? Where is that?"

"In here, too," she said as she flipped through the pages. Except there were no marriage licenses. None at all. "But they were all kept in here. My parents, my grandparents. I'm sure of it." She looked about the floor, knowing she hadn't seen the ancient pages scattered about but looking nonetheless.

Samuel helped her without a word. He quickly scooped up the scattered pages, scanning them easily before tossing them back on the floor. When she cried out at the mess, he shook his head.

"They can't know we've been here."

She grimaced. Of course. So she stood with him as they flipped through the pile of correspondence. None of them were the marriage licenses.

"But where could they be?" she asked.

"With Addicock, most likely," Samuel said grimly. "He was probably the one to ask to see your family history. Your father brings it down to show him, and in a moment's inattention, Addicock pulls out the marriage licenses. It would be enough to copy the signature to make the will appear real."

"But it's not real!" she ground out, even though she knew her protest was fast becoming reflex. "My father wouldn't sign everything over to some solicitor he barely knew."

"Of course not," Samuel said as he dropped the last of the correspondence on the floor. "But as the constable so assiduously pointed out to me yesterday, we need proof. Proof that would hold up in a court of law."

"But how if the signature appears real?"

He gently closed up her Bible. "I'll think of something. There are other ways to prove a will false."

She couldn't tell if he was just saying that to make her feel better or if he meant it. Either way it didn't matter. They didn't have time for her to sit around moaning about what had been done to her and to Tommy.

Pulling the Bible from his hand, she set it into her satchel. Then while he was closing up the desk, she headed for the back stairs.

"Where are you going?" he called after her.

"Upstairs for my clothes."

He caught up to her easily, taking the steps two at a time. Then he lifted the satchel off her shoulder.

"I'll hold the bag while you stuff. But we must be quick . . ." His voice trailed away as she stopped at the doorway to her bedroom.

Her room had been smashed to bits. Her bed, her dresser, even her shoes had been ripped apart as only a cobbler could. And then all the things had been thrown into the fireplace and burnt. Not well. The pile had been too big so it had flowed out of the grate. Penny could see the scorched remains of her mother's favorite candleholder in the center. Someone had kicked everything she owned into the grate and then tossed the candle—holder and all—onto the top of it.

The fire must have been bright. She hadn't realized how much clothing she had until it was all there in a pile, half ashes, half a sodden mess. Apparently, once the fire had threatened to rage out of control, someone had thrown a bucket of water on top. The fire had gone out, and the rest was left a half-burned mess.

"Yes," drawled Samuel from beside her. "I'll wager you got him more than solid with the broom."

"Yes," she answered as she leaned against his strong support. "Yes, I suppose I did. Enough to make him right furious."

He let his cheek set atop her head as he pulled her close. They stood there a moment while she struggled to breathe. Somehow this fire—this burning of everything she owned—was more personal than everything else. The loss hit her straight in her belly, and she was hard put not to sob.

"Come on," he said as he gently turned her around. "Is there anything else you want? Something of your parents? Or maybe Tommy's clothing?"

She nodded, unable to speak. He turned her toward her parents' bedroom, but she stopped him, guiding him toward Tommy's room. Everything of her parents had already been cleaned out. In the early days after their deaths, she'd had to sell what she could just to get food. If she hadn't found work at the dress shop, she and Tommy would have been in terrible trouble.

So she led him to Tommy's bedroom, pleased to see that Cordwain's fury had been limited to her. Though the room was a mess as he no doubt had searched for the bag of likes, nothing in there was destroyed. In fact, both her father's old wardrobe and the crib still stood solid as ever. Both had been made by her grand-uncle, and Penny was surprised by her tears of gratitude that the pieces still stood.

"They're beautiful," said Samuel as he watched her trail her fingers across the crib's carvings.

"It's bad enough that they stole the shoe shop. That's a future livelihood that can never be regained. But they took these things, too," she whispered. "Furniture that my grand-uncle carved for my parents when they got married. A lace scarf that had been my grandmother's and is now . . ." Her voice choked off. It was part of that pile of wet ashes in her bedroom. "I already had to sell the jewelry. Nothing that's left was of any value except for the shop location and the tools. But—"

"Of course it had value. It was your family's. It was your history passed down from generation to generation." He touched her arm, turning her toward him. "Penny, you don't have to apologize for being in pain. What happened is a crime. And I'll make sure to fix it. But—"

He stopped, his words abruptly cut off. It took her a moment to realize he wasn't looking at anything in particular but listening.

"Samuel?"

"But we haven't the time to mourn right now. Get whatever you need, and then we must go."

She nodded, knowing what he said was true. So she went to the wardrobe, opening it to grab what items she could. The furniture was large, meant for a man, not a baby. But since Tommy was the only boy in the house, it went to him. Her father had allowed her to use it when she was growing up, but the moment Tommy came to live with them, it had been moved to his room.

She'd been furious at the time. Her father's casual dismissal of her because she was a girl still burned. But all that resentment had been put away the moment her parents had died. She hadn't the energy now to devote to anything that didn't involve daily survival. So she handed the satchel to Samuel and began dropping clothes into the bag.

"Don't take everything. It's got to look like we were never here."

She nodded her understanding. She'd just take the few items that were left in the wardrobe and Tommy's winter coat. Then—

"Ooo-ee!" squealed a coarsely accented woman from downstairs. "You's a real gent!"

Penny whipped around, her heart abruptly beating in her throat. Someone was here!

"'At's right," returned a man's voice. "Me uncle trusts me with all 'is important things. 'E does the cobbling. I sees that it stays right and tight."

"Right and tight in yer pocket, I'll wager!"

Samuel grimaced, his eyes narrowed. "Jobby," he whispered. "Probably told to watch the place until Cordwain can move in."

Penny nodded, dropping the satchel as she headed toward the door. Meanwhile the bastard and his tart continued jabbering.

"Mebbe yes, and mebbe no," said Jobby. "Guess you'll just have to be nice to me to find out." There was no mistaking exactly what he meant about being nice. Especially as the woman trilled her answer.

"Ooo-ee! Mebbe it's me ye needs to be nice to. If'n ye want inside me skirts."

"Aw, come on, Mabel—"

"Two quid. 'Cause yer such an important mort now."

"One quid."

"Bloody bastard!" Penny hissed. Jobby had brought a whore into her home and they were dickering over the price in her kitchen! It was the last straw. Between one breath and the next, her fury boiled over and she lost all rational thought. She dropped the satchel and headed out of the bedroom. She didn't even have a weapon, but she'd grown up in this house. She knew where to find a knife or an awl. A bleeding chair would work as she smashed it down on his head.

That was the plan, but she barely made it a step past the door when Samuel grabbed her around the waist and hauled her back.

"Let me—"

"Shhhh!" His hand pressed hard against her mouth, cutting off her words. His other arm wrapped around her waist and pulled her off her feet in one swift move.

She kicked him, tried to bite off his hand, and was ready-ing to slam her forehead into his when he whipped her around again, this time toward the wardrobe.

"Listen to me, Penny!" he hissed into her ear. "This isn't the time! If we're caught here, we'll be the ones in the wrong. You can't fight him now!"

She didn't care. She didn't really hear him. Her mind was on Jobby bringing a prostitute into her parents' home. She could hear the woman's giggling squeal and Jobby's playful roar. He was chasing her. Probably to the stairs. Good God, she realized with horror. He meant to tup the tart in her parents' bed!

She lunged forward, but Samuel's grip was harder than iron. No matter how she struggled, he shoved her backward into the wardrobe. She fought him. She scratched, she kicked, and she connected more than once. But he was re-lentless as he shoved her to the back of the wardrobe and climbed in after her.

"Think, Penny! Think! We can't be found!"

The squealing bitch was on the steps now and Jobby's heavy tread was coming right behind. They were climbing the stairs, heading toward a bed. Tears of fury blurred Pen-ny's vision, and her breath was coming in harsh rasps from her nostrils. Samuel still had his hand over her mouth, and now his body pressed her hard against the back of the ward-robe. The door was ajar. He didn't have a hand free to close it. If anyone chanced to look into the room, then the game was up. They'd be found. Which made Penny even more determined. If they were going to be found, then she damn sure wanted to be caught when she was free to attack.

But Samuel didn't so much as flinch, even when she dug her fingernails into his arm hard enough to draw blood. All he did was lean in closer and whisper into her ear, his words not as important as the whisper of his voice. Soft. Nearly inau-dible. But the only voice of reason against her screaming fury.

"This is not the way, Penny. You're a smart girl. You know the truth. If we are caught here, then everything we do afterward is suspect. We have to work inside the law, Penny. You know this. If you want your home back, we have to wait. We cannot be found here breaking the law. Penny, listen to me. We have to be quiet. No matter what, we have to be quiet."

He was right. She knew he was. In truth, she'd known it from the very beginning. But Jobby had brought a tart into her home. He was even now defiling her parents' bed with low chuckles and loud smacks. Good Lord, did people sound like that when they tupped? It was awful! It was bestial! And it was happening in her parents' bed!

She closed her eyes, feeling her tears make Samuel's grip slippery. But her body was relaxing, giving in to the logic of his words. Now was not the time, but . . . Oh God. She could hear them.

"I'm so sorry, Penny," Samuel continued. "We'll make them pay, I swear it. It's cruel and it's terrible, but it won't last. We'll get the last laugh. Just a little bit longer."

How long? she wondered. She opened her eyes, and caught his gaze, silently asking her question. How long did they have to stand there and listen? She watched him bite his lip and think. Odd how his face shifted when he was doing calculations in his head. His brows narrowed and his eyes grew distant. His lips thinned, but not in an angry way. If anything, she thought there was a curve to his lips. Calculating was something he did very well, and there was a clear pleasure in his ability. And how odd that she was able to distract herself with these thoughts. How she could study the minute shifts in his expression rather than listen to what was happening right down the hall.

Then Samuel was whispering again right in her ear. "Are you calm now? Can you move quietly?"

She nodded slowly. She wasn't calm, but she wasn't going to run screaming at Jobby and his tart.

"It's best to go when they're in the thick of it, so to speak. But Jobby won't last long. We have to move with speed. Down the stairs and out the front door. Do you understand?"

She nodded, her mind doing her own calculations. And while Samuel was pulling his hand off her mouth, she was planning again, thinking logically. It would be winter soon. Tommy would need his winter coat.

"Through the kitchen," she whispered. "I need Tommy's coat."

He shot her a frustrated glance, but ended up nodding. Then they stepped as quietly as possible out of the wardrobe. Samuel grabbed the satchel, Penny snatched up Tommy's favorite blanket, then together they slipped down the stairs. A moment later, she'd grabbed Tommy's winter coat and her own cloak as well, which had been miraculously spared. Probably because it had been on the same peg with Tommy's. Then they were out the door. Two minutes after that, Samuel was hoisting the satchel on his shoulder while he turned their steps down the street in the opposite direction from the dress shop.

"Where are we going?" she asked, though the words came out harshly through gritted teeth.

"Put on your cloak. We're not going back to the shop just yet."

"Why? Where are we going?"

He stopped and took a moment to look at her. Not so much a glare as a long, considering look. "It is time you told me the rest."

"What rest?"

"The rest, Penny. Or at least more. And we're going to do it in the most private location possible given the circumstances."

"Your home?" she sneered.

"God, no. I expect you'll be screeching and screaming before we're done. That'd be noticed by my neighbors."

Then he reached out and forcibly wrapped her in her cloak.

"Then where?" she demanded as she swatted his hands away and finished with the cloak.

"We're going to do this in the basement of a brothel." Then he gripped her arm tight and started walking.

Chapter 13

❧

"*I'm not going to any brothel!*"

Samuel sighed, wondering if it was possible to forestall the coming argument. He doubted it, but he made an effort to convince her reasonably. "You would rather have an argument at the shop? With Tommy and Mrs. Appleton as witnesses?"

"Of course not—"

"Then we shall go—"

"I'm not having any argument with you at all!"

Well, that was obviously false. She had ripped her elbow out of his grasp, then planted her feet, dropped her fists on her hips, and started talking, her voice dangerously loud. He glanced about him uneasily. They were in a nearly deserted walk right off Bond Street. What they were doing right now was unusual to say the least, and would certainly attract attention if anyone were to walk by.

"You are not being logical," he began.

"You cannot—" she began, but he cut her off.

"And I do not as a rule allow anyone to screech at me in

public." He grabbed her arm and started pulling her forward. She followed merely because he was being rather rough. He didn't like it, but what help was there? What if Cordwain was coming back and saw them? What if Jobby had finished his business and was walking the tart home? Any number of things could happen, and he felt much too dangerously exposed out here.

Meanwhile, she moderated her tone to an angry hiss. "I do not screech."

"To answer that would require an accurate dictionary."

She was slowing, her steps catching in the street. Before long, he would be reduced to tossing her over his shoulder. He stopped first as a way of throwing her off balance.

"Penny, I would have a discussion with you. Now."

"I do not—"

"I don't care. It is imperative that we speak, and if you wish to have my help, then you will come with me and do as I ask!"

Even in the darkness, he saw her skin pale. "You aren't going to help me anymore?"

He groaned. Of course he was going to help her. But they needed to talk! "I need to understand some things. And if you will not converse with me in a place where we can scream and bellow and still be private, then I will be forced to follow you home. And then Mrs. Appleton and Tommy will—"

"As if I would argue in front of them!"

"You would not be able to control yourself." That was, in point of fact, the very problem: her inability to control her temper. "I assure you, I can be quite irritating when I choose."

"At least we agree on that!"

"Then agree on this: Penny, I mean to talk with you now. I assure you that you will be completely anonymous where we are going."

She bit her lip, her gaze flicking up the street where a

pair of dandies had just rounded the corner. It took only a moment for Samuel to identify them. Those two would not recognize Penny, and even if they did, they wouldn't care. But Penny didn't know that, and so he cast her a dark look.

"We need to speak in private," he stressed. "Can you not trust me in this simple thing?" The answer was obvious on her face. Penny did not trust anyone unless there was no other choice. She had been too self-reliant for too long. Or perhaps it was simply men she did not trust. After all, she had put her faith in the dress shop. But that had been as much desperation as faith.

"Very well," she huffed. Then she wrenched her hood over her head. "We will *talk*. And if you try anything else, I shall—"

"Good heavens! As if I had any inclination in bedding you right now!" It was a lie. The evidence seemed to indicate that he was interested in bedding her *all* the time, no matter the circumstances. He'd been terrified for their lives pressed up so tightly in Tommy's wardrobe, and yet his organ had still swollen up hot and hard for her. Even as she clawed and kicked him from head to toe, a part of him had wanted to pin her wrists and spread her legs right there.

Hell, that part still wanted it, but he was a rational man. He could control his urges. And so he took her arm and headed her down the street away from the dandies. It was that choice—to move left rather than right—that saved them. They had gone no more than three steps when a man came running through the alley they'd just left and streaked off to the right. If they'd walked the other direction, then the man would have collided with them. And if not the runner, then the four who followed closely after.

It was over quickly, as these things go. Samuel barely had time to step protectively in front of Penny when one of the pursuers threw a knife. The blade lodged deeply in the runner's throat from back to front. It was an incredible throw and Samuel might have admired it if it weren't so lethal. The runner was down, his blood welling into the street.

Three of the pursuers circled the body, standing still as the fourth hastily looked about.

Samuel tensed. He did not wish to be attacked by a gang of thieves, but he had nowhere to go. And no help beyond Penny, as the two dandies had taken off in the opposite direction.

"Don't be afraid," the man who threw the knife said in a cultured voice. "He was the thief, not I."

It took a moment for his heart to slow, but eventually Samuel recognized Demon Damon and exhaled in relief. The man was the owner of London's most infamous gambling den and as dangerous a man as could be. But he was also smart and did not kill indiscriminately. Therefore, Samuel and Penny had little to fear. Still, Samuel remained on his guard as he struggled for some way to ease the tension in the air. Flattery would probably work best.

"Very nice throw," Samuel said. As he spoke, one of the henchmen cleaned off the bloody knife and returned it to the Demon.

"I practice," came the calm response. Then the man's gaze flicked to Penny, who was still staring at the cluster of men around the body. "Have no concerns, Miss Shoemaker. The man was a footpad, part of a den of thieves that I have just recently discovered. He got what he deserved."

Penny nodded slowly, her gaze finally raising up to look at the Demon. It was only now that Samuel realized how very handsome the bastard was. Not tall so much as elegant, with dark hair and a white smile. Did Penny think him handsome, too? And how was it that the bastard knew her name anyway? He'd called her Miss Shoemaker.

Meanwhile, Penny swallowed and slowly folded her hands. "Why?" she asked.

"Why did he deserve his end?" the Demon asked.

She shook her head. "Why did you pursue him? Why not leave it to the authorities?"

"Because the constable has plenty to do, Miss

Shoemaker." Then he shot a disdainful glance behind him. "And this man stole from me."

Ah, that was the reason, thought Samuel. Only an idiot would steal from the Demon. In any event, he needed to get Penny away from this situation. "Come along," he said as he took her arm. "Let me see you home."

The Demon stepped closer. "I can escort you if you would feel safer."

"No," said Penny quickly as a small shudder ran through her body. "No, thank you. I am safe enough with Samuel."

A surge of pride warmed Samuel, especially as the Demon gave them a courtly bow and withdrew. Penny felt safe with him. In fact, she had chosen him over the obviously lethal and handsome other man. He would have crowed aloud if he hadn't been so intent on getting them out of the area.

They were barely more than a block away when Penny asked her question. "Do you know that man?"

"Demon Damon. A man who does not like to be crossed."

Penny drew in a full and shaky breath. "I wonder what was stolen from him."

Samuel shrugged. "With his kind, the item isn't important. Diamonds or food scraps, whatever it was belonged to the Demon. And he does not share."

Penny nodded and he was gratified to feel the tension in her arm release. She was feeling calmer.

"Better?" he asked, absurdly needing to hear her reassure him.

"Yes. I was merely startled."

She'd been a great deal more than that. Him as well. But at least it was over.

"We still need to talk," he said, cursing the timing.

"I know. Where are we going?"

"It's not far."

Four blocks later, they arrived at the Beehouse. Originally it had simply been Bea's House, as the madame's name was Beatrice. But that was many years ago. Bea was gone and Missy had taken her place. And Missy had reason to be grateful to him.

The woman had had a thieving employee—or so she'd believed—but he'd discovered the real culprit. It had been a dog who had a fondness for Missy's favorite purse. After he'd recovered her missing coins, the madame and he had developed a kind of friendship. Shared meals, shared secrets. Nothing to topple kingdoms—only a marriage or two. But she recognized the wisdom in having a smart gent in her circle of friends, and he liked having another place to loiter when he was bored.

Given their connection, Missy would let him do what he wanted in the basement of her home and say nothing to anyone about it. That is, assuming it wasn't being used at the moment and that he paid her ridiculous fee on quarter day.

Slipping through the shadows, he crossed to Missy's window and rapped twice. As expected, she was there, her eyes narrowing as she peered out into the darkness. He stepped into the light spilling out from her window and saw her eyes widen. A moment later, she jerked her head toward the back door.

He brought Penny round to the back, though he could feel her body tightening with every breath she took. She was a moral woman, he knew, and her judgment of this place would run deep. He had perhaps three minutes more to get her inside before she balked. So when Missy opened the back, he pulled Penny inside with him and quickly shut the door.

"We need to use the dungeon," he said quietly. "Is it available?"

Her penciled-on eyebrows shot nearly to her forehead. "You ain't never swung that way afore."

He shook his head. "Not for its usual purpose. We need a place to have a right good row where no one will think anything of it."

"Ah," she said, understanding. She tried to peer at Penny, but Samuel stepped in the way. Missy wouldn't talk—probably—but there was no sense in giving her more information than she needed.

"A right good row, Missy. And no one the wiser."

She nodded. "Yer in luck. We're not that busy, and them that are here don't seem to want to be whipped." She pulled an enormous key ring out of her pocket, pulled off the largest and most hideously ornate one, and handed it to him. "Ye got it for the night. But mind, if yer row turns bloody, ye'll owe me extra for the cleaning."

"Thank you, but I assure you there won't be bloodshed."

"I wouldn't be too sure about that," muttered Penny from behind him.

Samuel sighed, pleased that Penny's equilibrium returned, but saddened that he would have to fight through her anger. Missy, on the other hand, thought that the funniest thing she'd heard in a long time. She was cackling as she led them down the hallway and then hauled open the door to what once had been the root cellar. Bea—a woman with uncommon foresight—had remodeled it decades ago to look like a fanciful descent into hell. Samuel thought the ornaments cheap and rather silly, but one glance at Penny's face and he could see that he'd just confirmed her worst suspicions about brothels.

Well, there was no help for it now, and so he led her firmly down the stairs. At the base, they confronted a heavy iron door, which was unlocked by the ornate key. It was pitch dark in there, but he had a general idea where things were. A table nearby had a candelabra set at the ready. He dropped Penny's satchel on the floor, then fumbled to light the candles. A few moments later, he'd lit them and four sconces about the room. Then he turned to see that Penny was half a breath away from bolting.

"What is this place?" she breathed, shock and fear in her voice.

He turned, looking about to see the room from her eyes. Yes, he supposed seeing a torture rack against the wall and a restraining table would be rather startling to a well-bred woman. Especially after what they'd just witnessed. Add in the shelving full of whips and shackles, gags and . . . well, things that he knew the names of but most people didn't, and he feared his plans for a discussion were all for nothing. Still he had to try, so he strove for a calm, reassuring tone.

"This is a specialized room, Penny," he said as he shut and bolted the door. "And well used to screams, so you may screech at me all you like."

"I don't screech!" she all but shouted.

He nodded. "Excellent." He thumped the wall, which was heavy stone. "I'm sure no one heard that. And believe me, I have tried from above to see if any words could penetrate the ceiling. Nothing intelligible, I assure you." He frowned. She did not look reassured. "Truly, Penny, some gentlemen have rather violent tastes. Try not to look at the decor."

Her jaw went slack for a moment. "Try not to look at it? At what, pray tell, am I supposed to look? The meat hooks on the ceiling? The dark stains everywhere?"

"It's paint, Penny. For atmosphere."

She shook her head. "Not all of that is paint. The smell gives it away."

He grimaced. How could he forget that she was unusually perceptive? "Well," he said with a sigh. "I am very sorry that this disturbs you. Pray will you sit down." He held out a chair for her. Sadly, as he moved it, the shackles set up a rather loud clatter on the floor.

"I shall stand, thank you, Samuel."

He couldn't blame her, but neither could he let their conversation be deterred because of her sensibilities. "Very well," he said rather lightly as he settled himself into the chair. He knew for a fact that Missy made sure to clean the chamber regularly. And it wasn't as if he was going to have her strap him into the thing. "I have need of an answer from you. I'm sorry that it may be a rather painful answer, but it is imperative that we get to the bottom of it now. Truly, I fear for your safety—and your sanity—if you continue as you have been."

She frowned and folded her arms across her chest. "Very well," she snapped. "What is this all-important question?"

"Why are you so angry?"

She gaped at him. Her jaw dropped, her fists fell onto her hips, and she drew a deep breath with which to blast him. Samuel relaxed backward. It would take a while for her to get past the initial fury. He estimated twenty minutes at least. But then she surprised him.

She just huffed out her breath and leaned against the table. He wondered for a moment if the stains and the straps would bother her, but she seemed to have already dismissed them from her mind. Instead, she just shook her head.

"You are the oddest gent I have ever met."

He tilted his head, unsure how to take that statement. "No one but you has ever said that to me before," he mused softly.

She blinked. "Of course they have."

"I assure you, they have not. People as a rule are much more condescending when they speak to me. They are either angry and tell me to bugger off—"

"I can do that, if you like."

"Or they are amused and call me something like a sweet thing or a cute bean. I ask you, what bean would ever be considered cute?"

"So no one has said 'odd'? But you are."

"And is that bad or good?"

She shook her head. "It's just odd."

"And you, my dear, are avoiding the question at hand."

She grimaced and hopped up such that she sat on the table. In fairness, her grimace might be because of the table, not the topic. "I am not. Hell, Samuel, you're a brilliant man. Don't you think I have cause to be furious?"

"Of course you do. But this particular problem is only a couple days old. And your parents were killed not yet two months ago. Your fury is a good deal older than that."

"It is not."

"Those grooves set between your brows, the habit of clenching your fists tight to your hips, and the deep brackets around your mouth indicate differently. Those are patterns established very early, very young."

Her eyes widened and her hands went to her mouth. He almost smiled. Penny was the least vain woman he knew, and yet even she was horrified by what he'd just said. Could all that anger be carving itself into her face?

Of course it was, and so he stood and crossed to her. With gentle but firm fingers, he pulled her hands away from her face. It wasn't easy, especially as he could tell she was barely keeping herself from slugging him.

"Penny, you have been angry for a very long time. This last debacle has merely pushed you to the very edge. It makes you want to throw yourself at Jobby when you know it would do more harm than good. It makes you want to hurt me now when you know I am merely trying to help." He took a deep breath. "It makes you what to hurt everyone and everything, including perhaps yourself."

"That doesn't make any sense!"

"Very well, then perhaps it makes you want to hurt Tommy."

She blanched and he knew he'd struck a nerve. She was hot to deny it, but he pressed his hand to her lips. "Think before you scream at me, Penny. You can tell me everything, you know. I am the last person who would judge you."

It wasn't enough. With more strength than he'd expected, she shoved him backward. He stumbled, but fortunately caught himself on the shelving of dangerous implements.

Meanwhile, she leaped off the table to advance on him, spitting words like an angry cat.

"What do you know about life with a baby? There's food and teething and he wakes every night! Nappies to be changed, and he's in everything! I can't get anything done!"

"Of course—"

"But I would *never, ever hurt him!*"

"I believe—"

"He's the sweetest, funniest, smartest child. Everyone says so. He explores everywhere, most of them places he shouldn't be. He tries to eat everything, and my God, when he cries, I sometimes want to scream right back. Everyone thinks I'm a slut because of him. I used to get looks from people on the street. Kind ones, happy ones. Now they curl their lip, and I've been spit at. Spit at! Because they think I'm a tart. But they don't know me. *You* don't know me! Because I would never, ever hurt Tommy!"

There was more screaming. Every time he took a breath, every time he tried to move away from the shelving, she started up again. She loved the boy; that much was clear. But also the well of frustration and anger boiled out of her at the same time. She was a woman alone saddled with an infant boy. Of course she was exhausted and angry.

And yet, that wasn't the source of her fury. It was part of the problem, but not the source. So he waited, his hands raised in defense, his eyes watching to see if she lunged for any of the implements on the shelves.

She didn't, thank God, and eventually she stopped, her breath coming in ragged gasps as exhaustion took its toll. But she still had the strength to glare at him. Then she repeated what she had said before.

"You don't know me. I would never hurt Tommy. Don't you see that? Don't you see me at all?"

She stumbled backward, finally allowing him to move away from the wall. He would have caught her, but she was more likely to punch him than thank him for his help.

Besides, she steadied herself on the edge of the chair. Her back was to him, and he could see the clenched ripple of her muscles as she heaved in great gulps of air. Then he waited a bit longer, wondering if her good sense would return.

"Penny—"

"I would never hurt Tommy."

"I know."

She released a shuddering breath. "Then why would you say such a thing?"

"Because you're angry, Penny. And some of your anger is directed at him."

"Because raising him is *hard*!"

"And because there's something else about him that infuriates you."

She shook her head. "No! He's a child! It's not his fault!"

"What isn't his fault?"

She whipped around, her eyes narrowed and this time her fists were raised. "You're twisting my words!"

"You know I'm not."

She didn't answer. She stood there, her eyes glaring, her fists raised, and her body clenched so tight it was a wonder she could stand upright. And in that position, he knew she would never talk, never say the fury that was etched deep inside her. Which meant he would have to do it for her. Or at least try.

So he took a deep breath, raised his hands palms outward in surrender, and plunged on in. "Shall I take a guess, Penny? Shall I say that your father was an idiot? He never saw what you did for him, never appreciated how much of the work of cobbling you did? All he could see was that you were a girl and that he did not have a son."

"My father loved me!"

"Of course he did, but absently, in the way of all great artists. They see only their art, not those that support him day by day. If he had let you take your rightful place at his side, if he had let people know that you were his heir, then none of this would have happened. No one would believe that he'd given ownership to Tommy, which could then be sold to Cordwain. And even if they did, you could have been apprenticed to any of the other shoemakers. But he didn't do that. And he certainly didn't tell anyone that you had been making the shoes for months, if not years."

She swallowed, her eyes wide. There was denial in her face, and her fists had dropped down low as if she couldn't bear to raise them against her father. "It would have ruined him if word got out that he could no longer make boots."

"Maybe. But it would have been the making of you." He stepped forward, gently touching her wrists. When he went for her hands, she twisted the fists back and away from him. "Your father is the one who didn't see you, didn't know you. Of course that's not Tommy's fault. It was your father's. And your mother's, too, for not making him see his only child."

She turned her face away, but not before he saw what was in her eyes. It wasn't fury, as he had expected. It wasn't even the shimmer of tears. What he saw was a bleakness, an emptiness that told him that he had guessed right.

Meanwhile, she bit out six words, spoken in clipped accents as if she'd pushed them through clenched teeth. "My father was a good man."

He shrugged. "He was certainly a good shoemaker," he said quietly. "He might have been a good man, too, but he was a terrible father."

She flinched at that, but didn't speak. And the longer she stood there, body clenched tight, the more he began to worry. He thought that would be the release she needed. Finally, someone had said the words that were damned up inside her: Her father was an idiot. Her father hadn't valued her as he should.

Except her shoulders didn't release; her mouth didn't soften. If anything, she coiled tighter, and held back even more.

Which meant he'd been wrong. This wasn't the source

of her anger. He huffed out a frustrated breath. Damn, he was lousy at this type of conversation. Give him a set of clues, and he could make brilliant deductions. Scuff marks on the floor, a missing purse, even something spoken that was obviously a lie—all those things were clues that he used to make clever deductions. With Penny he'd done all that and obviously come up with the wrong answer. Which left him totally at a loss.

He touched her averted cheek, stroking his finger across her flawless skin. "I don't know what to say, Penny. And that is a rare thing indeed."

She didn't smile at that, though he imagined her expression lightened a bit. Then she released a long breath, but not as a woman finally letting go. Not even in a snort of frustration. More like a slow hiss from a pipe. Steady. Mechanical. Not a release, just a symptom.

Then she began to speak.

"My father loved me deeply," she said, her voice flat. "When I was little and got a new dress, he would take my hands and we would dance about the room. Whenever I was with the customers, he kept an eagle eye on me to make sure no man said anything wrong or touched me in any way. And when boys came to call, he tortured them mercilessly on their parentage, their prospects, their . . . everything." She shifted slightly, puffing out her chest as she mimicked her father. " *'The man for my Penny has to be worthy of her.'* That's what he said. That was his love."

"Were there many boys come to call?" he asked. It was not what he meant to ask. It wasn't in the least bit relevant, but neither was his irrational surge of jealousy at the thought of it.

She shrugged. "Enough. Among my set, I was considered quite a catch."

"You still are, Penny."

She didn't bother to argue with him. She merely shook her head. He knew what she was thinking. Everyone believed her a tart. She was now impoverished and had a baby to boot. Among most people, she'd fallen far from desirable.

"If only you could see this rationally, Penny. If only you understood how your skills, your determination, and your strength make you a prize."

Then she did look at him, and he saw fear in her eyes. A stark terror that froze the breath in his lungs.

"I once asked my father to let me sell shoes for him. Ladies slippers, much like what I am doing now. We would be Shoemaker and Daughter—shoes for lord and lady alike." She fell silent, obviously remembering. The fear hadn't left her eyes, and he knew they were getting close. But she'd stopped speaking.

"I assume he said no," he prompted, hoping to get her to continue.

It worked. She nodded slowly. "He said, 'What good would that do when you will be off and having babies with Wesley before the year's end?' "

He frowned, his belly tightening. "Wesley?"

"Wesley Barlow, the son of a baker my father liked. Wesley and I have known each other since we were Tommy's age."

"And your father expected you two to wed?"

She nodded, but the motion was more of a jerk. "I thought . . . I thought he was right. Wesley was my choice and I . . ." She looked down at her hands. Only now did he notice that they weren't clenched. Instead, they were limp. Almost as if she hadn't the strength to move them.

"Did you love him?"

"Yes."

A surge of fury washed through him. This boy—this idiot—had Penny's heart. "What did he do?" Samuel rasped out. "What did he do to hurt you?"

"He got a maid pregnant. They were wed two years ago."

It didn't take long for him to guess at the rest of the

pieces. "Your father always saw you as a girl, so when this wedding that he'd always wanted—the wedding to his friend's son—when it failed, he decided it was because you spent too much time making shoes."

"Mama said that, not Papa."

"But it was your father who made the decision. He declared that you would go be a girl. Go to parties and the like. Except he still needed you in the shop. So you worked for him as a shameful secret while your mother demanded that you be a beautiful girl to catch a man. And no one ever from the very beginning of your life ever let you just work as you wanted. As a shoemaker."

She bit her lip, her breath catching from strong emotion. But he couldn't tell if it was a sob or a scream. Either way, it didn't matter. And either way, he still had to point out the illogic of her fury.

"But you are doing it now, Penny. You have finally found a way to do exactly what you've wanted from the very beginning. You are making shoes, you are supporting yourself. You are—"

"Doing a man's work," she whispered. "A girl acting like a boy. I couldn't hold Wesley's interest. Every man who has looked at me has disappeared eventually. My father—" Her words choked off. She drew in to herself, collapsing against the table to the point that he grabbed her elbows to hold her up.

"Your father what?" he pressed. "Penny, this is important. I need to know what your father did."

"He called me unnatural. They both did, Mama and Papa. *Unnatural.* Because I wanted to make shoes." This last was pushed out on a sob as the tears finally broke free. She collapsed against him and he held her as her body shook.

Here at last was the source of Penny's pain. How well he understood this particular nightmare! Friends and family who didn't understand, who thought you an aberration because of what you loved. Because of what you found fascinating. But whereas his particular demon was unnatural, hers was simply a gift. The gift of being an artist. And as often happened with the lower classes, the artistry took a practical turn. She had a gift for shoes, and that was a marvelous thing.

He pulled her tighter into his arms. In truth, it was the only way he could support her body, but he didn't object in the least. He wanted to hold her as she sobbed against his chest. He didn't speak. He had to wait until she had control of herself enough for his words to make any sense to her. But in time she quieted, and he almost mourned the passing of her tears because she stirred against him, fighting his hold.

"You know it's not true, don't you?" he said into her hair. "You are not the least bit unnatural. And the men who abandoned you were fools. Every last one of them."

She didn't answer. Instead, she got more still, more frozen, and he cursed himself anew. He had said something wrong. Again.

"Penny, what is it? You must tell me."

She spoke so quiet he almost didn't hear, but he was listening very closely. "You are not a fool."

He frowned, not understanding. "Not often. But there are times."

He touched her chin, gently urging her to look at him. She did, though the movement was obviously reluctant. "You are not a fool," she said more strongly. "And you have no desire to lie with me."

He gaped at her. How could she possibly have read the situation so wrong? "Of course I want to!"

Her chin thrust out and an angry glint entered her gaze. "You said you didn't. You said it clearly less than an hour ago." And therefore, by extension, he thought her unnatural.

It took him a moment to think back to when he could possibly have said that. "Good God, Penny, you were trying to kill me at the time! Or run away. If I had told you the truth, we wouldn't be here now."

Her eyes narrowed and he could see she didn't believe him.

"Do you truly know nothing about me?"

The answer was obvious. She didn't know, which made the situation all the more ridiculous.

"I can see I shall have to be blunt. And sometimes," he added ruefully, "blunt requires demonstration."

So saying, he caught her hand. She wasn't expecting it, so he grabbed it easily. The resistance came as he gently forced it down. He was still holding her, so it required that he step back just a bit. Just enough to give room for him to press her fingers against his organ. But she was fighting him. Not out of any understanding, but out of habit. Which meant he had to be stronger than she was. Which meant she landed with more force than he'd intended.

The impact nearly brought him to his knees. But he measured the pain and groaned at the pleasure. And in time, she stopped fighting, softening her fingers until she had flattened her palm against him.

Eventually he managed to speak, but the sound was tight as his lust fought with his reason. "Yes, Penny, I want to bed you. I have wanted it from the very first moment I met you. I have created schemes in my head to seduce you. Even when you were trying to claw my eyes out, I wanted to throw you down and take you."

He took a deep breath, and in that moment, his body overtook him. Without willing it, he thrust against her hand. She gasped and started to pull away, but she was trapped between him and the table. And he didn't want her to soften her caress.

His body trembled, and he released a groan of delight. He saw her eyes widen in shock.

"You really want me?" She bit her lip.

He dropped his forehead against hers. "I cannot think

for wanting you, Penny. And believe me, that has never happened to me before."

He saw a ghost of a smile skate across her face. "I know this is ridiculous. I remember how you schemed to seduce me. But you didn't really know anything about me then. You were just being a man. And now that we are better acquainted . . ." Her voice trailed away.

"You think I will abandon you?"

She shrugged. "In two days' time, you have discerned more about me than my closest friends. Than even my family."

"Therefore, you think I will run from you. Because you are unnatural?"

She swallowed, her eyes canting away.

"That is a fear, Penny, and it is irrational." Then he pulled her gaze back to his. "I think you're amazing. Unusual. Beyond strong. Like a lioness defeating all foes as she protects her cubs. Like a waterfall for sheer beauty and power. Nothing can stand in your path, and even though you are falling, you are the winner. The rest of us are reduced to sand against you." Then he flushed. "And now you have made me poetic, and I am never poetic."

She looked at him, her eyes wide, her lips parted in amazement. She still had her hand pressed against him, and it was all he could do not to thrust against her like a dog.

Her eyes darted about the room, quick and nervous. "This room is not what I expected in a brothel."

He struggled to follow her non sequitur. "No. As I said, it is a specialized room."

"But there are things we could do here, aren't there? Things that . . . would keep me a virgin?"

Every muscle in his body clenched. He couldn't think; he wanted it too much. "Penny, do you know what you are asking? Do you know how easily I could lose control?"

"Maybe I could tie you down. So we wouldn't do anything that went too far."

He closed his eyes and groaned. The images that flooded through his mind nearly buckled his knees. But he didn't move. Instead, he forced out one word.

"Why?"

She took a hesitant breath, the sound both delicate and erotic. He opened his eyes to see her expression better and found instead a woman coyly stepping into her sexuality. And when she spoke, the words were halting, but honest.

"I want to know more," she said. "I want to *feel* more. You are the only one who sees me as a woman."

"I'm not," he rasped.

"You are the only one I know. And you are here. And . . ." She slowly pressed her lips against his. She was well tutored in kisses from before. And yet this kiss felt innocent, nervous, and so beautiful it was all he could do not to ravage her. So he kept himself still as she pressed her lips to his. And when she pulled back, she finished her words. "I want you to."

He nodded, though the motion strained his already tense muscles. His mind was racing, filling with thoughts of what and how and how much. But in the end, he decided on the simplest form of pleasure, the easiest protection for her.

"Shackle me to that wall."

Chapter 14

✣

Penny jerked at his words, even though she had been the one to suggest it. "You want me to . . ." She couldn't even say the words.

He nodded and pulled away from her. She watched him, seeing the strain on his face, but also the hunger. It was that hunger that thrilled her deep down inside. He lusted for her badly enough that he wanted her to chain him to the wall. The idea was thrilling. So she agreed, her eyes going to the bolts sunk deep into the brick wall.

He went to the shelves first, grabbing four cuffs. Two had short chains; two were connected by a long chain of at least eight feet. He handed her the lot.

"Attach the short ones low to the wall. They're for my ankles. The other threads through the higher bolt for my wrists. It's so I can move my arms, but not escape the wall."

She took them and nodded. She did as he bade while he squatted down and pulled off socks and shoes. Then he hesitated, standing up slowly as he looked at her. "You understand some nakedness is required. Especially if I am to be bound."

She nodded, her mouth very dry.

He began stripping off his coat and neckcloth. "I shall leave my trousers on—"

"No!" she said. It was more of a cry than a word, so she moderated her voice. "I should like to see all of you. If I may. I should like to . . . touch you again. If it is all right."

His eyebrows shot up such that they disappeared beneath his curly hair. "It shall be more than all right." He set coat and neckcloth aside before beginning with his waistcoat. "If you are sure."

"Yes," she said with as much breath as she could manage.

He didn't seem to hesitate as he stripped out of the rest of his clothing. But as she watched him work, she could see the slow darkening of his skin color to red. He was blushing, and interestingly enough, the blush did not stop at his neck, but spread lower down his torso. He was not a very tan man. His face had a softer, more golden color, but as soon as his clothing pulled away, she could see how pale he was. The candlelight added a warm tone, as did his blush, but all in all, he appeared more to her like marble than man. Sculpted marble in a lean body with dark, penetrating eyes.

It took her breath away.

He stood before her, his cheeks tinged red, then he gingerly stepped barefoot to the wall. Without so much as a word, he snapped the cuffs onto his ankles, then one wrist. But he had trouble with the second, and so she stepped forward. Amazing how her body worked without so much as a whimper of direction from her mind. She stood beside him and finished closing the cuff about his wrist, then stepped back to just look.

He was naked, standing tall before a brick wall, and she could do whatever she willed to him. With him. Right now, all she wanted to do was look. She had seen men without their shirts before. Even in London, an observant girl could see half-naked men. And there was a time that she'd been very observant indeed.

Samuel was not as bulky as many laborers. His muscles not so thick, but he had a crispness to his form. The muscles seemed longer rather than bulky, but still well defined. In the torchlight, she could see distinct hills and valleys across his body.

"You get enough to eat, but not much extra," she said, startled by her own words. That was not at all what she had been thinking.

He arched a brow and his lips quirked in a wry smile. "Damned by faint praise," he said.

"It wasn't praise at all. Just a statement," she said. Then she smiled to show that her words had been a tease.

"Of course," he drawled. "How silly of me."

She nodded, her gaze sliding lower now. His arms had enough chain to hang by his sides, and as her gaze dropped, she saw his fingers twitch. Something else twitched as well: his organ. It was thrust forward, thick and proud. And at the tip, she saw a glistening of moisture. She had no idea it could move like that on its own while the rest of him remained still.

She meant to look further, to see his long legs, his nicely shaped calves, even take a moment to absorb the shape of his feet. She was a woman who studied feet, and so his ought to have held some interest for her.

They did not. Instead, her gaze focused on the length and shape of his penis. She saw the dusky red that colored his skin, the thick veins and the smooth mushroom head. She noted the wiry curls at its base, and knew that a little farther back would be his sac.

Again, her body acted without her conscious intent. She stepped forward, her fingers stroking the smooth expanse of his chest, but only as a polite prelude. She wanted to touch it: his penis. And so, within moments, she let her hand drop until she could caress the smooth top, encircle the thick stalk, and eventually slip her hand beneath to find his sac.

She listened to his breath as she touched. After the first

gasp, his breath rasped out of him. His air came in soft pants and she knew he was holding back a groan.

"Is this good?" she asked.

"Yes."

"Everything?"

"Yes." His answers were tight explosions of breath. His eyes were closed, and his head was thrown back. She saw the muscles of his stomach ripple, and she decided she liked having him at her mercy like this. Shackled. Vulnerable. While she had the power to do whatever she wanted.

But what did she want? She didn't even know.

"What should I do now?" she asked, her words for herself as much as him.

"Undress, if you like. This was, after all, about you feeling things. That'll be hard to do through chemise, corset, and dress."

"You want me naked?" The idea was shocking. Titillating, too, but still unnerving.

He just raised an eyebrow, his silent statement obvious. After all, he was fully naked and chained to the wall. She was still fully clothed. It made sense, she supposed, that she should undress. At least some. So she started unbuttoning her gown.

The moment she began to work, his gaze riveted to her fingers. Then he took a step forward, only to be jerked to a stop by the shackles. Still, he was able to raise his hands at least, the chains rattling as he moved.

"Would you like me to help?"

Her fingers were fumbling, which made sense since her heart was beating so fast. She'd already nearly ripped off a button, and she could ill afford damaging this dress. Especially since it wasn't truly hers but one of Helaine's castoffs. So she nodded and stepped within his reach.

He was very gentle and very efficient. Her gown was sagging on her shoulders within a few seconds. She thought he would brush it off her, but he didn't. He finished with her buttons then let his hands drop away.

"You don't have to. This is completely about what you want—"

She shrugged out of the garment then kicked it aside. She was standing in corset and chemise, not to mention stockings and shoes. And suddenly, she wanted to take a deep breath. She wanted the restriction against her ribs released. But again, her fingers fumbled too much with the ties.

"Will you . . ." she asked, spreading her arms wide enough so that he could undo the laces.

Again, she was released within a moment. She took a deep breath—finally—feeling ribs, lungs, and blood moving freely. Glorious! She tossed aside the corset and a moment later bent down to unlace her shoes and strip away her stockings.

In the end, she stood before him in just her shift. It was a long one that covered her to mid-thigh. Compared to him, she was close to fully covered, but she still felt naked.

He must have seen her uncertainty. He touched her cheek gently, allowing his finger to stroke across her cheek and then down her neck. "You are beautiful, Penny. You have no idea what you do to me." Then he flashed her a cheeky grin. "Or perhaps you do. All you need do is look downward. I am completely on display for you."

He meant to remind her, gently, that he was as vulnerable as she. More so. But that didn't seem to make a difference to her racing heart.

"Samuel," she whispered. "Is this really wise? I cannot credit that I am doing any of this."

He tugged her closer to him, drawing her into the circle of his arms. She felt the chains fall against her legs, heard their rattle, but mostly she knew the tenderness of his touch. "None of this is wise, my dear. But you wanted to feel, and so, please, let me touch you."

She nodded, dropping her head against his shoulder. He

cradled her face in his hands, letting his fingers flow into her hair as he gently lifted her face. Then he brought his mouth to hers.

The kiss was perfect. Hard enough to feel his need, soft enough to soothe her nerves. She sank into the kiss, letting the sensations override her thoughts. His tongue thrust inside and she opened to him. He teased her tongue, stroked the roof of her mouth, even half growled against her as she teased, stroked, and growled back.

He spent forever in that kiss until forever became too long. And at that moment, she pushed her body against his. There was only the thin muslin shift between them, so when she pushed against him, she felt his every response. His skin was flushed hot, his organ pushed insistently at her groin, and just the feel of his hard body against her tightened her nipples to the point of pain.

His hands left her head to slide down over her shoulders. His mouth left hers to trail kisses along her cheek and jaw. The shift was bound with a simple tie at the neck. It was undone in a moment and he was pushing it off her shoulders. She had a moment's panic at the idea of losing that last barrier, but it wasn't strong enough to make her stop. Instead, her breath caught, she gripped the nearest hard thing at hand—the chain between his wrist cuffs—and then he'd pushed the garment down. It didn't even catch on her breasts, but slid straight down to her waist, where it stopped because her elbows were bent.

He kissed down her body quickly, his hands leading the way but only by a moment. She felt his palms and his fingers, stroking, flowing over her skin. And then in the same breath, she felt his mouth on her breast, his lips seeking her nipple.

He had one hand squeezing her breast, pinching the nipple. On the other side was his mouth, his teeth nipping slightly, then suction. These were things she noted with a detached sort of mind: his hands are doing this, his mouth is doing that. But what she *felt* was a thousand times less precise, and certainly not verbalized. She felt alive. She felt as if her whole body was waking up after a long sleep. It seemed that as she shucked her clothes, so, too, did she step out of all the things that named her. Any name. Daughter, virgin, shoemaker—these were the easiest to leave behind. Odd, unnatural, should-have-been-a-boy. These, too, slipped away. Then the rest faded as well, even the words he gave her: beautiful, strong, perfect. None of that held.

What was left was simply her. With a body on fire and a mind blanked to everything but how his touch made all sensations fill her being. She was breasts that ached. She was muscles that trembled. She was a belly that was liquid and aching.

Then his mouth ripped away. She felt him drop to his knees before her, the chains clanking as his hands dropped to her ankles. He lifted the chemise.

"Take it off, Penny. Please, take it off." But he didn't wait for her to comply. Instead, she felt his hands flow upward. Over her knees and between her trembling thighs. She clenched involuntarily, but released a moment later. She was lifting the chemise away and that allowed him to slip his hands between her thighs.

She cried out as he touched her there. She had no more mind to decipher knuckle or finger or hand. He was simply there, stroking her places that made her sob with wonder.

Then he was surging upward, hooking one of her legs beneath his arm as he moved. He raised it up and fitted himself to her. She felt the push of his organ, hard and insistent.

She wanted it. She wanted him there. But she was off balance, and that was what saved her. She stumbled, and he couldn't compensate because of the shackles. So she fell backward, out of his reach. Her one leg was still hooked in his arm, but the rest of her fell away. And when he tried to catch her, the chain snapped tight and he was jerked backward.

She landed hard on her bottom, her one leg caught at the ankle. She sat there, her eyes wide, her breath coming in rapid pants. He stood above her, guilt and hunger stark in his eyes.

"Penny, are you all right?"

She shook her head no. This was what she wanted. Still wanted. And yet, she was afraid. She twisted her foot out of his hand. She couldn't have done it if he hadn't released her. But he did, and she sat naked on the floor, trying to decide what to do. But all she could do was stare at his thick penis, still stretching for her.

"You said I would still be a virgin."

"And you are," he said gently.

She shook her head, her mind repeating the words bellowed from so many pulpits.

"It is sinful," she whispered.

He released a breath, the sound both frustration and resignation. "Will you stand, please, Penny?"

She nodded. The last thing she wanted to do was remain there sprawled on the floor. But as she straightened, her breasts moved, her legs felt weak, and she knew how desperately she wanted to return to a moment before. To the mindless sensation of it all.

"Trust me a little longer," he said. Then he reached out his hand, palm up. "Your virginity is safe. I swear it."

Such a stupid thing to worry about, she scolded herself. Most everyone believed Tommy was her son. If everyone believed her a tart, then what difference would it make if she tossed her virginity aside with Samuel? She had never felt so wholly herself except for a few moments ago. Or perhaps it was that she felt no restrictions, no worries, no *unnaturalness* in what they did. She was a woman, and she would feel what a woman did.

So she put her hand in his and let him draw her close. But when she would have pressed tight against his body, he gently spun her around. He was taller than her, and she felt him adjust himself such that his organ thrust up against her bottom and lower back. He was nowhere close to thrusting inside her and, in fact, would have to work hard to get it there.

That was, obviously, the point. So she allowed him to settle her back against his front. Then, at his urging, she let her head drop back against his chest. He took her hands then, gently lifting her arms as he encouraged her to grip a set of leather straps conveniently dangling from bolts to either side of his head.

"Hold on, Penny, and trust me."

She didn't answer. She couldn't because his hands began again to flow over her skin. While his fingers found and tweaked her nipples, his head dropped down. He began with her ear, nipping at the lobe, but eventually he pressed kisses to her neck and shoulder.

Against her bottom, she felt his organ pumping slowly, pushing up rhythmically. She didn't even know if he did it consciously, but she felt the steady thrust of it and began to counter his pressure. As he pushed upward, she pressed back.

He moaned softly against her skin, and one of his hands left her breast to skate down her belly. She whimpered, not sure of what she wanted.

His fingers slid between her folds. She was wet there, so his glide was easy. She felt every knuckle of his finger, every press of his hand as he slid inside her, then pulled slowly out.

It felt thick and rough. Not enough. The tempo was off. Her pulse was hard in her throat. And behind, he was pushing against her faster.

She wanted to say something. She wanted to control the sensations somehow. It was becoming too much for her. A scream was building in her chest, but there was no breath for it.

He pressed her forward to wrap his arm tighter around her. His finger went deeper. In. So thick. In. Then a rough pull out. His finger rolled high.

Yes!

Against her back, he was thrusting but she barely noticed. He was back inside her.

Not enough.

Out again.

A fumble.

Pinch.

Pleasure!

She must have screamed. She heard sounds, felt her body convulse. But mostly she was lost to pleasure. Wave after wave. For that blissful time, she felt like a pounding waterfall. It was a ridiculous image, but he had given it to her, so she held on to it. But in time, it faded. Waves became laps, which became ripples.

She returned to the awareness of her body. She hung limp in his arms and he was murmuring endearments to her skin. What he said, she didn't know. It didn't matter. It was soothing, and it eased the pleasure into a warm glow of happiness.

So this is why women marry, she thought. This is what they sought in a marriage bed. She wondered how many truly achieved it, and how many suffered terrible lovers?

Slowly she found her feet. He helped her stand. It took some time before she realized that her back was wet. He had released his seed there.

"There is a cloth over there," he said softly, pointing to the side shelf. "Right below the key to these cuffs."

She nodded and moved, stretching muscles that felt exhausted as she might after a long day's work. And yet never had she felt this happy after a long day.

She grabbed the cloth and cleaned herself. Then she gave it to him to do the same. But when she reached for the key, she stopped. Did she want to let him free so easily? Or was there something she could do now while he was still trapped? Or more exactly, something she could learn.

"Samuel," she said as she left the key right where it was.

He looked up, his expression open. Until he looked at her face. Then it abruptly shifted to wary. "Yes, Penny?"

"Surely these hooks and shackles aren't here for holding men back. There must be another purpose for it."

His eyes widened as his hands slowly lowered. He held the cloth over his organ, and his stance was decidedly defensive. "Some men and women enjoy being restrained. They like to be . . ." He swallowed and gestured to the shelves of implements. "They like being hurt," he finally said. "But I have never shared that feeling. I did this"—he shook the chains—"for your benefit."

She nodded. "Yes. Thank you."

He waited. "So will you unlock me now?"

"No," she said, surprising herself with her boldness. "No. There are a few more things I would like to know first."

"Such as?"

"Such as why you have been so generous in helping me."

He pulled back, his expression confused. "What?"

"You have devoted your life to this for the last two days. You have done nothing but help me. Without recompense."

"You will pay our wager when we are done," he said sternly.

She waved his comment away. "Money is not what motivates you."

"Thirty quid is good pay for a few days' work."

"And how much did this room cost?"

He blanched and glanced away. She had her answer there.

"More than a few quid, then. So it wasn't money. So why do you help me?"

He arched a brow. "You stand before me naked. I have just enjoyed the best, most unusual coupling in my life. And you can still ask me why?"

His words made her abruptly self-conscious, and she moved to pick up her shift. Even so, she was able to speak as she pulled it on. "You didn't know this would happen."

His lips curved. "Oh, but I have been dreaming of it from the first moment."

"Enough to invest two days' work to accomplish it? I don't believe it. You are friends with a madame. You could have any number of women."

His grin widened. "You underestimate your charms."

She shrugged and was surprised to find that her nipples were tight where they brushed against her shift. "Maybe," she answered. "But even I am not that charming. What is your game, Samuel? Why have you been working so hard to help me?"

He looked at her, his mouth tightly closed and his body tense. She saw anger in his expression, and a vulnerability she hadn't expected. She was probing into something painful for him, and that surprised her. She hadn't truly known what to expect when she began asking these questions. It was merely something that had hovered in the back of her mind, but she had ignored it. He was helping her. She hadn't the energy to question why.

But she did now, even more now because the questions pained him. And yet, she couldn't do this to him. She couldn't hurt him, not after what they had just done. Not after what he had just shown her. She couldn't do that to him.

So she flushed and turned away. "I'm sorry," she mumbled as she grabbed the key from the shelf. Then she handed it to him and spoke more clearly. "I'm sorry. Your reasons are your own. I should be grateful. And quiet."

Rather than take the key, he grabbed her wrist. He pulled her to him as if for a kiss, but he stopped short. He just looked into her eyes and held there, so still.

"Samuel?" she whispered.

"What else am I to do, Penny?" he answered. "What else should fill my days except you?"

She could tell that there was meaning beneath his words. Pain that she didn't understand, but she supposed she understood the basic essence of his statement. For all his brilliance, his life was empty, filled with one piece of nonsense after another.

She might complain under the weight of caring for Tommy, of trying to make shoes and provide for them both. But that filled her days to bursting. Whereas, perhaps for him, there was nothing. No family except his brother's. No occupation to fill his hours.

What did the man do with his time?

Chapter 15

❧

Samuel felt raw inside and out, and yet his mind had never been more at peace. He had just experienced the best sex of his life and it hadn't even been true sex. He had released against her backside, for God's sake.

And then she had asked him why. Why was he spending his time on her? Why did he do the things he did? Why did he wander through his days with no purpose at all? And right there was when he fell in love with her. Not a momentary interest, not a passing fancy, but a soul-deep worship of her. Because she asked the right questions. She saw him and that was what caused this unexpected feeling to fill him. Love. He was in love. And the moment the knowledge struck, his mind balked into a shocked and horrified silence.

He stared at Penny, his trousers on but not buttoned. He'd never been in love before. Not like this. In truth, he hadn't thought he was capable of it. He'd learned young that he played at love: seducing women, teasing maids, flirting in his own unique style. But that wasn't love. That was finding a way to entertain his mind and release his body. This . . . this depth of feeling for Penny was as unwelcome as it was unnerving.

He *felt* for Penny. He wanted to protect her, to solve all her problems, to bed her every night and wake to her kisses every morning. He wanted to see her laugh so hard her sides might split. And he wanted to be the one to make her do it. And he wanted her swelling with his child.

"Samuel?" she asked, her brows tightening in worry. "Are you all right?"

He blinked, forcing his mind to function. Yet more proof that feelings were detrimental to normal function. "Um, of course I am. Why do you ask?"

"Because you are holding your fall like you're gripping a dead cat."

"What?" He glanced down. His hand was on the fall of his trousers, the piece of fabric that buttoned to close the garment, securing it on his body. But instead of buttoning the damn thing, he had clenched it tight in his fist. Yes, he supposed this was exactly how he would hold a dead cat: with revulsion but a necessarily firm grip. Bloody hell, what was he thinking? Dead cats? "Why ever would I pick up a dead cat?"

"Why ever would you squeeze your fall to the point of ruination?"

He shook his head, unable to answer. He couldn't tell her the truth. By God, he couldn't even think the word anymore. He was not . . . that word. He couldn't possibly be in . . . that feeling. It would upset everything! And so with a conscious act of will, he unclenched his hand and slowly buttoned his fall. Sadly, he had creased it to ruination, but he'd be damned if he acknowledged that to her.

And here came the second most unwelcome surprise. On the heels of love came a kind of angry madness. One that was equally debilitating to all logic. But he was powerless to stop it. Soon after they had both finished dressing, he pinned Penny with a cold glare.

"Shall I walk you home now?"

She cocked her head, her expression deeply thoughtful. Bloody hell, was that what he looked like when he was thinking something through? No wonder his brother shuddered whenever that happened. It was downright terrifying to stand without a clue as to what was going on in someone else's brain. To cover how very unnerved he was, he bent to pick up her satchel. But that occupied only a few seconds. By the time he had straightened, she had come to whatever conclusion and was at his side.

"I can carry that," she said. "It's not heavy."

He stiffened, insulted to the core. Of course he would carry his love's bag. He was a man and that was what men did. They carried ladies' packages. But the damn woman was too independent and too used to being alone. She did not like anyone else touching the few things she had left. He understood that, and yet was still angry at her demand.

"I shall carry it for you. I shall walk you to the dress shop to see that you arrive safely. And then I shall surrender it to you. I assure you, I have no designs on keeping a bag of Tommy's clothes."

She pressed her lips together, but not before he saw a flash of hurt skate across her features. He had hurt her. He wasn't sure if it was his tone, his words, his actions, or all of them together. Damn it, he couldn't think clearly! "Penny, I'm sorry," he began. "If you wish to carry the bag, then of course, it's yours." He started to hold it out to her, but she flinched away from him. Then looked at him guiltily. God damn it all! What was wrong with the two of them? Life should not be so incomprehensible. Certainly not to him!

He growled and tossed the bag down on the floor. She started again, looking at him with wide, frightened eyes.

"Penny—"

"Just say it!" she snapped, her accent slipping the more vehement her words. "We had our fun and you wish to be rid of me now. You're trying to act the gent, but we're done."

He gaped at her, panic clutching his chest. "God, no!"

"Then what is it? Why're you so angry?'

He arched a brow, able at least to appreciate the symmetry of the situation. He'd brought her here specifically to ask about her anger, not his. But ironic or not, she deserved an answer. "I'm out of sorts, Penny. It has nothing to do with you," he lied. "I shall be better in a moment."

Again he was subjected to her heavy stare, and again he twisted inside, wondering what she was thinking. Every other woman of his acquaintance was damn clear in what she wanted. But not Penny. No, he suspected she would still keep him guessing even a century from now.

Then her expression abruptly cleared. Her eyes widened, and her mouth opened on a gasp. "Oh!" she cried. "It's because you didn't . . . Because you're a man and we didn't . . ." She bit her lip, and looked guiltily at the floor. "Oh," she repeated. "I've heard that always makes men angry."

It took a minute to follow her thoughts. Did she think he was surly because they hadn't actually made love in the usual way? It wasn't even remotely true, but in her innocence she believed it. And since he hadn't any other explanation he wanted to give, he grabbed on to it as a credible lie. "It is childish and highly ungentlemanly of me. I shall amend my mood immediately."

She shook her head. "No, no. I hear that it's normal. That men can't help it."

He snorted. Men on a whole were ruled by their passions, but he had once prided himself on being above all that. Obviously, that was no longer true. "It appears I am as fallible as every other man."

"No," she said, stepping close to him. "No. And I'm sorry."

He stopped her with a quick kiss to her lips. The motion was surprisingly easy as he pressed his mouth to hers. She opened willingly, but he refused to deepen it. It was too soon—for both of them—to begin a dalliance again tonight.

She had just begun and he . . . he was still much too unsettled to consider it. So he pulled back and looked into her
eyes. "Tonight was beyond special. Never apologize for it
or I will become angry indeed. Someday I may explain to
you exactly what has bothered me tonight. It is a nonsensical
male thing, I assure you. But one day, I may explain it to
you if you like."

"Yes—"

"But not tonight, I beg of you. Spare my tender male ego."

She smiled, a slight curving of her lips. "Of course.
And . . . you can carry my bag if you like."

"I should like it above all things."

"Thank you," she said, all sweet and shy. Then he did
kiss her. Lightly at first, then deeper. Stronger. He thrust his
tongue inside her and he expressed in that one passionate,
possessive kiss what he was truly feeling. Or at least he tried.
In the end, he pulled back, afraid of rejection, afraid of
things he couldn't even name, only to have her stare dazedly
back at him.

"Penny?"

"We can come here again sometime. If you like," she
said.

Immediately his organ surged forward, hungry as if it
hadn't just been satisfied not ten minutes before. "And if you
would like," he said by way of covering, "I should like to
take you to a party Thursday night. It's at a friend of mine's.
A ball of sorts, but with an entertaining guest list."

She blinked. "I can't go to a ball!" she gasped.

"But of course you can. You shall be my guest."

"But I'm a shoemaker! And a secret one at that!"

"But Thursday night, you shall be my guest. Say you will,
Penny. Please say you will."

"I—"

She was about to say no, so he kissed her again. Deeply,
hungrily, and with all the skill at his command. This time
when he drew back, she blinked at him in confusion.

"Say yes, Penny."

"Yes."

He grinned. "Excellent."

"But I can't go to any ball."

He dropped a kiss onto her nose. "Then it's not a ball. Just a gathering of friends where there might be dancing."

"But—"

"Penny, you must. I—I need you there."

She frowned. "Why?"

"Because . . ." Why? Why did he need her there? "I wish you expressly to meet someone. She has some rather unusual ideas regarding investments, and I should like your perspective."

"About investments? What do I know about those?"

"It is about female things, Penny. But she is a friend, and I do not understand the half of it."

Penny frowned at him. "You're lying to me."

"I swear I'm not." And he wasn't. Well, not entirely. He had already formed his opinion of Melinda's so-called investments. But still, learning Penny's perspective might be very interesting as well.

"Then we should talk to her some other time."

"Thursday night, Penny. It is the best time. Please, I want you to come."

It took a little more bickering, a little more pleading, but eventually she gave in. And then suddenly, they were climbing the stairs out of the dungeon in relative accord. It wasn't late by brothel standards, so as they topped the stairs, they had to stay back in the shadows to avoid being seen. Fortunately, they found Missy soon enough.

Then, once again, Penny surprised him. Just as he was about to hand over the key, she snatched it out of his hand. Her hood had been drawn over her face so as to hide her identity, but suddenly she tossed it back to glare at the madame.

"We're returning your room to you, but you won't be

charging him a penny for use of it. We didn't touch anything. Nobody wanted it."

"Penny," he said gently. "It's all right. Missy and I are friends."

"Not if she tries to charge you." She turned back on the madame, who was staring at them both as if they were mad. "Plain as piss he hasn't got a penny to spare. And no friend would take money he hasn't got."

"What?" Missy turned to Samuel in alarm. "You're broke?"

He held up his hands in a placating gesture. "No, I'm not. Everything's fine."

Meanwhile, Penny was stepping in between them, her expression fierce. "There are other ways for him to pay you. I'm sure he knows a gent or two who would love to use your dungeon. Throw a party in there or something." She turned to Samuel. "You do, don't you? Don't you know everybody?"

He quirked a brow, thrilled with the unaccustomed feeling of having someone else defend *him*. "I know *about* everybody. That's not the same as being able to influence them."

"But you can," she pressed. "You can find someone to throw a party here?"

He thought of all the men of his acquaintance. He'd never thought in that particular direction, but yes, he knew of someone who would enjoy the dungeon. And learning whom else the man invited would be highly interesting.

"Yes," he said with a slow smile. "I know just the man."

"Excellent," Penny crowed as she turned back to Missy, the key held out. "So he's square? No charge for tonight?"

Missy's brows were drawn together in a thoughtful look. Finally, she took the key with a careful hand. "Of course there won't be any charge, Samuel. But do say you'll swing around sometime soon. It has been so long since we had an afternoon's chat."

He grinned at her. "I'm afraid I'm rather full up this week. But soon," he promised. "I'll stop for tea soon."

"Oh yes," crooned Missy. "Make it soon." Then after a blithe wave and a longer, considering look at Penny, Missy disappeared back down the hallway into the main room. "Come along," he said to Penny as he lifted her hand to his arm. "I need to see you home."

She followed easily enough, their steps in rhythm, their spirits in accord. If it weren't for the late hour—and the fact that he carried a stuffed satchel—they might have been a lord and lady out for an afternoon stroll. Up until this moment, he'd never thought the activity had any merit. But for the first time in his life, he understood the need to just walk. In silence. With his . . . With a . . .

His mind balked. He could not label her his lover. He wasn't even sure she was his friend, truth be told. She was simply Penny, in his mind, and he refused to think beyond that. And then she had to spoil everything by asking a very awkward question.

"Just how tight are you?"

He flinched. "What?" he asked, though he knew exactly what she meant.

"How much money do you have? Enough to get by? Can you make your rent? You eat at your brother's. Your clothing is decent enough now, but it's getting on winter. Do you have a coat? Will you have enough coal?"

He turned to look at her, belatedly realizing that she truly thought him impoverished. "Penny, I have funds enough to meet my needs." Or he would after quarter day. He'd been investing lately, stretching his cash to a razor's edge more out of boredom than anything else. In truth, things were very tight until quarter day, when his investment would pay off. And pay off handsomely. But until that day, nearly a month from now, he had to live most sparingly.

"Francine's father paid her bill yesterday. Wendy made

sure I got what was owed me immediately. With Helaine's cast-off gowns and that sack of clothes for Tommy, I'm set for a while. More than set. Enough to share a meal or two with you. If you'd like."

He pressed his hand on top of hers, holding it there in a quiet squeeze. She was offering him her hard-earned money when she had just lost everything. The generosity of it touched him deeply. Coupled with how she defended him against Missy, he fell all the more in love with her.

"I should love very much to dine with you, Penny," he said softly. "But I have no need of your money. I swear."

She nodded and released a slow breath. She had truly been worried about him. "You can't live scrounging money off your brother all your life. And it's no good spending your time rescuing ladies."

"I rather like the lady I'm rescuing at the moment."

She flashed him a smile that warmed him more than any coal could ever do. "And I like it right back. But, Samuel, what do you do with your time? Doesn't it get—"

"Boring? Tediously so."

"I was going to say lonely."

He shrugged. "I have friends."

"Like Missy?"

"She's more of a friendly acquaintance."

"And me?"

He paused then. Not for long. Just enough for his step to hitch and for her to notice. Then he was walking again, trying to keep his manner smooth while his heart was racing and his mind all but exploded.

What was Penny to him? Good God, but he didn't want to answer that in his own mind, much less out loud to her.

She sighed. "You don't have to answer, if you don't want."

"I'm trying to," he said truthfully. He was all but mad with the search for the right words to say. Finally he reached for the easy way out. "What would you like to be?"

"You mean besides rich?"

He smiled. "You will be eventually, Penny. Give it a little time."

"Got to eat in the meantime. Got to find a home, too. We can't always live rent-free above the shop. Tommy will need clothes, and then there's schooling. I had a good education at an academy for ladies. Tommy deserves no less."

"Of course," he answered, startled anew by her background. So she had not spent all her days following after her father and his shoes. "But were you accepted at this academy? As a shoemaker's daughter?"

She shrugged. "It was a school for cits and by-blows right here in London. Some were the daughters of lords, but most of us were in trade of some sort. It was a happy time in my life." Then she looked down and he knew she was fighting of wave of frustration about her brother's future. "Tommy deserves no less," she said firmly.

"He will have it."

"Of course he will," she echoed, the determination obvious in her tone. "He *will*."

They walked in silence again, which gave her time to settle her emotions and for him to relax, hoping that she had given up her question. A moment later, though, his fears were renewed.

"So you understand, don't you," she began, "that I can help you if you need it. For a bit. Here and there. But I can't be with a man who just drains my money and my time. I liked what we did tonight. More than I should. But it's not worth Tommy's education money. It just isn't."

They had arrived at the dress shop, their steps slowing as she finished speaking. By the time they'd reached the door, she was turning to him, her eyes wide and her chin thrust out in stubbornness.

"You understand, don't you?" she asked.

"Of course I do, Penny. And I swear you will never have to support me with so much as a groat."

"I don't mind," she said honestly, her hand still on his arm. "All of us help out our friends, and everybody hits a rough patch. But it can't be all the time. I won't have it."

"No laze-about lovers for you. I think that's very wise."

She flinched at the word "lover" but didn't speak. Instead, she just looked at him, and he saw an unexpected anxiety settle into her features.

"I've never done something like this before. I don't know how to go about it."

He touched her chin, stroking his thumb across her jawline. Such a strong face she had, such a clear sense of purpose even now when she was beset on all sides.

"You amaze me," he whispered. Then he kissed her. Long and sweet, reveling in the taste and feel of her. He pulled her tight into his arms and felt her yield to his embrace. Strength softening for him. Nothing had ever pleased him more. Or left him randier.

He drew back for fear of taking more than he should, and right here in the street no less. "You should go inside," he rasped as he handed over her satchel. "Quickly before I drag you back to Missy's."

She flashed him a smile that was both coy and delighted, but she didn't leave. She didn't even unlock the door. "What happens tomorrow? Now that we can't prove the signature false?"

She was back to her case, to the return of her inheritance. He should have expected no less, and yet it stung a bit. Right after a kiss that left him thinking of nothing but her sweet body, she was already on to the next day's business.

"I shall have to make some inquiries, but I think our best bet is to enlist the aid of young Ned."

She frowned, obviously trying to place the name.

"Addicock's young clerk. If anyone can prove the solicitor a fraud, it will be the boy. Or the boy before him."

Penny brightened, her mind quickly grasping the

ramifications. "Another clerk! Of course! He might know all sorts of havy cavy dealing."

"Yes, but I must find him first. *You* must make any number of ladies slippers. Please, Penny, leave it to me for the moment."

She nodded. "But perhaps I could go with you to see Ned? He did seem like he was sweet on me."

Samuel's lips twisted into a wry smile. "Yes, he did. And yes, you will. But not tomorrow. Let me make some inquiries first."

"Very well. But you'll let me know what happens?"

"Of course. Just as you will be ready Thursday night for my friend's . . . er . . . gathering."

"You mean the ball."

He shrugged. "Whatever it is, you did promise."

"I did," she admitted. "And I will." This time she was the one who kissed him. Sweet, tender, and with every bit as much longing as he had. "Good night, Samuel."

"Good night, Penny."

Then she was gone. Inside the shop while he stood in the doorway like a lovelorn fool. In the end, he turned away. He headed toward his empty rooms on his silent street. He'd always appreciated the quiet before now. No servants, no impertinent neighbors. Not even a dog to yip at his heels. Was this what happened to men in love? Did they suddenly become morose? Did everything they value abruptly pale in comparison to the woman?

This would never do. Not because it wasn't acceptable behavior. It wasn't, but that didn't truly worry him. What bothered him most was what he saw when he looked in his mirror.

He saw a lanky, slouching man with hair too long by half, clothing that was creased and frayed. He saw his cluttered room behind him, and the haphazard piles of correspondence completely ignored on the floor by the door. Worse than that, he saw his own future stretched out before him like a boring game. Nothing there interested him. Nothing he saw excited him. It was all just endless days of games—investing games, flirting games, and secret games played by gentlemen for money, sex, or power. Tedious, which made him tedious by extension.

Or perhaps the better word was "unworthy." Because when he set up his own reflection against his image of Penny, he paled to nothingness. Whereas he wandered between wealth and poverty, a gentleman's pursuits, and a variety of brothels, she daily fought for her art, her livelihood, and now Tommy's inheritance and education. Those were substantial things. What he did was merely play games.

Never before had he felt so worthless. Never in his days had he breathed his emptiness so keenly.

But what was he to do about it? It had to change. It *had* to. Because how else could he win Penny? Only a man as substantial as she deserved to win her hand.

But how? How did a man who played at life find something *real* to do? It was a question that had haunted him long before he'd met Penny. But now he needed the answer with an urgency that burned in his gut.

He would find a way to be *real*. And then he would turn around and give it all to her.

Chapter 16

Penny slept well. That hadn't happened in such a long time. Not since before losing her parents. Not since the man who'd once said he'd marry her got someone else pregnant. That was perhaps the last time she'd gone to bed happy and slept peacefully until morning. So when she woke refreshed to the sound of Tommy babbling to himself in his crib, she was pleased indeed.

She had a lover, of sorts. A man who didn't see her as unnatural. When he looked at her, she felt like she was the most special woman in the world. She was still homeless, her life still in chaos, but somehow it all seemed better today. She wasn't unnatural, at least not to Samuel, and that made her want to sing. Or hum, at least, as she and Tommy began their day.

Nothing soured her mood. Cordwain couldn't do it when he came blustering and bellowing at their door. Wendy handled it easily. Anthony was spending some early hours at the shop doing the bookkeeping, so he held Cordwain off while Wendy went for the constable. Two finicky customers couldn't do it, even though they thought they knew more about what kept a shoe looking pretty than she did. And certainly Francine didn't sour anything as she settled on a stool next to the cobbler's bench and started to chat, much like Penny had done so many times with her father.

Except this time, the discussion wasn't about shoes or customers. It was a good deal more fun because it was about Francine's wedding.

"Mama is horrified, but who wants a party in the morning? It's a stupid law. Married in the morning. Why? I want a party with dancing. She says it isn't proper, and do you know what I said to her?"

Penny shook her head, barely able to keep her attention on her stitches. She was trying a new type of decorative stitching that would make the shoe stronger and prettier at the same time. "I hope it was that you were going to have a party first thing after you were married and she could come or not!"

Francine giggled. "I should have. Instead, I told her that I wasn't a very proper girl and that Anthony likes me just fine the way I am."

Penny gasped. She could just see the horror on Mrs. Richards's face at that statement. But it was no less than the truth. After all, Anthony and Francine had been caught in very improper circumstances. An engagement had been announced the very afternoon they'd been discovered, much to the couple's delight.

"Then I just walked away," Francine continued. "Right like that, I left her and went into the kitchen. She hasn't spoken a word to me since."

"Not a word?"

Francine shook her head, and for the first moment that afternoon, Penny detected a whisper of fear across her friend's face. "I just want a party, you know. A party with my friends and Anthony's friends. I want to have fun on my wedding day."

Penny giggled. "You're supposed to have your fun on the wedding night."

Francine sighed happily. "We've been having *that* for weeks now. Oh, Penny, I can't wait to be married so we can stop being interrupted! I want to sleep in a bed with him all night long!"

Penny looked down at the slipper she was stitching, but her hands were still. What would it be like to go to sleep lying against Samuel? To wake in his arms? She couldn't even imagine it. She remembered him naked and chained to the wall, and her blood heated as her heart began pounding. Could she actually *sleep* with him? As in close her eyes, settle next to his heart, and drop into a blissful night's rest? She wanted to think she could, but nothing about the man made her think of sleep.

Meanwhile, Francine must have noticed the change. While Penny was lost in her musing, her friend set her hand on Penny's wrist.

"Listen to me going on and on when you've been having such trouble. Tell me what I can do to help. How can I make you feel better?"

Penny jolted back to the present with a blush staining her cheeks. But one look at her friend's earnest expression and something broke inside her. For the first time in a very long time, she didn't want to keep her thoughts a secret. She wanted to share.

"Then tell me," she said softly. "How did you know that Anthony was the man for you?"

Francine shrugged. "I didn't. Not for the longest time. Father was pushing for a title, you know, and I felt so awful about myself. About everything."

"And did Anthony make you feel happy?"

"No. He did something much, much better. He made me

think. He made me stand up for myself. And then, he made me feel other things, too!" She giggled, her face bright red. "I don't think I discovered 'happy' until later." Then, proving that she was no fool, Francine looked harder at Penny. "You've got a man, haven't you? It's that odd gentleman Mr. Morrison, isn't it?"

Penny shrugged, finally abandoning any pretense at working. Normally she could pick up an awl or a scrap of leather and she was in her place. She loved nothing better than bringing one of her conceptions for a shoe to life. When things were at their worst—and there had been plenty of very bad times recently—she'd always found relief in one of her designs, sketching it on paper when she couldn't afford the leather.

But not today. Today everything in her heart and mind was centered on Samuel. So she set the slipper carefully down, trying to choose her words with equal caution. But she couldn't. So she opted for just talking. "Samuel and I—we've done things. Last night we . . . He . . ." She couldn't even put it into words.

Francine squealed in delight. "Was it fun? Did you feel . . ." She waved her hands vaguely in front of her belly. "Was it wonderful?"

"Yes. But we're not going to get married. He's a gentleman, I'm a . . . well, I make shoes."

"Beautiful shoes!"

She nodded, taking the statement as truth. "But what we did, it's a sin. It has to be."

Francine sighed. "You sure he won't marry you?"

Penny tried to picture it. She tried to imagine Samuel down on one knee before her, a ring in his hand, offering it to her. The picture was so beautiful it nearly broke her heart. But she just couldn't believe it would ever happen. "I don't think so."

"Oh." Her friend fell silent, sympathy in her eyes. "Do you really think God will damn you for it?"

"I don't know. I never really thought about God. Just what the priests say. And my mother. I keep thinking about my mother. She tried so hard to keep me sweet. That was her word for it. Sweet. She shooed all the gentlemen away and didn't like Ronald. He's the boy who got—"

"The other girl pregnant. It sounds like your mum knew what she was about with him."

Penny couldn't argue with that. But what would her mother say now? About her going to a brothel dungeon with a mad toff? She didn't even want to think of it.

Meanwhile, Francine pushed out of her chair, pacing about the room. Since becoming engaged, the girl had suddenly gotten four times the energy she'd ever shown before. She never sat like a sullen lump anymore. She was up and moving often. And right now, she wandered to where Tommy was asleep in a little nest of blankets and toys.

"You'll be careful, won't you?" Francine said in a low voice. "To not get pregnant."

Penny blanched. "We haven't even . . . We didn't . . ."

Francine turned back, her eyes serious. "But if he comes by again, will you step out together?"

"He's taking me to a ball tomorrow night."

Francine's eyes widened and she released a low whistle. "A ball! Really?"

"I shouldn't go. I'm not meant for that kind of party."

"But of course you are!" Francine crossed back to give Penny a firm shake. "If you have a gent who's willing to take you, of course you should go!"

Penny blushed and ducked her head. "Well, I already talked to Mrs. Appleton. She's airing out one of Helen's dresses for me. It's beautiful and Wendy said she'll make a few changes and it will fit me like a dream."

"So you are going!"

"I can't make myself say no."

"Of course not! You'll have so much fun!" She straightened and twirled in a happy circle. "You'll love dancing!"

"I don't know any dances!"

"Of course you do. You were taught them at school, just like I was."

"But I don't remember them."

"Yes, you will. I'll come back tomorrow afternoon. We'll go over the steps. You'll remember right away, I promise!"

Penny giggled. She couldn't help it. Francine was so beautiful when she was happy, all bouncing, giddy joy. She couldn't help laughing right along with her friend. Then Francine sobered.

"And make sure you have some of those French letters. You were right smart to tell me about them."

Penny's mood dropped straight down to her toes. "I have them," she whispered. It was all she could manage once she realized her friend just assumed she and Samuel would do more. Do *that*. It had made sense a month ago to help Francine get the condoms. Anyone with eyes could see that Francine and Anthony were in love. Nothing was going to stop them, and so Penny helped the best way she knew how: by preventing Francine from getting pregnant.

But that was an entirely different situation from herself and Samuel. Penny had known from the start that Anthony would find a way to marry Francine. Those two were just enjoying their marriage bed a little early. Samuel, on the other hand, was merely bored and looking for fun. There would never be a wedding between them, and so what they were doing was sinful. It had to be.

Francine dropped down before her, looking up anxiously into Penny's eyes. "Tell me honestly, Penny, if he wants to do what you did last night again. If he kisses you and touches you, are you going to stop him? Or will you want him to continue?"

Penny sighed. "I will want to do it again."

"So you liked it. It was good?"

Penny felt her lip curve into a smile. "It was wonderful!"

"Then who's to say what happens between you and him

is wrong? If you stop short or if you keep going. So long as you use the French letters, then no one will know one way or another. Your mum's gone, so she can't say anything. Most people think Tommy's yours, so no one expects you to be a virgin. What harm is there?"

"In being sinful?" she asked. That's what her father called it when Ronald got that maid pregnant: sinful.

Francine shrugged. "If you're sinful, then so am I. And I don't regret it for one second."

"You're going to marry Anthony."

"Doesn't matter as far as the priests are concern." Francine cocked her head, her brows drawn together into a frown. "Don't you see? You're a woman alone with a babe to raise. Everyone has already damned you. Not your friends, of course, but others. And your friends will love you no matter what you do. So if you make sure not to get pregnant, then what's wrong with being happy? It does make you happy, right? I mean—"

"Yes! Yes!" Penny cried. "It was the best ever! And I want to do it again and again and again!" She clapped a hand over her mouth in shock while her friend collapsed into peals of laughter.

"I hope you have dozens of letters."

"But—"

"Because using them is much more fun than stopping!"

Penny felt her jaw go slack in astonishment. She had heard some things, of course. From her married school friends and sometimes from overhearing her mother and aunt in whispered conversation. But no one had been so open about it. Not like Francine. So Penny abruptly made a decision. Not about Samuel, but about what she wanted to know. Which was *everything*.

Suddenly, she did the unheard-of act of putting away all her tools. They didn't have much time. Tommy could wake any minute. So she left her bench to sit beside Francine.

"Tell me about it. Tell me everything!" she begged.

And in the miracle that was this day, Tommy slept for a full hour more.

Samuel appeared after dinner with a tart folded up in his pocket for Tommy. Penny recognized the pastry as having come from his brother's home, and she wondered anew at the relationship between the men. "Doesn't your brother resent feeding you? And now Tommy, too?"

He looked up from playing tug-of-war with Tommy, his expression one of shocked surprise. "Heavens, no! My brother wouldn't care if I moved in with them. In fact, he's asked me to on more than one occasion. I've thought about it, if only to give Max someone intelligent to converse with, but Georgette and I would kill each other within days. So, my brother is content to have me visit and eat rather than murder his wife."

She laughed, but she still couldn't understand it. "What of the expense? Even if your brother forgets it, I'll wager Georgette doesn't."

He grimaced. "No, she doesn't. But I assure you, my brother will be well recompensed come quarter day."

She tilted her head. "What happens on quarter day? I thought your brother got all the money come quarter day. He's the baron, right?"

He nodded. "Many investments pay four times a year or quarterly. It's not just the land investments. Factories, mines, a lot of other companies pay quarterly. Or yearly. Didn't your father have customers who paid only after quarter day?"

She nodded, thinking back. "As a rule, Father was the one who went to collect debts. I merely kept track of the bills and monies owed."

Samuel frowned a moment. "You were your father's bookkeeper?"

She shrugged. "He didn't trust anyone else."

"My estimation of your intelligence continues to grow."

She flushed, pleased with the compliment. "Well, my *intelligence* desperately wishes to know what has happened today regarding my home and Papa's will."

"There isn't much to tell, but I shall explain what I have done."

Then he started talking even as he continued to play with Tommy, pretending to steal pieces of tart, only to give them back to the child a second later.

Penny listened as closely as she could. He had investigated the other signatures on the will from the witnesses. He continued to believe the signatures were false, but he had no way to prove that as yet. He'd gone to the pub where the documents had supposedly been executed. The innkeeper remembered nothing though certainly her father and Mr. Addicock had frequented the establishment. There was no more to be learned at the pub, so Samuel went to some of his solicitor friends. He'd also visited with the constable to learn the details of her parents' murder. On and on he spoke, the details merging together in her mind.

He saw the oddest things and thought them significant. One of the waitresses at the pub was stealing, but not from the till. She was pickpocketing certain customers and not others. The other waitress was pregnant and hiding it very badly. The constable was a smart one, though he was not aging well. An injury of some sort plagued his knees, not that he would admit that to anyone. Copper kettles tended to make tea taste odd. His solicitor friend's wife was gambling again. Samuel knew because the man's tick had reappeared and that inevitably meant debt. And the new clerk had a fondness for twirling his hair when he lied. Bad habit that.

There was more. An overflowing tide of more, and all too soon Penny listened with half an ear. Instead, she relaxed back in her chair and just enjoyed the moment. Soon she had her sketch pad in hand and was doodling as he spoke. The calm that came to her whenever she began thinking of her shoes merged together with the peace his words brought to her mind.

They were in the kitchen upstairs, which was really just a woodstove in the corner beside a table and chairs. Mrs. Appleton was in the workroom downstairs managing the receipts in her daughter's absence, and Wendy was done for the night. Gone early, which was becoming more frequent for her.

That left Penny upstairs with Samuel and Tommy. It was a cozy family moment, or felt like one at least. She had a full belly, Tommy was babbling happily, and Samuel was there nattering on about his day. If she closed her mind to reality for a moment, she could well believe this was her future. Samuel at the table, their children playing nearby while the water heated for tea. She could be sketching her latest shoe idea or perhaps stitching fabric to a sole. In a little bit, she would put Tommy to bed and then she and Samuel would sit together and   and   well, they would do what married people did. They would talk. They would share their lives. Then they would retire to bed to make brothers and sisters for Tommy. Or cousins, actually, not that anyone would note the difference.

That was the future her mind created for her, and she wanted it with an ache that left a dark hole in her belly. She wanted to believe it was possible, even though she knew it would never be.

"I won't bed you," she said abruptly, speaking more to that fantasy than to Samuel. "Not without benefit of a ring. I won't cheapen myself that way."

It took her a moment to realize she'd said it aloud, stopping Samuel's conversation mid-word. He was able to follow, of course. Or at least he pretended well. He cocked his head and smiled at her.

"Of course not. I would never try to cheapen you in that manner."

"You wouldn't?" She flushed, embarrassed and a little hurt by his answer. After all, didn't all men want to bed pretty girls? What was wrong with her that he would hold them back after everything they'd already done? Then she roundly chided herself for being so irrational. Why did she always leap to the conclusion that she was unacceptable?

He leaned forward, a grin on his face. "I would never ask, my dear. However, if you should wish to change your mind, trust me to be more than willing to participate in your deflowering."

She flushed, pleased by his frank words and his heated look. "But you won't ask it of me," she said.

"I want to. Believe me when I say that I wish for it like a starving man wishes for bread. But until the moment you ask, I have sworn to act as a true chivalric knight, worshiping you from a far."

"But if I were to ask," she said slowly.

His expression shifted into a seductive smile. "Then you will have no cause to regret our action, and we will enjoy a night of such pleasure. That, too, I have sworn."

She laughed because he was being silly. And because she wanted to cover the quiver that trembled in her belly. But when she looked into his eyes, she saw that he knew what he had done to her, the feelings that he sparked. He knew it as a man knows his own power. But she also saw a hunger there, a desire that quickened hers and had her thinking of what else could happen in the dungeon. Or in any room that contained a bed.

Thankfully, Tommy distracted them. He wanted down from his chair and to his toys. Which meant he had to be cleaned first, his nappy changed, and a host of other things that filled the time. Samuel stayed throughout her tasks, even helped with Tommy's bath. And all through the time, she was excruciatingly aware of how easy it would be to slide straight back into her fantasy. She could easily pretend that Tommy was not her cousin, but her child with Samuel.

That she and Samuel were wed, and five minutes after the boy was asleep, he would take her into his arms and kiss away all her cares. She would feel again that wonderful thing he did and more.

Oh, she wanted it. But it was never to be, and so she ended up shooing Samuel downstairs as she put the boy to bed. "Go away now. This is a time for family."

Her words were too harsh. She knew it the moment she said them, and seeing Samuel's face carefully blank told her she'd hurt him. Could it be? Could he have been pretending as much as she'd been? The idea was ludicrous, but she wondered as she watched him nod curtly toward her and step for the stairs.

"I'll just wait in the workroom, then. If Mrs. Appleton can watch Tommy, then we can leave as soon as you're ready."

She frowned. "Leave where?" The ball wasn't until tomorrow night.

"To speak with Ned Wilkers. You did say you wanted to join me when I speak with the boy."

"Oh! Yes. Of course." How could she have forgotten? That was what came of fantasies, she scolded herself. They made one forget what was important. "Ten minutes, and I shall be down."

"Take as much time as you need. I will wait." And with that he disappeared down the stairs. And she, idiot woman that she was, hated every second that they were apart.

"My God," she whispered to Tommy as his eyes began to droop. "What's to become of us? I've fallen for a mad toff!"

Tommy didn't answer, and ten minutes later, she was busy changing her gown and dressing her hair. She told herself it was simply to make talking to Ned easier. A pretty girl always got more information out of a man. But inside she knew the truth.

Especially since she selected a gown that unbuttoned easily down the front.

Chapter 17

Samuel hated waiting anywhere for anything. He truly despised having to do it while Penny was upstairs with Tommy and he was banished like an errant child. It wasn't a rational reaction, which made him all the more surly. The truth was, he had been enjoying his time with them and was now surly for being denied his treat.

So he sat downstairs, intending to sulk out his annoyance in the main parlor. But he could not keep his mind focused on it for long—especially since it was an illogical emotional response and not worthy of his brainpower—so all too soon he wandered to the back workroom.

Mrs. Appleton was there chatting with the buyer, Mrs. Irene Knopp, and the new apprentice, Tabitha, who had indeed gotten her glasses. He heard precious little of their discussion, but knew that it stopped immediately upon his entering the room.

"Discussing me, were you?" he asked lightly, though inside he sighed. He knew that women more than men valued the good opinion of their friends. And from the looks on the ladies' faces, they had precious little use for him.

Normally when faced with a hostile audience, he said his piece and left. Or just left. But for the first time in a very long time, he wanted someone's good opinion. The reasons why didn't matter. All that he cared was for them to speak well of him to Penny. So he did something he rarely ever did. He invited the women to vent their criticism.

"I can see that I have done something amiss. Pray enlighten me so that I can redress it."

The apprentice's eyes widened. It was clear she'd never heard words so big or ones spoken so sweetly. Not the case with the other two ladies. Their eyes narrowed and their faces grew tight. He was already mentally shifting his attention to something—anything—but the dressing-down that was to come when the purchaser did something that surprised him: she spoke rationally to him and in the language of money.

She began with the simplest of approaches. "I understand that you are a man of investment."

"I am not quite sure what that means," he lied.

She flashed him an irritated grimace, and he realized she was not a woman used to playing with words. "You invest in companies. In shipping ventures, in stocks, in a variety of ventures all designed to make money. You are a man who invests."

He nodded. "Yes, that is certainly true." Though how she had learned of it was beyond him. Perhaps from her father-in-law, who was also a man of investments, to use her language. If he recalled the details correctly, her father-in-law was the owner of Knopp Shipping. "If I might inquire, how did you learn—"

"You may not. What you can tell me is how you are faring lately."

He reared back. He had not expected such blunt speech from a gently reared lady. "I beg your pardon," he said stiffly.

"I apologize," though it was clear from her tone that she did not feel badly about what she'd said. "Let me express it differently. I understand that you are in arrears on your investments. Truth be told, you are in quite the soup."

Yes, that was indeed the image he presented. And truthfully, if things went badly—or more slowly than he expected—then quarter day would not be the salvation he envisioned. "My financial situation," he said stiffly, "is none of your concern."

"On the contrary, it is exactly my concern because I wish to offer you a job."

He was so stunned that he was robbed of breath. Imagine a woman—a cit's widow, to be exact—thinking to offer him a job. All his slim aristocratic heritage reacted to the insult, tightening his chest and flushing his face hot. He was just the second son of a baron, but still, the insult was a palpable blow. Had he truly fallen so far?

"No, don't answer. I can see it in your face. And no man wishes to work for a woman. But I need a man of some intelligence around. A man who can discourage ruffians and watch for sharks and shoals alike."

Her language was colorful and likely a product of her father-in-law. Still he understood her desire. She probably did need a man to help her in all the ways that a man was useful in business. Some situations were simply not safe for a woman.

Unfortunately, he was still feeling the insult to his very masculine pride. He answered with as much civility as he could muster. "Are you still being followed then? If so, I would look to your seamstress rather than to me."

Mrs. Knopp didn't answer, but Mrs. Appleton reared back in shock. "What does that mean?" And when no one answered her directly, she stepped forward. "What does Wendy have to do with this?"

"Only that Miss Drew is gambling. And when one dips too deep, all manner of difficulties follow."

"Preposterous!" the lady snapped. "Wendy despises gambling!"

Samuel merely shrugged. Willful blindness only irritated him. Meanwhile, the purchaser stepped forward, her head tilted as she studied him. "Reconsider, Mr. Morrison. It would allow you a reason to hang about near Penny, give you some stability as you await return on your existing investments, and most importantly, you might prevent a disaster that could destroy Penny's only means of income."

"So you wish to trade upon my affection for Miss Shoemaker to allay your fears. An endless dance, in my experience, for women are always dreaming up new fears. And what would I be paid for such a Herculean task?"

She named a small figure. Enough to significantly reduce his current financial strain, but not the loss to his dignity or the insult to Penny. On another day regarding a different woman, he might have considered it. There was a true mystery surrounding both her and the shop. After all, someone had been following Mrs. Knopp for some reason. And mysteries of that nature always intrigued him.

But the idea that he would barter a position just to remain close to Penny was insulting and vaguely dirty. He did not want the taint of commerce to pollute their relationship. Logically, such an attitude made little sense. After all, he had begun this dance with Penny as a wager. And gambling was perhaps one of the dirtiest form of commerce, as the seamstress was no doubt discovering.

But whatever the problem facing this shop was, he would not use it to court Penny. In truth, it bothered him that he was using their wager in just that manner. Which meant he needed to end the problem with Addicock, thereby removing the taint. The last thing he wanted to do was add yet another layer to their relationship. Purity was his choice, not further taint. And so he lifted his nose and spoke with as much aristocratic disdain as he could muster.

"You insult me and cheapen Miss Shoemaker. I would

think that, as her friend, you would want her to attract or discard men at *her* choosing without forcing the taint of commerce upon her relationships."

As expected, all three women reared back at his cold words. Even Tabitha, who didn't seem to understand his words. But it was Mrs. Appleton who narrowed her eyes in fury and spoke with a disdain he could not match.

"Taint?" she mocked. "You believe commerce taints her? Us? How bloody arrogant! This is how we live, how we survive, and no man can damn us for it!"

"And if I choose to lift my relationship with Miss Shoemaker above such mundane concerns, you have no cause to damn *me* for it."

Mrs. Appleton opened her mouth to say something, no doubt to blast him from here to eternity. But the purchaser held up her hand. The room held in silence as Mrs. Knopp studied him, pursing her lips as she thought. In the end, an incredulous laugh burst forth.

"You are trying to be chivalric. Good God, Mr. Morrison, you are styling yourself as a knight errant worshiping your lady fair from afar."

Samuel stiffened, though truthfully, he couldn't really stiffen any more. He had already postured himself as a man with wounded dignity. Now his body moved with natural shock at the woman's intelligence. Because the bloody female was *right*. He did want to be Penny's knight errant. He did want the purity of such an honorable and holy worship of his lady fair.

"And what is it to you if I do?" he asked stiffly.

"Because it isn't from *afar*!" snapped Mrs. Appleton. "I woke when she came to bed that night. I do not know what happened, but it wasn't noble or chivalric." She snorted. "You are no Sir Galahad!"

Samuel swallowed, knowing that she was right. Everything that he had done with Penny—and at a brothel no less—burned in his gut. The weight of his sins nearly crippled him. But he did not crumple. He was a man after all, and had his pride.

"I do *not* accept your offer of employment."

"No matter," returned the purchaser. "I have retracted it anyway. I would not have you in my employ. In fact, I do not wish to know you at all."

And she would counsel Penny against him, he realized with a heavy heart. Bloody hell, he should have remained in the main parlor for he had just turned all Penny's friends against him. There was nothing to do about it now but to execute a strategic retreat. So with a stiff bow, he turned to leave. Sadly, worst had come to worst. Penny stood at the base of the stairs. She had no doubt heard every word.

"Miss Shoemaker," he said, barely keeping the words from being a cry of alarm. "Are you ready to go? I believe time to get to Shoreditch grows short."

She nodded slowly, and he noted that her face was pale beneath the cosmetics and that her hand trembled where it touched the wall. Her gaze jumped between himself and the other women in the room. Sadly, the others made their opinion of him quite clear without any words at all.

How to turn her back to his favor? He didn't know, and that bothered him at a fundamental level. In nearly a week's acquaintance, he knew less and less of Penny's thoughts and heart. So he kept silent and simply held out his hand, silently praying that she took it.

She did, and the relief of that shuddered through him even as he guided them out the door and hailed a hackney headed for Shoreditch and Ned Wilkers. But once in the cab, the silence held dark and oppressive. She was thinking hard, and he was insane with the need to know her decision. Thankfully, she did not keep him in suspense for long.

"What does 'chivalric' mean?"

"Do you recall childhood stories of King Arthur and his knights?"

"Yes. They went out on quests. They did knightly things—defending the innocents, punishing the guilty."

"And they loved according to the Christian ideal. That meant—"

"No kissing, no touching, no marriage because Queen Guinevere was already married."

He nodded, no longer surprised that she easily cut to the heart of the matter.

"So you don't want to touch me anymore?"

He laughed, though the sound was strained. "I want to very much, Penny. But . . ." He sighed. It was good that they were sitting there in the dark. He did not think he could reveal himself were it the broad light of day. "I was very young when I realized that I saw things that others did not. That I understood a great deal more than others."

"You're the smartest man I have ever met," she said.

He took it as the simple truth. "But I used my intelligence badly," he said. "I made fun of others, manipulated events to show that I was smart and they were dumb. I made a farmer spend a day searching for imaginary gold. I sent my brother and father off chasing a leprechaun. I did so many bad things, Penny, you have no idea."

"What did the farmer do to you?"

He frowned. "What?"

"I doubt you were carelessly cruel. What did the farmer do to make you angry?"

"He, um, he beat a dog. It was his own dog and so he had the right. But . . ."

"So you sent him off chasing after gold. Did you save the dog then?"

He had. And he'd given the animal to a traveling tinker. "I saved that dog, yes. But it was theft, Penny. And besides, he got another dog and beat that one, too. I changed nothing."

"But you were young and your intentions were good."

"And my brother and father?" He knew the reasons why

he had done that. He'd known for years now, though he had never spoken of them to anyone.

"Families are difficult." She reached out and touched his hand. "I have lived with such anger that my father could not see past my sex to what I could do as a cobbler. Perhaps you were angry that your brother inherits everything merely because he is the elder. And you are left with only your wits."

"I used to be very angry," he said softly. In truth, the resentment still simmered. Especially on days when the hunger bit deep, when he had to dance attendance on some ridiculous society woman just so he could dine at her ball.

"What happened, Samuel?" she asked softly. "What happened to turn you into Sir Samuel, my knight protector?"

He laughed at her honorific, but he couldn't deny that it pleased him enormously. He did wish to save her from her dragons. Every single one of them. But honesty forced him to correct her. "I am no knight errant, as your friends will take great pains to explain to you."

"What happened," she repeated, "to keep you from becoming cruel and malicious? To bring you to help me instead of laugh at my woes?"

"Penny—"

"Do not fob me off, Samuel. I know how easily anger can turn to bitterness."

She was right. Something had changed the course of his life. Or more specifically, someone. "A tutor. He handed me the tale of King Arthur and his knights—in the original French no less—and he taught me."

"Taught you to be less bitter?"

"If I had what I felt I deserved—the baronetcy and all that it entailed—what would happen to my brother? He is not so smart as me. Kind and jolly as Father Christmas, but not so bright. He would be penniless in a fortnight. Too proud for a trade, too bumbling to manage on his wits, he would enter the army and be blown to bits equally fast." In his mind's eye, he noted the parade of young men he remembered who had suffered just that fate. "God was right to give him the title and me the ability to survive on my own."

"Are you?" she asked. "Are you surviving? I heard what Irene said. Are you close to debtor's prison?"

"No, my dear. No debts or at least not ones so substantial as to fear the law." Though if he were truly honest with himself, a disaster could indeed bring him to his knees. It was a delicate time for him, financially speaking. But he had faith that his investments were sound. He had studied them very carefully.

Meanwhile, she took what he said at face value, and the silence enfolded them again. Then he surprised them both by speaking.

"My mother caught me once teasing my brother. I'm afraid there were times I was very mean to him. She grabbed me by the ear and dragged me aside and said something I will never forget." He paused, remembering the exact moment and the force of her words. His ear even throbbed in remembered pain. "She said, 'To whom much is given, much is expected.' As I'd been given brains, I ought to find something better to do with them than trick Greg out of his best toy soldier.'"

He sighed, and acting on impulse, he tugged her across the seat and into his arms. He heard her gasp in reaction, but her body was pliant as she settled into his arms.

"I haven't," he said to her hair. "I've looked and looked, but I haven't found anything of value to do yet."

"You are getting me back my inheritance."

"I have been scheming to get you into my bed. I took you to a brothel."

He felt her body tremble at that, but she didn't speak. He had no idea if it was fear or anticipation.

"I am trying to be a better man, Penny. If you will but be patient with me, I will find a way to treat you as you deserve."

"Like Sir Lancelot treated Queen Guinevere? Loving her from afar?"

"You clearly do not remember the rest of the story," he drawled.

"I don't care about *their* story," she said as she pushed out of his arms. "I am not a queen. You *are* helping me. And Irene had no right to use your kindness for me to try and get you to work for us."

"It's not *kindness* I feel, Penny."

"Good. Because it's not what I feel either." And with that, she stretched up and kissed him.

His arms wrapped around her and his renewed determination to be a good man was not proof against her body pressed to his, her lips on his mouth. Especially as she began to nip at his lips.

Lust roared through him. He was already hard. It was a chronic condition whenever they were together. But now, a wave of hunger engulfed him. Where she was still teasing at his lips, he opened his mouth and thrust into hers. She was gripping his shoulders, encouraging closeness, but he rolled over her, pressing her back against the squabs as he began to take what he wanted.

He thrust his tongue into her mouth. He slid between her knees and ground against her. She moaned in response, which pushed him to further excess. One of his hands moved easily to her breast while the other sought the edge of her gown at her shoulder. He was intent on pushing it down, on stripping her bare, and doing what he wanted without regard to anything but the way she thrust her pelvis against his and gasped his name.

But they were in a carriage, for God's sake! All too soon they would arrive at the pub where young Ned passed his evenings. Penny was not a bored society matron reveling in a dashed tumble against the squabs. And he was not a beast to take what he wanted without regard to the woman beneath him.

But it was hard, so very, very difficult to pull himself back, to stop the way he grabbed at her gown, to force himself to sit back on the opposite side of the carriage. Especially since, even in the dark, he could see her red lips and disheveled gown. He could hear her rasping breaths, timed perfectly with his own. And he knew a thousand and one ways to manipulate her into his bed within an hour.

He knew them, but he could not. "I am a brilliant man," he rasped, speaking more to himself than to her. "And as a brilliant man, I have the ability to punish the guilty and defend the victims. It is immoral and irresponsible for me to take advantage of those who cannot defend themselves."

"And what does that have to do with anything?" she demanded. She had not moved an inch from where he had abandoned her for the opposite side of the carriage. Her skin was still flushed, her hair still mussed. And he was a breath away from returning to her. But her glare kept him fixed in place.

"Penny, I am trying to be honorable. I am trying to be a better man."

"Samuel, you are the craziest toff I ever met." And with that, she straightened up from the squabs, adjusted her clothing with swift jerks of her hands, and smoothed down her displaced curls. By the time the cab stopped at their destination, she looked as composed as any queen. And he felt as miserable as any Lancelot forced to worship his lady from afar.

Which was when he realized he was a damned idiot.

Chapter 18

Penny climbed down from the cab without even touching Samuel's hand. It was a pointed snub to him, but also kept her from flying back into his arms and begging him to kiss her some more. Hobnails and curs, what was she about? Begging a man to kiss her? All but spreading her legs and hiking her skirt in a hansom cab? Her gut twisted in shame. And yet even as she cursed herself as a tart, her blood hummed and her body still ached for his touch.

So it was best she keep her distance from him. Best she pretend anger at him rather than admit the truth: that she was ashamed of her own actions and her desires. And she was much too weak around him to be trusted with her own virtue.

"Ned should be inside," he said, his voice low by her right ear. She shivered in delight at the smooth tones of his very cultured voice. Then she felt his touch at her back as he guided her toward the door, and all her anger faded away.

"But what exactly are we doing here?"

"No one knows the secrets of a man's business better

than his clerk. If we are to gain evidence against Addicock, then our best ally is young Ned. Who, by the by, is known to be sweet on the pub owner's daughter."

She stopped abruptly, not two feet before entering the building. "But if he's sweet on a girl here, I cannot help you. He can't go soft on me if he's bent on impressing someone else."

Samuel nodded, his expression unreadable. "If you recall, you were the one who insisted on coming—"

She cut him off. "No, never mind. There's more than one way to turn a gent without flirting." His eyebrows went up at that, but she waved him off. She had no wish to explain something that was obvious to her merely because she'd spent a lifetime smiling at customers while still under the eagle eye of her parents. Ned was no more and no less than any number of men she had charmed.

So she bit her lip and forced herself to face the one question that had been hovering in her mind but she had not dared ask before. "Do you really think that Addicock killed my parents?"

Samuel flinched at her words, but he remained steadfast in his answer. "He had a hand in it, I am sure, though I doubt he did the deed itself." Then he frowned. "I just cannot understand why he says he has not profited from the theft. That is what we must learn, Penny."

She nodded, though she'd already dismissed the question. She understood it was important to Samuel, but in her mind, Addicock was guilty. Addicock did the crime. What he *said* was a lie.

"Perhaps Ned will know."

Samuel nodded. "That is my hope."

"Then let's get to it." So saying, she rubbed her eyes hard enough to make them ache. It hurt, but when she was done, she would have red eyes and a weepy appearance. Samuel glanced at her, obviously startled, but she just shrugged and tugged her curls into a wilder appearance before stepping inside the pub.

She instantly felt at home. Though this was Shoreditch, and therefore out of her usual circle of London, she knew exactly what she was about in a pub that catered to tradesmen. This one might sport a few more lean faces, a lot more of the poet types, but all in all, she saw the clerks and the artists alike and felt right at home.

She also saw Ned at a table, laughing with his mates. She headed in the opposite direction, making a show of looking at the patrons and appearing lost and confused. Samuel understood what she was doing or he had just learned to trust her enough that he hung back. Either way, he remained a step behind her, observing without speaking, while she worked.

It took Ned less than two minutes to recognize her and jump up from his table to touch her on the arm.

"Miss Shoemaker? Is that you?"

She spun around, her eyes and her motions a little too wide. "Oh, Ned! Oh, Ned, thank heavens." Then she took a deep breath and visibly pulled her thoughts and her body under control.

She could tell with a glance at Samuel that the man was surprised. Ned, too. Obviously few women of their acquaintance ever managed to control their emotions. But she was made of stronger stuff and Ned didn't need a wild show from a sobbing female to be persuaded. He'd seen her a little distraught so he knew she felt things deeply. And now, he would speak to her as a rational adult and be grateful that she wasn't a weeping, wailing woman.

"Ned," she said gently, "I would like a word with you, if I may. I would like to tell you something that has upset me deeply, and I hope that you might be able to help."

The boy's eyes widened, and he nodded. She could tell they'd gotten the attention of his mates at the table and she was loath to spread all of this before his friends. Fortunately it was late enough that there were open places about the pub. With a gesture, Ned moved them to a place near the door.

And as they were sitting, Samuel caught the eye of the barmaid.

"Three pints."

Penny smiled her thanks at Samuel. She wanted the ale and was grateful he wasn't cutting up stiff at her drinking it. Meanwhile, Ned was looking nervous.

"I don't know what I can do. I'm just a clerk. Addicock doesn't let me—"

She touched the back of his hand. Just a touch and then she withdrew, aware that a young woman behind the bar was watching them closely. Most likely the owner's daughter.

"I should like to tell you what I believe, Ned. You can make your own decisions then. I am putting my faith in you, that you're a moral man. That you go to church and you wouldn't do anyone harm. Not if you could help it. That's a hero in my mind, Ned. A man who stands up for what's right."

He nodded, his face going paler.

"Just listen," she said gently. "Then you decide. I don't believe that my father ever signed that will. I think it was faked. I think it was forged by Addicock and then you filed it with the courts not knowing anything was wrong with it. And then he ups and sells everything I own without a thought to me or little Tommy. Put us out on the street, he did, and kept the rest. Now I got a job with a dress shop, but it's barely enough to keep food in Tommy's mouth."

Then Samuel interrupted, his brow furrowed even as he was served his ale. "But where did the money go? That's the mystery, Ned. Why isn't Addicock suddenly flush?"

"Ain't no mystery," Ned muttered as he gazed into his own drink. "Man's always in debt. Can't pay me this week again 'cause he owes someone else."

Penny's attention sharpened to painful intensity. "His debts?"

Samuel, too, had suddenly looked up. "Owes whom, Ned? Is it gambling debts? At Demon Damon's?"

Ned shrugged. "Don't know where. Just that a few months back it got really bad. He hadn't been paying me and collectors coming around. Then suddenly there's a new friend. A man named Bill. Addicock hated him, but the man was always there. Then a week later, it all is fixed. No collectors, and I got everything owed." Then he looked her square in the eye, his expression apologetic. "But that was long before the sale of your shop. The two aren't connected."

"Are you sure? Was it about two months ago? Right before her parents were murdered?"

Ned slammed down his hand, his expression fierce. "There hasn't been any murder!"

The explosion was enough to draw attention again, so Penny touched the boy's arm. A soft press of her fingers, enough to calm him down. "Please, Ned, just listen. There has been a murder. Two of them. My parents."

Ned shook his head. "But Addicock shakes at the sight of blood. Full-on fit. It just started happening bad, not more than . . ." His voice trailed off and he took a hasty swig of his drink.

Samuel finished the statement for him. "So about two months ago something happens that rattles your boss. Something that makes him shake at the sight of blood. I think he witnessed her parents' murders. He might not have done the deed, but he knew about it. Was probably there."

"But why would he do that?" exclaimed Ned. "Makes no sense for him to go and murder a cobbler."

"'Course it does," said Samuel. "Your boss gets in deep. I saw the token in his office, so we know it's Demon Damon. He's got no way to repay his debt. So Damon comes to him and says, make a fake will and trust. I'll take care of everything else."

Penny shuddered, listening to Samuel outline the cold, calculated murder of her parents.

Meanwhile, Ned couldn't believe it. "He wouldn't do that."

"You mean *you* wouldn't, Ned," Penny said. "And you wouldn't work for a man who did such a thing. Not knowingly at least."

Samuel leaned forward. "Tell me more about this man Bill."

Ned grew sullen. "Don't know much. Just a man who came by. A lot."

"What did he look like? Do you know his address? Did he smoke cigars or dress strangely? Anything that would help us find him?"

Ned was starting to look alarmed, shaking his head with more vehemence after every question. "I don't know anything!"

Penny gripped the boy's hand, just for a moment as she tried to settle him down. "It's all right, Ned. I know you want to help." She glanced at Samuel. "Do you think this Bill was the one to do it? That he . . ."

Samuel twisted his glass around, staring into the depths of his pint without drinking. "It's possible. Or it's possible he was just another collector. What was the last time you saw him?" he asked Ned.

"Just a bit ago. He was all smiles, but I never did like the look in his eyes."

"What did he and Addicock speak about?"

Ned shrugged. "Don't know. Sent me off. Told me I could leave early, so I did."

Penny sighed with frustration. She knew there was something important here, but she couldn't figure out what. Worse, she didn't see how Samuel would discover what they needed to know. Thankfully, Samuel wasn't finished yet. He leaned back in his chair and studied Ned.

"When did you first see the will?" he asked.

"August fourteenth."

Penny felt her eyebrows rise. He knew the date exactly. Which told her that he'd been thinking about this even before she showed up. That he already suspected something was wrong. "My parents were murdered the very day before."

"'Course they were. That's what we do with a will. Once the person dies, we file the will at court. Nothing odd about that."

"Only that it was the first you'd heard of it," Penny pressed. "You'd never met my father, never heard about any will, and I'll bet you know everything that Addicock does."

Ned didn't answer except to take refuge in his drink while Samuel took up the tale again. "I think Addicock was there at the murder. Maybe Bill did it, maybe not. But let us say it is Damon who is orchestrating things. Damon would want Addicock there, to see it done."

Penny felt bile rise in her throat. "But why?" she choked out. "Why would he want a witness?"

"It's a threat to keep compatriots in line. A kind of insurance." Then he narrowed his eyes, obviously working through the details in his mind. "Once the forgery is made, Damon or his men kill your parents. Well, your father was the likely target. No profit in killing your mother unless they were together."

She closed her eyes, seeing her parents as they had been that last night. They'd been quarreling actually, about whether to hire a bookkeeper or not. But they were going to a pub to talk it out with their friends. That was the way of her parents. Good or bad, they always went together to the pub. To talk or to celebrate or just be together. Now that she thought about it, Papa rarely went anywhere alone.

"They always went out together," she said softly. "It would have been very hard to find him alone."

Samuel nodded as if he'd already guessed that. "So Addicock is there when the deed is done."

"He wouldn't do it!" repeated Ned. "Squeals when there's blood. Like a pig."

"But he would be there. Damon would be sure that he saw. So he wouldn't tell."

Ned didn't answer, just kept shaking his head.

"The rest would be easy. File the will, sell the shop, keep the money. Except he kept saying he hadn't profited a groat. Not a groat. That's what stops me. Where did the money go?"

At this point, Ned did look up, a puzzled frown on his face. Then he turned to Penny. "He doesn't understand about gamblers, does he?"

Penny shrugged. For such a brilliant man, Samuel was remarkably thick about the fact that gamblers *lied*. Not surprisingly, he read her opinion right off her face. Picking up his glass, he glared at them both.

"He was *not* lying."

"That don't mean it was *true*," inserted Ned. "If Addicock doesn't get coins in his hand, then it doesn't count. Just canceling out his debt isn't a real profit for him."

Samuel stilled, and Penny could see the shock hitting his body. "B-But . . ." He frowned. "But that isn't logical! And patently untrue!"

Penny knew he meant that Addicock's reasoning was untrue, and she gently pushed his ale up toward his mouth. "He's a gambler, Samuel. What's real to him and real to us isn't the same thing."

The man just shook his head right after taking a long pull. "But real is real." Fortunately, his mind was then able to leap to the reality of what happened. "So he does take the money but it all goes to cover his debt with the Demon."

Ned nodded, and Penny saw that he was sinking lower and lower in his chair. It was time, she realized. So she turned to face the boy square on.

"We know what happened, but we don't have the proof. I know you're an honest man, Ned. I know you would never be part of something so terrible. Can you find us the proof?"

Samuel, too, pressed forward. "Look for the marriage certificate of her parents. It's from her Bible, stolen to copy the signature. Look for pages where he practiced the signature. Anything that will help."

Ned didn't answer. In truth, his eyes were panicked, his expression as frightened as he was sullen. "I need a job. It ain't a great livelihood with him, but he does pay. Eventually."

"From stolen goods."

"And there are probably others," Samuel added. "Maybe not before Miss Shoemaker, but a gambler never stops. Not when it works once. Is there some other parent about to be murdered, Ned? We need you to look. We need you to find out."

Penny touched the boy's hand. "Please. We'll help you find another job. A good one that will impress the young lady over there. And won't she be excited to know that you stood up against a crime? That you helped someone who really, truly needed it. Please—"

"Fine," Ned cut in, the word half swallowed by his empty glass. "Fine. I'll look." Then he abruptly shoved up from the table and slumped away.

No more talking, no more explanation. Just a promise and a hope that he would come through for her. Penny looked after the young man and tried to keep her belief alive. This would work. She would get her home and Tommy's inheritance back.

Then she felt Samuel's hand, warm and comforting, surrounding hers. "Either way, you will be fine. Whatever happens, you will survive."

"I know," she said softly. And for the first time ever, she believed it. With his hand holding hers, with his strength by her side, she truly believed she had a future. And it could be a good one.

Then he destroyed it.

"Let's get you home. I've got other things to do tonight."

She gaped at him, all those lovely, half-conscious thoughts of what would happen tonight disappearing in a heartbeat. "But . . . but what are you going to do?"

"Talk to the constable first. Then there are other directions to investigate." He smiled. "I'm not relying solely on Ned, you know. I mean to find this Bill."

She nodded, though she knew nothing of the kind. "But—"

"I will see you tomorrow," he stated firmly as he dropped what looked like his last coins on the table.

She followed because what else could she do? He was sending her home. They went outside and hailed a hansom cab. She would have been happy to walk, but he shook his head.

"I'm not going with you, and I will worry too much if you are walking alone."

"But—"

He leaned forward and kissed her. It was a kiss that he kept light when she wanted to deepen it. It was a press of the lips that he refused to make into more.

"I will be worthy of you, Penny. Soon. I swear."

"Worthy of me? Bugger that!" she snapped, purposely making her words crude. "I'm not some bleeding queen—"

He kissed her again. And this time, he wrapped his arms around her and did what she liked. He thrust his tongue inside, he touched every part of her mouth, and his hands slid down to cup her bottom. It was horribly crass of her, especially as they were standing right beside the cab, not even climbing inside. But when she would have pulled him into the darkness inside the vehicle, he gently set her back on her heels.

"I will not fail you," he said firmly. Then he gently pushed her into the cab and shut the door. She would have argued, but she could see in his face that his mind was made up.

"Crazy toff!" she accused through the window.

He executed a courtly bow just as the hansom drove off.

"He just left you?" Francine gasped as she sat with Penny the next afternoon. "He just put you in a carriage and—"

"And I came back here. To make shoes for your wedding."

"Well!" harumphed her friend.

Penny echoed it and added a sigh for good measure.

"Did he at least kiss you?"

Penny nodded. "And tonight is the ball."

"Oh, right! The real society ball where you will have the best time!"

Penny closed off the stitching and leaned back to study her handiwork. It was a new pair of slippers for Francine's future mother-in-law. And it was a right pretty pair, even if she did say so herself. She was especially proud of the ribbon she'd added near the very toe. That had come as an inspiration early this morning, and it looked especially delightful. "Done," she pronounced, handing the slippers over to her friend. "Can you give them to Anthony to give to his mother?"

"Can you stop worrying about shoes and go get dressed? A real society—"

"Stop saying that!" Penny snapped, turning to the next upper that needed stitches to its sole. Just picking up the leather kept her hands from shaking. She felt secure when she was cobbling. Peaceful and happy. Who at this ball could possibly understand that? She'd be like a fish out of water there. "Maybe it won't be so bad," she said, trying to convince herself. "It's a party. I've been to plenty of parties."

"Not with nobs, you haven't," said Francine as she neatly grabbed the shoe parts. "Come on, Penny. Why aren't you beside yourself with excitement?"

Penny arched her friend a look. "Isn't it obvious?" she said morosely. "I'm a tradeswoman. I make shoes. I can't be—"

"You're smart, you're capable, and you've got a real live gent taking you to a party. Don't you be thinking you're less than anybody there. You go and have a good time."

Penny nodded, but inside, her entire body was depressed. Her heart ached and she nearly broke down in tears. She tried to cover it, but she couldn't. Francine noticed, and before Penny could say a word, she was wrapped in her friend's strong arms.

"What's wrong? Come on. Out with it!"

It took a while before Penny could force the words out. The realization had come on her last night as she climbed into her very cold and very empty bed.

"Something awful has happened," she whispered. Then before she could change her mind, she looked up at her friend and pushed the words out. "I've fallen in love with him!" she cried. Then she burst into tears.

Francine didn't say anything. Or if she did, Penny didn't hear it. She just hugged her friend and waited until the storm of tears passed. It did quickly enough. Unlike her anger, Penny's tears never lasted for long. Then when she had dried her face and blown her nose, Francine fixed her with a hard stare.

"You know, love isn't something to cry over. Love is a wonderful thing."

"Not when you're in love with a nob who won't even kiss you when you want."

Francine frowned. "I thought he took you to that dungeon place."

"He did," Penny said with a heavy sigh. "But yesterday he was all noble. Talking about being worthy of me."

Francine rolled her eyes. "The gents have weird ways of thinking. You're either a street tart to them or the Holy Mother. Seems to me, he's switched you from a girl he can bed to a girl to wed."

Penny stared down at her hands. Specifically her left hand, which would likely never sport a wedding ring. "He won't do either now," she said. "He's just a baron's son, but that's too high for me and we both know it."

"Are you sure? He's only a second son."

Penny shrugged, her mind twisting itself into knots trying to force herself to hope. But the more she convinced herself it was possible, the more her reason laughed at her. She was clutching at straws. Not only was she a tradesman's daughter, but worse, she actually *did* the trade. Her hands were rough and covered in scars. She worked long hours, and not at creating a nice home for a man. She had a babe in Tommy to take care of, and no man wanted to raise another man's son. The reasons piled up in her mind until all hope was extinguished and she was grabbing things to throw at the wall.

She didn't let them fly, though. She had control of her temper now, thanks to Samuel. Or at least better control now that Samuel had helped her gain some distance from her father's slights. But the unfairness of the world still ate at her. How dare anyone count her less just because she wanted to do a trade?

"Here now," said Francine as she gently pried the awl out of Penny's hand. "You're jumping to things that might or might not be true."

"No, I'm not. They're all—"

"Stop it! I won't hear another word about it—love or no love, will or won't marry. It doesn't matter. You've got a party tonight. A ball no less. And you're being taken to it by a man you love. That's cause to be happy, and to dress like a queen!"

Penny groaned at that. She didn't want to be Queen Guinevere. She wanted to be a woman. She opened her mouth to explain, but Francine just shook her head.

"Why do you look to the bad, Penny? You got cause, but really, something wonderful has happened. You're going to a ball! And with the man you love. Can't you celebrate that? Can't you be happy for one night?"

It took a bit for the words to sink in. Longer than it should have taken. After all, she had been happy once. She had gone to parties and enjoyed them. She had been a carefree girl once upon a time. Was it possible for her to remember how to do that again? To remember that she had food and shelter, plus people who loved her? No matter what happened, she and Tommy would survive.

So why not dance for one night? Why not enjoy Samuel's company for one blissful party? And why not take what pleasure she could with the man she loved? So what if he would never marry her. So what if the thoughts she had were considered sinful. Tonight was for fun. Tonight would be for her and Samuel's pleasure. No matter what happened tomorrow, she would enjoy herself tonight in whatever ways she could.

"You're right," she said firmly.

"Of course I am!" Francine returned. "So come, let's look at what you're going to wear."

Penny shook her head. "No, first I need to find some French letters."

"Oh, that's easy!" exclaimed Francine. "Anthony bought a whole tin of them!"

"Good! You must get me one."

Francine wiggled her eyebrows. "Just one?"

Penny paused. She'd never thought beyond the first time. "I thought it would hurt."

Francine shrugged. "Not if you do it right. Come on. Let's look at your dress and I'll tell you all about what I've learned from Anthony."

Penny agreed as she quickly put away her tools. If tonight was going to be an evening to remember forever, then she wanted to be armed with as much knowledge as possible. And that meant she had to prepare.

By the time Samuel arrived tonight, she intended to be a seductress the likes of which he'd never, ever imagined.

Chapter 19

✳

Samuel arrived promptly at seven o'clock at the dress shop. It was early for the ball, but he hoped to get a little time to sit with Penny and Tommy in private. It scared him to realize just how much he enjoyed that quiet evening he'd shared with them. He wanted more such nights—a lifetime more—and he was willing to make radical changes in his life to accomplish it. But first and foremost, he had to wait until quarter day. His investments would begin their return then and he could come to Penny with enough money to support all of them—Penny, Tommy, himself, and any new children—if not in high style, at least in comfort.

It would all begin on quarter day, which was only two weeks away. Still, he did not wish to appear like a pauper to his lady love, so he had borrowed some blunt from his brother to buy a couple gifts, and he'd managed to borrow a carriage. He intended to show Penny a proper evening in the style that would be their future. A carriage and a small gift, all in anticipation of their life to come.

So he appeared at the shop door in his best attire. He knocked, though he didn't need to. Mrs. Appleton was already pulling open the door and showing him in. And if her smile of welcome wasn't exactly warm, she hadn't slammed the door in his face either.

"Good evening," he said as he dropped into his most formal bow. Then he presented her with a bouquet of flowers. "I thought these might brighten up the shop."

Mrs. Appleton's face softened as she took the bouquet. They were hothouse flowers and came very dear. But it was worth it to see that softening in the woman's face. If he could get any one of Penny's friends on his side, he would count it a great victory.

"Oh!" she said as she buried her nose in the blooms. "They're lovely. But aren't they for Penny?"

"No. They are for you. I have something different for Miss Shoemaker." That piqued the woman's interest, but she said nothing. Then he gestured upstairs. "Might I go up? I brought a treat for Tommy."

"That boy is going to get fat with all the treats you keep bringing," she huffed. But she waved him upstairs. He took them two at time, anxious to see Penny, but stopped short when he topped the rise.

Sitting about the room in various places was every woman associated with the shop. Everyone, that is, except for Penny. He nodded to each in turn, mentally labeling them: seamstress, apprentice, purchaser, Mrs. Appleton coming up behind him, and Tommy. At least Tommy appeared delighted to see him. The boy crawled right over, no doubt looking for his treat.

Samuel passed it over even as he was making his bow to the room.

"Hullo, everyone. It is a pleasure to see you all this evening," he lied. Then he turned and lost all manner of speech.

Penny walked out of her bedroom with her friend Francine behind her. But he barely registered the other woman's presence. What he saw instead was a vision of shimmering gold. It was a simple gown of white with dark gold netting over top. There was very little decoration, and yet Penny needed nothing to show her as the diamond she was. The gown displayed her trim figure, the color set off her skin as not quite pale, but certainly not dark, and her hair had been brushed to the color of an old guinea—dusky gold with touches of red brought out by the fire. And if that were not stunning enough, her face was porcelain perfection. He detected a slight dusting of cosmetics. Powder for her face, kohl for her eyes, and she must have been biting her lip because her mouth was full and red, tempting him to forget the ball altogether.

Yet it was her eyes that held him transfixed. Pale blue, slightly pinched in anxiety, but without the hint of any anger at all. Penny stood before him open and vulnerable. She had no shield of fury to protect her nor even a purposeful task to occupy her thoughts. She was simply herself, a woman standing before him in beautiful glory.

"I cannot breathe," he whispered when that was not at all what he meant to say.

Penny's fingers tightened to white where she clutched them together. "Will I do?" she asked.

"No. There is something else you need."

He saw her face blanche and heard the gasps of outrage around him. But he ignored them. He drew out his small gift from his pocket, a jeweler's box offered to her on his open palm. "Will you wear this?" he asked. "I think it will match your eyes, but I could not be sure."

She took it from him, and he was not sure if it was her hands that trembled or his own. Either way, the box was opened, his token revealed.

"Blimey," she whispered and he felt his face heat with pleasure. She liked it.

He stepped forward, drawing the necklace out from the box. It was a simple gift, especially compared to what some of the ladies would be wearing tonight. He didn't even have the wherewithal to buy a chain for it, so the pendant hung from a black ribbon.

"Do you see?" he asked as he tried to get the aquamarine stone to catch the light. It was in truth a small stone, but the gold around it was what made it unique.

"It's a shoe," he said. "I know you are embarrassed about being in trade and likely nervous about the people you are to meet. But you must understand that they will know what you do. They will all know you are a tradeswoman and there will be sneering behind some fans and crass comments by some of the men. But if you wear this, it shows them that you are proud of who you are and what you do. And I am," he said. "I'm very proud of it." He held it up to her eyes and cursed softly. "Not quite right. But do you think it is close enough? I do not know that any gem would match the beautiful color of your eyes."

He was mentally comparing her eyes to the gems he'd seen in the shops, frowning as he discarded one after another. Then he felt her hands gently cup his.

"It's beautiful," she breathed. "I cannot believe . . ." She stopped, biting her lip as her eyes shimmered with tears. "But how could you pay for it?"

He smiled, the twist in his gut belying his easy words. "I am not impoverished, Penny. And you deserve beautiful things." Urging her to turn around, he tied the ribbon to her neck. He didn't have a mirror so he had to rely on the cues from her friend Francine as to exactly where the stone should rest. In the end, he managed just fine. The jeweled shoe settled in the center of her creamy skin, just above the shadow of her cleavage. And looking at it there, he desperately wanted to see her wearing just it and nothing else. The gem he bought for her while her body lay upon his bed as a gift for him.

The idea so overwhelmed him that he couldn't speak.

Which was just as well because all the ladies were crowded around looking and commenting for him.

"He's right, you know. Wear it with pride."

"Goodness, that's beautiful. The color is perfect."

"I know of a way to get a chain for that, and not so expensive. But for tonight, you look stunning."

Other phrases filled the air. Generally, the gift was approved, but in all that, Penny never said another word. That bothered him. He should have given her the thing in the carriage, but he hadn't been able to wait, and now he damned himself for his impatience. So he pushed all the women aside, forcing his way close enough to take Penny's hands.

"What is the matter?" he asked softly. If anything, her face had gone paler.

"Will I do?" she whispered. "Among your friends? Will I shame you?"

Lord, he wanted to kiss her so thoroughly that she forgot all her fears. But he couldn't do that. Especially since he could see the number of pins in her hair. She had likely spent an hour getting it to fall just right. So he had to content himself with lifting up her gloved hands and kissing them.

"I am an odd duck, my dear. You have said that many a time. It is more likely that you will find my friends equally odd and run screaming back here where it is sane."

"I would never do that," she said, her voice growing stronger with each word. "I have resolved to enjoy myself tonight."

"I have done the same!" he lied. In truth, tonight was more about showing her the life she might have with him. Once his fortune was established. "Come now. The carriage is waiting."

"Carriage!" she gasped.

"We could not walk all the way to Grosvenor Square."

"Of course we could!"

"We will have a carriage, and you will take my arm. And

when the butler pronounces your name, you will hold your head up high and I shall know that every man in the place is envious of me."

"Do you really think so?"

He smiled. "Am I not the most brilliant man you have ever met? You have said so dozens of times, you know."

"Of course you are, but—"

"Then trust in me, my dear. You will be the toast of the ball." So he took her arm and led her out to the waiting carriage.

Penny settled into the carriage, doing her best to quiet the quivering in her belly and the weakness in her limbs. Unfortunately, the carriage did not help. It was *expensive*. That was the only word for it. There was a crest on the side that she did not recognize, the squabs were almost new and in the finest velvet, and the horses seemed much too large to her. It was ridiculous, she knew, but everything about this fine carriage made her feel small and insignificant.

A liveried footman shut the door, and within moments, the carriage had begun to move. It was ponderously slow. Likely they would have arrived at the ball faster if they'd walked. But that wasn't the point. They were attending a ball—*she* was attending a ball—and people who did that arrived in carriages.

Samuel must have seen her stroking the velvet. "Do you like the carriage?"

"How did you get it?"

"It's the carriage of the Marchioness of Guillamore. She's our hostess tonight. She offered me the use of her carriage yesterday when I went to request your invitation." He passed her a sealed envelope that she knew was her invitation. She took it and felt its weight, knowing that never in her life had she held something so fine.

"A marchioness?" she whispered.

"A particular friend of mine. She styles herself as quite the egalitarian. She is also a patroness of the arts, extremely learned in alchemy, of all things, and has a fondness for the ridiculous. Which is why I am a favorite of hers, I suppose."

"You are not ridiculous," Penny said automatically. No, the one who would likely appear out of place was she.

"On the contrary," he returned as he took her very cold hand in his. "I make a point of being ridiculous. The more entertaining I am, the more parties I attend."

"But—"

"Hush, Penny. Stop worrying. It will be a marvelous night, I promise."

She had to take him at his word because she was already dressed and on her way. Short of jumping out of the carriage and running back home, there was nothing to do but see the night through. She had thought she would be excited by to-night. After her talk with Francine—and the placement of not one but three French letters in her reticule—she was beyond giddy with excitement. But as the moment drew close, she was hard put not to lose what little luncheon she'd eaten.

So she said nothing, but she gripped his hand as if he were her only lifeline in a very uncertain sea. And in this manner they passed a despicably slow procession to Grosvenor Square.

Eventually they arrived and the footman opened the door. Penny was forced to release Samuel's hand as she stepped out of the carriage. The night air was cool, but not unpleasant, especially as it hit her overheated skin. Then she chanced to look about her.

It felt as if every candle in London were lit about the stately home. A line of people waited on the walkway, and Penny had to stop herself from gaping. She recognized none of the women. Only the men who had frequented her father's shop. And of the men she knew, they were titled lords, every one of them, lined up with a beautiful woman on his arm.

"Samuel," she said, though it was more of a whisper. She had no strength in her voice or her limbs.

"You outshine them all," he said bracingly, and she shot him an irritated glare.

"It isn't about beauty!" she snapped.

"It is about being interesting," he returned. "And you will be the most interesting person here tonight. I swear it."

"Then you lie," she whispered, reaching for her anger as a way of putting strength in her knees. Fortunately he understood. He chuckled as he patted her hand.

"Tonight, you are a guest of the Marchioness of Guillamore. Hold your head up, Penny, and show everyone here that I am the luckiest man alive."

"You are a fool!" she returned, but she lifted her chin. Much too soon, they were inside and a few minutes later they arrived at the top of a ballroom stair.

"Mr. Morrison and his guest, Miss Shoemaker," the majordomo intoned in booming accents.

Penny tensed, waiting for the turn of faces and the look of scorn that would appear on lord and lady alike. But no one sneered. In truth, no one looked at all. They were busy chatting among themselves, preening in the way of fops as they waited to be noticed by their peers. It was rather startling, and the revelation froze Penny in place.

But Samuel did not allow her to remain for long. Within a moment, he guided her to the receiving line, where he introduced her to the marchioness and her doddering husband, who sat in a chair beside her. The marchioness was first. She was a stately woman with bright eyes and hair dyed brown. She was of middling years, but her eyes were keen as she smiled in greeting.

"Samuel, you didn't tell me she was such a beauty!" the lady said.

"Is she?" Samuel drawled. "I hadn't noticed."

"Don't listen to him, my dear," the lady said to Penny. "Samuel is known to have a keen eye."

"Thank you, my lady," said Penny as she dropped into her best curtsy. "And thank you for allowing me to attend."

"Pshaw!" the woman cried. "Samuel is always a delight, and his guests are always welcome. Provided, of course, that they do not land in the punch this time." She shot Samuel a severe look.

"A simple accident," he returned. Then he explained it to Penny. "A Russian acrobat with the bad sense to overindulge in brandy before his show."

"Oh," said Penny. "Well, I shall be sure to keep my feet on the ground tonight."

"Only if you want," the lady returned. "After all, the Russian made my party the talk of the *ton* for weeks!"

Then they were passed down the line. She was introduced to the marquis, who was easily twice the lady's age. His eyes were vague, his hands arthritic, and Penny thought he was about to drool. So the introduction was by necessity very brief.

Soon they had descended into the party at large. Samuel stayed by her side, speaking in low accents. He introduced her to poets and artists, to this lord and that lady. They all regarded her with some amusement before turning their attention to Samuel.

"Anything clever to do tonight?" they invariably asked.

To which he would always answer, "Not tonight." And then whoever it was would turn away in disappointment. And when Penny began to object to the question, he always patted her hand. "I told you I was here for their amusement. It's how I get invited to parties."

"By being amusing? Like a trained dog?"

He simply shrugged as if that meant nothing to him, then turned to introduce her to someone else.

Twice she tensed unbearably when he introduced her to one of her father's customers. Neither man even remembered her. Then the third—Lord Ferrers—narrowed his eyes in thought.

"Ah, yes, the pretty one with the clever hands. You've

grown up quite nicely, Miss Shoemaker. Quite nicely indeed." And to her surprise, he requested a dance.

She held up her card, sadly empty. Samuel produced a pencil, and suddenly there was a name on her card. It was only after they'd separated from Lord Ferrers that Samuel turned to her.

"I'm terribly sorry for not asking before. Do you know how to dance the quadrille?"

She nodded. "We had dance classes at my school. And I reviewed the steps with Mrs. Appleton this afternoon."

"There you go. I knew you were a clever girl. And what about the waltz? Did they teach you that at school?"

"No. But Francine showed me."

"Excellent." Then he took her card and scribbled his name on every waltz listed. Four of them to be exact.

"I haven't practiced it very much."

"Doesn't matter. Everyone knows I'm a terrible dancer so any errors will be laid at my door." Then before she could comment, he was all smiles. "Gillian, you are looking lovely tonight. Miss Shoemaker, may I introduce Gillian Conley, Lady Mavenford."

So it went. Everyone was cordial; no one sneered or laughed at her. In truth, they reserved all that for Samuel as they recounted exploit after exploit of his. She learned about how he recovered one lady's necklace, how he teased the Russian drunk, and embarrassed a cheeky by-blow who had just abused a maid. On and on it went. She spoke trivialities with titled ladies and impoverished poets alike. Once, at Samuel's prompting, she even gave business advice to a vague-looking woman who wanted to start a perfumery. Her name was Melinda and she was apparently the woman he'd expressly wished her to meet. But while the other guests chatted sweetly to her, they poked at him with a rather insulting good humor. He was their dancing dog, all his brilliance turned to entertaining party guests.

She was still mulling that over when it was time to dance.

Her fears surged to the fore, but it turned out, she could dance with a modicum of success. Eventually, she had other partners, most prompted by Samuel, if she had to guess. By the time the supper buffet began, Penny could hardly believe that the evening was more than half over. And more surprising still, she was becoming bored.

No longer a mass of anxiety, she was relaxed enough to realize that speaking among this set was no easier or harder than chatting with a customer. A few well-timed questions, and she had whoever it was nattering on about one thing or another. All she had to do was pretend interest and everything went well. There were even a few that she genuinely liked. A painter, a political writer, and the beautiful Gillian, Lady Mavenford, who had a surprising understanding of the life of the servant class. The woman was very excited about a school she was trying to establish in her home village in York.

Penny danced some, talked more, drank tepid punch, and even managed to finish a waltz in Samuel's arms with ease. He hadn't lied when he said he was a terrible dancer, but the joy of being in his arms was enough for her. In fact, they were in the middle of their third waltz when Penny realized she was enjoying herself!

"This is a lovely evening, Samuel," she said breathlessly. "Thank you for bringing me."

He grinned back at her and said something that sounded like, "Pigeon course." That wasn't right. He'd probably said, "But of course." Whatever it was didn't matter. Trying to talk and dance at the same time was too much for him. He stumbled, she caught him, and soon they were fumbling about. By the time they had recovered, Penny found herself laughing, especially since the others on the floor were chuckling as well.

"You still got two left feet, Morrison," one man drawled as he and his partner sailed by.

Samuel simply shrugged, flashed a sheepish grin, and

picked up Penny's arms again. They finished the dance without further mishap, and Penny felt yet another fear slide from her shoulders. Everything was well. And if she wasn't exactly accepted among these people, she wasn't reviled. So she smiled her most beautiful smile at Samuel and felt her heart swell with love.

"This is the most wonderful evening of my entire life," she said as he led her off the dance floor.

She was so caught up in her happiness that she didn't see the man step up to them. Samuel saw him, of course, and was in the middle of speaking a greeting when it happened.

Samuel said, "Oh, hello, Bingley—"

And then he was flattened by a facer direct to his jaw.

Chapter 20

~≫⊮≪~

Samuel felt his head snap back. He lost his balance and fell. He landed hard on his bum and barely kept his head from cracking on the marble floor. But that was nothing compared to the shock reverberating in his brain.

Carl Bingley, his best friend from school, had just hit him. Not only hit him, but planted him a facer that dropped him to the floor right in front of Penny.

"You bloody bastard!" the man raged as he stood over Samuel. "You bugger! You bleeding . . ." The list went on, all words that should not have been said in front of Penny. And all Samuel could do was stare up at his onetime friend.

The man was shaking with fury, his words more a reflex than conscious thought. And Samuel could see that Carl's fury was as much despair as it was anger. But that didn't lessen the pain in his face or the humiliation that Penny was now stepping between himself and Carl.

"Hey, now! What are you about?" To add to the disaster, Penny's hands were clenching into fists. A moment more and she'd raise them to defend him physically and that would put paid to any hope that she could move about in polite society. Ladies did not fight.

Samuel scrambled to his feet and tried to gently move Penny aside. But as Carl was raising his fists to plant him another facer, Penny didn't want to go anywhere.

"Carl!" he snapped as a way to draw the man's attention away. "What is the matter, man? What has happened?"

"They burned down, Sammy! Burned to the ground! I'm ruined! You've ruined me!"

Samuel counted himself a brilliant man, one who saw things with a keen eye and came to conclusions with extraordinary speed. But at Carl's words, his mind stuttered to a cold and ugly stop.

"W-What?" he stammered.

"Burned, Sammy! Both of them."

"Both?" He swallowed and it was a miracle he didn't drop to the floor right there. Two factories, side by side. Of course, if one burned to the ground, then the other was likely to go as well. Of course, that was obvious. But he hadn't thought about that when he'd invested in the two businesses. When he'd convinced his brother and Carl both to pour thousands of pounds into the investments. At the time, he'd been thinking economies of scale. That the two businesses could have one center for shipping and receiving. They could share security costs at night. They could negotiate for larger discounts by working together. That was all he'd thought about. Economies of scale.

He hadn't once thought about fire.

"It can't be," he murmured, even though he knew Carl would never lie. The man was too furious, too distraught for it to be false. "Quarter day is two weeks away. Just two weeks . . ."

"Not a groat left," Carl ground out. His fury was draining away to be replaced by a haunted emptiness. The man was married and his wife pregnant. And what about Samuel's brother? Greg had a wife and two children, not that Samuel thought about their daughter much. She was too little, but she would grow. Would they have to sell their London home? Would Max have to live back at the baronetcy?

"Two weeks," he mumbled again. "Two weeks and we would have recouped—"

"Nothing, Sammy! It's all gone!"

Samuel shook his head. He would not believe it. He straightened his spine. "I have to see it. I have to know—"

"Where do you think I've been? I was in Leister when I heard the news. Went straight there."

"There must be something left. Something to salvage."

"Burnt stubs and ashes." Carl's fists finally dropped to his side, and his shoulders drooped in defeat. "It's all gone. Will take years to rebuild. Years and a bloody fortune that I don't have."

"None of us do," Samuel murmured. Not he, not Carl, and certainly not his brother. At least Greg still had the baronetcy. That gave him a home. Carl's position was more tenuous, but his father-in-law would help. He would not be out on the street.

But Samuel . . . He closed his eyes. He'd put everything into those factories. *Everything.*

"You're sure?" he whispered without even opening his eyes.

"Burnt stubs and ashes."

Samuel bit back a moan. How could it have gone so wrong? How could he *not* have thought about fire? How could he have invested everything he had into this? Questions burned through his mind without relief. And into this agony came Penny's very calm, very rational voice.

"Come along, gents. Surely there's a room where you can put your feet up and have a brandy. Lady Guillamore, you have a place, haven't you?"

"Of course, of course," the marchioness said, but Samuel could tell by her voice that she was disappointed. Opening his eyes, he saw that everyone at the ball was watching his destruction with eager amusement and some satisfaction. Samuel had managed to be entertaining, after all. News of his debacle would be commonplace within an hour. "Come along, Samuel, Mr. Bingley. The room right over here. Miss Shoemaker, can I interest you in some strong tea?"

They shuffled along easily enough. The crowd parted slowly for them, but they did part. Samuel didn't speak. In truth, he could barely function. What he wanted most was to wrap his arms around Penny and hold the world at bay for a while, but he couldn't even touch Penny's hand. He hadn't the right anymore. His gaze fell onto the aquamarine at her throat. At least he'd managed to give her that before he lost everything.

She must have noticed his stare. She touched the necklace and gave him a wistful smile. "Never you mind about this. I'll take it back tomorrow. See that you get all your money back."

"The devil you will!" he snapped. "It's yours. You will keep it and wear it proudly!"

"Samuel—" she said, but he cut her off.

"I'm not done in," he lied. "There's a way out." But there wasn't. One couldn't make new investments without any money. And not only was he broke, but he was in debt, too. He started calculating all the expenses he'd accrued lately, all the creditors who were waiting until quarter day for their due. There was rent and a tailor bill now for the new coat and trousers he wore tonight.

Was he headed for debtor's prison? The very idea shook him to the core.

"You'll be fine," he said to Carl. "Your father-in-law, and all."

The man groaned in response, but didn't disagree.

"And Greg has the baronetcy. He'll have to share with Mother, but they always got on well."

"But what about you, Sammy? Where will you go?"

Prison, probably. He almost said it aloud with a hysterical

kind of laugh. Someone pressed a brandy glass into his hand. He opened his eyes. It was Penny, her expression calm, her eyes sympathetic. Giving in to temptation, he wrapped an arm around her and pressed his face into her belly. Last night, he'd pretended he could do this to her when she was pregnant with his child. He'd actually imagined listening for the babe's heartbeat.

Now it took everything in him not to weep. He could never have her. She deserved a man who could take her to parties and balls, who would support their children in style and send them to the finest schools in England. Samuel was so far from that man. He shouldn't even have been touching her, but he couldn't let her go. And when he felt her hand gently stroke his hair, he nearly sobbed out his despair right there.

"Hush, Samuel. There's always a way. Isn't that what you said to me? We'll find a way."

There was no way. "Fire," he mumbled against her belly. "Why didn't I think about fire?"

"Posh. Why didn't I think about a solicitor writing my father's false will? Because we don't think about these things. If we thought about all the bad that could happened, we'd never get out of bed. And we'd still miss things."

Samuel didn't answer. Instead, he inhaled deeply, smelling the scent that was Penny. Feeling the caress of her hand in his hair. And wishing for one last time for the things that could never be now. He wasn't her Sir Galahad. He was the court jester, and now it was time for him to withdraw.

He forced himself to straighten away from her. It was perhaps the hardest thing he'd ever had to do, but he was a man, damn it, and he would not wallow like a lost child.

"It's time, I suppose, to take you home. I shall ask Rachel for her carriage—"

"What? Don't be silly. It's a nice night and—"

"The evening should end as it began, Penny. A beautiful night to remember forever."

She looked at him then, her eyes calm and her body still.

She was thinking hard, he knew, but he hadn't a clue about what. Then the moment passed, and she was turning to the marchioness.

"Can you see to his friend?" she asked the lady, indicating Carl. "Can you see he gets home safely?"

"Of course," the lady answered.

"Then I'll take charge of Mr. Morrison." She gripped him under the arm and lifted. He obeyed quietly, having no strength to do anything else.

Rachel stepped forward. "I'll summon my carriage—"

"No need," interrupted Penny. "I can call for it. You make sure Mr. Bingley gets home to his wife."

"Of course, Miss Shoemaker. It was a pleasure meeting you. And, Samuel," she added with a bright smile, "I must thank you again for keeping my party lively."

She meant it as a joke, and Samuel took it as his due. He was the court fool. Entertaining was what he did and would likely have to do for many a year to come. After all, parties were the only way he would find food. And with that thought in mind, he drained the brandy in his hand. It would likely be the last he had for a very long time. Then he turned to Penny, a little startled to see the look of cold disgust on her face. For a moment, he thought it was directed at him. It should have been. But instead, she was looking at the marchioness.

"We'll be leaving now," she said curtly.

Rachel nodded to them. Then, mindful of his role as Penny's escort, Samuel offered her his arm. She took it as regally as any queen, and together they walked through the gauntlet of intrigued stares and superior snickers. Samuel kept his face calm—as did Penny—and eventually they made it outside.

"Damnation," he cursed. "We forgot to call for the carriage."

"No matter," she said, not slowing her pace at all. "We shall walk."

"Penny—"

"Hush, Samuel. I am determined to walk, and so you

may accompany me or summon the carriage for yourself. I'll not ride in that woman's carriage again."

Her tone was sharp enough to surprise him. "Has the marchioness offered you some insult I didn't notice?"

"Insult to me? No! But imagine her thanking you for making her party entertaining."

He winced. "She was joking."

"She was not. At least not fully. How many of them in there see you as a prancing dog? 'Tell me about my watch, Morrison.' 'I hear Warwick is in the suds again. Do you think he'll recover?' 'Do you recall the weather three days ago?' Blimey, but they were dreary. And you call them your friends?"

He blinked at her, startled to hear the defiance in her voice. Was she really defending him? When he had just proved to everyone of the *ton* how inadequate he was at supporting a family?

"That is the role I play at these things," he said honestly. "I am invited because I entertain."

"But you call them your friends!" she snapped.

"Well, they are. Some of them. Not all, but some I like quite well." He slowed, turning her to look at him square on. "I wanted to take you to a ball. To dance with you and see how beautiful you were in a gown made for the very wealthiest among us. And you were, you know. Stunningly beautiful. Up until Carl gave me that facer, I was the envy of everyone there."

She snorted, but he could see that she was pleased by his words. Reaching up, she touched his face. "Samuel, will you walk with me?"

"Of course." Then he frowned at the streets. This was not the way to the dress shop. "Where are we headed?"

"To your rooms."

He swallowed at that, but she kept her expression steady.

"Penny . . ." he began, not knowing what exactly he wanted to say.

"And as we walk," she said firmly, "I should like you to explain what happened. If you would."

Of course he would. He could deny her nothing. But still it was hard to expose his failing to her. The event was so new.

He patted her hand and they began to walk again, their steps slow. Fortunately it was early enough by *ton* standards that there were still people about. That gave them the illusion of safety and respectability. Though he did keep a wary eye out for footpads.

"Samuel, what happened?"

"I invested in two factories. They made furniture. Good, sturdy, cheap furniture such that could be created in a factory and shipped throughout England, perhaps onto the Continent. Nothing that required art or decoration. The one made desks and chairs. The other made tables and bed frames. Nothing elaborate. Just simple and cheap."

"And now they have both burned down."

He nodded, his spirits turning morose. "We have had problems aplenty. The workers didn't understand, always wanting to put time into making the things lovely."

She smiled at that. She would, of course, being an artisan herself.

"But that wasn't the purpose of this furniture. No man should have to sleep on the floor or squat on a rock in his own home. I thought to make simple, affordable furniture. For everyone."

"So you had problems?" she prompted when he fell silent.

He nodded. "A shipment of wood went awry. Someone fouled the paint. That sort of thing. Annoying, certainly, but we got it sorted out. Had the mischief makers arrested, in fact."

"Then things went well?"

He nodded. In truth, he hadn't paid that much attention. The Season had started and all appeared to be running smoothly. "I hadn't heard of any problems. The first load went out to the stores a month ago. Sales were just as expected." His brother had checked on that. Greg was very careful with that sort of detail. Usually Samuel checked things out at the beginning. Greg followed through to make sure it all went as it ought.

"So it was doing well."

"Expected the first profits—"

"On quarter day."

He nodded. It was the day he had meant to propose to her. Now he hoped that he would spend the day free of prison.

"Damned timing, isn't it?" she asked. "Are you sure you caught all the mischief makers?"

He glanced at her, startled anew by her intelligence. "Of course we did. Or rather, I thought we did."

She nodded. He was already following her logic, thinking through the possibilities with an eye to sabotage. After all, if someone wanted to destroy the factory, he might start small: fouling the paints, misdirecting the supplies. But when that didn't work, he would have to take more drastic measures. Perhaps to the point of setting the factory ablaze.

"I have to see the ruins," he said to himself.

"What?"

"The fire. There are signs when a place is deliberately set ablaze. Every fire takes a predictable, logical path. The science is relatively simple once you learn the basic principles. There are ways to tell if the blaze was an accident or a deliberate attempt at sabotage."

He looked up at the sky, thought about the time, his remaining coins, and the different ways to travel to his destination. His brother and Carl would want to join him. They were equal investors. Not that solving a crime would save any of them. The factories were destroyed, but perhaps there would be satisfaction in seeing the guilty caught and punished.

"I will have to leave in the morning," he said to himself. "Greg won't be up before then. And it will give me a chance to apologize to them. And to Max." He sighed. "Poor Max will have to leave London." He didn't know who would mourn that more—himself or the boy. Damn, he had loved having them here. His mind spun off on what he might say to the boy to make things better. To Max, to Georgette and Greg. At least the little girl was too small to understand. Though she would realize when everyone had to up and leave for the country. It was all his fault—

"So you set the fire then?"

He frowned. "What?"

"I'm looking at your face, Samuel. I can see you feel responsible. But if you didn't set the fire, then how can it be your fault?"

"I'm the smart one," he said honestly. "They invested because I said to."

"And seems to me they took a risk right alongside you. Not all businesses work out, you know."

He kicked at a stone, his mind spinning beneath the onslaught of guilt. This investment would have made all of their futures, Penny's included if she had accepted his suit. Now . . .

"Stop it!" she snapped, pulling his face to hers. He hadn't even noticed that she'd stopped, but now she stood directly in front of him and her eyes were practically blazing with fury.

"You're not a trained dog, like those blighters at the party think. You're not an all-knowing god, like you seem to think. Just like I'm not a queen, you're not a knight errant. You're just a man, Samuel. A good man with a good heart. But that doesn't keep you from making mistakes."

He looked at her, saw that her eyes were hot and her breath short as she grew furious on his behalf. He saw that she was beautiful in her clothing, but all the more amazing because she understood his thoughts without him even expressing them. When had he last known a person—man or woman—who could know what he was thinking and talk to him so clearly?

Never. Except perhaps the one tutor when he was a boy. Never in his adult life, and never a woman. Not until Penny. "I would have married you," he whispered. He wanted her to know that. "I would have showered you with gifts, given you and Tommy everything you wanted. I would have done that for you."

She said something under her breath. A curse, he thought, except that why would a woman curse after he said that? He couldn't reason it out, especially since she didn't give him the time. She stretched up on her toes and pressed her mouth to his.

He wanted to hold her off. He wanted to be an honorable man. If he couldn't marry her, then he shouldn't . . .

But her mouth was insistent and her body was warm. He felt her arms slip around his torso and her breasts press against his chest. So he gave in to temptation. He tightened his hold, he bent her slightly backward, and he plundered her mouth with all the desperation he had burning through him. He poured it all into her, and she took it and turned it into passion. Within a second, he was rock hard.

"Penny!" he gasped, breaking off the kiss and knowing he was a few breaths away from doing things to her that were certainly *not* in the chivalric code.

She twisted slightly, bringing her lips to his ears. She spoke softly, but with a determination that rang through her words and her body straight into his.

"I have French letters," she said. "And I want you to be my man. Tonight."

"Penny," he murmured, trying desperately to hold on to his better judgment. "I cannot—"

"I'm not some bloody queen," she huffed. "Now take me to your rooms or I shall strip you naked right here in the street."

She wouldn't, of course, but one look in her eyes told him she was in earnest. She would absolutely attempt to seduce him right here on the street.

"You are the most amazing woman."

"And you are the strangest toff." She gripped his ear and pulled him close. "Now take me to your bed."

So he did.

Chapter 21

≫⊀≪

Penny *was not an impetuous woman. She did not make* decisions lightly. She weighed them in her mind, thinking through possibilities, testing the feel of the decision in her gut long before she acted. This decision—the one that made her what everyone already thought of her—came so easily she wondered if she was lying to herself. Was it really so easy to step into sin?

Yes, she realized. Yes, when the heart was in love. So she walked calmly with him to his flat. She had already headed them in that direction anyway with this thought in mind. And when he took her inside the building to the two rooms he let on the top floor, she felt a sense of inevitability settle around her. They had been headed here since the first day that he'd rescued her bag of likes from Cordwain.

"Penny," he began when he'd finished lighting the candles.

Lord, would the man never stop talking? She waved him to silence as she took in her surroundings. Clutter. That was what she saw. Books, bizarre bottles, a mishmash of odd toys or tools or she didn't know what.

"I'm sorry. I didn't clean," he mumbled as he grabbed a pile of papers off a bench and dropped them on top of a tray of something that . . . well, she didn't know what it was. An experiment of some sort, she supposed. And a failed one at that.

It took her a moment to realize that he had almost no furniture. A table and a bench. Presumably there was a bed in the other room. Everything else was in piles.

"This is why you bought a factory to make furniture," she mused.

He shrugged. "I don't entertain. No need to have much." He stepped close to her, stroking the backs of his knuckles across her cheek. "Penny, we don't have to—"

She kissed him. She was tired of all the thoughts. His head, her head, all the words that spun around and around. It was exhausting. She had made her decision, so tonight—to make this a perfect night—she would end it in his bed.

She pressed her mouth to his, she teased his lips with her tongue, and she pressed her body against his. He grabbed her tight, hauling her hard against him, but he didn't immediately dive into her kiss. There was a reluctance that she understood.

"I wanted this to be our wedding night," he whispered against her lips.

She stilled, pulling back slightly as she looked into his eyes. He had said that before, but she thought it was a result of his shock. Now she looked into his eyes and saw that he was earnest. That he had planned on the when and the how to marry her.

"Penny, answer honestly. Would you marry a man who might be headed toward debtor's prison? One who had nothing, not a groat to his name?"

Her mind was scrambling for an answer, but her body

was already doing it for her. Before she could even formulate the words, her head was shaking, no. No, she wouldn't put herself or Tommy at such risk. Whole families disappeared into debtor's prison, never to come out. She would not marry a man who put them in such peril. She just couldn't.

He dropped his head to her forehead, despair already in his face. "I'll find a way, Penny. I swear it."

Then she found the words. She knew what she needed to say, and so she cupped his face and pulled his gaze back up to hers. "I won't marry you, Samuel, but I will love you. I do love you. And because of that, I will bed you."

"No—"

"Yes." She stepped backward, and her fingers found the buttons of the gown. This was one of Helaine's designs. It had the buttons along the side, and so it was awkward, but easily undone without help. She unfastened the dress, and let the gown fall open. The shift was part of the design, and so there was nothing to stop the reveal of one breast to his gaze as a triangle of fabric fell away.

She looked up then, a little uncertain as to his reaction. One glance reassured her. He stared as if mesmerized, but his fingers jerked as if wanting to touch, but still holding himself back. And his eyes, Lord, his eyes stared at her with such hunger. He wasn't looking at her breast, but at her face. And she could not mistake the desire in his eyes.

Then she shrugged her other shoulder out of the dress. The fabric slipped down over her arm, revealed her other breast before catching on her hips. A shimmy next, and the dress pooled at her feet. She stood before him in stockings and slippers. Then to make sure he absolutely understood, she looked him in the eyes.

"I'm sure, Samuel. I have been for a while now."

He took a moment—a long moment—when he studied her face, then let his gaze travel the length of her. Then he just shook his head in wonder.

"You make everything in me grow silent. Everything. Silent with awe."

She didn't know how to answer, so she didn't. She just felt the way her blood simmered in her body in response to him. The way her nipples tightened and her legs grew weak. This man—this brilliant, mad toff—was looking at her as if she were a goddess. And—

Her mind stuttered to a stop and she squeaked in surprise. Faster than she thought possible, he had closed the distance between them, scooped her up, and now was carrying her to his bed. She was lifted in his arms, well able to kiss him. She did so as soon as she could capture his face. And he returned it with a thrust that left her breathless.

She didn't know what she expected at this moment. She had heard any number of stories from her married friends. She certainly didn't expect to be lowered reverently to his bed. She didn't know that he could do that without breaking the seal of their mouths. And she also hadn't expected the sudden power in her very gentle toff.

He possessed her mouth with a kind of command, just as his hands began to possess her body. She couldn't explain it with words, just that this time when he stroked her body, she felt it as a caress *and* a brand. When he shaped her breasts, she felt the exciting touch of passion, but she also felt as if he was laying claim to her. When his fingers pinched her nipples, she gasped as fire shot to her womb, but she also felt as if her nipples where his to tweak, to brush, to suck. And he did all of those things while her body gloried in his possession.

So caught up was she in the sensations that she didn't even realize when he left her mouth and her neck. He'd been kissing her, stroking her skin with his tongue, but when his mouth found her breast, she began to gasp with such hunger. Her skin was on fire, her legs restless, and her back would not stop lifting and lowering as she ached to have him closer. *Deeper.*

He was sucking on her nipple, drawing it into his mouth, pulling on her strongly. Each pull had her lifting off the bed, each stroke of his tongue had her toes curling in delight. And when he nipped at her tip, she cried out. Oh, God, she never wanted it to end.

She tried to touch him. His face was tucked away from her, but she stroked his hair, flowed her fingers down his neck.

"Take off your clothes," she gasped. "Please."

He lifted off enough to shuck his shirt and cravat. She saw pale skin turned golden by the firelight. He was a lean man, but she saw muscles gloriously defined, corded and strong. She stroked across his torso, knowing the feel of him already, the scent that was him, and the power that lay in his frame.

"All of you," she said as her hand tugged at his trousers.

He shook his head. "Not yet. I will go too fast."

"Samuel—"

"In this," he said firmly, "I know best. Relax, Penny. Let me show you what you can feel."

"I—"

He found her nipples again. Pulled sharply on one of them, and she cried out at the lightning that seared through her blood. His other hand was not so far behind, stroking and shaping her until her breasts were like twin flames, molded and owned by him.

Then he let his hands slip lower. Her legs were already restless, and so he easily knelt between them. His hands flowed over her belly, pressing deep into her muscles in such a way that her entire body tightened then released. Tightened, then released open. So wide and aching for his touch.

His fingers touched her hips, her thighs, and then slid underneath her knees to lift them up. Then before she could process the vulnerability of her position, his thumbs slid between her cleft.

She cried out, shamelessly lifting herself into his caress. He took his time, and again she felt the echo of his demand. His every stroke seemed to ask questions: *Who owns you? Who has the right to touch you like this?*

She answered silently. *You do. Take me, I am yours.*

He rolled his thumbs up and down in the longest caresses. High up, making her gasp as her body thrust down against him. Then lower, deeper, and inside. She had felt this before, but now she wanted it with a desperation that was completely mindless. She simply wanted. More. Thicker. Deeper. Harder. Yes.

Soon, it became just *yes.*

His mouth replaced his thumbs. She felt his fingers deep inside her, while his tongue began tracing, licking, thrusting. Again, he owned her. Every inch, every place. She was spread wide before him, and he took thorough command of every part.

He licked, and her body hummed. He sucked, and she arched. His tongue was a constant delight, and her body climbed higher and tighter.

Then one last push with his tongue, and she flew.

Pleasure suffused her. Like a wave of light that flowed through every cell in her body, she was alive with joy. But it didn't last, and it wasn't complete. And it was something she experienced alone.

So when she at last settled enough to breathe, when she collapsed boneless and sated on the bed, she looked at Samuel and gave him a wistful smile.

"Come with me. Love me," she said. It was as much as request as a command, and she watched as his eyes lightened with delight.

He straightened up from the bed and stripped off his trousers with quick, efficient strokes. She watched his glorious body appear, and she wanted to touch him, but she was too relaxed, still floating in a warm pool of delight. About the time when she was beginning to feel the cool air, he returned to her. He kissed her ankle and then her knee as he drew it up.

She started to sit up, reaching finally to touch him, but he held her off.

"If you touch me, I shall explode."

"But—"

"Shhh," he said as he kissed her silent. Then when he broke away, he whispered into her ear. "Trust me," he said.

She did. In everything, she already did. So she let him push her back into the bed. She watched in curiosity as he pulled a French letter out of a tin and slowly rolled it onto his organ. He was very large, she thought, and she wondered for the first time if this was even possible. But she didn't ask the question. She knew that the smallest show of doubt from her and he would stop. So she kept silent as he gently knelt between her legs.

One leg was drawn up, bent at the knee, and he began stroking that leg. Long, sensuous caresses that had her sighing in delight. How could a touch be both too light and absolutely perfect at the same time?

He drew up her other knee as his touch went deeper, into the muscles of her thighs. His hands crept higher and she felt herself tense. But she was no match for the steady kneading of his fingers.

Upper thigh. Inner thigh. The crease between groin and leg.

By the time he was stroking the flesh there, her buttocks were tightening into his touch, her breath had grown short again, and her skin was flushed.

He leaned forward and pressed a kiss into her belly. She felt her flesh quiver beneath his caress, and then he moved to one tight nipple. One breast. The other breast. And then, up to her mouth. He thrust his tongue into her and she all but sucked him inside. She wanted him in her. She wanted the play of teeth and tongues.

But then she felt him down below. Hot and thick and right

at her opening. *Finally!* She pressed against it, smiling as he slipped easily in. A bit. A bit more.

She had stopped kissing him, so intent was her focus on what he did below. So he rained light touches against her eyes, her cheeks, before whispering into her ear.

"Say yes, Penny. God, please, say yes."

"Yes." The word came without thought, and then he slipped farther in.

He was big. Huge even. Or so it felt. She gasped at his invasion, and he stilled, waiting as she breathed in tight pants. Another gasp as he pushed deeper still.

Her hands clenched his back, then slip upward, wrapping around his shoulders to draw her up and away.

It was too much. He was too large.

Then he pushed in a little more.

"Ah!" she cried, though it was more of a gasp than a cry.

He stilled again. He found her lips again. She had no breath for anything, no awareness of much beyond him thick and hard inside her.

"Look at me, Penny."

She did. She had no strength to refuse him.

"I am yours," he whispered. "Forever." Then he thrust the rest of the way in.

The pain was real, but it was also very quick. She cried out. She must have because, a moment later, he was kissing her face and whispering soothing words. She had no comprehension of what he said, only the soft sound of his voice, low with concern but also husky with desire.

At first she responded to the soothing notes, but in time the pain faded. In a moment, she began to feel him thick inside her and not so unpleasant. In a minute, she wanted to experience something a little different, so she shifted her hips. The friction that created was nice. The press of his hips into hers was very nice. And his weight—ah, his glorious weight—was extremely nice as he pressed against her.

She came into more awareness of his whole body, most especially his mouth right next to hers.

She kissed him, sucking on his lip when she could not get an angle to nip at him. She felt his reaction tremble through his whole body and straight back into her, deep inside where he was embedded.

It was so wonderful she wanted to do it again, but she didn't have the chance. With a groan, he began to slide back out.

"No!" she cried. She liked him where he was. But then she liked the slick friction. "Samuel?" she whispered.

"Trust me."

"Yes."

He pulled nearly out, froze a moment at the very edge, and then thrust back in. She thought he meant to go slow. She could read it in the hesitant jerk to his motion. But he was losing control. His arms were trembling, his breath was short and uneven. He pushed inside, and she released a soft sound of delight.

It felt good. *He* felt good.

"Yes," she whispered again, speaking more to herself than to him. Yes, this was what she'd wanted before but was missing. Yes, this felt right. Him inside her. Him trembling as she tightened. Him withdrawing again, only to have her wrap her legs around him. Him gasping her name as he thrust into her again.

"Penny."

"Yes."

Then there were no more words. He thrust into her; she pushed up against him. His breath shortened; her body tightened.

His tempo increased.

She arched.

The coils tightened.

Pleasure!

Thrust.

"Yes!" he cried.

Together. They shared the light this time, and it was . . .
Wonder!

"Mmmmm." Her voice was a low rumble against his
chest, and Samuel smiled. He'd managed to shift positions,
pulling her on top, then adding a blanket to keep them warm.
But beyond that, he'd been too blissfully happy to do anything else.

She was his. She'd said it. *Yes.* He'd said mine, and she'd
said yes. Or perhaps it had been different words—he
couldn't exactly remember—but it didn't matter. In his heart
and his mind, she was his. She loved him. And he . . .

And he . . .

Hell. He loved her, but he couldn't support her. Worse,
with his current debts, he would be a burden to her and
Tommy.

"You're thinking," she murmured, her voice drowsy and
absolutely adorable.

"I am not," he lied.

"You are. Your heart is speeding up and your breathing
is tight." She lightly punched his shoulder. "Stop."

"Anything you command," he answered, though it would
be impossible for him to comply. He had to find a solution.
He had to find a way that he could be worthy of her. He had to—

Her sigh cut off his thoughts. And when she started to
roll off him, the mental silence shifted to alarm. "Penny!"

"No, Samuel, let me hear what it is that bothers you so."
She paused and bit her lip, her gaze dropping to the bed and
their naked bodies. "Are you ashamed of me now? Have I
fallen from queen to—"

"Don't even say it!" The snap in his voice startled them
both. Then he touched her chin, drawing her eyes up to his.
"I still worship the very ground you walk on. And if this
hadn't been your first time, I swear to you now, you would

have no respite from me." His gaze dropped meaningfully to her breasts and lower. Lord, he was already stiffening up again and he could tell by her hitched breath that she could see it, too.

"Then what, Samuel? What is it that makes you think so very hard?"

He laughed, though the sound was tight. Did she not understand the least thing about him? "I think all the time. It is a miracle that you silence my brain as much as you do."

She nodded, as if she already knew that. "So what are you thinking about now?" She grabbed the pillow and braced it behind her back, then pulled the blanket up to cover her luscious breasts.

He flopped onto his belly to hide his erection, then— because she had taken his only pillow—tucked his other blanket beneath his chest so he could easily see her. She waited patiently while he moved, but he could see she would have her answer. Sadly, the problem was not so easily discussed. Or perhaps it was because, a moment later, words began tumbling forth.

"I have failed. I have failed you, my brother, and my friend. I think of myself as a smart man, but in everything that matters, I have failed utterly."

She blinked, and he could tell she was startled. He waited while she formed her thoughts, but in that time, more words tumbled forth.

"My mother is the one who told me—repeatedly—that I must use my intelligence for good purposes. Then she told me exactly what that purpose should be: seeing to the safety and stability of my brother, Gregory."

"She told you to look after your older brother?"

He nodded. "Greg is the most amiable and good-hearted of men. Excellent as a baron, generous with his tenants, and a rather perfect father as fathers go. But he is not smart. Without me beside him, he got rooked left and right. Without me, he probably would have purchased magic beans."

"Good Lord, he cannot be that daft."

"He is, I assure you. Now to his credit, he would tell you that he knew there were no such things as magic beans, but that the poor fellow selling them was so delightful that he hadn't the heart to say no."

Penny rolled her eyes. Obviously, she knew people just as foolish. "So you looked after your brother."

"I did," he said with some pride. "And then a terrible thing happened."

She tilted her head, waiting for the rest. He released a dramatic groan.

"He met Georgette, a woman as managing as it is possible to be. It was a match made in heaven and Greg fell deeply in love. I was released from my duties because she had taken over the task, leaving me suddenly free to pursue my own goals."

"That must have been very painful," she said, her eyes filled with sympathy.

"Painful?" he mocked. "I was free! How could you—"

She touched his arm, silencing his protest. "From the earliest moments of my life, I was raised to be a shoemaker, and yet the more work I did, the more it was denied me because I am a girl. I know the pain and fury of that."

"I am nothing like—"

"But you are," she pressed. "From the earliest moment, you were raised to take care of your brother. And then suddenly, you were free." She shook her head. "That would be like someone taking Tommy away from me. I would be free, but it would tear my heart out."

He blinked, processing her words, slowly understanding what he had never voiced aloud. No one else could understand why he didn't dance at his brother's wedding. Why he tried to be happy but could not. No one else saw what this woman did.

She stroked her thumb across the back of his hand, and he quickly flipped it over so they could entwine their fingers.

"What did you do after Gregory married?"

He snorted. "I did what all good second sons do: I went into the military."

He felt her body tense, though she didn't say a word. But their legs were touching. Indeed, the steady heat of her soft length was a sweet distraction. And the more he focused on that, the easier it was to talk about his past.

"I thought I would bring my intelligence to bear to aid England against her enemies. But I hadn't counted on the one indisputable fact of the army." He flashed her a rueful smile. "The military, as a rule, has no interest in logic or reason from the lower ranks. Superiors ask for obedience, and as we had no money to buy me a higher commission, I left as soon as it was possible."

"But that's not failure," she said. "That's making a different choice."

He shook his head. She didn't understand. "I saw battle, Penny. I saw men under my command die for no good reason. I saw illogic everywhere I turned, and I saw men—many of them just boys—perish in the most horrible ways. I couldn't stomach it, Penny. So I left."

She had no answer to that. He could see it in her eyes. The same helpless futility that dogged him in the mirror. The stupidity of the military was not something either of them could change.

"Then what?" she asked.

"Then nothing. I came back to London. I nattered about and I am still nattering about."

"You invested in those factories."

He nodded. "And they are now ashes. As are my brother's fortune and Bingley's."

"And yours. That was to be the making of you, wasn't it?"

He sighed. She understood. And as soon as it was daylight, he would have to deliver that awful news to his brother and Georgette. And Max. What would he say to Max?

He heard her sigh, and then she shifted on the bed. She pulled the pillow down to his head. He rolled to his side and settled her on his shoulder. He tucked her under his chin and tried to burn every sensation into his memory. This was a moment he never wanted to forget.

"With a fortune, I could marry you. Without it, I have failed you, too."

She didn't deny it. He knew she wouldn't risk marriage to a man in debtor's prison. Instead, he felt her leg slide against his and her lips press tender kisses to his throat.

"There is an answer," she whispered. "To all of it. Addicock and my shop, the factories and your fortune. All of it has an answer, Samuel."

He didn't say anything. She was wrong, but he would not take away her hope. He had no solution to proving Addicock a fraud. Not an immediate one. Certainly not one that would come to fruition before he was tossed in jail.

Then she lifted her head to look directly into his eyes. "You'll find your place, Samuel. It's not as your brother's keeper. It's not in the military. It's somewhere else. You'll find it, Samuel, and when you do, I'll be waiting."

He looked at her, her words flowing into him like a slow and steady pressure. Water, pushed between the cracks of his heart and mind, tiny drops at first but more and more with every second that passed. As he lay there against her, he felt all the weight of his failure lift up and wash away. The great load of his mistakes—one after another—just floated away. Because she would wait for him.

"I cannot ask that of you," he whispered. "I have no idea how long this will take. How many years before I am clear of debt and can come to you as a man, not a—"

She cut off his words with a kiss. It was swift and fierce, just like her. Then she pulled back and looked into his eyes. "You didn't ask, and what I said—it's not a promise. It simply is, Samuel. I love you. I will wait because my heart will not choose any different."

"I won't fail you," he swore. "I'll find an answer."

"I know," she said. Then she smiled before she echoed

back the words he had said to her so often. "No matter what happens, Tommy and I will be just fine."

But it mattered to him. It mattered a great deal. He didn't say the words. He had made the vow enough times that he didn't need to repeat himself. Especially as she stroked her fingers across his forehead, smoothing the furrows he knew were there.

"I want you to love me again, Samuel. Right now. Please."

"It's too soon—"

She didn't let him stop. She took charge, kissing him deeply, sweetly, and with enough demand that he was all too happy to comply. He took what time she allowed, stroking her body, kissing her skin, sucking her nipples to tight, hard points. This time, she helped him with the French letter. This time, he took her to her peak twice before he finally thrust inside. And when they both shuddered with their release, he knew that he would do anything, say anything, become anything if it meant he could have her forever.

"Wait for me," he said just before he slept. "I'll fix everything."

"Tommy and I are fine," she murmured into his shoulder. "Fix yourself. Then come find me."

Chapter 22

~×~

Penny went with him the next morning to talk to his brother. He didn't want her there, but in this she knew he needed her. Not to say anything. He had words on top of words. No, she would be there to look Georgette in the eye and let the woman know that she would not be laying the blame for this on Samuel's doorstep.

That was the trouble with smart men. They thought they had all the answers, and then when life knocked them aside, they thought it was all their fault. Couldn't be that life didn't always work out. That sometimes evil won. Samuel saw that as his own personal failure, and there was nothing she could say to change that.

But she could sit there in the library as he explained things to his brother and Georgette. She sat with folded hands and a serene expression. And whenever Georgette opened her mouth, Penny glared the woman into silence.

It worked. Never before would Penny have thought that she could silence a nob. Certainly not a baron's wife who was as managing a woman as could ever be. But Samuel had given her a new strength. The way he looked at her, the way he *listened* to her, gave her a confidence that had slipped in to replace the fury that had been so much a part of her life. Thanks to Samuel, she was no longer angry. She was strong, so in thanks—and in love—she would use that strength to defend him.

Until the moment he abandoned her. Which was at nine o'clock that morning.

He'd finished giving the news to his brother and Georgette. He'd spoken quietly and calmly to Max. And then, finally, he'd turned to her. She'd smiled at him, expecting that he would drive her back to the shop, that he would tell her that last night meant as much to him as it did to her, that he needed to see her again tonight. Any of those things.

Instead he took her hands and pressed a long kiss to the back of her knuckles. "I have to leave now. As soon as the word gets out, I will have creditors dunning me. My brother and I are going to see the factories. If nothing else, I will know if it was a crime or simply bad luck."

She nodded, remembering that he had said that was his intention yesterday. In fact, it had been her idea. But in her lovestruck haze, she'd forgotten it. She'd thought he would stay in London with her, solving her problem with Addicock.

"Of course," she said. Because she could see that he could do nothing for either of them if he was in jail. "When will . . ." She couldn't even say the words. She swallowed the lump in her throat and tried again. "Will you come back to London?" *Will I ever see you again?*

"Yes," he said. The word sounded like a vow, but her head knew that some things didn't go as predicted. Some things even a mad toff couldn't control.

"I'll watch for you," she said. She'd intended to say that she would wait for him. And sadly, she knew she would. Possibly every day for the rest of her life. But even she knew that was a promise that she might not be able to keep. Vows spoken in the sweet of night when their bodies were entwined were one thing. But she was a practical girl with a child to support. And she would not tie her heart or her body to a man who would threaten her security. She just couldn't.

So she promised the truth. That she would watch for him because she knew she would be doing that. She just might not be able to wait.

He noticed the shift in her words. She saw the realization hit him like a blow. His body jerked slightly and then his eyes dropped to the floor with a nod. He understood. He knew her so well, he probably knew what she was thinking even before she'd said the words. But that didn't stop her from feeling like a witch for what she'd said. Or failed to say.

Then he drew her forward to the butler. "Braxton will see that you get home. Greg and I need to leave immediately."

She nodded. There was nothing more to say. And in front of the servants, she didn't feel as if she could even kiss him good-bye. Fortunately, that didn't seem to matter to him. He wrapped his arm around her and pressed his mouth to hers. She responded immediately, pouring all her love into that one kiss. She pressed herself to him; she clung to his lips and his tongue; she even sucked him inside when he might have pulled back. She told him without words how much she wanted him.

When they finally broke apart, his eyes were dark with hunger. She matched his need. Her body throbbed with it. But then his brother came down with a bag packed and their time was over.

With a last look, Samuel left.

"He's not coming back. I'm so sorry, Penny, but you have to know the truth. He won't be back in any meaningful way. Not in the way you want or need."

Penny didn't answer. She knew Irene was trying to be

kind. After all, how many times had she delivered bad news to a friend in just this kind of way? Blunt, to the point, and exactly the truth as it needed to be said. But it wasn't the truth. Or at least she prayed it wasn't.

So she sat back and eyed her handiwork instead. She was fitting Irene—Mrs. Knopp, their purchaser—with a brand new pair of walking boots. The woman had apparently walked her way through all her other footwear and needed more boots.

It was kindness work, but Penny wasn't too proud to take it. With Samuel gone, she had the time on her hands and needed the money. So she made the boots and a right fine pair they were. They molded to the woman's wide foot and hugged her calves sweetly, giving the appearance of slender strength. Penny had put on a small heel for beauty, but maintained a sturdiness for long wear. All put together the boot was both beautiful and functional, and she was very proud of the design. She might have spent a few seconds more admiring her handiwork, but Irene wouldn't let her. The woman continued to be nice, though her every word grated on Penny's nerves.

"I can see you're not ready to hear the truth yet. I understand. Believe me, it was weeks before I was able to accept the truth that my husband had died."

Penny straightened up so she could look the woman in the eye. "It's not the same. Samuel hasn't died," she said firmly. "He's just—"

"Running from creditors." Irene reached out and took Penny's listless hand in hers. "I know this is hard, but I know his type. My father was such a one."

"No—" Penny began, but Irene wouldn't be stopped.

"How many of his creditors have rung your door since he left? Five? Six?"

It was eight in the last twelve days. Eight ugly men who demanded to know where Samuel was hiding. She didn't know, and she had no idea how they had connected him to her. But they had found her and they never believed a word she said. It had gotten so ugly that Wendy had hired a new "footman" to help lift and carry work. In truth, the man was big and brawny—about the size of a draft horse—and he frightened the bad element away.

"Samuel will be back," she said firmly. "When everything is in order."

"My father used to say things like that. And yes, he did return. When the creditors had gotten tired. When he had won that night at the faro table and was feeling flush. When he was home, we had such a wonderful time. But it never lasted. He was never a man we could count on. Eventually he would lose again, debts would pile up, and he would disappear, leaving behind a mess for the rest of us to clean up."

Penny blinked away the tears, knowing that for Irene, that had been the truth. For Helaine, too, for her father had been an equal scapegrace. But that wasn't Samuel. "He doesn't gamble. He hasn't lost at faro."

"He gambles on investments, and that is just as bad." Then the woman squeezed Penny's arm. It was a friendly gesture, and truthfully, when Penny looked into her eyes, she saw only warm sympathy in a face too used to being hurt. "I know the type," she said gently. "Love them if you must, but don't ever marry them—"

"I'm not planning to—"

"And don't ever trust them. They will fail you. Whether on purpose or by accident, it happens nonetheless."

Penny didn't answer. She wanted to. She wanted to scream loudly at this austere woman who saw too much. But what came out instead were tears. The slow, steady leak of despair. She wanted to believe Samuel would return to her. That he would find a way to fix everything, and all would be well. But as every day passed, more doubts crept in. With every creditor who pounded on the door and every night she crept into a cold bed without him, she doubted a little more.

She still loved him. Her heart still screamed his faithfulness. But her mind was growing louder every day. How long before she lost her love to the reality of living alone? How long before she proved herself as a faithless lover who no longer believed in her love's ability?

She was ashamed of her weakness, but as each day passed, she couldn't deny it either. How could one man—even as brilliant a man as Samuel—succeed when everything was stacked against him? Against her?

Irene didn't say anything. She just handed Penny her handkerchief and then hugged her tight.

"I know how hard this is," Irene said, and Penny could hear the break in her voice. After all, the woman had lost her true love at sea. "It's so easy to just fold into yourself and hide. But you have Tommy, who needs you. You have work, which is a godsend. And you have us, Penny. Never forget that. You have us to help you and strengthen you. We won't abandon you whatever happens."

Penny nodded. She knew that. She knew that she would survive no matter what. Samuel had given her that gift at least. He'd made her see her own strength such that she believed in her own future if not hers and Samuel's together.

"Thank you, Irene," she said as she slowly pulled away. "I know you mean well—"

"But you're not ready yet to give up. I understand. But I've learned something in the last few years. You don't need an aristocrat. In fact, they're the last type of man for you."

Penny stiffened slightly. "You mean stay in my own class."

Irene pulled back. "No! Of course not! I mean that you're much better than the stupid men of the peerage. You need a man who knows what it is to work for his money. That's the kind of man who will value you and value the work you do. That man can't be found in the aristocracy. They're lazy, born to wealth and expect worship as their due. Lord, no!

Even if the Prince Regent were to bow down before me and ask for my hand, I'd turn him down flat."

"He's already married."

Irene waved that away with a smirk. "Well, even if he wasn't, I'd still refuse him. Damned privileged idiot. I wouldn't want him or any of his friends. Penny, you need a man who knows your worth. And that can only be a man who's had to work for his supper."

Penny listened. She couldn't help herself. And as she listened, the words sank into her skin. Perhaps Irene was right. Perhaps no toff—mad or otherwise—could understand her worth. Or perhaps Irene was speaking more about herself than about Penny.

"Is there a man, Irene? Is there someone you're thinking about who has nothing to do with me or Samuel?"

"What?" the woman gasped. It might have been convincing if she hadn't colored up to her ears. "Of course not!"

"Who is it? What has happened?"

"Nothing! Nothing!"

Penny could see that the woman was lying. But they weren't friends enough yet to share this. Or perhaps it was too new for Irene to tell anyone. Either way, it didn't matter. The lady stood up and neatly pulled out money from her reticule.

"This is for these wonderful boots and the slippers for Francine's wedding."

"Irene!" Penny cried. "You don't have to pay me now. All the clothing and the shoes come out of our pay. Wendy has said so." She had to say so; otherwise Penny would have been working in the shop naked. She'd had only the clothes on her back when she was tossed from her home. She'd had to find an arrangement for clothes somehow, and Wendy had decreed that all employees could be advanced the price of their attire.

"Yes, yes, I know. But I have a different arrangement with the shop. And besides, I have the money. Best take it before I spend it on a new hat. I saw one just the other day that I can't stop thinking about."

"Then you should go buy it and wear it to the wedding."

Irene laughed, and Penny saw at last how beautiful the woman could be. The austerity left her face, hiding the sadness that dogged the woman's expressions. Instead, she was young and lively as she must have been as a child.

"I might just do that. But only if I can afford it after paying you." So saying, Irene pressed the notes into Penny's hand. Then her expression sobered. "We know your value, Penny. I saw Francine's wedding shoes, and my God, they are gorgeous! You have a gift. Don't sell yourself short for any man."

Penny nodded, swallowing down the lump in her throat. She knew her friend was right. She was valuable. She was a good, hardworking woman. She deserved an equally honest and true man.

But what about Samuel? cried her heart. What if he was exactly the man for her, but just needed a little more time?

Chapter 23

꩜

The morning of Francine's wedding dawned dreary. The clouds overcast everything, making the world a perfect match for Penny's mood. She was happy for Francine. Ecstatic really, but a tiny part of her was so jealous she couldn't stand it. Why did Francine get to be lucky? Why did she get to have wealthy parents who loved her, a husband who thought the moon and sun set on her whim, and a future that overflowed with happiness? Why did Francine get those things and Penny did not?

It was a mean feeling and only a tiny part of her heart. But in the gloomy darkness before the day began, Penny looked at the sky and agreed completely. Life was awful. She would never see happiness. And . . . And . . .

And Tommy was awake. Not crying for his breakfast, but happily talking nonsense to himself. She didn't know what he was doing, but the sound of it sparked the happiness inside her. It took at least five minutes to do it. She was human enough to hold on to her sulks for that long. But eventually, the truth of her life asserted itself.

She and Tommy were healthy, had a home, a job, and a good life. And if her existence didn't include the man she loved, well, then that was simply something she would have to live with. She was a shrew indeed to begrudge one of her dearest friends the love of her life.

There it was, plain and simple. So Penny got up, bathed, and dressed as quickly as she could before Tommy began to think of his stomach. Soon Mrs. Appleton joined them in the prewedding preparations, and eventually a miracle happened.

Penny was soon over-the-moon happy. Not for herself, but for Francine, who today would see one of her dreams come true. Francine and Anthony would marry this day, and with the sun starting to peak out behind the clouds, the day would soon be fine. All would be well, if not for Penny, then at least for Francine. And that would just have to do.

They made it to the chapel in plenty of time. Mrs. Appleton took Tommy, and Penny rushed to attend the bride. Francine was stunning. Her gown draped down from her figure like the robes of a queen. She'd lost a great deal of weight since first entering A Lady's Favor dress shop, but that had little to do with the radiance that shone through every pore in her body. Francine was grinning when Penny arrived, and the squeals of delight that followed as they hugged made everything wonderful.

She had other attendants besides Penny. Eight in all, each with a special pair of slippers made by Penny's own hand. As if on cue, all the girls raised their gowns to show off their shoes in a line. Penny displayed her own, and then they cheered. Beautiful. Shoes, gown, attendants, and bride—all giddily happy. This was her life, Penny decided with a smile, and she would not allow a missing mad toff to dampen any of it.

The ceremony began and Penny had to admit that Anthony was a handsome devil. As he stood tall and proud, she wondered if Samuel would look so desperately happy at their wedding. Would his eyes sparkle and would his every expression say he couldn't believe how lucky he was? Anthony did, and in her imagination, Samuel would as well.

The service went as planned with vows spoken strong enough to be heard in heaven. And if their kiss was a bit scandalous, no one seemed to mind, least of all Francine. Then there were hugs all around and the wedding breakfast.

It went exactly as it ought except that, every once in a while, Penny would catch a glimpse of a lanky man with wild hair. She thought it might be Samuel, but when she looked closer, she didn't see him. She'd mistaken someone else or imagined something entirely different from what it was. In those moments, her heart twisted painfully, and she worried that this, too, would be her life for the next however many decades. Would she forever be looking for him, only to be painfully disappointed?

Hours later, Tommy was beginning to get cranky. He needed his nap, and Penny needed the quiet. She would rest with him or perhaps work on some shoes. Anything to take her mind off Samuel and weddings.

Mrs. Appleton was having too good a time, so Penny refused to let her come home early. She collected little Tommy and hailed a hackney, then settled back into the squabs with a sad sigh. It didn't matter what her mind told her or how many times she resolved to be happy. Her heart loved Samuel, and like it or not, she would remain true to him. God willing, he would be true in return and one day come to her a whole man. One who did not question his value to her and one who also remained blessedly out of debtor's prison.

She hadn't even realized she was crying until Tommy's hand brushed at the wetness on her cheeks.

"It will work out," she reassured the boy. "It will. Someday." Then she dropped her head on the boy's and cradled him close as they made it the rest of the way to the shop.

She disembarked, juggling Tommy in one hand and her

bouquet of flowers in the other. The shop was closed for the day as everyone was at Francine's wedding, but she had the key to the back workroom so she headed there. She was barely two steps into the alleyway between buildings when she pulled up short at the sight of Ned Wilkers pacing in agitation right outside the workroom door.

"Ned?" she gasped. What would Mr. Addicock's clerk be doing here?

"Miss Shoemaker! Thank the Lord I found you!"

She rushed forward, seeing that his hair was pulled askew, his eyes were wild, and he clutched a satchel as if his life depended on it.

"Ned, what has happened?"

"It's all true. I went looking like Mr. Morrison said, and it's all true!" This last ended on a wail loud enough to startle Tommy, who had been drowsing on her shoulder.

"Come inside. Tell me everything!"

"No! No! We have to go to the constable. Addicock found me. He knows what I have!" So saying, he jerked the satchel forward, but he didn't release his grip on it.

"Is that proof?"

He nodded, though the motion was wild. "The marriage license from your Bible. Practice signatures. The fake will. Everything, but there's something else. He's going to do it to someone else, too!"

"What?"

"A baker with a young son. It's terrible what he plans! And when I found out—"

Fear tightened Penny's chest. "Oh, Ned, you didn't confront him, did you?"

"Lord, no! I grabbed everything! Couldn't let him do it. Not to somebody else. But he came back from lunch too soon and he saw me. Miss Shoemaker, he *saw* me!"

Ned's fear was palpable and Penny fumbled with the keys to the shop. They had to get inside, out of the open. Finally she rammed the key in and twisted, unlocking the door.

"Inside," she hissed.

Ned dashed inside, but once there he obviously didn't know what to do. They had to go to the constable; that was certain. But she had Tommy in her arms and a damned bouquet of flowers, which she immediately dumped on a worktable. Bloody hell, where was everybody?

At the wedding, of course. And their new footman, Foster, had the day off. She and Ned were on their own. Damn! She'd just have to take Tommy with them. Juggling the boy, she turned to Ned.

"We'll go to the constable now. You have all the proof in there?" she asked, gesturing to the satchel.

He nodded, but his eyes were frantic. "You don't understand. He saw me take these! He followed me!"

Fear gripped her belly. "But you've been waiting outside the shop. He couldn't have—"

"I ran, Miss Shoemaker. I ran faster than him, but he's got a gun. I've seen it. He's got a gun, and he said he'd kill me." The boy was shaking with terror, and his fear was ratcheting up her own.

"We have to stay calm. You say you outran him? Does he know you'll come here?"

Ned shook his head. "No."

But at the exact same instant, a thick voice said, "Yes."

She whirled around. The workroom door was open, and there stood Addicock, looking almost as wild as Ned. But only "almost" because the hand holding the gun appeared damn steady to her.

"Give over the sack, Ned," he said calmly as he stepped inside. "No one needs to get hurt."

Ned shook his head, and Penny could hear the way his breath had shortened into tight pants of panic. "You killed her parents! You stole her shop!"

"I didn't kill anyone," Addicock snapped. "It was all him! He made me!"

"Who?" Penny asked. She didn't really want to bring the

man's attention to her, but the question was startled out of her. "Who killed my parents?"

"The same bastard who will kill you if you don't shut up. Now give me that bag, Ned!"

Ned's eyes hopped between Addicock and Penny. Then he abruptly straightened. "No, I won't! And it don't matter anyway. Soon as I can, I'm going to the constable. I'm going to tell them everything!"

"You bloody idiot," Penny groaned. This wasn't the time for the boy to get noble. Not with a gun pointed at them! And Tommy still on her shoulder! "Give him the bag and swear you won't say a word!"

Ned's eyes practically bugged out. "What?"

She looked at Addicock, keeping her voice steady. "I'm going to set Tommy down now. He's getting heavy and then we can work all this out."

"Don't move!" he snapped as he swung the gun in her direction.

She tried her best to smile reassuringly at him. She couldn't get agitated. It would wake Tommy and that was the last thing they all needed: a screaming toddler in their midst. "I'm on your side here," she lied. "I've got a good situation in this shop. Don't want anything changing that." Then she took a step to the pen they'd set up for Tommy in the workroom. "I'm just putting him down." With luck, it would keep the child safe from whatever was about to happen.

She shifted the boy, settling him down in the pen. He stirred, but didn't wake, his little mouth pursing as he found his thumb and began to suck. Penny spent the whole time holding her breath while her back prickled with awareness of the men—and the gun—right behind her. All three of them remained absolutely still, waiting to see if Tommy would drop into sleep. None of them wanted a child in the middle of this.

The boy settled, thank God, and Penny turned to face Addicock. Except the man was no longer alone. Slipping up silently behind him was their new footman, Foster. She did no more than open her mouth in shock, and then it was over. Foster pressed his own gun to the back of Addicock's head and spoke low and menacing.

"Hard to miss killing a man at this distance," he said. "Now stop waving that pistol around and give it here. You'll wake the boy if it goes off."

Addicock was frozen in terror, his body and his breath completely cut off. It was left to Foster to reach around and pull the gun out of the man's hand. Easy enough to do, thank God, and in a minute Addicock was pushed hard against the wall so Foster could tie his hands tight behind his back with a rope.

Meanwhile, Ned collapsed into Tabitha's chair, his breath escaping in a stuttering exhale. "Thank God. Thank God."

"No," she said firmly. "Thank you, Foster. I don't know what possessed you to be here on your day off, but I am extremely grateful."

The man flashed her a grin. "It weren't my day off, actually. I was hired to watch you and the shop, and that's what I did. Now, if you'll give me that bag of proof, Ned, I'll make sure it gets to the constable."

Ned straightened, his eyes narrowing in suspicion. "No one touches this but—"

"I'm a Bow Street Runner, boy. Hired on by Mr. Morrison. Now it suits me just fine if you come with me to see the constable. But whether you come or not, that bag of proof is coming with me now."

Ned's eyes widened. Likely Penny's were just as huge. "You're a Runner?" asked Ned.

"Hired by Samuel?" asked Penny.

The man nodded. "Owed him a favor," he said by way of answer. "He saw me just before leaving town. Told me what was up, and I swore to watch you, miss. But I couldn't find that Bill person. Hard to investigate while watching out for you."

Finally, Penny's knees gave out. She'd thought Samuel had abandoned her, but he'd found a way to keep her safe nonetheless. And if Ned really had proof just like he said, then everything was set right. The shop, the false will, everything would be straightened out.

"Have you heard anything from Samuel?" she asked, too afraid to voice her real thoughts: *Was he safe? Was he in jail?*

"Not a word. Sorry. But he's a smart 'un. He'll be back. Especially once he hears about what happened here."

She straightened. "But how will he find out? How will you tell him?"

The man just shrugged. "Won't tell him, but he'll find out, never you fear. He's a man who knows things. Especially when it's important." Then he grabbed Addicock and jerked him toward the door. "Come along, Ned. It's a long walk to the constable's and I mean to have a nice hot supper as soon as it's done."

So it was over. Foster took Addicock and Ned away, leaving her future if not assured, at least remarkably hopeful. Tommy was asleep. The dress shop was quiet. She had at least a couple hours before her in which to celebrate.

Instead, she dropped her head onto the worktable and sobbed.

Where was Samuel?

Chapter 24

꧁ꕥ꧂

Two days later the shop was busier than ever. The day after Francine's wedding, they'd received news that Helaine, now Lady Redhill, would soon be returning from her honeymoon. Somehow that news leaked to the rest of the *ton*, and the number of appointments increased even without the lady home yet. Apparently, her notoriety brought in customers. With customers came new shoe orders, and Penny was quickly scheduled for the next three weeks for measuring and creating likes. Now she had to get an apprentice for sure, but she was too busy to search.

So it was that she was in the workroom, carving a block of wood, when a knock at the back door startled her. She glanced at Wendy, who was present today, stitching a dress with quick flicks of her wrist. The two women exchanged a shrug, and Penny went to answer it.

The man waiting on the opposite side had her breath catching in her chest in fear. He wasn't a large man by any means. Foster was easily a couple stone heavier, but something about this man's dark hair, slick smile, and slow nod of greeting made every inch of Penny's body recoil.

She gasped and instantly took a step back. He didn't seem surprised, and thankfully, he didn't take advantage either. He simply stood there with a set smile on his very smooth face. It was Wendy who reacted, straightening up from her worktable with palpable anger.

"You have no right to be here!" she snapped as she rushed to Penny's side.

He didn't respond except to nod and bow almost insolently at the seamstress. But then he turned back to Penny. "I apologize for the intrusion, Miss Shoemaker, but I believe I have inadvertently wronged you. I am here to make amends."

Penny frowned. His tone was kind, but the way Wendy was reacting made her very suspicious. "I'm sorry. I don't understand," she said as politely—and as coldly—as she could manage.

"Allow me to introduce myself. I am Damon Porter. I own a gambling den some miles from here."

Wendy piped up. "He owns three gambling dens and most people call him Demon Damon."

That's when she remembered. He was the man who'd killed the footpad some weeks ago. The night Samuel had first brought her to the brothel. Mr. Porter looked different in the daylight, but he was definitely the one who'd thrown a knife through the footpad's throat. Samuel had said he was a dangerous man and at the moment she believed it. Especially as his smile grew wider, as if he enjoyed his demonic nickname.

"Yes, well, men with debts will point at all sorts of devils so long as the finger never points to themselves."

Penny straightened, finding her voice despite her memories. What she wouldn't give to have Samuel beside her right now. "What has brought you to our back door, Mr. Porter?" she asked.

"It appears that a Mr. Addicock created a false will and trust and then sold your property out from under you."

Penny straightened. "Yes, that's true."

"Well, he did such a thing so as to pay off a debt to me. The constable informed me of the illegal nature of his transaction, so I have taken steps to remedy his crime."

Penny shuddered. The way he said "steps" gave her the chills. But as he appeared to be waiting for her reaction, she forced herself to whisper, "I don't understand."

He handed over a piece of paper. She took it slowly, looking down to see a great deal of legal language, which she couldn't process with Wendy standing beside her radiating fury and Mr. Porter in front of her looking so bizarrely charming.

"It is the deed to your store. To the building and the land as should have been your inheritance from the very beginning."

She gaped. That was all she could do. Just stare at him, and then down at the paper that still made no sense to her. It was Wendy who spoke, her voice trembling with some emotion that Penny couldn't name.

"Why would you do such a thing?"

Mr. Porter flashed them both a warm smile. "Because that is what should have happened in the very beginning."

Finally Penny found her voice. "But Cordwain is there. He and Jobby—"

"Have both been removed. I cannot speak to the state of your home. I am sure that there have been things broken or changed. I understand there was a fire in one of the rooms."

Penny bit her lip, remembering the way all her things had been burned. "But he's gone now? It's mine again?"

Mr. Porter held out a key. "It is yours. Mr. Cordwain and his associates have been told to keep away, and I believe they will listen." He flashed a smile that showed his teeth. "I have some influence with them, I think."

She took the key and held it in her hand. She felt the weight and size of it, and in that moment her world shifted. It settled back into a familiar place. Was it possible? Was it truly over? "And Mr. Addicock—"

"Is dead."

She gasped, as did Wendy beside her.

"I apologize for speaking so bluntly. It appears remorse hit Mr. Addicock in the late night hours. He was found dead this morning."

"Dead?" she whispered. She didn't have any idea how she felt about that. Certainly she hated the man. But . . . dead? He kept claiming that he wasn't the one who had murdered her parents. Foster and the constable both had promised her that they would find out the truth of a great many things from Addicock once the man was incarcerated. Now he was dead?

"Yes. Quite dead, I'm afraid." Then he flashed a rueful smile. "Or not afraid since surely that is the man's just deserts. After everything he did to you and young Tommy? Let us all pray that he made peace with God before he died."

Penny nodded because that was what good Christian women did. But her mind was still reeling.

"But what about my parents?" she whispered. "He was supposed to tell us who killed my parents."

"As to that question, I believe I have an answer. Tell me, do you perhaps recognize this?" He pulled a simple bracelet from his pocket, holding it aloft such that nicked links of gold caught the light.

"Mama's bracelet!" Penny cried, rushing forward.

He handed it to her and once again, she felt the weight of it, heard the clink of the metal, and for a brief second she believed her mother was there with her, as if that horrible night had never happened.

"Papa gave this to her at Christmas when I was eleven. She wore it every day after that. I never thought I'd see it again."

Mr. Porter cleared his throat. "Do you perhaps recall that I was pursuing a thieving ring?"

"Yes," she whispered, wishing again she could forget what she'd witnessed that night.

"This was in their treasure. I made some inquiries and guessed it might be your mother's."

"Everyone knew it was hers," she said, holding it as if it were the most delicate thing.

"And now it is yours," he said.

"So, my parents were killed by footpads? It had nothing to do with Addicock? What about that man named Bill?"

Mr. Porter shrugged. "There was a man named Bill in the thieving ring. Bill Worsley."

Her hands tightened into fists and the bracelet bit into her palm. "Where is he? This Bill Worsley."

"Dead, Miss Shoemaker. And unable to harm you ever again."

She blinked. Another villain dead, both her mysteries solved, and her property returned to her. She should be happy, but instead she just felt overwhelmed. And inside, there was that soul-deep longing for Samuel. He would understand this.

"But surely this is a happy day," Mr. Porter pressed. "You have your home back. Your life. You should be celebrating!"

"Yes," she said, though her heart wasn't in her words. This was too much, too fast. And Samuel wasn't here to explain it to her. Thankfully, the thought of him was enough to settle her mind onto some very solid facts. First off, that this was indeed excellent news, but it wasn't her life.

She straightened and was gratified to hear that her voice rang strong. "This is good news, Mr. Porter, and I thank you for arranging it. But my life was never in question. I have friends, family—" An absent lover. "With or without my home, I would have been fine." She said the words and finally believed them with her whole heart. Thanks to Samuel's efforts and her own strength, she and Tommy would be fine.

"Of course," he said.

"But . . ." she continued, lifting the deed to the shop in her hand as well as her mother's bracelet, "I thank you for this. You have been very kind."

He flashed a grin that was all teeth. And even odder, it wasn't aimed at her but at Wendy. "I can see that you are indeed an extraordinary woman, Miss Shoemaker. I am pleased to have some small part in restoring your home back to you." And with that, he gave them both another small bow and left.

Penny watched him go, keeping an eye trained on Wendy. There was something between those two. Wendy made no attempt to hide her glare as the man sauntered away, a jaunty whistle filling the air. Penny waited until he turned the corner out of sight before turning to her friend. She meant to ask for an explanation, but she never got a chance. The seamstress was pulling on her cloak.

"Wendy?"

"I need some more thread. Might take me a bit. Got to match the color exactly right."

Penny knew a lie when she heard it. Wendy had thread of every color and make already at her station. But the woman's face was pale and her jaw was set. Whatever was going on would not be discussed now. So Penny didn't argue. She just watched as her friend gathered a swatch of fabric with shaking hands. Then when Wendy turned for the door, Penny stepped into her path.

"You have all stood by me these last weeks," she said. "Without all of you, I don't know what I would have done."

Wendy's expression cleared. "Don't be silly. You would have managed without us. Didn't you handle things all those weeks alone before you came to work here?"

Penny shook her head. "I was at my wit's end, and you

know it." Then she boldly touched the woman's arm. "I hope you know that I would do anything for you. All of you. You need only ask."

Wendy blinked, and for a moment, there might have been tears shimmering in her eyes. But a second later, they were gone and Wendy was holding up the swatch of fabric. "What I need is good thread that matches and won't break."

"Wendy—"

"Don't you wait up for me. Don't know when I'll be back." And with that, the girl slipped around Penny before rushing out the door.

Hours later, Wendy still hadn't returned, but Tommy had woken from his nap. He'd played with Mrs. Appleton as Penny whittled a block to make a like. Then there was dinner and soon bedtime for the boy. But not for her.

"I'll put him to bed," said Mrs. Appleton as she bent down to pick up Tommy. "You go on. I know you want to."

She did. But she had left the boy in Mrs. Appleton's care too many times. "It can wait."

"No, it can't. It's your home. Go. Make it yours again."

Penny felt her lips twist into a rueful smile. "I don't know that that's even possible. And I certainly won't be able to do it in a single night."

"Never you mind that right now. Go while there's still light. And mind you keep a sharp eye out. I don't know that this Demon Damon has done all he said."

Penny pulled on her cloak, stopping long enough to press a kiss to the boy's forehead, and then another to Mrs. Appleton's cheek. "I couldn't have done any of this without you. I still can't," she said.

"Oh piffle," the lady huffed. "I should be thanking all of you. I was a dried-up old prune, hiding in the shadows and dreaming of earlier days. If it weren't for all of you, I would have wasted away years ago with no one to mourn me."

"That can't be true."

"It can, and it was. But that's different now, thanks to all of you. I've got little Tommy to play with, Wendy to teach reading and writing to—when she's around, that is. And my daughter's a lady again, just as she ought to be. That's all thanks to you girls."

"You're a part of us," Penny said, meaning every word. "A part of the family."

Mrs. Appleton smiled, her cheeks turning bright. For a moment there, Penny saw the beauty she'd once been years ago. Then the lady waved her away. "Go on now. Go find out what damage they've done to your home."

Penny nodded and left. Twenty minutes later, she was pushing into the dusty interior of the shop that had once been her father's and his father's before that.

It was stripped bare. Cordwain hadn't left her anything of value. And what he couldn't take, he'd smashed. She stood in the middle of ruins. Except, of course, that she didn't need any of it. She had her own tools now and her own workbench. Her father's lay at her feet in splinters, but that didn't matter. Her memories remained. The things he'd taught her remained as well.

And if she looked around and saw the debris of the men's shoe store that had once been, part of her also saw how the space could be redone. It would take a while, but she could change this into a lady's shoe establishment easily enough. She'd need new furnishings, new displays, new everything fit for a lady of the *ton*. And now she had the space to do everything she envisioned. And what she saw in her mind's eye was glorious indeed.

She was still thinking, tabulating costs in her mind, when she heard a noise. The sound came from the front door, which she knew she'd closed and locked. She whipped around, seeing a dark male figure stalking toward her. In his hand, he carried a large sack. She drew breath to scream even as she was reaching for the largest piece of wood to use as a weapon. But just before she released it, the man stepped into the light.

"Samuel!"

Chapter 25

✦

He looked good, Penny thought, as he slowed to a stop about two feet away from her. At first, she wasn't sure what was different. His hair was just as wild, his body still as lanky, like sticks stuck together. But his eyes were steady instead of hopping around. And though his shoulders were high in a kind of awkward shrug, his face looked softer somehow.

"I knocked but you didn't hear me," he said by way of greeting. "So I—"

"You picked the lock."

He dropped the satchel on the floor by his feet. Now in the light, she could see that it was her bag of likes. The one Max had been hiding for her. "I had to see you," he said. "I went to the shop and Mrs. Appleton told me you were here."

She nodded. "Did she tell you that the shop is mine again? I even have my mother's bracelet back." She held up her wrist to show it to him. "It has all worked out just as you said."

He snorted. "Not just as I said, Penny."

"You told me that I would be fine. That Tommy and I would have food and shelter, and we do. We are."

"You had that without me."

She nodded, knowing it was true. "But without you, it doesn't feel as good. In fact, without you, it feels unstitched."

His eyebrows went up. "Unstitched?"

"Like I have all the pieces, but they don't hold together." She looked at him, only now realizing what she should have understood from the beginning. "Oh, Samuel, I was so wrong. I don't care if you're in debt. I don't even care if you're going to prison. I will have enough money to get you out. And you'll be here with me and Tommy. And I want that. I want you. I love you."

There. She'd said it. She'd laid her heart bare for him as she never thought she would for any man ever. She looked in his eyes, wondering what he thought. Did he want the same—

His mouth was on hers. Somehow he'd crossed the distance between them in one breath. His arms were around her, his mouth was on hers, and he was lifting her up. She didn't even know why, but she didn't care. She was in his arms and they were kissing.

Their mouths were still fused as he started walking. She was not a small woman, but he carried her easily.

"Samuel," she gasped, breaking apart enough to ask her question. "What are you doing?"

"I'm not going to prison," he said as he carried her to the stairway and started climbing.

"What?"

"No prison. My debts are paid."

She framed his face in her hands as she searched his expression. No deception. No embarrassment. "What? How?"

"I have a job, Penny. A good job that pays me well. Or well enough this time."

"A job?" she echoed, the idea beyond bizarre. What sort

of job could he get that would pay him that much that quickly?

They were topping the stairway when his momentum seemed to stall out. He set her feet down gently on the floor, his expression tender as he looked into her eyes. "I have missed you so much. Every second I was gone, I thought about you."

"Samuel—"

"It was arson. Just like you thought. The factories were deliberately burned down."

She blinked, trying to sort out his words. But in the end, she gave up. She knew he would get to the point soon enough. And he did, though not in the way she thought.

"I love you, Penny. Please say you will marry me. I have a job now. I can support us, though I think you will be making much more than I. Still, I will work very hard every day to—"

She didn't let him finish. She kissed him with everything she had, everything she was. She kissed him and she didn't stop even when she began fumbling at his clothing. But he did. He pulled back enough to look into her eyes.

"Where, Penny? I cannot take you right here in the hall."

He could. She was that willing. But they didn't need to. Instead, she grabbed his hand and hauled him into her parents' bedroom. The furniture was intact. Apparently, Cordwain's fury hadn't made it all the way upstairs.

"Are you sure?" he asked. "After the last time—"

She didn't want him talking about Jobby or what had happened the last time they were here. So she just shook her head and grabbed the linens from the mattress. Within a minute, she had the bed stripped clear.

"Mrs. Appleton says I must remake this place into my home again. My parents are gone. Most of everything that was, is gone. But I can build it again, Samuel. I want to build it with you."

So saying, she climbed onto the mattress and turned to

face him. And as he watched, she began unbuttoning her gown. His eyes grew intense, and she saw his nostrils flare, but he didn't move toward her.

"Penny, I'll never be rich. I'm just a second son of a baron. I don't know that either of us will ever be accepted into the *ton*."

"I never cared about that."

"I know," he said as he stepped up to the bed. "But I wanted to give you so much."

"Then give me yourself." She stretched up to claim his mouth. And as she did, her gown fell away. He met her with an intensity that was all Samuel, and she reveled in it.

His hands started at her jaw, framing her face, steadying her. But as he began to take control of the kiss, as she began to melt into everything that was him, his hands slipped down over her shoulders and to her breasts. She gasped when he stroked her, squeezing her nipples just as she liked.

"It has been so long," she murmured as her head dropped back.

He didn't waste the opportunity as he shifted to rain kisses on her cheek, her jaw, and her neck. He pressed her backward into the mattress, and she was soon stretched out beneath him. He'd already shucked his coat and cravat. Now she pulled at his shirt and trousers. She wanted to touch all of him. To feel all the long, lean, wonderful length of him against her.

"Penny . . ." he began, but she shook her head.

"You talk too much," she said without heat. "It's time to undress."

She fit action to words, stripping out of her shoes and stockings. He grinned and worked equally fast. Soon they were both undressed, both delightfully, deliciously naked. She pulled him onto the bed, feeling his heat and the hot thickness of his organ. She lifted her knees, trying to angle him where she wanted, but he pulled away.

"Condom," he gasped.

"I don't care," she said.

He stilled, his gaze going especially hot. "You would risk a baby, Penny? With me?"

Yes, she realized with some shock. Not only would she risk it, she wanted it. His child. Perhaps a little boy as smart as he. Or a little girl with clever hands. "Yes," she whispered. "I want that, too."

"Then you'll marry me?" he gasped.

"Of course!" she cried. "I love you!"

"I love you, too," he whispered. She loved it when he whispered to her. He always made the words reverent like a vow. Then, while she was still softening from his words, reaching up to kiss him in her joy, she felt his organ push against her folds.

"Yes," she whispered. "Finally!"

He grinned and pushed all the way home.

He filled her. Body and spirit, he brought all her pieces together. She would have said more. She would have told him she loved him again and again, but he left her no breath for words. He kissed her. He thrust inside her. And when she could barely breathe, he pulled back enough for him to stroke her right above where they were joined.

Her body tightened, her back arched, and . . .

He thrust.

Her body exploded into bliss.

He joined her, his body shuddering with his release.

And when the bliss began to ebb, he was right there to catch her, to hold her, and to make sure her pieces reassembled in the right order: as his wife.

"Penny?" he asked sometime later. They were resting in each other's arms, a blanket pulled on top of them. Bodies sated and eyes heavy, they spoke in low, slow tones.

"Mmmm?"

"Don't you want to know what kind of man you'll marry?"

"I already do know. You're my mad toff."

He chuckled. "I'm a Bow Street Runner."

It took a moment for his words to sink in, but when they did, she thought it was brilliant. Absolutely brilliant. She lifted her head off his shoulder so that she could see him more clearly. "How?"

"I wasn't the only investor in the factories. And it wasn't just me, Greg, and Bingley. There were two others. Two men of some means and influence. They arrived at the site soon after I did."

"Well?" she prompted when he fell silent. "What happened?"

"It was Greg's idea. Or Georgette's. It's hard to tell. But Greg was telling them that I would solve the crime. I'd already determined that it was arson, you see."

Of course he had.

"And so Greg said I was a Runner. I'd already been talking to him about it on the way there, but I hadn't decided. In any event, these men offered me a great deal of money to solve the mystery."

"And you did?"

He stiffened in mock insult. "Of course I did. How else do you think I could pay off my debts? And now as soon as a certain beautiful shoemaker pays me my winnings from our wager, I shall have enough to buy said young woman a beautiful wedding ring."

"But wait, that was just one job. Have you become a Runner in truth?"

He smiled. "I have. I talked to Foster about it when I asked him to look after you." Samuel's expression abruptly sobered. "I should have been the one watching you. I'm sorry—"

"He did an excellent job. I was well protected."

"But—"

"Ack!" she gasped as she hit him in the shoulder. "Tell me about the job!"

He chuckled even as he rubbed at his shoulder. "There is no more to tell. I am a Runner now, and one with an excellent reputation, I might add. Especially after solving the arson. It was the owner of a competing set of factories. We have seized his assets, you know. It's all rather complicated and will take some time getting through the courts, but in the end we'll all have our money back. Greg, Bingley, and the others, too. We'll probably make a profit."

"You'll have nobs coming to you left and right," she murmured, thinking of the possibilities.

"I already do, truth be told," he said with a shrug. "I've had people coming to me for years. The difference is now I'll charge money for it, and the mysteries will be more substantial than silly parlor games at a *ton* ball." He tightened his hold on her. "You were right, Penny. I wasn't my brother's keeper, and I'm definitely not a soldier. I solve crimes." He flushed. "I think I'm rather good at it."

"Of course you are."

"And I owe it all to you. Without you, I think I would still be wandering the streets of London, seeing all manner of secrets, but never doing anything with it. You have given me purpose, Penny, and I can never thank you enough for that."

"You can love me, Samuel. You can marry me."

He grinned. "I will. I do. Just as soon as we settle up our wager. Thirty quid, I believe."

"Thirty quid!" she cried, belatedly remembering that she had agreed to double their wager. "But I haven't got that kind of money right now."

"No matter," he said as he rolled her over and settled once again in the place she most loved him to be. "I think I can take it in trade."

"Well," she gasped as he easily, wonderfully seated himself. "I am a tradeswoman."

"You are the woman I love. I will do anything for you, anything you want."

She smiled. "You," she whispered. "I want you."

"Done."

And so their bargain was sealed. And in the best possible way.